NO OFFENSE

Francesca D'Armata

Published in the United States of America.

Eccellenza Communications International, Inc.
5773 Woodway Dr. #295
Houston, TX. 77057

For information regarding bulk purchases, please contact sales@fdarmata.com or visit our website at www.fdarmata.com.

ISBN: 0692783547
ISBN 13: 9780692783542

CHAPTER ONE

The job that no one else in the family wanted was hers. Bookkeeper, or as Jack Hunter, her father-in-law, put it—chief financial officer. She could calculate numbers faster than you could input them in a machine. Decked out in faded jeans and a cotton top, her brown locks, which highlighted her amber eyes, would have to be ironed if she wanted them straight. Snappy casual, Steely was appropriate for any event in Grey County. She sorted through mail at the kitchen table, glancing back and forth between the utility bills and her view of the den.

The new bride hadn't expected to spend her days alone with her mother-in-law in the backwoods of central Texas. It was the first time she had ever lived outside of the Houston city limits. If Beatrice Hunter had screamed there the way she did here, the neighbors would be calling the cops. Early in her sixties, aging hadn't mellowed Bea or her cantankerous hair. She was jagged.

Beatrice was doing what she did most of her waking hours, sitting upright in her recliner and facing a TV loud enough to scare the coyotes out back. She wadded the newspaper in her lap and threw it at the wall, startling Steely, who still wasn't accustomed to her outbursts.

"Mr. Keaton again?" she asked.

"That backstabbing crook started his own foundation with ten million dollars from our company!"

"At least he's giving it to charity," Steely said, sorting through invoices.

"Charity? He's probably his own charity! That money will disappear just like everything else he stole from us!" Bea swung her hands in the air. "I'm here sitting here in the backwoods with the squirrels while he's spending my money! And one of state's most admired CEOs is mowing grass in a field—who knows where." Bea began shaking. Her heart had become accustomed to spikes in pressure in between long periods of almost no activity at all.

"I never liked that no-good dirty dog, but blaming Jack for almost collapsing the company is something I'll never forget." Bea exhaled and settled back down.

Losing a $600 million company she and Jack started with nickels and dimes would throw anyone into a tizzy. But not Jack Hunter; he didn't appear to be anxious at all. He almost seemed to be enjoying the country life.

Allowing Bea to sporadically vent seemed to help her cool down faster. Steely knew to nod at the appropriate time. The venting backfired if she didn't. Still Bea managed to stun Steely when she suddenly flung up out of the chair.

"Was that thunder?" Bea yelled.

"Could have been. It's raining hard."

Bea's brow crinkled. "It sounds like somebody's throwing rocks on the roof."

"It's getting rough outside. The guys should be here soon."

Steely's phone chimed.

"Are you going to answer it?" asked Bea.

"It's a blocked number again." Steely tapped a button. "Hello?" She set the phone back on the table. "Hung up again."

"That's a bunch of nonsense, disturbing people and then hanging up like that. Let me have it next time. I'll tell them something that'll make their head swim."

"Probably make my head swim too."

Steely packed the invoices into a kitchen drawer. She pushed a chair over to the kitchen counter, climbed up to open a cabinet, and reached for a cup.

A loud explosion rattled the house. Two cups shot out of her hands, soaring into the air. One of them clunked down on her head, sending her toppling to the floor, seeing stars.

Bea flung the remote control across the room and vaulted up. "What was that?"

Steely squeaked, "Sounded like an earthquake." She got to her feet, holding onto the chair, with two walnut-sized lumps rising on her skull.

"We don't have earthquakes around here. We have dust storms and droughts."

"Then something blew up."

"There's nothing around here for miles."

"It sure wasn't thunder," Steely said, shaking her head. "Definitely wasn't thunder."

"Well, then what was it?"

Steely pushed back the curtains. "The sky is red...like the sun tumbled down."

Bea was concerned enough to retrieve the remote, cut off the TV, and hike over next to Steely. "There's not a thing out that way."

Steely kept her apprehension in check. The last thing she wanted was to get Bea even more upset before Jack and David got home, but what she saw looked like the aftermath of some kind of explosion powerful enough to blow a hole straight through to China. She opened an entry closet and retrieved the binoculars.

She placed them in position and focused on the sight. "It's a massive fire. Flames are blazing up in the sky."

"Let me look." Bea grabbed the field glasses and scanned the area.

"Could it be a bomb?" Steely shivered, rubbing the goose bumps that had popped out on her arms.

"A bomb in the middle of the hill country?" Bea passed the binoculars back to Steely, went for her cell, and rapidly tapped in a number. "I'm calling Jack."

"I'll call David."

Neither answered.

For the next few days, Bea slept. She couldn't eat. She just stayed in bed. She didn't want to see anyone. Steely hadn't been away from the house since the accident, except to make the burial arrangements.

There was no reason to delay the service. It might even make things worse for Bea. The service was scheduled the day after the bodies were retrieved. Autopsies were not needed. No one could survive driving off a cliff and the fireball from the impact of the vehicle.

On funeral day, Bea hadn't come out of the bedroom all morning.

Steely heard very little stirring behind the closed door. Only when Bea came to lock the door could Steely confirm she was up.

Steely walked back to her bedroom, down a short hall from Bea's, and slipped into a black knit dress. She pressed her back against the bedroom wall, holding the zipper in place. The first time she learned how to pull a zipper up on her own was in her senior year of high school. The stretchy thing sagged from the five pounds that had suddenly melted off her body.

She placed the hanger back on her side of the closet, gazing at David's clothes, pressed together, as if he were coming back to

4

wear them. There were two rows of shirts making a path to the long items hung at the end. Shoes were coupled along the floor. She reached under a sweater, folded on a shelf, and dug around until she found a small square box with beat-up corners. Inside was a silk drawstring pouch containing a silver chain and cross. She hooked it around her neck. Then she stepped into practically new, eight-year-old black patent-leather pumps. She'd worn this outfit to only one type of function: funerals.

The space between Steely's bedroom and Beatrice Hunter's was only a few short steps. She tried the door again. Still locked. Bea never locked her bedroom. She'd chastise Steely for locking her own bedroom. If Steely fell, they'd have to break the door down to get inside, Bea argued. Fortunately Steely hadn't the need for a busted down door yet.

Steely tapped lightly on the wooden frame. She knew better than to knock. Bea didn't tolerate loud noises well, unless they came from her. She placed her head near the crack between the door and the frame. "Miss Bea, I don't want to push you, but we need to leave now."

Bea didn't answer. It's hard for anyone to talk when they're crying their eyes out. She'd made it clear she didn't want comfort from anyone, especially from someone *barely kin,* like a daughter-in-law.

Steely hurried to the living room. She checked out the front window. Pepe Martinez was waiting, his car idling now for over thirty minutes. He'd grown up with Beatrice and Jack, known them most of his life. He was the only one Bea would allow to drive them. He knew how to keep his mouth shut.

She tapped on the bedroom door again. "Miss Bea, I'm sorry but—"

"Quit beating on the door!" Bea's voice was hoarse, dulled by a tissue. "You're making me nervous!"

"Miss Bea, I don't want to do this." Steely swiped her swollen eyes, took a deep breath, and pressed her forehead against door.

"Last week, I'm sure you would've never thought you'd be going to a funeral today for your husband and son. I sure wouldn't have. I want so badly for someone to shake me and say, 'Wake up! Wake up! It was only a nightmare.'"

Steely paused for a few seconds, not for dramatic effect but contemplating what to say next. "But the nightmare is real. I wish it wasn't, but it is real." She shut her eyes tightly, squeezing out tears. "You had thirty-seven years of marriage to a loving husband. Very few people get that kind of love and dedication. You could act crazy or say kooky things, and your husband stuck with you. Not many would."

The sobbing stopped.

Steely scrunched her face, realizing what she'd admitted, and quickly said, "And you raised a son, who grew up to be a fine man. A mighty fine man, who loved his mother. He looks just like you, Miss Bea. He was kind to me from the first day we met. Generous too. You've been greatly loved, Miss Bea. Now, it's time to go honor your husband and son, who cared so much about you."

Bea was breathing loudly, which meant Steely had either helped her or made things significantly worse. But she was stirring.

Steely rushed to the kitchen and turned on the faucet to camouflage the noise she'd make going out the back door. She crept around the back of the house to Bea's bedroom. She cupped her eyes to take a look in the window between the frame and drapes. Bea was lying across the bed but fully dressed.

Steely jogged back inside, turned off the water, and attempted one last try at nudging her mother-in-law. She gingerly tapped her knuckles on the door and whispered, "Miss Bea, may I please come in?"

Five miles. An eight-minute drive. I'll be eight minutes late if I leave now.

"Miss Bea, I don't want to do this. But I'm going on. I'll drive myself. I'm sure Mr. Martinez will come in and stay with you, so you won't be alone. If you can't do it, you just can't do it. You can only—"

Bea flew out of the room and shouted, "Why were you peeping in my window?"

"I was making sure you were OK."

"Don't you know mature women need their privacy?"

Steely spoke fast. "You can have all the privacy you want, Miss Bea, when we get back."

Bea stuck a wadded tissue in her purse and snapped it shut. She was ready to go. Hair sprayed in place, gray dyed out. Black dress and black leather pumps, which she'd only worn on the same occasions as Steely. Bea looked sternly at Steely. "Don't be rushing me."

Steely nodded.

Bea made it down the short hall and through the den before halting at the front door. "I'm nailing a sheet over that window. I don't want you seeing my business. When you get older, everything drops."

"Miss Bea, believe me, I don't want to see anything dropping. But we need to pick up and go."

"Hold on a minute," she whimpered. "I need my rings."

"Let me get them." Steely ran to the kitchen. She opened the fridge, reached to the very back, and scooped up a plastic butter tub. Then she darted back.

Bea popped the lid off the tub, slipped on her wedding rings, and gazed at them. "We didn't have a lot of money when Jack bought me these. He offered to buy me some bigger ones. I didn't want them." The side of her face glistened.

Steely gave her mother-in-law a few seconds to compose herself. If they missed the entire service, they'd just have to miss it. She was giving Bea the moment she needed.

It wasn't long before Bea lifted her head and motioned that she was ready to proceed.

Pepe popped open the car doors. Steely helped Bea along the sidewalk before she pulled away. "You don't have to walk me around like I'm ninety."

Bea's knees buckled halfway between the house and the car. Steely firmly held her up. She had to get through the day, keep her mind off herself, and then go home and crash. This wasn't the first time Steely had lost family. Mother, father—now husband and father-in-law. But she had never lost a child. She recalled seeing Mrs. Yost right after she lost her oldest daughter to cocaine. Her eyes were as red from rubbing as if they'd been cut.

Martinez met them a short distance from the car. He took Bea the few remaining steps, helping her into the front passenger seat. Steely slid in behind her. Bea leaned over her shoulder and murmured to Steely, "He got it from me."

"What?" Steely asked.

"Generosity."

"That's right, Miss Bea. Not a stingy bone in him."

Bea left the window down, rested an arm on the door, and breathed in new life.

Steely cradled her head against the back seat.

They had briefly come up for air.

CHAPTER TWO

About a mile after he passed the county line, Nick spotted the sheriff's office. Hail pellets slid off his hood like marbles when he stopped and cut the engine. The former all-American defensive back hobbled up three short steps to the front door, turned a beat-up knob, and pushed his way inside. "Hello? Anybody here?"

A man yelled from a back room, "Have a seat; be right with ya."

"Yes, sir." Nick scanned the room. There was no finding a seat. The office looked like it had been ransacked. He eyed the two jail cells. Shouldn't really be called "cells." Neither had a door. They were more like waiting rooms than cells.

Boots shuffled along the floor until a man appeared from a dark hallway. He strode toward Nick. "May I help you, sir?" the man asked, with a twang. His slick silver hair, pressed jeans, and plaid shirt were made Nick think of a ranch hand. He held a manila folder with an air of authority in one hand.

"Sir, I'm Nick Dichiara."

"You're Vince's son?"

Nick nodded.

"You were a toddler the last time I saw you."

"Then you can help me. I'm trying to find the sheriff."

"I'm Sheriff Tucker."

Nick winced.

"Excuse our mess. We're in the middle of a remodel. Not much to do around here except keep people from meddlin' in other people's business, so we're takin' our time and doin' it right. This place will last another hundred years once we finish."

"Umm..." Nick glanced around the room, hoping the sheriff was one of those genius types—a disorderly mess but an expert in his field.

"Mr. Dichiara, I doubt you came to check out our remodel. What can I do for you?"

"I'm trying to get some information about the accident involving Jack Hunter and his son."

The sheriff strangled the folder. "One of the worse I've ever seen."

"What happened?"

Tucker's voice cracked. "Missed a curve and landed in a canyon. Son, I've known Jack and Bea all my life. The worst thing I ever had to do as sheriff was tell Bea and that young widow what happened. It was horrible, just horrible. Made me sick, lookin' at the wreckage at the bottom of that canyon. Still can't retrieve it. Almost lost a deputy recovering the remains, the way the vehicle jammed up in the rocks. Gonna take special equipment—maybe a hydraulic crane—to haul it out."

"Something isn't right. Jack knew the risk of hauling a trailer with a heavy tractor. Any rupture in the gas tank could cause a massive explosion. He wouldn't speed. He was almost home. It just doesn't make sense."

"Accidents like that are tragic. They never make sense." The sheriff released his grip on the folder, which would never lie flat again.

Nick shook his head in disagreement. "Driving off the side of the cliff?"

"Speed and terrible road conditions—that's a deadly combination."

"Sheriff, have you ever given Jack Hunter a speeding ticket? I've never seen him speed. He even walks slow."

Tucker pondered, tilting his head to one side.

"Have you ever even seen him speed?"

The sheriff slammed the folder on a desk. "Young man, let me tell you, I'd take the risk—go down in that canyon myself—if I thought it was anything but an accident. And I promise you this: I'll get that vehicle out. It'll take some time, but I'll get it out. And when I do, I'll go over every inch of that truck myself. You can count on it."

"OK, Sheriff, OK. And after you finish, what will happen to it?" Nick leaned close enough to the desk to view the tab on the rumpled folder—*hunter fatality*. He wished he had a copy of it.

"We'll send it to the salvage yard." The sheriff reached for his jacket dangling on a rack.

"Which one?"

Tucker became agitated. "Are you the one callin' for the wreckage?"

Nick was taken aback. "Someone wants it?"

"They sure do. It's poor taste for people to call wanting it for scrap metal, when Hunter and his son aren't even in the ground." The sheriff opened a desk drawer and pulled out a wallet, his badge pinned on the outside.

"Sheriff, which salvage yard?"

"Matt Berry Scrap Metal."

"Sheriff, if you don't find anything wrong with the truck, I'd like to pick it up and bring it to Houston. And I assure you, it won't be for profit."

"That's up to Bea." The sheriff put on his jacket, dropped his wallet in a side pocket, and checked the time on a dusty clock hanging cockeyed on the wall. "Aren't you going to the Hunters' service? It's about to start."

Nick's face tightened. "Isn't it tomorrow morning? Everyone is driving in tomorrow."

"No, it's right now."

"Stinkin' Keaton gave us the wrong date!" Nick took off for the door and stopped. "Sheriff, may I follow you?"

"Get your car going, and I'll come around front."

Eight minutes later they turned on a one-way street toward the cemetery and lined up behind the last car. The sky was rowdy, but the rain had stopped. The sedan carrying Steely and Beatrice whizzed by.

CHAPTER THREE

M artinez took the spot always saved for the closest kin be-
hind the hearse. He turned off the ignition and opened
Steely's door. Noting Pastor Weldon had stalled by singing hymns,
Steely sighed. Then she hurried over to him, under the small tent
that covered two caskets and a few chairs, to whisper in his ear.
This had to be the shortest service he ever performed.

Weldon understood.

The few gathered respectfully rose to their feet when Bea wobbled out of the car. Pepe had one side, and Steely took the other,
making sure Bea remained standing. They practically carried her
across the lawn to a front-row seat. Every person was wet from the
rain. They were good, caring people.

Weldon condensed the service to ten minutes. He concluded
with a prayer while every head bowed. "Father, we ask You to comfort Beatrice and Steely. For we know when we are weak, You are
strong. Give this family Your strength today. You alone are their
comforter, their healer, the restorer of their souls. We lift them up
to You and trust You to take care of them. We ask these things in
Jesus's name. Amen." As eyes opened, people circled around Bea.

The pastor and his wife accompanied Beatrice Hunter for a last good-bye. In a few minutes, the metal boxes would be forever lowered eight feet below. A backhoe with a warmed-up engine waited in the background ready to replenish the soil.

Bea ran her hand gently across each casket, as if she was touching the remains inside. She lifted a rose from each spray on top, clenching them tightly to her chest. Steely waited to the side. She wasn't touching the caskets. She'd seen what was inside. If Bea had seen them, she most likely wouldn't be standing at all.

Steely felt frail, as if half the blood in her body had been drained. It took all the strength she could muster to get her and Bea there today. She turned away. There was no need to see the hole, exposed, when the wind blew the drapes tapered around the coffins.

Steely caught a glimpse of Nick and the sheriff, their heads bent together, listening to Tucker's radio. Suddenly both men perked up. Tucker jumped in his cruiser and U-turned, throwing up a small tornado of dust. Nick cast his gaze back at her.

He's family to me.

Nick moved toward her, his steps purposeful, until he touched her arm. "Steely, I'm so sorry…"

Her eyelids slowly closed.

He cupped her face in his hands, as if he was holding her heart.

"Nick." She huddled in his grasp. He held her securely. Her body trembled.

"You're freezing." He took off his coat. "Put this on." He wrapped her up. They sloshed through the sparsely laid grass for a few yards. She latched onto his arm.

"I don't understand," she uttered.

"I don't have the answer. We may never understand why. But if we could ask any of them if they wanted to come back, they'd say no. If I don't know anything about what happened, I know that much."

She agreed and held onto his arm. He placed his hand on top of hers, steering her.

"Miss Bea was against our getting married."

Nick glared over at Beatrice Hunter, still lingering by the caskets.

"I was told she thought I'd be a terrible wife—you know, because of my circumstance." Steely felt numb as she repeated her mother-in-law's unfavorable assessment.

Nick briefly stopped. "You're the perfect wife."

Steely almost edged out a grin. They slowly walked on.

"Steely, if there's anything you need, please call me. I don't care what it is. Anything. Call me. You know I mean it."

She did. But she wouldn't call. Her world could be crumbling beneath her, as it had before. She didn't call then. If she had, she would have made nonstop calls between the eighth grade and her freshman year in college.

"Did anyone else from the company come?"

His lips pursed, and he silently shook his head.

"Miss Bea said they're nothing but a bunch of dirty dogs. Are they?"

"Some are."

"Good thing Mr. Keaton didn't come. She'd do something she might later regret."

"I'm about there myself."

They took a few more steps.

"She said they wouldn't have the guts to show up."

"A few had the guts. There was a problem with communication. The newspaper said the service was tomorrow. The sheriff just told me it was today. I came up early to talk to him, or I wouldn't have known."

She scrunched her face. "The sheriff?"

"I wanted to get some details on what happened." He kicked a chunk of mud.

Steely tightened her grip. "Nick, I've had my share of peculiar deaths. Something's not right here. It's just not right. Do you trust the sheriff?"

He tightened up. "Yes. He's doing his job."

"Jack driving off a cliff just doesn't feel right. This isn't the first thing that didn't feel right to me."

He wiped a tear from her face. "I guarantee you: we'll find out what really happened." He refrained from blabbing about what had plagued his mind since the moment he heard Jack drove off a cliff. The truth was he wasn't sure of anything that'd happened the last two months. The memorial service was not the time to speculate. "How long are you going to stay in Grey Canyon?" he inquired, changing the subject.

Steely's tone settled. "I'm not sure. I'll stay with Miss Bea for now."

They stopped and faced each other.

"I know Mrs. Hunter is hurting badly." He looked over at Bea and then back to Steely. "She was my mother's college roommate. For some strange reason, they get along. But you're hurting too, Steely. You've been through a lot. Is staying with Mrs. Hunter the best thing for you?"

"I'm going to get her situated. Then I'll move back to Houston. She really doesn't want to live with me anyway."

"I see. Then I suggest you respect her wishes."

Martinez caught Steely's attention. He motioned that Bea was ready to go.

Steely acknowledged him by returning the nod. She unwrapped herself from Nick's grasp and began to remove his coat.

"No, you keep it." He placed the coat back onto her shoulders.

She peeked inside, revealing a label. "This is an expensive coat."

"It's just a coat. It will keep you warm."

"Thanks, Nick." They briefly embraced.

As she left, she glanced back at him on her way to the car. Martinez held the door until she was settled in the back seat. Bea buckled up in the front.

Nick stared at the exiting car, catching a last glimpse of her through the rear window. He stood frozen for a few seconds until she was totally out of sight. Then he jogged to his car, pulled out his cell, and punched in a number. "Pierce better get back fast. We've got a mess to untangle."

CHAPTER FOUR

Nick stared blankly out the window in Pierce Thibodeaux's twenty-fifth-floor office, watching the attorney fiddle with a glass jar perched on a bookshelf. The last few minutes had grated on him. He had waited for weeks to get the opinion of the chief counsel for Jack Hunter Industries (JHI) on Jack's departure and the stability of the company. And he wasn't leaving, even if he had to watch Pierce piddle around all morning.

Pierce would have an iron-clad opinion, although it sometimes conflicted with Nick's. His South Louisiana upbringing gave him a boldness that resulted in more run-ins with Harry Keaton than Nick. Pierce finally placed the cylinder packed with sand next to a row of books. He pawed the wreath of dust growing around his head.

Pierce poured liquid from an insulated jug. "Coffee?"

"No, thanks. I've had all the coffee I can handle today." Nick pushed a chair closer to the desk and then sat again. He was ready to throw the chair out the window if he could gain Thibodeaux's attention. "Can we get going here? I feel like I've aged waiting on you."

"I don't know what to say. I walk in the door and find out Jack not only resigned but died. I feel like I got hit by a cement truck."

"Pierce, it was worse than that. I was afraid to drink the coffee in the board room."

Thibodeaux unbuttoned his jacket, rolled out a chair, and sat. His face belied trouble. Clearly, the relaxation he received from the longest vacation of his life had severely diminished.

"I tried to reach you for two months. You're supposed to be a workaholic."

"Not anymore." Pierce poked a pass code on his keyboard, gaining access to the most secure area on the JHI intranet: accounting. He leaned back, distressed, elbows fanned out on the arms of his chair. "I can't imagine this place without Hunter."

"The ship has been commandeered by pirates."

Pierce shook his head and sipped from the cup.

"You should have been here."

"How was I supposed to know the company was about to crater?"

"You sure didn't need to vacation right now."

"That's what you think. I had to do something drastic. I promised my wife no electronics. Just family time. The entire world could have fallen apart, and we wouldn't have known." Thibodeaux added another pass code; an antivirus program began scanning his system.

"Did you need to take a blackout vacation?"

Irritated, Pierce responded, "Nick, when I left, everything was rolling along great."

"I told you four years ago the LLCs were sketchy."

"They're still sketchy. Jack told me to go. And I went. My wife has put up with a lot. After what just happened to Hunter, it's vacations from now on for me. Only God knows how long any of us have left." He tapped a few more keys.

"Are you having a midlife crisis or something?"

"Just getting my priorities straight."

"What happened?"

Pierce's countenance changed from troubled to ticked. "I came home early one day and saw our neighbor Billy Mick talking to my wife. He got all up in her personal space."

"He hit on Muffy?"

"His wife works. He's at home all day baking cookies." Thibodeaux banged the keys, putting in another code. "That cookie maker better keep his cookies to himself. Nobody's baking with my wife but me. He tries that again, and Billy will never bake again."

"So, you can take the baker. Impressive. Now, Pierce, can we focus here?"

Pierce leaned in to his monitor.

"Where are your glasses?"

"I broke them." He hit a few keys and turned toward Nick. "Go ahead tell me how this went down."

"Keaton threatened to collapse unless Jack resigned."

"Couldn't you stop him till I got back? We can delay anything for ninety days."

"Stopping Hunter when he's made up his mind is about as easy as going a year without sinning."

"Why'd he transfer his shares to Keaton for nothing?"

"Keaton held the company hostage until Jack resigned and gave up his interest."

"What about your dad? He's Hunter's personal attorney. Couldn't he help?"

Nick flinched. "Pierce, some days he doesn't remember his name."

Thibodeaux shook his head. "I'm sorry, man."

They stared at each for a few seconds until Nick spoke up. "You know, we came within a day of filing chapter seven."

Pierce smacked the arms of his chair. "That's garbage! If this company were a bank, it'd have enough reserves to satisfy the FDIC!"

"Not according to my audit."

Pierce lifted the clipped papers in front of him and thumbed to the last page. "Your audit stinks!"

"Sure it stinks. It's all red ink."

"Did you trace the assets?"

Nick lunged over at the jar on the shelf and dug out a fistful of sand.

Pierce flew up. "What are you doing?"

Nick pitched the sand in the air. They watched it vanish into the carpet. "Trace that!"

Pierce sat, agitated. "I hope the blood worms don't mind you messing with their habitat."

Nick looked surprisingly back at the jar. "Well, they should feel right at home with the parasites in the executive office."

Pierce tossed the report across his desk, scattering a few envelopes. "You need to leave my worms alone and figure this out. Keaton could walk away with two, maybe three hundred million, plus Hunter's interest in JHI. Why is he still here?"

"I don't know."

"You're the senior VP of finance. You better get busy, or Beatrice Hunter will never see another dime from this company."

Nick slung the report back across the desk. "Thousands of transactions are hitting the books every day. I'd have to freeze every account just to catch up. You're an attorney. File a petition for an injunction and shut down the insanity!"

"For what?"

"I don't care for what. Just file a stinking lawsuit." Nick rose and moved around like he wanted to leave, but he didn't. He stopped behind a chair, angrily hammering the back with a fist. "Isn't that what attorneys do—file stinking lawsuits?"

Pierce hollered, "You want an implosion? We'll ruin the company for sure if I make an accusation against the CEO. You give me something that will get Keaton out. I'll get him replaced and file the stinkiest suit ever filed!"

"Fine then. I better get back to work. But I'll tell you. I've had it with Keaton giving me the runaround about the flash drives."

"You still haven't found the account statements?"

"Nope. Statements from nine years ago until I got here are still missing. Keaton claims Jack had them."

"You believe him?"

"Not unless Jack lied to me."

Pierce shook his head.

"Keaton's stonewalling. I don't think I even have all the accounts. I've been contacting our clients to make sure they're being invoiced to a legitimate JHI account. It's the craziest thing. Hundreds of LLCs out there are collecting our revenue in unknown accounts."

"Order dupes."

"Don't think I haven't tried. Keaton is the only man who has the authorization to get at them."

"You mean to tell me Nick Dichiara, who went around town playing a teenage superhero, can't get a few account statements?"

"Oh, I'll get them. And I'll get the assets back too. And I better not hear any complaints about my methods from anyone, including you, Mr. Thibodeaux." Nick took two abrupt steps toward the door.

"Nick, will these statements show a crime was even committed?"

Nick swung back around. "I've been told no."

Being a head lower than Nick didn't stop Pierce from getting in his face. "I want Keaton too. But you better watch it. If you go after him, he'll go after you. He could even point the finger at you."

"Let him."

"I'm serious, cowboy. Don't go getting yourself indicted. If we ever get someone to investigate this, they'll dig into you. They'll pull every bank record you've ever had. They'll know if you ever took a kid's milk money."

"Am I supposed to be scared?"

"I hope so. Maybe a little fear will keep you from getting reckless."

"You're the guy that chews on jalapeños," Nick responded. "I'm surprised you didn't punch the guy who wanted to bake with Muffy."

Pierce rolled his eyes.

"You did? Didn't you? That's how you broke your glasses. You punched him!"

"He ran like his cookies were on fire."

Nick snickered and then turned to leave.

Pierce yelled, "Keaton can't touch you, unless you're indicted for fraud. You might want to warn your parents. Keaton might go after them. Your father is a wealthy lawyer. He set up the first few LLCs. Your mother was the best county prosecutor in my lifetime."

"My parents are junkyard dogs. You want to know what they taught me? I'll never be successful without taking risks."

"Great. Probably the only thing you remember." He patted Nick on the arm. "Just be careful."

"I'm going to get Keaton," he said, leaving without agreeing. The only way to be careful in this situation was to do nothing. And that was something he wasn't capable of doing.

CHAPTER FIVE

Steely Paupher grew up in a tree-towering neighborhood. She was the only child of parents who not only cherished her but also each other. Middle school at Juan Seguin was drama-free until the eighth grade. A perceptive math teacher told her in the first week of school that she had the common sense of a forty-year-old. Steely may have been on the fast track to maturity, but she was barely thirteen. And in middle school a kid needs a best friend more than books. Someone she can count on. Someone who will defend her no matter who's around. If there were a middle-school survival kit, a best friend would be a staple. Steely's staple was Erin Fitzpatrick, a girl her age who also grew up near their downtown Houston neighborhood. "Reliable at all times" defined her friend Erin.

One day after school, Steely and Erin pedaled their bikes to Memorial Park. Along the two-mile stretch, Erin teased Steely, saying she had some big news. After several minutes of taunting, Erin stopped, propped her bike against a tree, and squatted.

Steely set her bike up too. "What's going on?" she probed. "Tell me the good news!"

Erin grinned broadly. "In a minute. Let's rest; then I'll tell you."

Steely sat, crossed her legs, and waited a few feet away.

Erin recited something to herself that Steely didn't understand. Like she was rehearsing a speech in her head. Her mouth moved, but nothing came out.

She stretched in the leaves, spacing out in a daydream. Steely went from excitement to anxiety trying to figure out what was going on.

Maybe it's nothing more than a family vacation. The past year, Erin's family had covered the earth vacationing. Steely pondered every possible scenario. Several more minutes passed with not so much as a hint. The wait was tormenting. Steely pressed again. "Come on; tell me what's going on." Steely wadded a few dry leaves, crumbling them into tiny morsels.

"Well..." Erin flailed her arms, as if going for a kill shot in volleyball. "My dad's CPA firm has a new client that's paying him crazy money. He said we're rich!"

"That's great!" Steely looked over at her friend's bike, figuring this wasn't the big news. Erin's new bike, with more gears than she knew what to do with, was a financial statement to an eighth grader.

"Things are so good that—" Erin stopped short for a few seconds before continuing. "We're moving!" She clapped, giving herself a rah-rah.

Steely had heart palpitations. "I'm happy for you." And she was—deep down inside. She was happy for her. "I know you wanted a new house, but where is it?" She nervously waited to hear if Erin's new home was even in the continental United States.

Erin crossed her arms under her head, resting hammock-style.

Steely's bronchial tubes tightened. She dug an inhaler out of her pocket. Two squirts brought some relief, but her thoughts raced on. She wished she had an inhaler for her mind. She pressed. "Where, Erin? Where are you moving?"

"Pecan Valley Estates," she puffed.

Steely cheered. "That's great news! There are some nice homes there. And it's only a short walk from here—that won't affect anything. We can ride bikes and hang out just like we've been doing!"

Erin laid back.

Steely was right. It was only a short walk. But it was on the other side of the tracks.

Erin grinned. Sneered. Grinned again.

Steely's wide mouth smiled. "Erin, we might move too. My dad's been working so hard. Really long hours the last few weeks. I've hardly seen him. He's so smart. My mom said he's on the level of a genius. Dad didn't say anything about being rich, but we have more than we need."

Erin hiked a leg, scrunched her face. "The Cricket said your dad was a garbage collector." Then she tilted sideways, waiting for a response.

"Garbage collector? Well, I guess you could say that, but he only collects the most important garbage."

"No garbage is important."

"He securely shreds papers. I told you that—"

"I'm getting hungry. I'll race you!" She leaped up for a head start.

"You're on!"

They pushed and pulled along the narrow sidewalk, crossing carefully at each corner. The roads were much too busy to ride in the street along the curb, which they sometimes did. Erin held the lead with five blocks to go. They made a sharp turn to find a five-foot-six obstacle on the sidewalk.

"Move!" the girls screamed in unison.

Cricket Mauder heard them, making matters worse. They would have been better off saying nothing and attempting to maneuver around her. Cricket venomously positioned herself in place. They weren't getting past her.

Erin swung right, landing spread-eagle in the grass.

Steely's split-second choice was running Cricket down or veering into oncoming traffic. It was as if she was moving in slow motion, but she wasn't. She was out of control.

The driver smoked his tires on the asphalt. Steely attached to the car like a magnet to metal. Then she peeled off a side panel, dropping onto the street. The man jumped out of his car and knelt beside her. She looked up at him, dazed.

"Thank God you're alive!" he said. "Are you bleeding?"

She wasn't interested in triaging her body for scrapes and bruises. Her pain was suddenly anesthetized when she locked eyes with his emerald greens.

"I'm so sorry. Are you able to speak?"

She lifted up on her elbows and muttered, "What's your name?"

"Nick Dichiara."

Nick Dichiara…I'm so glad I crashed into you.

He helped her sit. "Stay here a minute. You don't want to get up too fast." He unfastened her helmet and slipped it off. "Good thing you had this on."

Steely blinked in agreement.

Erin groaned and spit out a few blades of grass, attempting to draw attention.

The Cricket had the consoling ability of Job's friends. "Pauper, you need to watch where you're going! You tore up our grass and almost ran me down!" She stooped and uprighted an overnight bag. "You better not have broken anything. My mother is picking me up to go to Dallas."

Steely attempted to stand. Nick reached for her. "Let me help you up."

His arms are bigger than my body.

"Your knee's bleeding," he said. "Let's get it checked out. I'm calling nine one one."

"No. Really, I'm OK. I can't go to the hospital every time I bust a knee. Would you mind helping me over there?" She pointed to the grass.

"Of course not." Emerald Eyes wrapped one arm around her back, the other under her knees, and cradled her. She rested on his well-endowed shoulder and closed her eyes.

Erin's mouth dropped.

Cricket propped her hands on her waist. "She's OK," she complained. "Don't put her in my yard!"

Nick placed Steely on the grass. He was deaf to Cricket, standing a few feet away. "Are you sure you don't need an ambulance?"

"No, no. Really, I'm fine." Steely felt sorry for the poor guy. He looked worse than her.

"Pauper, you're a complete idiot," nipped Cricket. "You don't tell someone who hit you with a car that you're not injured."

"It's the truth," Steely insisted.

"I think you cracked your head open and lost your brains!"

"Cricket, you need to leave," said Nick.

"This is my yard!" she barked.

"Call the cops!" Then he looked back down at Steely. "Do you live far?"

"Only a few blocks." She moved her legs. Still worked. "I can make it fine."

"I'll drive you home."

Her face broadened. *Drive me in his car? What kind of car is that?*

Erin drooled. Cricket snarled.

"I want to talk to your parents." He checked out her bike, compared it to his back seat. "I'll put the top down. It'll fit."

"She's faking." Cricket folded her arms. "She can ride her own bike home. Nick, give Cricket a quick ride around the block. Hurry, my mother will be here any minute."

Nick glared at her. "I've told you a hundred times—you're too young to ride with me."

"What about her?" Cricket extended a finger at Steely. "We're in the same grade, but I'm a year older."

"I have a question for you." He kept his eyes on Steely, but he was talking to Cricket. "Why didn't *you* move out of *her* way?"

Cricket flashed her lanky lids. "Pedestrians have the right-of-way. She could've seriously hurt Cricket."

Nick shook his head in disgust. "You heard her scream. I heard her scream!"

"And you may have been speeding."

"I hope I wasn't."

Cricket unfolded her arms and moved closer to Nick. "When Pauper stops seeing stars, she's going to see dollars. My memory is already getting foggy. Maybe you were speeding? Maybe you jumped the curb and hit the little tot. I'm the perfect eyewitness. All I need is a ride to school once a week, and you're in the clear."

"Looks like the Cricket's attempting a middle-school shake down," said Nick, staring at her sternly. "You better go inside and wait for your mother before I call the cops!"

"You're making a big mistake!" Cricket stomped off, crossing paths with an ant mound. She deftly swung her foot back and decimated the colony. "You don't have any more business sense than Pauper."

"Nick, I'm not suing you," whispered Steely.

"Don't worry about it. I have insurance if you did."

She arched a brow.

Don't worry about it? Is he for real?

"Just rest here," he said.

They stared at each other for a few seconds.

"Nick, it's getting dark. I need to go on home."

"OK." He set up her bike. "Here we go." He opened his car door, pressed a button, and wound down the top. His license tag was still a paper one.

This man is putting my bike on his leather seat. Steely caught a glimpse of his onboard computer system. *This car could drive itself.*

Her cuts and bruises weren't nearly as painful as telling him, "I'm sorry. I can't ride with strangers."

"I understand," he said.

"You do?" she said, high pitched.

"I should've known you can't ride with people you don't know."

He's understanding...

Erin finally dusted herself off and got up. "Nick, I'm Erin Fitzpatrick, your new neighbor. I'm moving down the street in the big two-story with the giant windows in front."

"Then welcome to the neighborhood, Erin." Nick offered a handshake. Then he directed his focus back on Steely.

Steely rationalized. Riding with the finest looking man she ever saw in the finest looking car on the road. *Erin knows him...It's not much of a ride. Just a few blocks. No one would know...I can't do it. Even the most gorgeous eyes I have ever seen, the most perfect brown hair, and enormous muscular body doesn't mean he's not a serial killer.*

Preparing to get up, Steely brushed the remaining dirt off her shorts.

"Let me help you." He placed his left hand on the center of her back, his right one under her elbow, and lifted her smoother than hydraulics. "I should have paid more attention to my surroundings. It's been a tough evening. My mind was somewhere else." He smiled. "How about this—let me walk you home? Would that be OK?"

Her best friend pushed for a wise decision. "Steely, don't be paranoid. For once in your life, take a risk. I know him." Erin stood her bike up.

What kind of pressure is that? Calling me paranoid in front of a man who shaves?

"May I walk you home?" He helped Steely to the sidewalk. "Would that be all right?"

"I think it would be nice." Steely glanced over at the car and spotted a William Travis High School sticker on the windshield. "Are you a junior or a senior?"

Junior...please junior.

"Senior," he answered.

"You'll be gone before we get to Travis next year."

"We can still be friends."

Both girls nodded.

Nick moved his car to the curb. He'd mention the huge gash on the front end. He gripped Steely's bike like a plastic toy, pushing it alongside of her. Erin was relegated to tagging along behind.

Two and three-quarters of a second later, I would have missed him. He's so fine.

Steely dismissed the fact that two and three-quarters of a second sooner and she might have been face to face with Jesus.

They strolled together, much slower than the ants Cricket evicted. As they got closer to her home, she abruptly dropped the small talk in lieu of gathering vital information. Her first question was of ample importance: "Are you married?"

He looked over at her. "Not yet." He was almost pretty but manly at the same time.

Erin butted in when possible, which wasn't often since Steely talked nonstop. "Steely, he's not old enough to get married," Erin scolded.

"Erin, you can get married at eighteen," Steely said. "Or even before with parental permission." She swished her head back at Nick. "Are you eighteen?"

"Yes, but I'm going to college before I get married."

"I'm going to college too. Where are you going?" Erin asked.

"Texas Tech."

"Me too! Both my parents went there. We'll be in college together if you take grad courses. Are you getting a grad degree?"

"I'm not sure yet."

"After college I'm getting married. I'm going to have a happy home like my mom and dad," she said confidently.

"Me too," said Steely. "Age doesn't matter among college students. Does it?"

"That's right," he said. "I believe you'll have that happy home," he remarked, cloudy eyed.

Erin took the opportunity to pass the yappy couple when they crossed to the next corner.

Their journey had dwindled down to the last block. Steely slowed down and conversed faster. "And I'm going to have two children and a pug."

Erin had had her fill and blurted, "Steely, quit boring Nick with all your business. I'm surprised you haven't told him how you threw up when you had the flu."

"Why would I?" Steely blinked fast at her.

Nick patted Steely on the shoulder. "You're not boring me. I think you're a fascinating young lady."

Erin clenched a fist and mumbled, "I should've gone left."

Steely agreed.

"Is that knee holding out OK?" Nick asked Steely. "I can give you a piggyback if it's hurting."

The girls briefly stopped breathing.

Erin dropped her head and whispered, "Say yes, and let me dream."

Steely caught her breath. "I...think...I can make it."

He paused, looking puzzled. "Wow! You're the first girl who ever turned me down."

Why'd I do it?

Erin kicked her and whispered, "You lost your mind?"

They were a few steps from the last turn.

I have to keep my head on straight. He's an older man. He'd be a weirdo if he liked an eighth grader. I'll probably never see him again.

She kept her eyes glued on him.

Erin led the way around the last corner, cutting to the right onto their street. Her face lit up. She yelled back, "Steely, the cops are at your house!"

"Nick, did you call the cops?"

"No. Steely, what's your last name?"

"Paupher."

He shrunk. "Steely, you better run ahead inside. I'll put your bike up."

She stared at him curiously for a second and then took off.

CHAPTER SIX

She burst open the front door and found an officer standing alone in the living room. The house was still. Even the officer stood motionless. Something had happened, and it was not good. Officers don't wait in your home to deliver good news. "Is everything OK?" Steely asked. "No, I see it's not."

The officer grasped her hat and moved it to one side. Looking peaked, she briefly shut her eyes, keeping them closed longer than a normal blink. She hesitated for a few seconds and then asked, "Are you Steely?"

Steely trembled. "Yes, officer. Please tell me why you're here." She had a clear view of the empty kitchen. The bathroom door was open. No light on in there. The house only had two other rooms, and they were bedrooms. "Where are my mom and dad?"

"Steely, I'm Officer Montgomery. May we sit down and talk, please?"

The only way Steely could sit was if the officer knocked her down. She wept, releasing some of the hysteria building up inside. "Please…where are my parents?"

"Your mother's in the bedroom lying down. I didn't want to leave until you got home. It's your father…"

"What?" She stopped crying briefly and rambled, "Where's he? Did he have an accident? He's a good driver, except he drives too slow. Says he's being careful. I told him not to drive so slow. Is he in the hospital or something?" Then she abruptly stopped. "You wouldn't be here if he was just in the hospital." She felt her knees buckling. "Would you?"

The officer placed her hand on Steely's shoulder. "Honey, I'm so sorry. Sometimes things happen that are out of our control. We tried—"

"Tried?" Steely said frantically. "I want to talk to him. Where is he?" She took her cell out of her pocket. Her dad bought her the phone. It was for one purpose: to call him or her mom, any time, any place. Dad always answered. His number was the first one stored on speed dial. He set it up himself. Her finger wobbled as she pressed the single digit. Tears trickled past her face down to her neck. She brushed them off with the back of her hand. "My dad will answer. You'll see; he'll answer."

The phone rang four times. Then it went to voice mail. Steely cringed upon hearing her father's recorded voice for the first time. She looked up at the officer and then slid down to the floor and crunched forward.

"I'm so sorry." The officer stooped down beside her. "Your father had an accident at Curley's Bar."

Steely dropped her head and rocked back and forth. "What? My dad doesn't even go to bars!"

The officer placed a hand on Steely's back. There was no way to lessen the load she had just dumped on her. "We'll get to the truth. We have detectives interviewing witnesses now. They're telling us your father fought with a man—supposedly over a woman."

Those were gut-wrenching words. "A woman?" she whimpered. "There was no other woman." Her face overheated. Her body perspired profusely.

The officer had delivered the most stinging news an eighth grader could ever hear: her father died in a bar fighting over a woman who wasn't her mother.

Steely jumped up and ran for the kitchen. She leaned over the sink and poured her insides out.

Montgomery stayed with her. "I had to tell you because it's already hit the news." Montgomery opened a few drawers until she found a washrag. She ran cold water over it and dabbed Steely's burning face. Then she rinsed it and placed it around the back of her neck.

Steely lifted her head a few seconds later. Her body was briefly cooled, but inside she was still a raging furnace. One thing she was confident of: she knew her dad. No one could convince her otherwise. No way he had some other life. No way he was some other person she didn't know. She respectfully responded. "I don't care what anybody says. I know my dad. There was no woman for him except my mom."

Montgomery wasn't there to debate her father's fidelity. She was there to carry out the worst part of her job by delivering the news. "I believe you, Steely. I don't believe everything I'm told. I hope you don't believe everything you hear on the news." The officer held Steely's chin up. "Your mother really needs you now. Why don't you go in and see her. I'll let you know when we have more information."

Steely wiped her face again and hurried to the bedroom. She cried in bed with her mom until her mom fell asleep. She eased out of bed so as not to wake her. Next, she booted up her laptop. She read every news report she could find. The stories were just as the officer said. She read through each of them over again and then watched the video reports over and over but learned nothing new.

The only confirmed fact was that her dad had passed. It didn't matter to Steely that every one of the witnesses gave the same account of what happened—Fred Paupher was in the bar fighting over a woman. Steely wasn't buying it. No matter what the witnesses or news reports said, she didn't believe it.

Her mother was devastated. She and Fred had been together since high school. He was not only her husband but also her best friend.

The police had made many arrests at the cantina. The manager, along with over forty patrons, were picked up for drunkenness. Most had crossed over the legal blood-alcohol limit hours before the fight.

Detectives questioned everyone. But they couldn't identify who'd shoved Fred into the wall, where his head took the fatal blow. The only thing all of the witnesses agreed on was that a woman started screaming for Fred to leave her alone. And then a brawl broke out. The medical examiner ruled Fred's death a homicide. Tests revealed his blood-alcohol level was zero. Steely was stumped trying to figure out what brought her dad to the bar that afternoon.

Steely's mom slid deep into depression. Before long, she was unable to work and almost homebound. The responsibility for her and her mother had suddenly been passed to Steely. She was her mom's unofficial guardian. She wasn't old enough to be official and feared telling anyone since someone might trigger having her mom committed to the state psychiatric hospital in Rusk. Steely would then become a ward of the state. Motherless and fostered until she was eighteen. Steely protected their home at all costs, telling no one about the situation.

CHAPTER SEVEN

Steely was sitting on the edge the sofa. The checkbook tumbled from her hands, landing between her and the coffee table blanketed with bills. Her mother lay under a blanket on the adjacent sofa watching a game show. Contestants dressed in humorous costumes for a chance to win a grand prize or to walk away with a dud was the scope of her entertainment.

Steely had learned how to clean the toilets. The toilet cleaner label gave clear instructions. Pour it in and scrub. These were directions she could understand and follow. But there was no guidebook on how to make up a budget shortage of a thousand dollars each month. She had used coupons and bought discounted sale items. Every time she got close, somehow the shortage grew.

"Mom, do you know if Dad had any other accounts?"

"No, just those I gave you."

Steely gathered the bills together. She stacked them in a pile. They were the liabilities. The family's checking-account statements were lined up next to them. The measly two pages accounted for their only liquid assets. There was no need to include the savings account with its zero balance. She folded her hands together and stared at the table. Seconds later she took a deep breath and exhaled as if she had run a marathon.

"Mom, have you seen the most recent statements?"

"No, only the ones I gave you from last month. There's a lot of money in those accounts. Dad even paid off the mortgage."

"Yes, it's paid off," she sighed.

"I know he was saving to build a new home. He wanted to tear this one down."

Steely gazed at the middle of the living-room floor.

"The trees are beautiful, but they can destroy a foundation," said Mom. "Dad talked about getting a beach house too, and maybe a boat. He said we could pay cash by the end of the year." Her mother caught Steely's distressed face. "Is something wrong, dear?"

"No, it's fine."

But it wasn't fine. The bank accounts had a total of $575.23. Fred had emptied them. Steely pulled the previous twelve statements and carefully lined them up. Fred's income had shot up to $25,000 a month. Two days before he died, he'd withdrawn $273,042.18 in cash. The money had vanished. And there was no record as to where it went.

I'm not telling her. After the report about the woman, she'd think Dad was running around on her for sure. I have to find a job.

Her granddad in Pensacola had told her about his childhood a few years before he passed. By the time he was fourteen, both his parents had died. Granddad lived at the YMCA for four years before he joined the army. After two years of service, he came back and started his own business, selling cooking pots door-to-door. If Granddad could make it, so could she. But not by selling pots door-to-door. It wasn't a good idea to knock on a stranger's door and ask if they wanted to buy some pots.

Over the next two weeks, Steely applied for work at fast-food restaurants, bookstores, home-cleaning services, and finally at a library. She was ready, willing, and able to work. But no one would hire her. The reason for her rejection was as clear as the toilet she had scrubbed. She was only fourteen. Every prospective employer gave Steely the same story. "You're too young." She couldn't get a job doing even the simplest task.

There was no business left to call, no place to apply—until Jenny Dix caught her after school at her locker. The halls were nearly empty; only a few students remained fifteen minutes after dismissal. Steely didn't know Jenny well. She had one class with the girl whose signature outfit was chains—big ones around her neck, arms, legs, just about everywhere they could be hung. Back in the sixties, Jenny would have most certainly been present at Woodstock wearing nothing but long hair and chains. Steely had a signature outfit too: faded jeans and a knit pullover.

Jenny fanned her hand past her nose. "Steely, your books stink. What kind of cheese did Cricket put in your locker?"

"I don't know. I'm taking them home this weekend to air out in the backyard."

"Hey, you ready to call my guy for a job? He's got only one opening."

"Thanks for the offer, Jenny." Steely shut her locker and spun the combo lock. "No offense, but it sounds a little sketchy."

"It's not!" Jenny said defensively.

"I've filled out forty-three applications. They all said I'm too young. Nobody will hire me. There's something about their insurance that stops them from employing anybody under sixteen. Everything will be all right. I'll figure something out." Steely headed down the hall.

"Hold on." Jenny caught up with her. "He's a successful businessman who will hire you today. He's made a ton of money." Jenny searched her phone. "Here, call this number."

"Why would this man be different than anybody else?" Steely was resistant to even make the call.

"He's unconventional. Call him."

"I don't know…"

The girls moved down the hall toward the exit. Two boys passed, gawking at Jenny.

"What are you looking at?" she snapped.

One of the boys taunted, "Did you escape from the zoo?"

Jenny fired her math book at him. The boy dodged it and walked off chuckling.

Timmy Kipps came up from behind. Small for his age, he was not an ounce over ninety-nine pounds. He picked up the book and handed it back to Jenny. "Don't pay any attention to them. They just like getting you stirred up."

Jenny agreed.

"Thanks, Timmy," said Steely.

He shyly ventured, "Steely, I'll wait out on the sidewalk if you want to walk home together."

"Sure. I'll be out in a few minutes."

Timmy grinned and shuffled off.

Steely and Jenny continued on.

"How well do you know him?" Jenny asked.

"Just met him a few weeks ago when I was cutting the grass. He lives a block from my house. He offered to help me that day and has been helping ever since."

"He's ticking off the wrong people."

"I don't know how. He's a supernice guy."

"Anyway, let's get back to business. This man will hire you. He's easy to work for. His boss is weird, needs a good waxing, but you'll never see him. I only saw him once by accident. Are you interested?"

Steely shrugged. "What kind of job is it?"

"Delivery. You pick up and deliver packages. Easy stuff."

"Like a courier?"

Jenny gave a thumbs-up. "That's the idea."

"Is it dangerous?"

"Nope. It's exclusive. Someone got promoted, and he has an open spot. You don't want to miss this opportunity. Hurry, before he hires someone else."

Steely paused. "Do I need a car? I can't get a provisionary license for another ten months and twenty-seven and a half days. You have to be fifteen."

"You don't need a car. He prefers that you walk or ride a bike. Easy to get around."

"Will he need to talk to my mom? You know, to get permission?"

"Steely, were you harvested in a shell? If you go around asking questions like that, people will think you're slow."

"It's a legitimate question." Steely popped open the door and tapped down six steps.

Jenny hit every other one, trying to keep up. "Call him. He's really nice, except for one thing."

"Is he a pimp or something?"

"No! I told you it's a delivery business."

"I wasn't sure if I was the package."

"I'm not a prostitute!"

"OK, then what's the catch?"

"He's very private. He just doesn't like it if you ask too many questions."

"What am I delivering?"

"What did I just say? Do your job, and don't ask questions."

Steely set her books on the sidewalk between her legs. She took out her cell, input the number, and placed the phone next to her ear. "I don't care about his idiosyncrasies, as long as it's not illegal." Steely looked point-blank at Jenny. "Is it illegal?" The phone was ringing.

"Of course not," assured Jenny.

He answered.

Steely had her first job.

CHAPTER EIGHT

The Houston Police Department wasn't the place Steely expected to be on a Friday evening. It wasn't where she expected to be at any time. She was there for only one reason. She was in trouble. If someone at HPD needed to talk to her, she would've rather they did it by phone, just like her dad did when he reported a minor car accident. Steely was getting the idea that she was the only thing minor about what happened.

Officer Montgomery ran Steely past the detainees lined up in chairs along a wall. Men and women were mixed in together. Handcuffs and fetters held them in place but didn't stop the obscenities from pouring out of their mouths. Those arrested were innocent. Every one of them said so.

HPD had run a sting that netted a bumper crop, way more arrests than they had officers to process. Those picked up were drugged out, liquored out, totally spaced out of their minds—some without the help of a mind-altering substance. Every detainee had the same attitude, the same angry look, and the same rough appearance, except the girl donning a white cardigan with heart-shaped buttons.

Montgomery placed Steely in the chair next to Sergeant Donovan's desk and informed her that Donovan would be right back. Everyone else was in line for a padded interrogation room.

Donovan towered over Steely while getting to a chair that disappeared when he sat. His hand swallowed up a pen. The six stripes on each sleeve were earned from consistently locking up more bad guys than anyone else in the department.

Steely was calm until Sergeant Donovan read Officer Montgomery's report out loud. She wondered if she would be the next one seated in the chairs lined up on the wall.

"Let's start from the beginning," he said, in a deep, brassy voice. "What were you doing meeting with Sling?"

"Working." She clenched her sweaty hands in her lap. Then she unclenched them and stuck one under each thigh. "Why did Officer Montgomery bring me here?"

"She doesn't want you to die before you get to prison."

Steely sniffled. "Well, I don't want either one. I need my inhaler." Steely took the canister, pressed two squirts, and returned it to her purse.

Donovan pulled a tissue from a box and passed it to her. "Steely, listen to me. I can't tell you what's going on, but I can tell you this much. Don't ever call that number again. Don't ever—I mean never."

"Yes, sir," she squeaked.

"Never ever."

"I won't. That job is over. I quit!" Steely closed her eyes tightly.

He set the report down and eased back. "Good. May I tell you a story?"

"Am I under arrest?"

"You're being questioned."

"Why don't you arrest Mr. Sling, if he's breaking the law?"

"We want his boss. Slings are like weeds. His boss can always find another Sling."

"Am I a person of interest?"

"No, not in that sense."

"Do I need a lawyer?"

"No. May I tell you my story?"

"Yes, sir. Please proceed." She sniffled, dabbing her nose.

"My dad died in the Vietnam War when I was a little boy, much younger than you."

Steely regained her composure and listened intently.

"It was me, my momma, brother, and two little sisters."

She sighed.

"My momma was a cook, worked late almost every night. My brother, Eddy, walked my two sisters and me to school and picked us up each day. He was fifteen. Momma didn't make enough money for us to live on—a little short each month. Eddy got a job at the movie theater ten months before he was sixteen."

"How'd he do that?"

"Well, I'm not recommending you do this. He told them he was sixteen."

Steely's face widened. "He lied?"

"Yep." Donovan raised his hands. "He only worked there eight months before they found out and fired him. Then he could never work there again."

"But that was eight months your family got the money they needed to pay their bills."

"You understand what I'm saying, don't you?"

"Exactly." Steely perked up. "I'll be fifteen in a few weeks. I'll find a job! Thank you, Sergeant!"

"You're growing up fast, aren't you?"

"Yes, sir." Steely was almost bubbly. "I'm all As. I have to work hard in English. It doesn't come naturally, like math."

Stone-faced, Donovan quipped, "That isn't reflected in your verbal skills. Now, listen closely. This is extremely important. You must remember to follow a few rules." The sergeant spread out five fingers. He held down the first. "Don't hang around anyone older than you. Do you understand that?"

"Yes, sir."

He held down the next finger. "Only be where you're supposed to be, at the time you're supposed to be there, with whom you're supposed to be."

"Yes, sir. Right place, right time, right people. I've heard that before."

He held down the next finger. "Go to church."

"Yes, sir. I do. Twice a week."

"Don't ever deliver anything for anybody."

"Yes, sir."

He held down the last finger. "And don't ever call that number again."

"Yes, sir."

"You promise?"

"Yes, sir."

"I don't want to find you near anybody like that man again. Ever again."

"Don't worry, Sergeant Donovan. I won't. He was creepy. Handing out lunch sacks sealed up like they were gold. I knew this wasn't some free-lunch program. I was told it wasn't illegal. You have to be careful who you trust, Sergeant. I'm sure Jenny doesn't know how bad it is. My courier days are over. I'm never delivering anything like that for anybody again, no matter how much they pay me. Period."

"Good then. We understand each other. Now Officer Montgomery will take you home."

"Sergeant?"

"Yes, Miss Paupher?"

"Did he get arrested?"

"Who?"

"Your brother."

"No, since he was fourteen, it wasn't against the child labor laws for him to work."

"Really?"

"Yeah. But remember, I'll personally send you to juvenile hall if you ever call that number again."

"Sergeant, if I was starving to death, living under a bridge, I wouldn't call that number."

"Good." The sergeant stuck Montgomery's report in a machine, disintegrating it. He stood, indicating they were done. "Now scoot before you get hurt. This place is dangerous."

"Yes, sir." Steely started down the hall with him beside her. "Sergeant Donovan, you're really nice. People shouldn't say those bad things about you. You're nothing but nice."

"Nothing but nice?" He smiled and shook his head. "Officer Montgomery, come take this young lady home!" He winked at her. "I don't ever want to see you in here again."

"Yes, sir." She flashed her eyes at the wall of offenders and then back at Donovan. Cupping her hands by her mouth, she whispered, "Don't worry. I won't tell them you're nice."

"Get going!" he said.

Montgomery swooped up behind Steely and ushered her out.

CHAPTER NINE

Steely found a job within a week at the posh Westminster Theater. She was selling little bags again. But this time, they were filled with buttered popcorn. Her first weekly paycheck netted $68.78. It was still short of what she needed, but she wouldn't end up in juvenile hall or get a tag with her identity tied to her toe.

The job had good perks too. Free movies, popcorn, and sodas made with real syrup. A month before her sixteenth birthday, Steely passed her driver's test for a hardship license so she could drive herself to work. When the theater needed cleaning after each showing, she was the first one inside to pick up. Most of the time, she'd finish before any of her older coworkers even showed up. There were no issues, until one Saturday afternoon.

The new sci-fi movie, *The Jupiterian*, was about to begin its second showing of the day. Steely was in the auditorium when she spotted a group of kids coming in the theater. She didn't recognize any of them, except one. The Cricket. She shot right over in Steely's direction. There was nowhere to escape. So she did the only thing she could: she ducked between two rows of seats. But it was too late.

"Pauper?" Cricket said, looking down at Steely curled up on the floor. "You weirdo. What are you doing down there?"

Steely reached for the back of a chair and pulled herself up, popcorn stuck on her knees, soda dripping from her sleeves. "I'm—" She didn't get another word out before Cricket spotted the blue skirt, white blouse, and name tag pinned on her left shoulder.

Cricket lit up with excitement. "What are you doing working here?" Before Steely could answer, Cricket pointed and razzed. "You're only fifteen! Today is my lucky day!"

Steely knew better than to try to reason with Cricket. But she had little choice. "Please be quiet. I've had no problems here. Everybody likes me."

"Do they like liars? 'Cause that's what you are—a deceiver. You're not old enough to work. You're breaking the law." Cricket was purposely loud enough to draw stares from the surrounding guests.

Steely said, quickly rattling off her excuses. "It's not against the law. I'll be sixteen soon. Please don't say anything. Throw my lunch in the toilet again. Stick some more blue cheese in the cracks of my locker. I don't care if my books stink. But please don't say anything."

"I'm a reasonable person."

"Really?" Steely said under her breath.

"Maybe we can negotiate."

"What do you want?" Steely prepared for any menial chore or degrading favor. Cleaning Cricket's locker. Washing her sweaty gym clothes. Serving her lunch in the cafeteria.

Cricket sneered. "I want to better my education."

Steely whispered, "What you do want from me?"

Cricket slid close to Steely, where no one else could hear. "You're supposed to be the smartest algebra student in the city."

"I did win a contest—"

"Mrs. Dryer always says, 'Let Steely help you. She's an angel,'" snipped Cricket. "Looks like the angel has fallen."

49

"You want me to tutor you? Sure, I'll help you. No problem. Let's meet every day after class. I'll help you all the way to an A. Algebra is easy once you get the hang of it. It's a deal!" She held out a hand, which Cricket promptly brushed away.

"That's not exactly what I had in mind. I don't need algebra to get me where I want to go in life. I need a higher GPA."

"Algebra can help in many ways. Just about any type of business. Calculations will go faster with algebra. It's my favorite subject."

"Will you shut up and listen?" Cricket glanced around and squeezed in tight. "Mrs. Dryer has only two different tests for all her classes."

Steely put her hand on her forehead. The Cricket didn't want to learn. She wanted to cheat.

"I'll get you copies of both tests each week. You fill in the answers. You help me, and I'll help you. We help each other." Cricket crossed her arms and waited for a response.

"Let me teach you. I know I can help you. Then you will have earned your grade."

"There is nothing I want to learn from you. You need to learn from me if you want to get ahead in life. Give me an answer key for the tests, and I'll forget about your deception."

Steely raised her voice. "The only thing I've learned from you is what *not* to do." People turned and stared as she walked off.

Cricket hollered, "You're as dumb as you look! You Paupers don't know a good deal when you see one!"

The manager terminated Steely on the spot. He said he hated to do it but had no choice when Cricket threatened to call his boss.

Before Steely made it to the car, her cell was buzzing. It was her mother. "Steely, I don't feel well. Can you come on home?"

"I'm on the way, Mom."

Four minutes later, she rocketed the car up the driveway and ran inside. Her mom was sitting on the sofa. She could tell her mother's heart was beating rapidly, but she was breathing better.

Steely had made her doctor's appointments twice. One of the best medical centers in the world was in walking distance. But her mom wouldn't go. Steely thought about having her picked up against her will. But she couldn't force her mother into the hospital without a court order. She'd checked. And she was too young to get one.

"Are you going back to work, baby?" her mom asked.

She said casually, "No, ma'am. I'm done."

"I hope I didn't get you in trouble."

"Not at all, Mom. You're never any trouble." Steely sat on the sofa with an arm around her mother's shoulder. She glanced over at the kitchen. "Did you eat your lunch?"

"I wasn't hungry. I've been feeling so good until the last few days. I've just had a setback."

"It's only a temporary setback. Are you sure you'll be OK if I go to Erin's surprise party tonight? I can skip it if you need me here."

"You've been going to her parties since you were five. I'll be fine." Her mom looked away. "I'm getting off this couch and finding a job."

"I got you, Mom. You took care of me all my life. Take all the time you need. But if you feel bad again, promise me you'll go to the doctor."

"We'll see."

CHAPTER TEN

Steely gave her hair a squirt of antifrizz and darted to the kitchen. Her mom was cozy in her pajamas on the sofa watching her dramas, the ones where the stories were crazy enough to cause her to forget her problems.

Her mom perked up when Steely came in. "Your hair looks so cute."

"I straightened it. It doesn't look stiff, does it?"

"It's perfect, but I like it curly too. I'll tell you this: my girl will be the prettiest one at the party."

"Thanks, Mom." Steely retrieved an already prepared sandwich and a glass of milk and set them in her mother's lap.

"Baby, you quit making my food."

"It's the only way I know you're eating. Make sure you drink your milk."

"Next week I'm looking for a job. You do way too much around here. I want you to quit your job and enjoy your life."

"I am, Mom. Everything is fine." Steely dashed to the front door. She checked the gift bag again.

"You make a mighty fine PB and J." Her mother took a bite, clipping a corner of the sandwich and downing it with a swallow of milk. "Oh, Steely, we got another cashier's check in the mail. It's on the table by the door—beside the gift bag."

Just in time. Steely flipped the envelope over, checking for a return address. "No name again." She opened it and held the check up to a lamp, looking for any clue that would reveal the sender.

"I called the bank. It's real. They said to bring them in."

"I'm going to take them in the morning." She set the check on a corner of the table. "I'll only be gone a couple of hours, Mom." Rearranging the tissue stuffed meticulously inside, she peeked in the gift bag again. "I'm walking since I'd have to park a block away because of the surprise. I'll catch a ride home."

"Erin is going to be shocked that you found a candle just like yours."

"She was so excited when I won mine at school. I just had to get it for her."

"This one cost way more than a buck for a raffle ticket."

"It's worth it to see the look on her face."

"I hope she hasn't gotten snooty."

Steely smiled. "She's the same old Erin. Just with a bigger house."

Mom raised her voice. "She better appreciate you!"

"Gotta go now. Love you, Mom!" Steely took off with the gift bag in tow.

Already a few minutes late, it wouldn't have mattered if she took the car instead of making the ten-minute walk. The sidewalk and road were both blocked by a crossing train. It was six endless minutes before the caboose chugged past and the crossing bars lifted. She hurried along, bouncing the gift bag at her side. It wasn't long before she heard music and smelled steak sizzling over mesquite.

Erin's street was strangely desolate. There was not a person in sight, which you would expect for a surprise party. But oddly every curb had a car against it. Many had parking citations blowing from the wipers. The metal no-parking signs on one side of the street were currently being ignored.

The partiers could be seen dancing through the life-sized living-room windows. The fun was underway.

Erin must have gotten home early.

Steely sprinted up the sidewalk toward the front door. She almost slipped when Erin popped out, startling her. She quickly regained her balance and prepared to greet her friend. "Happy birthday, Erin! Sorry I didn't get here in time to surprise you."

Erin took a step forward under the porch light. Something wasn't right. Steely had read Erin's face most of her life. She knew when Erin was happy and when she wasn't. Clearly she was annoyed.

Erin planted herself between Steely and the front door. "Steely?"

Steely usually avoided confrontation, but she was always ready to defend her friend if the situation called for it. "Was someone rude to you? Tell me what happened." She spread her arms in preparation of their usual greeting. A hug.

But Erin clammed.

Steely's arms flopped to her sides. "Was it those same girls from last week? You know—the ones who called you hefty?"

"Nope." Erin folded her arms, slightly tapped her foot.

Maybe I didn't dress right.

"Erin, your dress is beautiful. I didn't know the party was dressy. Are my jeans and knit top OK? I can go home and change."

Erin was unresponsive, simply glaring at her.

Steely tried again. "You're not mad because I'm late, are you?" She could have guessed all night and would not have figured out why the girl was agitated. Her apprehension grew. "Come on, Erin. What's wrong?"

The birthday girl tightened the grip on her crossed arms. "What are you doing here?"

Steely's stomach suddenly ached. Her eyes moistened. "It's your birthday, silly. I'm coming to your—"

"Steely, this party is only for a certain group of friends. It's invitation only."

"Uh?" Steely was puzzled. "Wasn't it a surprise party?"

"Surprise? I totally planned it myself."

"I got an invitation."

"No, you didn't," Erin snipped. "We'll do lunch next week. OK?"

Steely had a visual of the Cricket inside, buckling in laughter. Her invitation to a "surprise party" was a counterfeit. Steely gripped the handles of the gift bag. "Aren't we best friends?"

"Sure we are," whispered Erin. "But sometimes we have to expand our relationships."

She replied with restraint. "You mean you're expanding me out?"

The sky rumbled above them.

The invitees stopped dancing. They started gawking at the scene in the front yard. The moment escalated when the Cricket barged out. "Erin, come back in. We're about to start the dance contest!" Cricket acknowledged Steely with her usual contempt. "Hey, Pauper, are you part of the catering service?" Cricket's verbal assault set off an eruption of cackling inside.

The gift bag edged off Steely's fingers, landing between them. "No, Cricket, I'm her best—"

Erin cut her off. "She's on her way home." With one swift motion, Erin scooped up the bag. "Everything is good. Go back inside, Cricket. I'll be right there."

But Cricket wasn't finished. She yelled, "And, Pauper, quit googooing over Nick."

Steely rolled her lips tightly together.

Erin looked away.

"You better quit stalking him before he calls the police," Cricket ranted. "You know his mother wouldn't dare let him date a freak like you."

"Cricket, please go inside," Erin said. "I'll be right there."

Cricket took a few steps and lowered her voice. "You have one minute to get back inside. You embarrass me again, and I'll make sure you're trashed so bad no one will speak to you until college."

Erin swallowed loudly, as if she was choking.

Steely stared silently at her.

Cricket went back in and slammed the door.

Lightning flashed above them. Steely wished rain was streaking down her face. But it wasn't.

Erin was now visibly uncomfortable and slowly moving toward the house. "Now, let's be mature about this." Erin fidgeted, attempting to give an anemic explanation. "Give me a break here. I've worked hard to get Cricket to accept me."

"Cricket's the social mafia! Why do you need her to accept you?"

"She's who you need to know if you want to be popular."

"Is that what you want, Erin? To be popular with people who control you with threats?"

"You always take things the wrong way—you're just too sensitive," she whispered. "I'll still hang out with you. Just don't be selfish and mess up this opportunity for me."

"I'm not going to mess up anything. I think you have more in common with Cricket than I realized."

"Good. I feel better now that we understand each other."

"Perfectly." Steely blotted her face with her sleeve. She could have entered any emergency room, and they would have assumed she had been physically beaten.

"Now that everything's OK, I'll open your present." Erin dug around the tissue paper and lifted out the candle. She didn't jump up and down with excitement. She inspected it.

Is it broken? What's she looking for?

Erin threw a hip to one side. Cradling the candle in one hand, like a softball, she said, "You gave me a regift?"

"A *regift!*" Steely was boisterous enough to send the partiers back to the window.

"Shh!" Erin waved, trying to let them know everything was fine, even though it clearly was not.

A light drizzle sent Erin running to take cover under an awning. Steely ran off.

Erin slung another verbal punch. "Steely, you can wait in my garage till the rain stops!"

Steely wished she hadn't heard her. She didn't care about the rain, and she didn't care about the risk of being electrocuted from the lightning now shooting around her. She would have rather run through a hurricane with rain pelting her body like bullets than hear another word from Erin.

She ran two long blocks before dashing into a pizza joint. The restaurant had a small game room on one side and dining tables on the other. The restroom was beside the ordering station in the middle. Her hair was matted. Her makeup had washed down to places where it wasn't originally placed. Rain speckled her knit top, leaving it more wet than dry.

Steely kept her head down, using a hand to conceal her identity. She went straight for the ladies' room, where there were three stalls. All, with half-opened doors, appeared to be empty. She chose the last one in which to roll up in the fetal position and wail.

Ten minutes later, she stood facing a chipped mirror over a sink. Her face was ruby red. With her eyelids hugely swollen, she folded some paper towels together and ran them under the water spigot. Then she gently laid them over each eye. She leaned against the wall for a few minutes before swabbing the remainder of her face. Another look in the mirror showed minor improvement. She still looked beaten up and feared she might never look normal again. At least not tonight. But she was ready to get out of there.

She peeked out the door. Six giant steps, one leap, and she'd make it if she ran like crazy. She squeezed out the door to get a clear view of her exit. Then, right by the door, at the video games, she spotted him. Any other time, she would have planned for an opportunity to run into Nick Dichiara. But not tonight. There was no way around him. He was flapping pinballs under glass next to the exit.

Her only choice was to lower her head and take off. But she underestimated who she was eluding. She could have worn a mask and put on stilts, but it wouldn't have mattered. He blocked her path, situating himself between her and her escape.

"Steely, are you all right?" he asked.

She acknowledged by nodding and hoped that would be the end of it.

He bent closer, examining her face. "Are you sick?"

"Nick, really, I'll be fine." She tried unsuccessfully angling around him.

"Steely, you don't look fine to me." Nick was a detailist with a photographic memory. He'd be the best eyewitness a trial lawyer could put on the stand. He pressed her. "Steely, what's going on?"

"Really. I'm fine now." She gave him a half smile. It was the best she could do.

"Then why aren't you at Erin's party?" In just one shot, he'd hit the bull's-eye, leaving her no wiggle room. Even if she didn't answer, he'd figure it out in a matter of seconds.

She took a deep breath. "I wasn't—"

He held up a hand. "Hold it! You came from that direction. What did Erin do this time?"

Steely shrugged, hoping he'd heard enough.

His face reddened. His ears turned purple. "Never mind."

His mother picked up two boxed pizzas from a counter a few feet away. "Nick, are you ready to go?" Mrs. Dichiara's voice was mighty, like her stance. Her gray hair tightly tapered around her neck. Her chest size included triple letters.

Nick said, "I'll be right back. Don't move." He hurried to his mother and whispered into her ear. She nodded. Then she fired a few words off in Italian that didn't need translation. They paired up and descended upon her.

"Steely, we will take you home."

"No, please. I can walk." Steely wasn't certain what to think of Nick's mother. But she didn't seem the way Cricket described. "Really, I'll walk."

Nick ended the discussion when he took off his jacket and wrapped it around her wounded heart. Mrs. Dichiara apparently wasn't one to argue. When she spoke, there was no dissension. She put an arm on Steely's shoulder, as though they were old friends. "Honey, you look like a wet puppy. We're not about to leave you here." She passed a box to Steely. "Take this pizza home for you and your momma."

"Thank you, Mrs. Dichiara." Steely choked up for the second time that night.

"You're welcome. Nick, drive us, please." Mrs. Dichiara tossed the keys in the air. Nick snatched them on the way down.

"Steely, you're going to love my driving!" he boasted.

"Son, make it uneventful," his mother said.

"Mother, I've been driving for—"

"I don't care how long you've been driving; I almost got whiplash on the way here."

"Mother, really?"

"My head bopped around every time we stopped and started."

"Mother, you're going to scare Steely."

"My brains were doing the cha-cha." Mrs. Dichiara winked at her.

Mrs. Dichiara's dry sense of humor wasn't what Steely had expected. She struggled to contain her laughter. Nick grinned, holding the car door open for them. The rain had stopped. The ground glistened. The tears had ceased.

Steely hopped into Mrs. Dichiara's back seat, wrapped up in her son's jacket, feeling like family with somebody she had just met. She didn't really understand it. Maybe it was because she knew Nick. And she could see him in his mother. Caring. Concerned. Handing her a twenty spot, ordering Steely to take her mother to see a movie. Steely smiled effortlessly on the short drive home. She didn't allow Erin's party to drain her of another ounce of emotion.

Later that evening Steely and her mom sat on the living-room floor eating pizza and laughing at fifty-year-old sitcoms. It was the best night they had spent together in a long time. Shortly after midnight, Steely went to bed right after her mom. She rested quietly in her bedroom, reliving the five-minute ride home. She laughed again at Mrs. Dichiara's brains doing the cha-cha. She had drifted off for about twenty minutes when her phone rang.

It was Jenny Dix.

CHAPTER ELEVEN

Steely stirred, squinting just enough to see who was calling before picking it up.

"Hey, Jenny. I had the best night ever. Nick's mother bought me a—"

"He's after me!" Jenny's voice was partly drowned out by cars and blaring music. "I'm afraid he'll kill me."

Steely squeezed her eyes together and sat up. "Slow down. Did you say *kill?*"

"Yes!"

"You better get out of there!"

"Please come and pick me up. I'm too scared to move. The boss has a gun."

Steely flew out of bed and flipped on a light. "Where are you?"

"Greenville Boulevard at McCaney," Jenny whimpered.

Steely threw a sweatshirt over her gown and pulled on her jeans. "McCaney?" She stepped into her shoes. "I don't know where it is."

"Head out Eastside Road and call me."

"Got it!" She tiptoed to the kitchen and scooped the car keys off the kitchen counter. It was impossible to move a ring of keys without making noise. She wished she'd left them in her pocket the night before. In another few seconds, she'd be outside and in the car. But opening a seventy-two-year-old door was noisier than an alarm system.

"Going somewhere, dear?" her mom yelled from the bedroom.

Steely exhaled. Climbing out of a window might have been the better choice. "Guess your hearing is still keen, Mom."

Draped in a terrycloth robe, her mother rushed out of the bedroom. "Answer my question, please."

"Just giving a friend a ride. Go on back to bed. I'll be right back. No need for you to lose any sleep over this." Then she pulled the door open enough to get outside.

But her mom stood firm. "Who needs a ride at this time of night?"

Jenny's terrified voice resounded in Steely's mind. Running out the door was a thought, but not an option she was willing to take. "Just a friend who needs a ride home. Mom, I really need to go. I told her I was coming."

"Steely, this isn't a difficult question. Who is this friend?"

"Jenny Dix. She needs me to pick her up."

"From where?"

"Corner of Greenville and McCaney."

"I see. Guess you're planning on walking there, since you only have a provisional license. I sure haven't given you permission to drive at this time of night."

The door was open. The car was in sight. Jenny was waiting. "Please, Mom, it's an emergency. She's in trouble."

"Did she call nine one one?"

Steely shook her head.

"Didn't you tell her what Sergeant Donovan said?"

Steely indicated she had.

"She didn't listen to you, did she?"

"She will now."

"You're not going."

"I can't leave her there alone."

"You're not going."

"Mother, please. Her life is in danger."

"Mother? We're suddenly formal. Steely, sit down and call Sergeant Donovan. He can get someone there faster than you can drive." She pulled out a chair from the kitchen table.

Steely reluctantly planted herself in it and called Donovan from her cell.

He answered on the first ring. "Donovan here." He was awake.

"Sergeant Donovan, this is Steely Paupher."

"What is it, Miss Paupher?"

"Jenny Dix is in trouble. She's at Greenville and McCaney. She's running from a man with a gun."

Her mom's face expressed concern.

"She wants me to pick her up."

Donovan became anxious. "You're not there, are you?"

"No, sir."

"Good. We have officers on the way. Shots were fired in the area. The description of the victim fits Miss Dix."

Steely choked.

"Steely, there are some people we can help, and there are some we can't. I'd hate it if anything happened to Miss Dix. But we warned her, just like we warned you, to stay away from there. You listened."

Her mom held her hand.

"Sergeant, she was desperate."

"Desperate?" said Donovan unsympathetically. "Well, thank God, most of us would rather starve to death, live under a bridge if we have to, than destroy another person's life selling drugs. I have another call. But don't leave your house tonight. For any reason. Don't leave your house."

The shooting dominated the morning news. Jenny Dix never had a chance. Six point-blank shots blew her heart right out of her back. She died on the corner seconds after she called Steely.

The police discovered that a customer had complained that his order was short by ten grams. The boss took his dissatisfaction out on the courier. Within hours, Donovan arrested a forty-three-year-old college professor, but he was not the shooter. After one night in lockup, he was ready to spill his guts. But he could only rat out Sling. And Donovan needed more than a two-bit Sling to obliterate the person really responsible. He needed the boss. But no one seemed to know any more than his street name. The boss.

CHAPTER TWELVE

Nick shifted the coupe in reverse and maneuvered his car out of the driveway, avoiding his mother's SUV. He kicked up a little dust, staying within the speed limit but arriving faster than anyone else. The midnight-blue two-seater with pitch-black leather was an oddity. There had been only twelve in production in the last year. He couldn't maintain that baby at just any grease shop. Every part was a European special order. There were only three dealers in the United States. Fortunately for Nick one was in the Bayou City.

Jason Wilkerson flagged him down from a corner. "Nick, stop!"

He screeched to a halt at the curb. A neurotic driver behind him sat on his horn and zipped past him, shouting things he might not have been so brave to shout if Nick's windows had been down. He pressed a small lever to scroll down a window. Jason lifted his shades and leaned in. "How about a ride?"

Nick unlocked the door. "Come on, before someone else wets their pants."

Jason situated himself inside. "Where we going? Not that I care. I'd go anywhere in this beauty."

"Golf." Nick shifted, getting them moving again. For a few seconds, the G force restrained them tighter than a seatbelt.

"A game?" quizzed Jason.

"Don't have time. You want to hit a few?"

"You bet."

"In a suit?"

"One sec." Jason tossed his jacket into storage behind the seat, followed by his tie. He rolled up his sleeves, lowered his shades, settled into the concord seat, used his hands to rearrange his hair, a few spikes up, and he was set. He briefly shut his eyes, envisioning a pilot saying, "We're cleared for takeoff."

More pressure on the accelerator sent the ground hugger slicing through the wind. Nick's mother claimed the car crawled around the ground like a cockroach. His father pulled a muscle the first time he got out of it. If the aerodynamic coupe were any tighter, he'd have to ride with the top down.

Jason gawked at the dash. "You taking this to Lubbock?"

"No. I'm keeping it here to use when I'm in town. I had to skip the summer session. Trained all summer with Mr. Hunter. Just flew in to meet with him. Didn't you start at UT this summer? Why are you still here?"

"Job hunting. I was going to call you today. I'm transferring from UT to UH."

"Didn't you get the scholarship money for tuition?"

"Yes, but there wasn't much time for fun."

"They kicked you out?"

"Recommended that I depart. They have no hospitality."

"At least they didn't press charges—hacking into their server like that. Was it that much fun e-mailing half the faculty that they were terminated and not to set foot back on campus?"

"Not anymore."

"How many didn't show up the next day?"

"Eight. Forty-three called to check. They should've known better. Everyone else went."

Nick glanced over at Jason, who was looking out the passenger window. "You're a software expert. You'll find somebody who doesn't care about your transcript."

"Looks like Mr. Keaton doesn't care."

"Mr. Keaton at JHI?"

"Yep. He wants to hire me permanently."

Nick veered toward a curb and then straightened back up. "Doing what?"

"Wire transfers. I worked all day yesterday setting up a series of transfers."

"Doesn't he know how to wire money?"

"I guess it was too cumbersome for him. The company sends hundreds of wires every day."

"To where?"

"I don't know. I set them up, and Mr. Keaton inputs the account and routing numbers. Easiest grand I ever made. I guess they pay more for contract work."

Nick swung his head at Jason and then back straight ahead. "They paid you a grand to send wires?"

"Yeah. Can you believe it? Mr. Keaton keeps the account information in a folder locked in a safe. I told him I could put it on a jump drive. He could just plug it into his computer. He didn't go for it. Hey, guess who gave him my name? Cricket, of all people."

Nick looked puzzled. "Cricket? She despises you."

"Guess she came to her senses. She probably has a crush on me."

"How does she know Keaton?"

"Her step-step-step-step-step-father had a business deal with him. By the way, Nick, is it true?"

"You mean working in Saint Stephen's Island at Christmas at break? It's true."

Jason fiddled with his sunglasses. "Put my name in if you need an associate."

Nick turned the car sharply to the left, sending them right. "You'd have to take a pay cut. Mr. Hunter wants me to check out our subs there."

"If I get this job working with Mr. Keaton, I'm going to be the best at whatever he asks me to do. This is my big chance. I just can't fail again." He snapped his head toward Nick. "Mr. Keaton is ticked you're in his biz. But what Mr. Hunter wants, he gets. Why'd your dad do the legal work on Saint Stephen's Island instead of Mr. Thibodeaux?"

"He isn't familiar with international law like my dad."

"It's one of the biggest projects in JHI history."

"This deal is small potatoes, less than one percent of the operating budget."

"People wonder about Mr. Hunter's shooting a nineteen-year-old to the top of the executive ladder—before you even graduate college. How does that look?"

"Like you better quit whining or I'm dropping you at the next curb."

Jason glared at Nick. "Can't we have a discussion?"

"I'm making twelve fifty an hour until I graduate. You want me to tell Mr. Hunter you want to be treated like me?"

Jason squeezed his brow together. There was silence for a few seconds before he changed the subject. "Do you think Mr. Hunter will sell the company? I've heard rumors."

"Anyone would sell anything for the right price."

"To Mr. Chevoski?"

"Never. Mr. Denison showed me Chevoski's proposal. His offer was an insult."

"I heard he thinks Mr. Hunter is his papa bear."

"What? I never heard that."

"You ever met him?"

"No. And don't care to." Nick approached a corner, took a right, and sent them left before careening back in place. "Something's not right with that guy. His business is obscure. He claims he represents investors. Mr. Denison doesn't think he has any investors."

"What do you think about Mr. Keaton pushing to take the company public?"

"You sure know a lot about what's going on, for a contract worker."

"Rumors."

"Hunter will never give up controlling interest." Nick shifted down, turning into the Pecan Valley Country Club. He rolled in between two white lines and cut the engine. "I'll get the balls. You get the clubs." Nick had one leg out the door and paused. "Congratulations on your job, Jason. But you better be careful about what Keaton asks you to do. He and Qualls are the two in senior management that I can visualize in handcuffs."

"You're not fair. You have nothing on him. Do you?"

"No. But I can feel it in my gut."

"So I shouldn't work with the guy just because of your gut?" Jason smirked.

"You're a smart guy. You need to think about why Keaton paid you a thousand dollars for a job he can get a clerk to do."

"It's not any different than Mr. Hunter propelling you to the executive office. He's hiring the person he wants to train, just like Mr. Hunter. I'm sure Mr. Hunter's relationship with your dad was a factor. But he wants you, Nick. Now Keaton wants me bad enough to pay me a chunk of cheese. What's wrong with that?"

"It's peculiar. Mr. Hunter seems uneasy. He won't say why. But I think it's the reason he's chasing after me."

"Maybe his gut is bothering him."

Nick pointed at Jason. "You need to do two things. Find out why Keaton is overpaying you. And get the clubs." Nick got out of the car and slammed the door.

CHAPTER THIRTEEN

The Pecan Valley Church pantry had two sides—one for food and the other for clothing. Virginia, a widow who ran the place, befriended Steely as they prepared weekly sacks filled with some of her favorite nonperishables.

"Hi, Miss Virginia," Steely said, entering. "Do you have any good news?"

"Hi, princess!" Virginia waddled around the counter, wrapped her marshmallow arms around Steely, and squeezed.

"Well? Are you getting married?"

Virginia covered her giggle with a hand. "We're just going to stay friends. He has his, and I have mine."

"Kids or money?"

"Both." Virginia opened a cabinet. Passed a loaded sack to Steely.

"I guess that keeps things simple."

"I'm sixty-six years old. I'm not doing complicated."

Steely set the sack by the door.

"I got in the pajamas and new suit you wanted."

"That was fast." Steely followed Virginia to the next room, where it appeared the church could clothe all four million people in Harris County, if needed. The room was a mini department store. Racks of clothes lined the walls. Tables in the middle of the room held folded items.

Virginia pointed at two pairs of silk pajamas. "Like them?"

"Very nice." Steely cuddled them in her arms. "So soft."

"Hold on to them." Virginia lifted a suit off a rack, holding up the timeless white jacket and skirt, already pressed and covered in plastic. She checked the tag under the right sleeve. "She's a two, right?"

"Yes, ma'am," Steely said timidly.

"I wish I was a two," Virginia teased. "I have to add a zero. Now, you don't go telling anyone."

Steely shook her head. "They couldn't drag it out of me."

"I don't think I have anything to worry about. You don't gossip, do you?"

"Not on purpose. Sometimes things just slip out."

Virginia handed Steely a shoe box. "Words just flow out of me."

Steely lifted the lid to view the white pumps. "They're like new."

"Sure are! We're not spreading any fungus around here. We clean and disinfect our things. I don't even want to think about what some people have growing out of their toes."

Virginia popped open a brown paper bag and packed up the shoes and pajamas. She kept the suit on the hanger and passed everything to Steely. "How about I fix you up for Easter?"

"I'm good. I need to be going. Mom will be worried." Steely headed toward the door. "Thank you so much! These are really going to make Mom feel better."

Virginia asked, concerned, "Is she still sick, dear?"

"She was getting better. I think she had a relapse. You know, like when you have a cold and then you overdo it. She's been trying to find a job. She's a really good mom."

"You do a good job taking of care of her."

"We take care of each other. Who knows what I'd be doing without her."

Virginia muttered, "Probably sharing your food with the indigent." She held the door opened. "You come see me anytime you need anything. If we don't have it, I'll find it. Understand?"

"Yes, ma'am. Thanks, Miss Virginia!" Steely lifted one of the bags in an effort to wave and then scurried off.

Steely shoved a hip at the unlocked and slightly open front door of the house. Sometimes her mom stood at the threshold for a few minutes and looked out to see what she was missing.

The television was off. "Mom!" Steely set the groceries in the kitchen. "Mom!" She wasn't in the living room or the kitchen. The bathroom down the hall was empty. "Mom! You sleeping? Wait till you see what I got you!"

Steely turned the corner. As expected, her mom was there in bed. She burst in the bedroom at full speed.

"Look, Mom! Look at these beautiful things!" She spread the pajamas and suit across the bed. She rearranged them to give her mother the perfect view. The shoes were hidden on the floor, in preparation for surprise number two. "I don't know if I want to give you these pajamas." Steely rubbed them up to her own face. "You might not ever want to get out of bed!" she said, giggly.

Steely moved closer, rubbing her mother's back. "Mom, are you OK?" Steely gently patted her back but received no response. "Mom?" She felt her mother's face. "Mom?" She tugged on her robe. "You're freezing." Steely slightly shook her. "No!" she screamed. "Mom, wake up! Wake up!" Steely pulled on her mother's robe, ripping off a piece of the pocket.

"Mom, please!" she cried. "It's time for Easter, and I'm going to graduate in a few weeks. You said you'd go with me. Please wake up." Steely grabbed the phone from the nightstand, accidentally knocking off an empty medicine bottle. She hit three simple numbers.

An operator answered, "Is your emergency police, fire, or medical?"

"I need an ambulance for my mom. She's not breathing."

"Are you at 5750 Saint Ambrose Avenue?"

"Yes, please hurry. My mom is all I have."

"Go open the front door. A unit is only a few blocks away." Steely dropped the phone, tore out of the room, and threw open the front door. The sirens already faintly blared.

In fewer than two minutes, three paramedics, saddled with equipment, were inside and ready to work. They laid her mother flat on the floor and placed two large paddles on each side of her chest. The medics shocked her multiple times, propelling her several inches into the air. They waited a few seconds each time for a response. When there was none, they hit her again with an electronic force strong enough to jump-start a car. Each time her mother's body leaped off the floor.

One of medics looked up at a shaken Steely. "Are you here alone?"

"Yes," she sniffled. "Is she going to be OK?"

The medic tilted his head at his associate. "We're taking her in. You can ride with us." They packed up her lifeless mother, placed her on a stretcher, put an oxygen tube across her face as if she were breathing, and lifted the gurney into the ambulance. Sirens blasted all the way to the Northwest Regional Hospital.

Steely curled herself into a chair in the crowded emergency room, holding tightly to the fragmented cloth from her mother's robe.

A nurse dressed in blue scrubs approached her. "Honey, would you like to go and wait with your mother until the coroner comes?"

Steely's nose ran. Her eyes dripped. All she could do was stand to indicate assent.

"Come with me." The nurse directed Steely down a hall to her mother's room. There was no heart monitor attached to her mom; the machine stood powered off beside the bed. No oxygen mask covered her mom's face; it hung ready for use on the wall above her. Her mom's silver cross dangled around her neck. She lay peaceful, never to be in pain again.

Steely climbed onto the bed. This was her last chance to lie beside her mother, rub her face, hold her hands, and tell her how much she already missed her. She didn't know if her mother could see her from heaven or not. But she felt somehow that her mother knew she was there.

A week later, Steely stopped by the pantry. Virginia cried more than Steely when she told her that her mom didn't wear her new suit to the Easter service as planned. Mom did better than that. She wore it to heaven.

When Steely was leaving, she heard music coming from the sanctuary. Inside, several musicians stood on a platform, practicing for the Sunday service. She peered in an open door and proceeded to a back pew. She lay on her side, tucked her hands under her head, rolled up, and closed her oversized eyes. The musicians practiced for an hour. Then they packed up their instruments and left a few candles flickering on a table up front.

Steely wasn't sure how long she had slept. Maybe an hour—maybe two. She dropped to her knees and put her head down. "Father, it's me, Steely, again. I still call for Mom every time I get home. It seems like I can't get it in my head that she's gone. I know she's not there, but I keep calling for her. Took me over a year to stop calling for Dad. The house feels so empty. Why were their lives cut short? Mom was just getting better after what happened to Dad…I'm just trying to understand. Maybe I never will. Just like Mrs. Yost's daughter. She never understood it. I'm sure if I needed to know, you'd tell me. I trust you, Lord…Good night for now."

She rested back on the pew. Time no longer mattered. No need to rush off. There was nowhere she needed to go. No one waiting for her to get home. Thoughts about her parents ran through her mind like she was watching a video. But she no longer felt anxious. Her heart no longer tried to beat itself out of her chest. She lifted her head, went down the aisle, and skipped down a dozen steps in the front of the church before a striking thought caused her to slow at the last one and then abruptly stop.

What am I going to do now?

CHAPTER FOURTEEN

Curley's Bar started to crowd up at dusk. Many of the same vehicles parked in the acre-sized lot daily. Steely recognized the stickers on bumpers and the stuffed dice and beads hanging from the rearview mirrors. Going by there to spy on the customers made her feel that she was doing something worthwhile. It got her mind off of her mom's death but back on her dad's. Her mom's passing wasn't something she was ready to absorb. And there wasn't a Curley's Bar to ponder at for her mom. Or to wonder why people lied about her. Her death was just what it looked like—an accidental overdose. Nothing more to understand or do. Just to miss her.

But that was not the case with her dad. His death was no accident. It was intentional and purposeful.

Every time the door swung open, she leaned out of the car to see inside. She'd have gone in if the beer-bellied man standing outside in a Curley's T-shirt wasn't checking IDs. Underage kids using fake IDs had caused so much trouble; they'd almost lost their liquor license. Steely wasn't there to cause trouble. She wanted to find out what caused her dad's trouble.

She pushed the gear out of neutral and stirred up the loose gravel while getting to the road that took her home. The short drive wasn't long enough to get her mind back on track. It made it worse. Her garage didn't help either, since it was exactly how her dad had left it. And everything in it was a reminder of him. She cut the ignition and thought about everything she knew about her dad's death, which was practically nothing.

Right after Fred had passed, Steely went through every drawer, cabinet, shelf, and box, anything she found that might have led to information about what he was doing besides shredding paper. She didn't know what she was looking for then and still didn't know now. But she was certain what happened to her dad was somehow connected to his business. And what was left of his business was stored in the garage attic.

She unlocked the door leading from the garage to the kitchen. It was hard for her to go in. The house felt chilly, just like outside. Mom's bedroom door was shut and would remain that way until she was ready to open it. The sheets had been stripped and thrown away. There was no need to go in that room ever again.

Steely fired up the furnace, changed into a gown, tossed a pillow and blanket on the sofa, and crawled under it. Physically she was done, but the *why*s and the *what*s would not let her rest. *Why would someone want Dad dead? What drew him to that bar?*

There wasn't going to be any sleeping until her thoughts stopped swimming around in her head. She pushed the blanket aside and went back to the garage.

It was time for a second look. Maybe she could catch something at eighteen that she hadn't seen at fourteen. She picked up a hammer and then went up the ladder created by nailing two-by-fours to the studs. Then she gave the plywood floor a couple of whacks with the hammer, staying in position to hightail it down if she spotted a rat. She paused, heard nothing, and then pounded the floor again. Paused again. Then she crawled up onto the floor, stood, and stared at empty cabinets.

Most of the attic was covered with plywood. Where it ended Steely balanced herself on two-by-fours crisscrossing above the sheet rock stuffed with insulation. The ceiling sloped as she moved deeper into the space where two sagging cardboard boxes were tucked away. She scooted toward them and dug through the contents. The boxes held the papers she thought were most prevalent to her dad's business but hadn't yet told her who wanted him dead.

For the next two hours and twelve minutes, she reexamined the contents of the boxes. Nothing seemed odd enough to catch her attention. Fred's business of secure shredding for corporations was low stress and certainly should have been low risk. He had no employees. He never had a complaint from a customer. If something was amiss, Steely wasn't recognizing it.

She repacked the boxes and pushed them back in place. She carefully maneuvered her way out. One misstep on the boards could send her through the sheet rock and plopping down on the car. She made a few cautious moves on the plywood—before she slipped. Her hands groped for a rafter, keeping her weight on one foot while balancing and trying to get herself back in place. But when she stepped down, she hit something that was not insulation. She knelt to brush away the fluffy stuff, uncovering a metal utility box.

The box was locked. There was no key anywhere near it. Shaking the box did nothing more than shuffle its contents. Tugging and pulling on the latch didn't help either. The box wasn't opening. She stared at it for a few seconds. She thought about pitching it on the driveway and running it over with the car but wasn't sure if that would damage what was inside. Struggling with a metal box wasn't what she wanted to be doing in the middle of the night. She tucked it back in place, flipped off the light, and headed downstairs. She hesitated on the first step, took a second look, and then hurried down the ladder. She picked up a screwdriver and crawled right back up.

The screwdriver was narrow enough to wedge into the lock. The lock popped when she hammered it with a fist. Inside were bank statements. She quickly flipped through them. Looked like a few hundred of them—all from different LLCs. Fred had hidden the first page of each account.

Steely lined up ten pages along the floor, examined them, searching for a connection. Then she repeated the process and dug out another stack. All different account numbers. The only common factor was all accounts were in Saint Stephen's National Bank in Saint Stephen's Island—213 accounts. The last page in the stack was quite different from the rest. It was a photocopy of a cashier's check for $273,042.18 payable to Flash Away, LLC. The check was the amount her dad had withdrawn from the Paupher family checking account. Flash Away apparently was his biggest client. Copies of invoices to Flash Away were in a corner box. It hadn't meant anything to her until now.

Dad gave the money back.

Steely choked up. She was relieved but still puzzled. The check answered some plaguing questions, but it also created new ones. Whatever happened between her dad and Flash Away was serious enough for him to sever the relationship and return the money they had paid him.

Steely put the statements and the copy of the check back in the box and covered it back up. She scampered down the ladder, lifted the garage door, and drove off. Nobody was there to stop her from doing something she knew was irrational. Waiting until sunup wasn't an option. She wasn't sleeping tonight anyway. Armed with a name and an address, she was going to find Flash Away.

It was a quarter till one when she drove to the back of the two-story brick warehouse near the Houston ship channel. Her head-lights illuminated a wooden dock where semi trucks could back in and load or unload their contents. The building appeared abandoned. A couple of trucks were parked at a similar warehouse a few doors down. The inside of the building seemed to be as dark as the night sky. Her cell provided enough light to locate a side door, which she opened and went in.

There was nothing in the facility except thirty to forty bulky plastic trash bags, piled up against a back wall. Those bags would have all gone home with her if she could've stuffed them in her car. Since that wasn't going to happen, she started at one end of the room and began digging. She'd stay there all night if she could find anything significant. She rummaged through the first twenty bags fairly quickly. They contained nothing but real garbage.

The search was uneventful until she reached the end of the wall, where several bags were stacked higher than the rest. Pulling the three bags down, she uncovered a three-foot-high gray bin. She pushed more bags away, revealing Fred's markings on the front side. Her dad had been there. She gripped the container with both hands as if it might take flight on its own and disappear.

Then the front door opened.

She quickly dove in between the bags.

A man entering shouted, "Make one more misstep, and you're a dead kid."

Steely hoped he wasn't talking to her. She took shallow breaths and froze in place. A sliver between the bags gave her a visual of two people but only the backs of their heads.

"I just want to quit and go back to school," the boy pleaded.

The man was not yelling at her.

Just sit tight. But what if he hurts the kid?

"Go back? There's no going back. I own you. You do what I tell you to do." The man took out a gun and pointed it at the boy's head. Steely ruffled a bag. Maybe the boy could run. She didn't want to see him get his brains blown out.

The man yelled, "Who's there?" Then he rushed toward the bags. The boy didn't try to escape. He followed the man to the back.

"You start in the middle," the man said. "I'll get the other side." The man kicked several bags around from left to right. The boy worked his way to the end.

They shoved bags around, getting closer with every one. There was no way she could run. The man unlocked the gun's safety. He could fire off a round with nothing more than a low-pressure squeeze. She wasn't going to die stuffed into trash bags like a dead cat. There was a back door.

Can I make it? Stop shaking…Breathe shallow…Jesus, help me…I'm going to make it. When they get to me, I'll run! Stay low and don't look back…I can do this; stay still…Then run like crazy.

The boy lifted the white bag that made her cover. Most of the bags were light. This particular bag was heavy. It took both of the boy's hands to nudge it for a good look. He dropped the bag back into place before she could react.

Steely abandoned her plan and stayed put.

The man suddenly fired three quick rounds from the .45. The boy dropped another bag on her and twisted his head toward the man. "What ya shooting at?"

"Maybe a cat," said the man.

"Glad it wasn't me." The boy backed away from Steely.

"If I shot you, it'd be the last thing you heard."

"Guess that was the noise." The boy took a few more steps away. "Nothing here."

The man followed the boy's lead toward the door. "Now get to work. I don't want any more trouble out of you."

"I understand."

Without any provocation, the man swung his arm back and pistol-whipped the kid in the head. The boy floundered a few steps and collapsed.

"You mess up again, and you'll get the other end," the man said casually as he left.

Steely squeezed around the bags and tumbled out. She ran straight for the boy. He wasn't moving. She caressed his face with a violently shaking hand. "You're going to be OK."

He opened his eyes and touched the purple golf ball growing on his head.

Steely said, "I lost my cell in the trash. I'll go find it and call for an ambulance."

"No," he moaned, sitting up. "I'm getting out of here."

"You need to get your head examined."

"That's what my mom said." The boy wobbled to his feet.

Steely helped him gain his stance. "Who was that man?"

"Sling."

"That's not Sling."

"There's more than one."

"Well, thanks for not telling on me."

"I didn't want to see your insides splashed all over those white bags."

"Me neither," she said, exhaling.

"What ya doing here?" he asked. "This is where Sling brings you if you need an adjustment."

"I'm trying to find out who killed my dad."

"I'm sorry. What's his name?"

"Fred Paupher."

"Never heard of him." He blotted his bloody head with his white T-shirt. He went to a window and checked outside. "You better go. He might be doing some more adjustments tonight."

"Call HPD and talk to Sergeant Donovan. He'll help you."

"Talk to the cops?" He laughed. "I might as well shoot myself in the head."

"Nobody can make you do something you don't want to do. Tell Sergeant Donovan."

"You haven't been in this world."

"I've been close enough."

"Then you should know the only way to get away from these guys is either in a box or move where they can't find you."

"That's why they get away with it. Nobody will report them."

The boy rubbed his head, indicating that he was in pain. "Didn't you just hear him? I know what I'm talking about. You need to go."

"I'm going…in a minute."

He opened the door and looked around. "OK, but you better hurry up." He raised the collar on his jacket and took off.

Steely ran to the back and tossed a few bags out of the way to make a path for the bin. She tilted it on its wheels and tugged it toward the door. She carefully rolled it down the few stairs at the dock and then pushed it across the lot to her car. She tipped the bin on its side and shoved it into the trunk. She took off with the trunk wide open and the lights off for the next few blocks.

Avoiding the major streets took her twice as long to get home. But she couldn't risk drawing unwanted attention. Speed was not her top priority. It was getting home at all. She backed into the garage. She wrapped a rope around the handle of the bin and then to a bench that was braced to the wall. She drove the car forward just enough to yank the bin out of the trunk, ran back, set it upright, and rolled it back inside the garage. The next problem was the heavy metal lock on the hard plastic lid. Prying would be difficult. That was the purpose of the lock.

The plastic component of the bin would be tough to cut. She looked around the garage. Tools were hung on the walls and laid out on shelves like a hardware store. In one corner above a table was a chainsaw. It was electric and could cut down a tree with the flip of a switch. She lifted it and brought it over to the bin. The teeth of that saw would definitely spit plastic bits everywhere. It would be a mess, but it'd work. She placed the saw next to the container and was stretching the cord over to the electrical socket when she spotted two keys on a clip.

The one that fit the bin was obvious, round with a metal piece sticking out, almost like a safety deposit box. The same key fit all her dad's bins. The other key was for the utility box.

She inserted the key and turned. The lid easily lifted off. Inside was a stack of papers two feet high. She leaned the bin on its side and pulled them out. They were all bank statements, some identical to the ones she'd found in the attic. Some she'd never seen, from accounts in Geneva.

For several hours, she studied the Geneva statements, comparing them with the ones she'd found in the metal box. There was a pattern. Funds wired in; ninety days later, funds wired out. She mental mathed the ninety-day average at over two hundred million. They were into something sinister. And she knew exactly what it was: money laundering. Steely was now certain her dad's involvement with Flash Away had gotten him killed.

Discovering the facts about why her dad died meant learning whatever she could about Flash Away. And money laundering. Neither of which she knew much about.

CHAPTER FIFTEEN

Flash Away was not a registered US company. It was not listed in any corporate database nor advertised anywhere. Neither were the LLCs. It was as if all the businesses listed on the account statements were nonexistent. Steely found nothing.

She called the banks in Saint Stephen's Island and Geneva. Security concerns kept them from helping someone with no authority on the accounts and from telling her who did.

The assets were out of reach unless you were an agent for the FBI. She suddenly knew what she wanted to do with her life. Become a special agent with the FBI. Her goals quickly developed. For her application to be considered, she needed a college degree.

There were several major course options. She chose finance since no university had a major called How to Stop Money Laundering and Find Out Who Killed Your Dad. The advanced college courses she needed were all junior and senior level. Her plans had navigated from community college to a four-year university.

Now she found herself frantically searching through her desk for the response from the only school where she'd applied. Texas

Tech. The letter had been stuffed into a drawer to its deepest corner, under coupons that expired months ago. She took it out and ripped it open, speed-reading the prepared response congratulating her for being accepted for the fall semester. She searched for a cutoff date. Seventy-two hours was all she had left to confirm acceptance, or her invitation would be null and void.

She called the toll-free number and informed the admissions office she would be attending the fall semester. They urged her to sign the letter and overnight it to the campus.

The next week, as promised, Tech delivered a welcome package with scholarship information. If she qualified for the maximum amount, it would cover the tuition, books, and fees, but not housing.

The admissions department had one cancelation, making a dorm room available. The bad news was it was priced like a presidential suite. Staying on a household budget was diddlysquat compared to the cost of college housing. Class started in eighty-two days. If she was going to Tech, she had to find a home. A cheap home. Fast.

Steely called every potential rental in the area. Garage apartments, spare rooms—anything she could find. She even checked on maid's quarters. Houston had plenty of them. The boarder would clean the house for free room and board.

But none of those options existed.

Two weeks before class was to start, Steely rented out her family home. The income would be enough to pay for the taxes, insurance, and maintenance on the property, but not much extra.

The car was loaded, and she took off on the 529-mile trip to Lubbock. The next day she had an appointment with Mrs. McCollum, one of the school admissions counselors. The only thing Steely needed counseling on was where to lay her head.

McCollum greeted Steely in the school hallway. Stiff as her blue hair, she offered no hope when she said, "You're too late. There's nothing I can do for you. Drop this semester, and get your housing application in for next year." Steely didn't ditch the semester. She ditched the advice. She settled in on the top floor of a parking garage and slept in her car. School hadn't started yet. This was the safest place for now since she found out cheap hotels were not that cheap.

For the next week, Steely stopped calling about housing and started driving. She circled around the school daily and then spread out. There were a few apartments available but more than double what she could afford, even working two jobs. Her daily visits to McCollum's office, checking for cancelations, were unproductive. She heard the same story every time: No cancelations. No suggestions.

Five days before school was to start, she went back again to the counselor's office. Steely's tenacity was not helping. It was backfiring. She had become an irritant to McCollum. But the counselor finally offered a suggestion: "Why don't you become an RA? You'll receive a huge reduction in the cost of housing."

Steely was ecstatic. "I would love to become an RA!" she told McCollum. "What's an RA?"

"A resident advisor. You work in the dorm. Therefore, you have a reserved room. You'll need to see Ms. Blackwell, who runs the program. You better get going now."

Steely thanked her, but she wasn't sure if McCollum had been more interested in shooing her out than finding her a home. Either way, she left to pursue the only suggestion she had. Becoming an RA was now more important to Steely than her college entrance test.

Blackwell was commanding, with her chopped hair, black dress, and sharp-toed red pumps. But her looks were deceiving. Since Blackwell was a graduate student, she had almost no authority to make a decision about anything. And she was less encouraging than McCollum, if that were even possible.

"I can't help you," Blackwell said. "The RAs were chosen months ago. It's too late." Then Blackwell gave her the most interesting reason yet. "We make our decision on a need basis. We pick the most qualified students who need the job the most."

Steely explained that she wasn't hiding a trust fund. Blackwell was a wax figure, showing no emotion. "You're too late," she said.

The start of school was now imminent. Four days away and still no housing. The director of housing's schedule was packed, helping students who had reservations. "Those who planned ahead." She chastised Steely for not doing the same. Blackwell became less impressed the more Steely persisted.

"You're here almost as much as I am," Blackwell complained. "It's time for you to face reality. There's no housing here for you. None. Every spot is gone. It's not going to work out." Go away, she insinuated. "You need to withdraw and apply for next year. I'll let you apply to become an RA."

Steely just stared at her, contemplating her next step.

Then Blackwell threatened her: "In the two years I've been here, I've never had a student removed from my office. You're about there. Leave my office right now." She twirled her finger. "Turn around, walk out that door, and don't come back unless I call you. I'll put your name on the list to be next in line if an RA drops out."

"That's great!" Steely perked up. "How often does an RA drop out?"

"Never! Now get out!"

"Ms. Blackwell, just please put my name on that list. It's all going to work out. I promise I won't come back until you call me. It's all going to work out." But she didn't know how.

Blackwell opened the door, crossed her arms, and tightened her face.

Steely went outside and sat on a bench with the perfect view of the lowest-priced dorm on campus. The parking lot across from the dorm was packed with cars. Parents drove in with their students and unloaded their luggage. Some laughed. Some cried. Empty nesters were the criers, she figured.

That night, she slept on the bench. Slept on it every night until the day before orientation. The birds knew her. The squirrels hovering in the trees knew her. Everyone who passed by that bench knew her face. She would have camped out on the bench the entire fall semester if security hadn't chased her off.

After reexamining the situation, she had two choices: a sleeping bag under a bridge or a shelter. After only one night, the bridge was ruled out. It was scary waking up with a man she did not know snuggled next to her. So she searched for a shelter.

CHAPTER SIXTEEN

Nick showered and dressed. He declined a cream tie. He picked a green one from a metal rack and wrapped it around his neck.

The corporate world of suits and ties was not his first choice. He wanted to go pro. Just a few months ago, he had quarterbacked Tech to a bowl win and himself to an ACL tear. An operation to repair the damage would be his second surgery. And he didn't want a third. He already walked with a slight limp.

Working with Jack Hunter was as close as he was getting to following in either of his parents' footsteps. He sure wasn't going to law school. That went without saying. He loved Jack Hunter, had known him all of his life, but he hated ties, suits, and the humdrum that went with them.

Jack Hunter had no idea how close Nick came to ditching a business career and pitching a pigskin. Hunter would have tried to convince Nick that working at Jack Hunter Industries was far less risky than playing football.

After interning three summers and a few days a month, Nick was groomed as the vice president of finance at JHI. His corner office on the executive floor at the JHI Tower was between the board room and CEO's suite.

Nick buttoned up his jacket and glanced out the window. She was watching him again. Her second-floor bedroom—one down, across the street—had the perfect angle to see into his. Cricket troubled him for several reasons. Why was she aiming a telescope powerful enough to see Mars into his bedroom? On a clear day, when the oaks were trimmed away from the window, the angle was perfect for a not only a view of this room but also his bathroom. The entire bathroom.

The morning was clear. The trees, trimmed.

Nick showered with the bathroom door shut.

But it wasn't her setup that disturbed him the most. It was her checking out his bedroom when he wasn't there. The night before, he had thrown a ladder against the side of the house. One adjustment to the home security camera and he now had a video proving his theory to be a fact.

He had too much on his mind. No time to ponder why Cricket acted the way she did. Who could figure that out anyway? He rushed out of the house to his car, pressed the keyless ignition, and shifted to reverse.

Cricket dashed across the street toward him, waving. "Nick!"

He checked his watch and then lowered his window. "Hey, Cricket." He wouldn't tell the voyeur what he knew just yet. Her not knowing gave him an advantage he was not ready to lose. He'd be dressing with the bathroom door closed for a while longer.

Cricket Pouty-Face whined, "Nick, Cricket's car is acting up. Would you give her a ride?"

Nick glanced at the time again. "I have a meeting." He squinted out the window at her. "Where to?"

"UH downtown."

"Get in. It's on my way." He shifted to park, trotted to the passenger side, and opened her door. Cricket moseyed in. He ran back and got in. He was about to hit the gas when Cricket caught his hand. "Nick, I can't seem to get the seatbelt fastened. I think it's stuck."

"It's tricky." Nick reached around her. "There's not really room for two."

She pressed forward, making it a tighter squeeze. "Take your time."

The belt clicked. He leaned back in his seat and hit the gas. "Isn't your car new?" Nick asked, looking over at her.

"Yes, but I'm already having trouble with it." She eased closer to him. "Maybe it's a lemon."

"It's under warranty, right?"

"Yes, but they take forever to fix something."

He stopped at a light and glanced at her. "Why didn't you go to UT?"

"I made a mature decision to stay close to home."

Nick looked to see if she appeared serious. "Really? I wouldn't have pictured you doing that."

She gushed, "I prefer to stay close to my family and friends."

"Is that right?" he said, in a doubting tone.

"My grandmother is getting older. She would do anything in the world for me."

"There's nothing like grandparents. All mine passed. You won't regret staying."

"I'm sure of it." Cricket caressed his arm.

"I'm curious about something. How do you know Mr. Keaton?"

"I have connections in high places."

"Close enough to get Jason a job?"

"Just trying to use my influence to help out an old friend."

"Friend? You spit on him after he called you a narcissist."

"I'm a forgiving person."

Nick looked over at her. "Really?"

"People can change, you know. Now, would it be too much trouble to give Cricket a ride until her car is fixed?"

"I'm only staying with my parents until my downtown condo is ready." Nick glared at her. "I value my privacy."

"Sure you do. It'll be a couple weeks, right?"

She read the paperwork on my desk.

"How'd you know?" He looked for a reaction.

Unfazed, she walked her fingers up his arm. "Oh, a little birdie told me."

The traffic came to a standstill. Nick shifted to neutral.

"Nick, let me pick out the colors in your condo."

"Got it all done but the bedroom."

"I'm an expert in bedrooms. When I finish, you'll never want to come out of the room."

"I hope we're still talking about the decor."

"We'll make a day of it," Cricket sang. "We can get the linens and everything. Go out to lunch. It will be fun! I'll do some special decorating for you."

He shifted gears. They were boxed in.

"Nick, you realize Cricket's in college. Right?"

"Yep."

"Just don't forget; Cricket is a grown woman now."

He pressed tightly toward the door. "I prefer clean earth tones."

"You need to add at least one jewel tone. Like your tie. Looks way better than a cream-colored one." She winked.

He swung his head toward her and then back at the road. *What's she up to?*

CHAPTER SEVENTEEN

Finding a women's shelter in Lubbock wasn't easy. They not only didn't advertise; they were shrouded. Steely finally found someone who gave her a hotline number. The hotline wasn't much of a hotline. A directory assistant screened her before providing another number to call. It took all day for a call back. After answering dozens of questions, she finally was given an address.

The facility was located only a few blocks from the university. All she needed was somewhere safe until she could find something more permanent. It would be somewhere that campus police wouldn't run her off. The dorm bench and her car were not considered acceptable sleeping facilities.

Two circles around the block advanced her no more except to realize the street number did not exist. She parked and walked, checking every door until she found a midrise cinder-block building. The name and address of the Henderson Women and Children's Center might have been left off the building, but they remembered to install a reinforced-steel door.

To the left of the door was a glass window, a good two inches thick. She tried pushing the door, but the slab of steel didn't budge. She stood, staring blankly, until a light lit up the window. Her eyes caught the *BULLETPROOF* sticker in the lower right corner.

The lady inside spoke through a speaker.

"Yes?" the woman asked.

"I'd like a room, please," said Steely politely.

"Do you have a bed reserved here?" She popped a mean piece of gum as she spoke.

"Well, no, not yet. But I would gladly pay a reasonable rate."

"Honey, this ain't no hotel."

"I just need a place to stay for a while."

"Come in." The door cranked open with ease. The structure resembled a family resort. An indoor playground was the focal point of the first and second floors. Several mothers watched as their children played. The women were smiling, but their faces were worn.

"Come over here, please," she said.

Her name tag read "Jane," but that was clearly not her real name unless everyone who worked there had the same name. The drawer beside her was full of "Jane" badges.

"Yes, ma'am."

"Is your life in imminent danger?"

"Danger?" Steely flashed her eyes toward the playground and then back to Jane.

"Has someone threatened you and/or tried to harm you and/ or your family and/or caused you and/or your family physical or emotional harm?" This was clearly not the first time Jane asked those questions.

"No." Steely took an extended look at the mothers. This facility was on lockdown. The mothers were smiling, but they hadn't always smiled. Most of them had some sort of visible bruising.

"Then, sorry, we're full," said Jane. "We're only taking life-endangerment cases right now."

Life endangerment? "Miss, I'm sorry to have bothered you." Steely turned toward the door and waited for it to open.

"Young lady?" Jane said.

"Yes?" she said, not turning back.

"You don't have any place else to go?"

"No, but I'll be fine."

"You can go to the general shelter. They'll take you since you're homeless. Turn right at the next light. You'll see it on the left."

Steely glanced over her shoulder and nodded. "Thank you. I'll give it a shot." She made a quick exit. As she walked away, a young mother with two small children approached the same door. Her right arm was in a cast. The door opened without a question asked. The young mother had been there before. She knew the routine.

The general shelter was easy to spot. The lighted sign above the front door was clear about what was inside. They had plenty space for Steely or anyone else who dared to enter. But Ron and Bethany, the couple who ran the place, blocked her from taking further steps inside.

"This place isn't for you," Bethany said firmly. "It's too dangerous."

"We put our lives at risk every day we're here." Ron shook his head. "Someone could lose it and go berserk. Some of the people here are barely functional. Many have fried their brains with drugs. Some unfortunately are still users. We're here to help them. You can't stay here."

Steely listened. Then she decided to get real with them. "Is it safer than living under a bridge? Because so far, that's my only other option. I'd sleep in my car if I could find a safe place to park. It's a weird feeling waking up hooked onto a tow truck. It cost me sixty-five dollars for a ride I didn't want to take."

Bethany poked Ron. They agreed. "You can go to the Henderson Women's and Children Center," Bethany said. "You'll be safe there."

"It's really nice." Ron picked up a phone.

"No, I can't go there," Steely rebutted.

"Don't worry," Bethany said. "We can get you in Henderson."

"I really appreciate it. But no, I can't do that."

"You sure?" asked Bethany.

Steely nodded.

Ron set the phone down. "OK. If this is what you want."

"But you must keep to yourself," Bethany instructed. "Don't be friendly. Don't speak unless you're spoken to. Avoid eye contact with everyone. We'll put you in the far back. It may be a little safer in case there's trouble up front."

Steely took a deep breath and exhaled, nostrils flaring. "Thank you." She lowered her head and maneuvered to the back. It didn't take but a few steps before she looked into the eyes of Ron and Bethany's objections. Space didn't mean a private room with a bed and a mattress. Space meant a cot. And a general shelter meant anyone generally human—most of the time—qualified for a cot crammed up next to another. There were some road-rage-looking people cohabitating in the open, square room. Most were men. Only two other women in the entire place. They must not have been in imminent danger, or they surely wouldn't have been there. Not one person stayed at the shelter because his or her life was good. Everyone had trouble or was trouble.

Steely took her place on the eighth cot in the ninth row, with her allotted blanket and premium pillow. The cot was made of a washable canvas. It was clean but tough. No problem. She was tired enough to rest on a bed of rocks.

Within a week, Steely learned how to sleep with one eye open and one leg hanging off the cot. By the end of the first month, she was educated about life in a shelter: First, you don't get any sleep at the general shelter with people fighting spontaneously throughout the night. Second, you learn how to get out of their way fast. The cops were called almost every other day to maintain order. Third, they don't do background checks. If they did, they'd have to kick out many of the occupants. On any given day, fifteen to twenty of the residents had a device strapped around their ankles with a tiny blinking light. They were the convicted felons on parole. You don't get that kind of leg accessory for a misdemeanor.

After school started, Steely spent most evenings at the campus library. It was open around the clock, and its lounge chairs (big enough for a bear) were more comfortable than a bed. She studied each day until she fell asleep. She'd leave at sunrise, so she could get back to the shelter and change clothes before class. The occupants usually weren't throwing punches at six in the morning. They were either worn out or passed out. Either way, it was the most peaceful time of day.

Thanksgiving week proved to be the most peaceful week. Everyone left, except Steely, Ron, and Bethany. The couple set a small table with a traditional Thanksgiving dinner. Ron and Bethany held hands and then reached over the table for Steely to join them. Ron gave thanks and passed Steely a plate.

The couple seemed balanced, smart, and loving. Steely wondered how they ended up running a place that most people wouldn't set foot in. They spent every day working with people who had more problems than could be named.

Maybe Steely should have worked up to the question, but she didn't. She asked pointedly. "Why are you here?"

Ron looked over at Bethany. "When we got married, we pictured a family with children and a puppy. You see, we both were only children, so we wanted at least two."

Steely set her fork down. *They can't have children.* "I'm sorry, I shouldn't have asked."

"No, it's a normal question," said Bethany. "I'd be wondering too."

Ron said, "Steely, my parents died in a car accident right after we got married. Then Bethany's mother died of breast cancer two years later. Her dad passed from a stroke a few days after that."

"I'm so sorry."

Bethany tightened her grip on Ron's hand. "We were just about to consider adopting a baby when we saw Jeri, our next door neighbor, get beat up by her boyfriend."

Steely's face broadened. "Did she survive?"

Bethany nodded. "She got a restraining order and took off with their baby. Ron and I started thinking. What if she hadn't had the money to leave? She'd have been homeless unless someone took her in. An average of three women each day are killed by domestic violence."

Ron looked around the room, spreading his arms. "We didn't want to live just for ourselves. We can't help everyone, but we can help some. The biggest problem is drugs."

Steely looked down at the table. Steve's credit card sat on top of a grocery receipt. She bent close enough to read it and then shot her gaze back up at the couple. They didn't need to be working at the general shelter. They didn't get paid either. Their last name was Henderson. They were trust-fund babies.

The shelter went back to its daily ruckus until the week of Christmas. Again, everyone left except Steely and the Hendersons. She expected a quiet Christmas Eve, her first without her mom or dad. This was before the choir from Outreach Christian Church poured into the building. It wasn't the gifts or the carols that helped her the most. It was the people who cared for her—a stranger housed in a place she never thought she'd be at Christmas.

Staying at the shelter helped Steely realize how easy it would be for some to end up homeless. The people there had some of life's worst problems. Not all caused their own problems. Some had other people who caused their problems. Either way, they all found themselves with no place to call home.

Steely began the winter semester by establishing a routine. She spent her days at school. Evenings at the library. Then she went back to the shelter to shower and dress. The library served two purposes: study course work and research financial fraud. The court cases she studied were way more interesting than her school books. Especially the ones the prosecutors won.

One morning during the first week of class, Steely came back to the shelter to clean up. Everyone was asleep except one woman who appeared to be in her midthirties. This was the first time Steely had seen her. The woman targeted Steely from the moment she entered the facility. Steely ignored her as instructed, making her way through the cots to her spot in the back.

The woman followed.

Steely kept moving. They didn't lock eyes until the woman was a couple of feet away. Steely waved awkwardly and moved on. The woman didn't wave back. She tracked Steely until Steely reached her cot in the back. Then she got right up in Steely's face.

Steely glanced around the room. Everyone was asleep. Ron and Bethany were out of sight, most likely asleep. She hoped the woman was normal enough to handle eye contact. Since there was nowhere to escape, she did what she did best—act normal. "May I help you with something?" she asked.

The woman growled, "If I ever see you near my man again, I'll make skinny-girl stew out of you. Throw in a few potatoes, carrots, and onions and you'll taste like chicken."

"Not everything tastes like chicken," Steely snickered nervously.

The woman wasn't amused and continued staring at her through dilated pupils.

"Ma'am, I don't know your man," Steely calmly replied. "And I know I haven't been around him because I haven't been around anybody. I'm antisocial."

The woman swished out a five-inch blade with an equal-sized handle.

"Ah!" Steely flung back against the wall. Her mace was within reach. Fighting a razor with a squirt of mace most likely would not be productive. The woman might not even flinch, even if Steely emptied the entire canister on her. Her teeth looked big enough to chew up the can and spit it back at her.

"I'm telling you, I don't know your man. I don't know anyone here except Ron and Bethany."

"His name is Ron." The woman moved the blade closer to a vital vein in Steely's neck.

"Oh no! There are two Rons."

"Don't lie to me." The woman squeezed in tighter.

Steely thought it might calm the woman if she just confessed and agreed. There was no time to convince her there were two Rons there. She had to speak without moving her jaw. "OK. I promise I'll never do it again."

The woman pressed the weapon on Steely's neck. The blade was dull and would take additional pressure to slice through skin. "There's still blood on this from the last skank who said that."

Maybe that was a bad call. Maybe reason?

"Look you don't want to go back to prison, do you? You could get the death penalty."

"Didn't get it last time. They said I wasn't fit for trial."

"Never mind then." Steely leaned as far away as she could without falling sideways. Dicing someone up was certainly a parole violation. The assailant would be able to begin preparations for that stew before anyone monitoring the device strapped around her ankle was alerted.

The woman kept the weapon on Steely's neck. "I can handle a knife better than a butcher. One slit and you'll never speak again. That is—if you survive. You understand me?"

Steely was a mannequin.

The woman came closer. "Don't let it happen again."

Steely blinked twice.

The woman flipped the blade back in place and left.

Steely left too.

The next three weeks, she bedded down in a sleeping bag in the back seat of her car. The days were short and the evenings frosty. She could shut both eyes at night with no concern that someone might threaten to make a fresh batch of skinny-girl stew. The twenty-four-hour café, where she parked, didn't mind her taking up a space.

Steely unzipped herself from the bag, sat up, opened her backpack, and took out an envelope with a paper listing her grades. They were good. Certainly they could have been better. She was fine with them as long as they were good enough to stay on scholarship and keep the upper-level accounting classes she scheduled for the summer. Housing would be plentiful then.

She rolled up her bag, grabbed a small tote, and headed to the ladies' room inside the restaurant. Scrubbed her face, brushed her teeth, and changed her clothes. She was about to leave when her cell beeped. Ms. Blackwell's number flashed on the screen. She hadn't talked to her in six months.

"Hello?"

"This is Julia Blackwell," she snapped. "Steely, you sound like you're in a tunnel. Where are you?"

She darted out the restroom and headed for her car. "Does that sound better?"

"Are you trying to get me fired?"

"What? I think we have a bad connection."

"I told you to withdraw your application."

"I just—"

"Don't you know freshmen are required to live in campus housing or at home with parents? The rules were fully covered at the spring open house for prospective students."

"Ms. Blackwell, I had no idea. Nobody said anything—"

"Where are you living anyway?"

"Close by. You're not expelling me because of a technicality, are you?" Steely reached the car, opened the door, dropped her bag in the back seat, and got in.

"It's a good thing for you that I received your letter of recommendation."

"You know some people are unstable. Wait—was it good?"

"Of course. And I found a spot for you as an RA, as long as you don't gamble. You don't, do you?"

"Gamble? No—"

"Then the room is yours."

Steely hadn't been in contact with anyone socially since she'd arrived in Lubbock. If a serial killer had grabbed her, no one would have known she was missing. The letter of recommendation did puzzle her. *Who would have sent it?* It didn't matter. She had a place to sleep with a home address, and nobody there had mandatory leg bracelets.

The dorm room was private, since she was replacing two girls, not one. The two previous RAs had been expelled. The school didn't care much for RAs running a casino out of the dorm. By the end of the fall semester, every student in the building owed them money. Parents complained. Police were called. They were out.

The room had a second-floor view of her favorite bench and a private bathroom with a shower. The bed wasn't much softer than a cot, but it was a bed. On top of it was her first piece of mail: an envelope containing a cashier's check, identical to the ones she and her mom received after her father passed. Anonymous had found her.

During her junior year, one of the girls in the dorm invited Steely to a weekly Bible study, where she met another junior from Houston. David Hunter had grown up a few doors down from Nick Dichiara.

She had met him briefly before but didn't really know him. He asked if she would like to study with him. She did. The next week they were dating. The relationship quickly progressed from casual to serious. They spent every spare minute together. Within a few months, she was loved and in love. By the middle of their senior year, they were engaged.

Jack Hunter, David's father, was thrilled for the young couple. Steely met Mr. Hunter numerous times when he came up to take her and David camping at Buffalo Lake. She quickly grew very fond of Jack for many reasons. He reminded her of her dad.

Steely was anxious to meet Mrs. Hunter too. It seemed odd that two months after the engagement she hadn't yet met David's mother, Beatrice.

CHAPTER EIGHTEEN

Nick and Jack rounded a circular table in Jack's office. It was where Jack did his strategic planning. He'd usually call in the heads from each department when there was a problem. They'd sit there all day, if needed, pondering the best course of action. Nick had insisted that none of the others be invited to this meeting. The CEO was the only one who needed to hear what Nick had to say just yet.

Meetings in Hunter's office always ended with Jack's giving Nick a good-job pat on the back, along with instructions to keep doing what he was doing. That wasn't going to happen today. If they kept doing what they were doing, a billion-dollar company would cease to exist. That's why Hunter didn't merely glance over the balance sheet, as he had done in the past. He fixated on it.

Black-suited, hair combed to a mess, Nick had more questions than clarity. Things had been going on that shouldn't have. Assets had disappeared. Equipment purchased and then vanished. The company had moved from vast profits to draining cash reserves.

Jack grew up on the oil fields of West Texas. He dressed like he had never left. The man knew his business whether he wore a white collar or not. He was trying to wrap his mind around something he had never seen before in Jack Hunter Industries. Fraud.

Nick said, "Sir, I don't understand why we're wiring our assets to the subsidiaries in Saint Stephen's. Harry has been giving me the runaround since I got here. Now we're at a dangerous point. The subs have drained our capital. It won't be long before we're unable to operate."

Hunter looked intently at the bottom line, stared at the figures as though they would change if he gazed long enough. Jack was just short of a panic—and he wasn't the type to panic. "What's going on in Saint Stephen's?"

"Crates are shipped in and out. Who knows what's in them. I can tell you for certain that I don't see tens of millions in assets there. Not in the warehouse or the little bank on the island. They didn't even recognize our name. We don't have any substantial assets there."

Hunter dabbed his forehead with the napkin from under his coffee cup. He returned the cup to its saucer and looked over at Nick. "Your dad set up the LLCs."

"His practice was mostly personal litigation. Why'd he set up the LLCs?"

"It was a favor for an old friend. I know Vince structured them correctly. I'd trust him as much as I trust myself."

"Yes, sir. You must realize we're not talking about just those companies. The number of assets funneled from our US accounts is one hundred times more than expected. And they are not going to those three little bank accounts connected to the three LLCs he set up."

"One hundred times?" Hunter's tone matched Nick's. "That's unacceptable. Everyone in this company knows we have to stay within budget."

"I agree, sir. And where's the end? There are no profits from any project on the island. Absolutely none."

"Harry's been handling this." Hunter pushed the report aside. "Have you asked him?"

"I have, sir."

"What'd he say?"

"Nothing."

"He didn't answer?"

"He said nothing but a bunch of useless palaver. He's deflecting. I don't believe he likes a freshman VP questioning his projects."

"I don't care what he likes. Have you asked Charlie?"

"Not since his doctor told him to slow it down or he wouldn't see his next birthday. Between you and me, I don't think he could have caught this with the antiquated way the financials are set up. The system was fine when everybody was doing what they were supposed to do. The number of daily transactions is so far off the target. We need to update our systems to keep up. The way things are now, we can think everything is fine, perfect, when it's really falling apart. I need Mr. Keaton pinned down long enough to explain."

"I'll talk to him Monday. He'll answer your questions, Nick."

"Thank you, sir." Nick sighed. "May I upgrade our system?"

"You upgrade anything you need."

"I'll get it done immediately."

"I'm going to Lubbock for a few days. David got engaged a few weeks ago."

"Congratulations, sir."

Hunter gazed off.

"Aren't you happy about it?"

Hunter turned back to Nick. "Yes, but don't tell anyone until I tell Bea. I should've told her before now."

"I won't say anything."

Jack tilted his head at Nick. "Tell me how you're ever going to find someone with you working so much?"

"I found someone, sir. But she doesn't know yet."

"What are you waiting for?"

"I'm surprising her next week. And offer to help her move back home. I'd go this weekend if I didn't have a fund raiser tonight. But I have to warn you, sir. I won't be working this much if she says yes."

"You better not." Hunter held out a hand for Nick to shake.

Nick locked up his office. He was ready to look at something other than dollar signs. He swung by his condo for a quick change of clothes and then took off for the Pecan Valley Country Club a few blocks away.

He left his car running at a side door for the valet. A hostess led him to a table where his name was written in calligraphy on a place card. A quick dinner was served for him, along with another three hundred fifty guests. Then everyone was led out of the ballroom to various events around the club. Bingo, a silent auction, live auction, and carriage rides functioned simultaneously.

Nick chose the latter.

He had already spent more time than he wanted in conditioned air.

The night was crisp; the air, sweater cold. Two palominos pulled a carriage around the entrance of the Pecan Valley Country Club. The coachman's rugged gloves and vest looked more like an nineteenth-century stagecoach driver than a cowboy giving romantic rides in the city. He pulled on the reins, bringing the carriage to a halt. A young couple stepped down from the buggy. Nick and Cricket were next. They were not on a date. Cricket arrived early and switched her place card with the ninety-year-old gentleman who was to sit next to Nick.

The coachman offered Cricket his hand. She gathered her glittered gown and then scooted across the cold bench.

Nick stepped in beside her. Only two events could get Nick Dichiara in a tux. A wedding and a fund raiser. He was decked out tonight for the benefit of the residents at the Star of Light Assisted Living Home. Many of its residents were healthy enough to outlive their retirement funds. There could be no other reason for anyone to pay a grand for a thirty-minute carriage ride around the grounds of the club.

The coachman whipped the reins in the air. The horses trotted in a semicircle down the main entrance. The riders had a perfect view of the laser lights spotting the grounds like snow.

Cricket purred, "Nick, Cricket is getting chilly. Can you move your manly self a little closer?"

Nick stayed put and unfolded a blanket under the seat. "This should do the trick." He laid it across her.

She moved over, tried nuzzling his arm atop her shoulders. But his arm wasn't going anywhere. It was a barrier. Then she pressed herself close and pulled the blanket up, tucking herself in. "That's a little better," she cooed. "Don't be greedy. You need to share your body heat."

"I don't like the sound of that." Nick was more interested in the stars than the moves she was making. "One day, I'm going to buy a telescope."

"Yeah?" Cricket cleared her throat. "The stars are so romantic, don't you think?" She looked up at him with lips slightly puckered.

"Guess so." He turned away.

Cricket rolled her eyes.

"You didn't just howl like a coyote, did you?" Nick asked.

The coachman chuckled.

"Very funny."

"I wasn't sure." Nick whispered, "There it goes again. Coyotes are out there with the other nocturnal creatures."

"I used to be nocturnal," she murmured.

The coachman shook his head.

Nick moved an arm over the side of the carriage. "How's your grandmother, by the way? Is she here tonight?"

Cricket straightened up. "No. She isn't up to all the excitement."

"Too bad. I hope she gets some benefit out of tonight's event."

"Right…"

"I'd like to meet this wonderful grandmother who caused you to skip UT."

"She's not big on company, especially when she isn't feeling well."

"I understand. I have to admit, your dedication to her makes me think a tad better of you."

Cricket tilted her upper body, her chest out. "Nick, you know I'm no longer a child. Can't you see the difference?"

"I keep thinking about how brutal you were to Steely."

"Pauper?" Cricket said, irritated.

"See? You know her name is Paupher."

"Me and sweet little Steely have no problems. There's no reason for me to ever say another unkind word to that child." Cricket spread her lips. "She's not concerned about my silly high-school antics. She certainly wouldn't be thinking about that when she's about to marry David Hunter."

Nick fell back against the bench.

Cricket moved in tight. "Didn't you know? Shocking, isn't it? Mrs. Hunter will probably drop dead when she finds out."

"I didn't know they were dating," Nick said, flustered. "The last couple of years have flown by. I thought she was graduating and coming back home."

"Yeah, she is but as a married woman. I'm sure she thinks she'll be sitting pretty for the rest of her life. But you never know…"

Nick dropped his head in his hands.

"You look stressed," Cricket said, in baby talk. "Hard day at work?"

He didn't answer.

"Here." She eased over.

"Please don't," he said.

"At least let yourself relax for a change. Just lean back and let Cricket make it all better." She twisted him toward her and massaged his shoulders.

He resisted, but not fully. The carriage rounded the last lap and trotted into the driveway. Nick walked Cricket to the door and left.

CHAPTER NINETEEN

Nick shuffled down the hall to Jason's cubicle. The clutter on his desk was gone. His wastebasket overflowed onto the floor. Boxes stacked at eye level were packed and ready for hauling. "Did you get those account numbers for me?"

"No."

"Why not?"

"Mr. Keaton never took his eyes off me. He doesn't just hand them over and take a nap."

"Don't mess with me. You could have at least memorized one."

"I need time."

"You know how to complicate what you're doing, so Keaton doesn't know what's going on. I need that information today."

"What's wrong with you? You look like your dog got run over." Jason taped the last box, set it on the desk, and patted Nick on the shoulder. "You should look better after taking a few days off."

Nick shrugged and stuck his hands in his pockets.

"Didn't you chill at your parents' beach house?"

"Chill? No." Nick stared at the boxes. "How'd you get Jack to overlook your public intoxication charge and move you upstairs?"

Jason whispered. "He doesn't know."

"He'll find out when Benita does your next background check."

Jason grinned. "Mr. Keaton had one done prior to my little infraction."

"Jack's going to hit the roof."

"He'll never know. Mr. Keaton's going to take care of it."

"He'll probably get you a fake background. Then—"

"Nick, face the facts. You're no longer the only one under thirty on the executive floor! I'm getting Mr. Qualls's old office. He's getting an office down the hall. I have everything but a title."

"I see." Nick peeked in a box. "What'd you do, just dump everything in there?"

"This stuff's going to the Dumpster." Jason knocked Nick's hand out of the way and closed the box. "I'm working alongside Mr. Qualls in the venture capitalist group. No more IT for me."

Nick looked concerned. "You know Mr. Keaton's projects are draining the company," he said, irritated. "I'm not making this stuff up. It's real."

Jason patted Nick on the shoulder. "You don't understand how venture capitalists operate."

Nick lectured. "They invest capital into startups or existing companies that want to expand. The investment can turn massive profits or massive loses—usually nothing in between."

"So you know a little."

"Ask him some basic business questions. He doesn't know squat. And then to work with Qualls…" Nick shook his head.

"Why not?" Jason opened the desk drawers, making sure they were empty. "He does his part. I'll do mine. Keaton is my manager. Period."

"Qualls looks like a serial killer."

"What do you look like? Someone drinking chocolate milk?"

"You mean a café mocha?"

"I'm surprised they don't put it in a baby bottle for you."

"You're making a big mistake."

Jason threw a plastic cup in the trash. "Mr. Hunter will never promote me like Mr. Keaton. Let's face it, Mr. Hunter acts like you're his first-born son."

"We're upgrading all our systems. You can write some of the programs. Hunter will allow you to patent them. No company does that."

"There's not enough money in it for me."

"No money in software? It's scary when you say things like that."

"I mean here at JHI. Excuse me now." Jason went around Nick, ripped his name plate off the cubicle, and shot it toward the trash but missed. "I have to report upstairs."

Nick lifted two boxes. "These aren't heavy; put another on top. I'll help you take them to the Dumpster."

"Put that down. Monte's coming to get them."

"He's a maintenance engineer—been here before you were born. He's not your personal gopher."

"Put 'em down." Jason yanked the box out of Nick's grasp, dropping it to the floor. "You have to act like an executive if you want to be treated like an executive." Jason straightened his tie and headed down the hall with Nick diagonally behind him. "Come check out my office. Mr. Keaton bought me an espresso machine."

"I don't drink his espresso, and I wouldn't work for Keaton."

"Better watch what you say." Jason shifted his brow. "You may have to drink it instead of your chocolate milk."

Nick looked away.

"Loosen up, pal. You're so uptight." They stopped at the elevators. Jason buttoned his jacket. The elevator cranked open; he held it. "You coming?"

"Not yet."

"Fine. But you look like your world has come to an end. Mr. Hunter isn't concerned about Mr. Keaton, and you shouldn't be either."

Nick started to say something but then stopped.

Keaton should be concerned. Jack should send him and his stinking coffee packing!

"There are times when you need to sit back and enjoy yourself." Jason let go of the door. It closed.

Nick kicked the elevator. *I'm going to find out what's going on here.*

CHAPTER TWENTY

Steely had looked forward to meeting her future mother-in-law until Jack explained that surprises made Beatrice Hunter nervous. Steely doubted Mrs. Hunter would get nervous over a good surprise. Their first meeting ended with Bea being taken away in an emergency vehicle. Steely hoped history didn't repeat itself today.

There was nothing left to do except get out of the car and go inside the house. Steely had butterflies in her stomach, and watching David poking around inside the car made them worse.

Is he stalling?

She popped open her door and got her first earful of Beatrice Hunter's megaphonic voice that sent neighbors to their windows. David honked twice, announcing their arrival, and then hurried over to Steely and tugged her up the sidewalk and into the house. There was no welcome party waiting at the door. Beatrice was no longer heard.

David probed out the window. Steely leaned over to see what caused him to squeeze his eyes together like he was getting an injection.

"Why are the paramedics here?" she asked.

"They come to visit sometimes. Dad?" he called out in a worrisome tone.

"Visit?" said Steely, taking a second look out the window.

Jack came out of a back room.

"Hi, kids. I didn't hear you come in." He gave Steely a reassuring kiss on the cheek. He shook David's hand and gave him a side hug.

David inquired, "Did Mother call the paramedics again?"

Again?

"Huh?" Jack asked, mirroring the same anxious look as his son.

"Dad, they're here." He motioned outside.

"When did she do that?" Jack opened the door. "I've been with her for the last two hours. She hasn't been out of my sight, except when she had to go to the—" He shook his head.

A uniformed woman and two men approached the threshold. The woman acknowledged Jack. "Scottie, good to see you, but we don't need you today." Hunter attempted to close the door.

He knows her by name?

Scottie held her place. "Mr. H, we got a call from Mrs. H again."

Mrs. H?

"Really?" Hunter stepped aside.

"The bedroom, sir?" Scottie poked her head inside.

"Yes," Hunter muttered. "You know the way."

She knows the way?

Steely darted to the door. "I think I should leave."

"No, no," David said. "Mother will be fine."

Hunter followed the medics to a back bedroom. "Coffee, anyone?"

Steely whispered, "Is she really sick?"

"Probably not. She doesn't cope well."

"I'm not coping too well at the moment. She doesn't want us to get married. Will she do this on our wedding day?"

David shook his head. "I doubt it."

"You doubt it?" she said in a high pitch. "We can't take that risk. We can't have a wedding with your mother not showing up. And we might not know until the last second? All I'd be thinking about is will she or won't she? Let's elope. I prefer to elope anyway. Are you OK with that?"

"Elope?" David glanced at the back hall. "Maybe we should."

"Well, it's not exactly eloping since they already know. But you know what I mean."

They held hands for a few minutes before they heard wheels rolling and walls being bumped. The paramedics were heading out with Mrs. H in tow. Steely moved out of the way, far back into the kitchen. She preferred her first sight of Mrs. Hunter not be with straps holding her in place. The medics could have turned the stretcher upside down, and neither Beatrice nor her puffy hair would budge.

"We're taking her this time only as a precaution," announced Scottie. "You know, because of her age."

Beatrice moaned, "Sure hope I'm not having a heart attack."

Jack kissed her. Scottie and another attendant pushed the stretcher down the sidewalk into the open ambulance. Jack waved from a few feet away. "You're in good hands. I'll check on you after dinner. Bye, Bea."

"Hold it!" Beatrice shrilled.

Scottie held the door, leaving her a squinty view out. "We have to lock up now, Mrs. H."

"Wait! I changed my—"

Click. Scottie snapped the door, jumped in the driver's seat, turned on the siren, and hit the gas.

Eloping for sure.

CHAPTER TWENTY-ONE

Beatrice Hunter didn't have a bad heart. She had a bad gall-bladder. Good thing Bea's doctor didn't require her to stay calm and quiet when she got home because she was not. Her hair was on fire after hearing about "the elopement." Suddenly, she was in a tizzy to talk with Miss Paupher. Bea called Steely and told her they needed to meet for lunch immediately to straighten some things out.

Steely wondered what wasn't straight. Everything seemed crystal clear to her. Beatrice didn't want her marrying her son. She did accept Bea's invitation and promptly went over to see her. Steely took a practical precaution and parked the car a few houses down, just in case the medics showed up again. She was running for the door if she heard sirens.

Bea casually greeted her at the door. They went past a warm kitchen table and proceeded to a stately dining room. Five chairs were on each side of a twelve-foot table with Bea at the head. Steely's place was set to her left. A white rug covered most of the floor. The lunch consisted of BLT sandwiches, chips, and iced tea.

Steely became concerned. "Mrs. Hunter, should you eat that much bacon? The mayonnaise is oozing out the sides. I don't want you to get—"

"I've been eating bacon all my life." Bea used a piece of bread to spread out the dressing. "My gallbladder was dumped in a plastic bag. It won't be giving me any more problems. It's odd you don't eat bacon. You could slap a piece of bacon on anything and make it taste good."

"I don't want to overdo it and make my stomach hurt."

"Well, my stomach already hurts."

Steely leaned to one side, getting a better view out the window. "You expecting someone?"

Steely nervously said, "You feeling OK?"

"Is that supposed to be a joke?"

"No, ma'am." Steely cleared her throat.

Bea dabbed the corners of her mouth with a napkin and pushed her plate aside. "Steely, you seem like a compliant child."

Steely coughed.

"I'm sure you don't want to start off a marriage by disappointing your fiancé's mother. Will you do one little thing for me?"

This was no ordinary question. This was a trick. "What is it you want?"

"Postpone the wedding?"

Steely took a bite out of the BLT and swallowed it without chewing.

Bea stared at her for a few seconds.

"Your skin is bleaching like you're going to pass out. Maybe I need to call the medics for you."

Steely shook her head and then sipped the tea.

"I've seen people look better than you in the ER," Bea said.

"I'll be fine." Steely scooted the dish off the placemat and set the tea on the indention. She took another quick sip.

"Let's just cut to the chase," Bea said. "Are you sure you're ready for marriage?"

Steely covered her mouth with her napkin, cleared her throat. "I believe I am."

"It's not easy."

"I know."

"How long have you known my son?"

"Two years."

"I knew Jack all my life."

"Long time."

"You get married and then find out what you got, like a grab bag."

"Grab bag? Then nobody would marry."

Bea shook her head. "Many shouldn't."

"Are you saying we shouldn't?"

"Don't put words in my mouth."

"Mrs. Hunter, what exactly do you want?" she asked firmly but politely.

"Temper, temper. You sure get bent out of shape fast. A quick temper is not a good thing in a marriage."

"I'm fine. Well, not exactly fine. But what do you want?"

"One year."

"A year?"

"To give my *only* son a decent wedding."

"A decent wedding—with me?"

"He can marry you. I don't stick my nose into his business."

"I wasn't sure—"

"Give me ninety days."

"Well—"

"Sixty? Don't you want a nice wedding? Every woman does. Unless you're planning on getting divorced."

"Mrs. Hunter, I'm not planning on divorcing. I'm planning on eloping." Steely cringed.

She's still breathing.

"Eloping?" She pitched down her napkin. "I'm sure this is nothing more than a thoughtless spur-of-the-moment blip. I'm certain you'll come to your senses."

"I don't think so."

The housekeeper peeked out the kitchen door and then tiptoed off.

"This is the only wedding my son will ever have."

"Mrs. Hunter, you have to understand—"

"*You're pregnant!*" she shrieked.

"Mrs. Hunter!" Steely said, raising her voice.

"This would make sense if you're pregnant. This elopement nonsense."

"Mrs. Hunter, you have to have sex to get pregnant."

"Eee, I don't want to hear about sex!"

"I'm definitely not pregnant."

"Then there's no reason why I can't have the wedding I've always dreamed of for my only son."

Steely stood. "Mrs. Hunter, I'll discuss this with David."

"He already said it was OK with him."

"I need to discuss it with him."

"Do you think I'm lying?"

Juan Rios, Mr. Hunter's assistant, passed through the room behind Bea. Steely could see him. He raised a tight fist in solidarity and support.

"Mrs. Hunter, there really isn't anything for me to discuss with David. We're eloping. I'm glad I was able to meet you before we left. If we hadn't announced our engagement, I would have met you afterward. You're not really supposed to tell anyone when you elope."

Beatrice twitched every time Steely said "elope."

"Thank you for lunch, Mrs. Hunter. Lunch was—it was enlightening. I must go now." Then she went for the door.

Bea flung her chair backward, going after her. "Steely, wait. You need to think about how you're disappointing me. This isn't a good start!"

"The last thing I want to do is disappoint you," she pronounced with authority. "But I think eloping would be best, and this is our final decision. Good-bye, Mrs. Hunter, and thank you for lunch." Then she bolted.

Definitely eloping. Beatrice Hunter would have to birth another baby to get the wedding of her dreams.

She pleaded, cried, and begged for a wedding. Steely compromised with a simple ceremony in the Pecan Valley Christian Church's prayer garden, attended by only Bea and Jack. Steely was radiant in a white laced gown. Bea never knew she picked it up from a resale shop for thirty-five bucks. She had already heard what Bea thought about resale shops. "All they sell are dead people's clothes." Steely hoped someone died in a bridal grown.

After the wedding, the newlyweds made their home, temporarily, in the apartment above the Hunter's garage. Steely and Beatrice had become neighbors.

CHAPTER TWENTY-TWO

Nick didn't wave Hunter down. Or yell to get his attention. He jumped in front of his car. He had chased Jack all morning. He was either going to have a chat or get run over in the JHI parking garage.

Jack slammed on the brakes, barely missing him. Sliding his window down, Jack bellowed, "Nick, where'd you come from? I almost hit you."

Nick pressed on the hood with his fingers and went around to the driver's side. "Sir, you're the most careful driver I know."

"So what caused you to test my skills?"

"Would you please squash Mr. Keaton's audit request?"

"Nope, give him his audit. It might be to his demise. You're the one who's been questioning why the subs are way over budget. Harry keeps dodging the questions. I've given him every opportunity to make this right."

"I think it's gotten worse, sir."

Hunter cringed. "Harry gave me the same hogwash he's been giving you. It's hard to imagine that someone you've known all your life would do something like this. It's criminal."

"Do you mean embezzlement?" Nick's countenance brightened.

"Maybe worse."

Nick slapped the car door. "Now you're talking, sir! Let's shut him down right now!"

Hunter shook his head. "Complete the audit first. Then I'll have clear grounds to dismiss him and whatever else I need to do. I can sell what is left of our assets in Saint Stephen's. Charlie's doc won't give him the OK to come back. He's only on the board, so it's up to you."

"Sir, if we're going to do this, then let's hire a team to do an investigative audit. They can dig deep enough to account for every dollar."

"Nick, isn't the new system set up?"

"Yes, sir, but—"

"Get this done. Then you can bring in the team you want." Hunter checked the time on the dash. "I'm late." His window went up. The discussion was over.

Nick paced down the driveway behind Hunter. He stuck his hands in his pockets and kept moving. Cars buzzed around him until he stepped back onto the sidewalk. He needed to think and to let out some steam. Mostly let out steam. He already called the audit team he wanted. They were booked for the next forty-five days. And it could take another six to nine months to report their findings. There was still one question he couldn't get out of his mind.

How's this audit going to benefit Keaton? He wouldn't want it unless it did.

He pounded the pavement for almost an hour and then hustled back to the tower and swiped his security card to get a lift to the top floor. His office was left; Jason's, right. He turned right. Maybe Nick could squeeze something out him. Jason would defend Keaton. Nick was certain that wasn't changing today.

Jason wasn't sitting back in his leather chair sipping from his favorite mug. He was slamming his desk drawers. He dug around inside one and then shoved the drawer back in place. He barely looked up when Nick threw the door open.

"Jason, did you get the account numbers?"

"No! Quit asking me. I can't get them."

"What's the deal with this audit Keaton wants?"

"He just wants an update on where we are." Jason looked under a desk pad and then a lamp. Nothing but wax.

Nick jerked a chair from the desk and placed himself in it. "So why can't we wait another six months?"

"Mr. Keaton said Mr. Hunter has made some bad decisions that need to be addressed."

"Have you been watching cartoons again? The only bad decision Mr. Hunter ever made was hiring Mr. Keaton."

Jason repeated his search, opening every drawer, looking inside, and then forcing each back in place. He threw his hands in the air. "You complain about everything Mr. Keaton does." Jason swung around, searched the top of his credenza. He swung back around. "You let your feelings about Mr. Keaton get in the way of your objectivity."

"It's hard to be objective when my gut is attacking me."

"Tell your gut this: he gave over two million to charity last year."

Nick leaned in. "It was company money." He sat back. "What are you looking for anyway?"

"Nothing."

"Well, it isn't in your desk or credenza." He stood and turned toward the door.

"Nick, I'll catch up with you later. I'm having a bad day."

Nick nodded and then headed to his office. He slammed the door, leaned back in his chair, and rubbed his eyes with two fists. Suddenly, he paused and opened them wide.

What'd he lose?

He sneaked back down the hall and peeked in Jason's office. Jason's jacket was off, his tie loosened and underarms drenched.

Nick air walked to the elevator and pressed eight. He took the next ride down to the eighth floor, got off, and no longer walked lightly. He sprinted down a hall to Jason's old cubicle.

Monte was tossing a trash bag into a cart. Jason's desk was torn apart on the floor. Nothing there but partitions, metal rods, and a light attached to the barrier wall. Monte did a double take at Nick's stampeding toward him. "Is something wrong, Mr. Dichiara?"

Nick huffed. "What are you looking for?"

"A toy. Mr. Wilkerson called me in a panic. Said to get down here and tear his desk apart. Good thing I had tossed the boxes. I had to dig through a trash bag. I have more to do than look for his toys and pick up his laundry. He thinks I'm his butler!"

"Monte, what else did you find?" He pointed to the cubicle. "In there?"

"A bunch of dirt."

"That's what I'm looking for." Nick picked up a piece of the desk, slowly turned it over. "I need to see the trash."

"It's all in there." Monte passed the bag to him.

Nick dumped the contents across the floor. It was mostly candy wrappers, coffee cups, and holes punched from papers. Nick sifted through each item. "How about the toy? Where'd you find it?"

"In that crevice of the desk." He nodded at the corner. "I don't know why a miniature bear had him so worked up." Monte cupped the bear in his hand.

Nick tilted his head to one side. "May I see it?"

"Certainly, sir. Maybe it has some sentimental value."

"Jason?"

"No." Monte shook his head. "I guess not."

Nick turned it over and examined it. The miniature figure was similar to a toy out of a gumball machine. Nick held the tiny figure up to the light. He rotated it around and pulled the head with one hand, the claws with the other, separating the body. "It's a flash drive. Who knows you found this?"

Monte smiled. "Only you, sir."

Nick reattached it and closed it in his fist. "Will you follow me?"

Monte nodded. "Anything you say, Mr. Dichiara."

They raced up to Nick's office. Nick stuck the device into his desktop. The only thing on the drive was a series of numbers. Nine numbers clumped together separated into columns totaling 216 sets.

"Did he say anything else about this?"

"No," said Monte. "Just sounded like he'd get his head chopped off if he didn't find it."

Nick plugged in another flash drive, made a copy, and ejected the bear.

"What are all those numbers?"

"I know what they are. I just don't know where they are." He passed the bear to Monte. "Please take this to Jason."

"Yes, sir."

"And, Monte, please don't say anything about the detour to my office."

Monte nodded.

Nick moved up close to his desktop and stared at them until the numbers blurred together. He finally pulled out the duplicate and slipped it into his pocket. The device wasn't leaving his sight.

CHAPTER TWENTY-THREE

Meeting with Hunter in his office at 6:15 a.m. was only for one reason: to have a discussion with Hunter that Nick did not want anyone else to hear. His back ached. His eyes strained. They became more irritated every time he rubbed them. He looked gaunt, as if he had the flu and hadn't eaten for a week. He felt even worse than he looked.

Nick fidgeted, waiting for Hunter's reaction from across the desk. Hunter rocked back and forth for a few seconds and then leaned forward. Nick had plenty to say, but he was giving Hunter time to digest the indigestible. Hunter knew there were problems but never dreamed anything would put the company in jeopardy. The dam had broken, and the audit revealed the aftermath. For several minutes, they both stared at page six of six until Nick broke the silence. "We're operating in the red."

"I can see that."

Nick knew Jack never worried about JHI. He had never needed to stress. Any time a situation cropped up, he quickly and efficiently fixed it. That was one of his duties as CEO. Problem fixer.

Jack scratched his forehead. He was always smiling or at least having a peaceful look on his face, but he had neither this morning. "Our sales are up. So is our revenue. Definitely some embezzlement going on here."

Nick glanced at the door. It was shut and locked. He and Hunter were the only ones privy to the audit. He preferred to keep it that way. "Definitely, Harry is responsible. How'd he funnel out two hundred thirteen million and nobody know it?"

"I don't remember authorizing him as a signer on the reserve account."

"We can get the bank to pull the signature card."

"What about the revenue? Where is it?"

"I don't know. Assets are going out, and we don't even know where. We need a team of auditors in here ASAP to investigate."

"Call them."

"Done. They'll be here next month."

"We need them now."

"The only group with the capacity for something of this magnitude can't come until next month. It'll take them six to nine months to go through every subsidiary in Saint Stephen's. They'll trace the profits and the reserves. There are accounts we didn't even know existed. I need the names of the banks. We may have to sue Harry after he's dismissed."

"We'll do whatever is needed."

"This mess will be cleaned up before our regularly scheduled audit. We can make it until then using our line of credit. I'm sure of it. Can we call Mr. Keaton in and fire him now?"

"Not yet." Hunter clenched his teeth, paused a few seconds, and then ordered, "Nick, I want you to e-mail a copy of this to the board. And tell them I'm requesting an emergency meeting this afternoon at three. You be there too."

No! "Sir, why give this to the board? It's like passing out cyanide."

Hunter raised his brow, a definite sign of his disagreement.

Nick felt feverish. "Sir, this could be calamitous. The stock will tank. Our reputation damaged. Everybody will lose if that happens. The stockholders...the employees. This information needs to be trashed."

"I can't ignore it. The employees' retirement accounts are invested in this company—others invested their life savings."

"Sir, I admire your transparency, but this report is a sham."

Hunter glared over at Nick. "You prepared it!"

"Let me rephrase. The numbers are skewed from embezzlement. You said that yourself."

Hunter pointed at the wrinkled papers. "That's where we are right now. Correct?"

"But we're not compelled to disclose this to anyone. These numbers don't have to leave this room. I can drag Harry along, just like he has done, with the flash drives." Nick's assessment was correct. He didn't need to explain the risk to Hunter.

Hunter looked steadily at Nick as they engaged in their most combative conversation. "Regulations set boundaries. Lines you don't cross or laws will be broken. I'm not only doing what is legal; I'm doing what's right. Every day new funds are invested in our stock." He glanced over at a framed portrait of himself and his father and then back at Nick. "You think I'm making an irrational decision, don't you?"

Life in the office briefly stopped. No one even blinked until Nick responded, "Sir..." He stammered, "Well...yes. I do."

"You've got backbone."

Nick cleared his throat. "Sometimes my backbone gets me into trouble."

"You're not in trouble. But you need to understand that I made this decision when I started this company."

"Sir, you never thought your childhood friend would embezzle a couple hundred million from you."

"Doesn't matter. I decided long before a crisis what I'd do if the bottom falls out. When the truth could cost me everything."

Nick slumped slightly.

Hunter took the six clipped pages and slid them across the desk. "Now e-mail this to the board."

"Yes, sir." Nick got up to leave.

"And, Nick…" Hunter walked along him. "You may not understand today, maybe not even tomorrow. I hope I live to see the day when you'll know I was right."

Nick's eyes filled.

"Don't worry. We'll straighten this out. And, Nick, even if things spiral down like you think, this is still the right thing to do. As long as I'm CEO, we're doing the right thing. Got it?"

Nick acknowledged Hunter and left. He went to his office and prepared the dreaded e-mail. No explanation was given, just: "See attached report and be at the board meeting this afternoon." Pressing send was more painful than tearing an ACL.

Just before he conked out, Nick e-mailed Jack a bulletproof spiel for the meeting. He hoped Jack would memorize it. All Jack needed to do was point a finger in Keaton's direction, fire him, and proceed to build the company back up. Simple. Then they could spend the next year going after the assets while they recouped their balance sheets.

A few hours later, he sprung the chair back from his desk and checked his watch. He had surpassed his catnap by an hour. He dashed to the men's room, rolled up his sleeves, turned on the water, splashed his face a few times, dabbed it off, and ran back to retrieve his jacket. He was due back in Jack's office.

Donna, Hunter's assistant, was stationed outside. The middle-aged woman, with flipped hair, was loyal to her boss of sixteen years. "Mr. Hunter came out a second ago looking for you," she said gloomy faced, when Nick entered the suite.

Nick acknowledged her with a nod and went straight into Jack's office. He didn't need to say anything. Donna had made copies of the audit. She knew what was in it.

Jack stood gazing out a window. He had witnessed most of the surrounding buildings crop up like weeds. He and Bea rode out their first hurricane in his office. The building swayed, but not a single glass broke. "Nick, I've made a decision," Hunter stated as he turned around.

"Yes, sir." Nick had a hand in his pocket, shuffling a few coins.

"You're not going to like it."

"I'm not...sir?" Nick stared up at the ceiling, figuring Hunter was right. "Aren't you firing Mr. Keaton? That would get my happy face back on." Nick edged out a chuckle.

"Nope. Not just yet."

"Sir?"

"Bea thinks Harry wants me out."

"Probably would make his day. Fire him. Just fire him."

"No. Nick, when you want to catch a fox in the henhouse, you watch and wait for the fox to come back. That's when you nab him."

"Sir, are you going to base this decision on a fox stealing hens? I'm not so sure that's the best thing right now."

"I'm leaving Harry in place until the company's back on stable ground."

"Sir, no! Please no." Nick passed his hand through his hair. "We talked about this."

"Why hasn't Harry taken off?"

"I've pondered that question myself."

"He can't get to the assets. Wherever the assets are, he can't get to them. That kind of money can't just suddenly show up in his account—he'd be caught."

"Then what can you do to prompt him to fix this?"

"Take a vacation."

"Seriously, a vacation?" Nick looked as shocked as he sounded. "Sir, are you feeling well?"

"A leave of absence."

Nick shook his head. "No, sir. Please, no."

"Harry caused this mess. Therefore, he can pull this company out of it quicker than the auditors can get here. I'm going to put him in charge while I'm gone."

"How do you know he won't destroy it?"

"Because he needs this company. He would have already left if he didn't. Listen very closely to what he says today. Oh, and one more thing."

"Yes, sir?"

"Don't defend me."

"What if I'm asked a question?"

"Won't happen. This meeting won't be a fact-finding mission." Hunter bent, scraped a wad of dirt from his shoe, and tossed it into the trash. Getting up, he buttoned his jacket. "Now let's go."

The hallway was silent from Jack's office to the boardroom. Hunter entered to a sudden hush. They had been talking about him, most certainly, not in a good way. Hunter took his seat at the head of the table. Nick pulled up a fold-out chair a few feet to the left of Hunter.

Keaton was to Hunter's right. His suit jacket hung on the back of his chair, and a red tie was wrapped around his neck. Next to Keaton was Thomas Qualls. A frown never left his face. He was a ditto stamp for anything Keaton proposed. Bill Clayton was across from Keaton. Fifty years ago, he was a steer wrestler; last forty, a successful wildcatter. He chartered a bank and funded it himself. Next to Clayton was the former CFO, Charlie Denison. Charlie had been with the company twenty-plus years before a forced medical retirement.

"Good morning." It was the first time Hunter addressed the group without putting a smile on every face in the room. "Let's keep this informal. You've seen the audit Mr. Dichiara put together. Bottom line—we don't have enough capital to complete the next month. We're operating in the red. Basically broke. I don't know what else to say, except I take full responsibility. I'm making the appropriate moves. We'll use our line of credit until we get everything back in order. The company will back on track within six months. Any questions?"

Any questions? They should have a thousand questions.

Keaton broke the silence. "Jack, we're heading to bankruptcy."

There he goes. Fire him!

"Bankruptcy can be avoided," reputed Jack.

"I've come up with an alternative plan," Keaton said. "A plan that will save us from bankruptcy."

Nick was coming unglued, making sharp, erratic moves. Clayton and Denison didn't seem shocked by Keaton's suggestion—not a good sign for Jack. They had been prepped. Suddenly the haze cleared. Jack had been set up. Keaton had tainted the board.

"Jack, you're the largest shareholder," Keaton said. "Transfer your shares over to me and let me fix the problem, or the company will fail and our stock will be worthless."

Keaton's such a con man.

"Harry, we don't know what's going on yet," argued Hunter. "If you know something I don't know, you need to say it now."

All eyes turned to Keaton.

"Well, no," he said, shifting. "But do you know what bankruptcy means? A change in management. If you want this company to survive, we must have a regime change." Keaton sounded like he was orchestrating a Third World coup.

Hunter muttered, "I'll agree to a leave of absence."

"That's not good enough. You need to transfer your interest and resign."

Transfer him to a jail cell!

"You want me to give you my shares?"

"I'll give you what I can, but everyone in this room will lose if we file for bankruptcy. Investors might get a penny on the dollar. You don't want that to happen, do you?"

Nick cleared his throat, trying to get Jack's attention.

Hunter, fire Keaton now.

Clayton had heard enough. "Jack, what happened?"

Hunter covered his mouth, dropped his hand, and said, "I don't know."

Denison said, "I hate to say it, but Harry is correct. The company could file bankruptcy. It may be the best thing, whether Jack stays on or not."

Keaton interrupted. "Jack has to go and relinquish all interest in the company. We can make the necessary changes and be back on track by the next quarter."

"That's absurd," Hunter said. "You're straining out a gnat and then swallowing a horse!"

Harry pointed a finger at Jack, the same finger Nick advised Jack to point at Harry. "You must resign!" he blasted. "I'll take on all the risk, only if I have total control. But you absolutely must resign!"

Hunter slapped the table. "Fine. I'll resign, if that's what you want, Harry, but I've got something I want you to sign in my office."

What's he doing?

"Sure, Jack, anything." Keaton passed a prepared document and his gold pen to Hunter. "Sign here."

Hunter's hand convulsed, opening and closing several times, before he picked up the pen, tightened his grip, and signed away Jack Hunter Industries. With a few strokes of a pen, the man was out.

Jack had been sucker-punched. Beaten down. And he tapped out. Nick expected something slimy from the leech. Clayton and Denison sitting quietly by watching Jack get slaughtered was shocking.

No one offered Jack a gold watch—not even a worthless plaque—celebrating his tenure. The only thing they gave Jack Hunter was a boot out the door. The meeting was adjourned. The CEO was replaced.

Jack swung around and confidently tilted his head at Nick. Then he walked out. Nick stared, in wonder, at Jack's submission to the dysfunctional board. Then he left. He stopped in the hall outside his office and looked back at the conference room. The noise from board members conversing easily carried itself down the slick walls. He took a few reverse steps back.

Clayton had gripped Keaton's tie. "I don't care if I lose every dime I have in this company. Jack was man enough to stand down today, but you better remember that he's my friend, and I'm bringing him back. I don't like hurting him, so you, Mr. Keaton, had better be a fast performer. Because one way or another, Jack Hunter will be back within a year. And you can count on that."

Keaton gagged. Clayton finally let him loose.

"You have nothing to worry about," Keaton said, easing the compression around his throat. "I know how to whip this place back in shape." Keaton's apparent self-confidence hadn't impressed anyone, especially Clayton.

Denison was up next. "You took full advantage of my absence. Let me tell you, I'll be watching every move you make. Twenty-one years as CFO. The worst thing I had to deal with was missing toilet paper. I still think you were the culprit."

Harry shook his head.

They stood down.

Hunter, Clayton, and Denison were all ex-military. They knew when to stand down to an enemy. And this was one of those times.

CHAPTER TWENTY-FOUR

Jack Hunter began liquidating the family's remaining assets. He sold everything of value, except the family farm. He had co-signed all JHI notes, and he wasn't going to let them default. He would have sold the farm too, if it hadn't been in a trust that made it unsalable. He left Houston with little to nothing but owing no one anything.

The farm where Jack was born, in Grey County, was an hour and a half northwest of Houston. The twenty dense acres had a two-bedroom, one-bath, fourteen-hundred-square-foot wood-frame home on the front side of the property. Most everything in it was over half a century old, including the family portraits scattered along the walls. Pine trees clustered around the exterior, creating a distinctive aroma.

After supper on their first night, the family gathered on the front porch. David and Steely nestled in a swing on one end, his head in her lap with his eyes closed. Bea and Jack moved back and forth in wooden rocking chairs.

"I like it here," Steely said. "My parents took me to a dude ranch once."

"This is not a dude ranch," Bea snipped.

"I still like being out in the woods," said Steely.

Beatrice slapped her arm and then her leg. "The mosquitos are eating me up. Jack, will you please tell us why we're out here, before I get the virus?"

"I found a job clearing brush for Energy Oil. It's an hour away, but it will be steady work. I start tomorrow."

"Brush?" Bea said. "Jack, you're in your sixties!"

"I can still work. David will go with me. Steely, you still want to keep our books?"

"I'd be glad to."

Bea threw her head back. "I feel like I'm in la-la land!"

Hunter patted Bea on the leg. "Honey, we're going to be all right." Then he gave her a peck on the cheek.

Bea rose abruptly, which was customary when her emotions ran high. "OK, you and David are cutting grass. She's keeping the books. I'm going inside before the cobbler gets cold."

Steely learned the first week that her challenge wasn't in taking care of the company finances. She was fully equipped to pay the bills of the small company. She wasn't equipped to keep Beatrice Hunter from becoming "overly nervous." Some days were good, but some days she'd rather be riding on the tractor in ninety-nine-degree heat, with 90 percent humidity, getting a red neck, than be in an air-conditioned house with her mother-in-law.

The guys had already been gone several hours before Bea rolled out of bed, garbed in her flowered shift. She strolled to the kitchen, poured a cup of coffee from the pot Jack had made, and headed for the living room. She stood by a window, took a swig from the cup, and said, "I'm going to lose my mind if I don't get out of this rathole."

Steely stretched out on a mat in her shorts and tank top, briefly stopping her routine. "Miss Bea, the exterminator's coming the week after next to check for any critters in the house."

"You like saying that, don't you?"

Steely tilted her head. "Saying what?"

"Critters. Does that make you feel like a country woman?"

Steely scrunched her face. "What? The exterminator is coming in two weeks to check for rats. That's all." She stretched an arm over to one side and repeated the routine with the other.

"Everybody moves in slow motion in the country. It takes a week to do something that should take a couple of hours." Bea raised the cup to her lips. "They'll probably come riding up in a horse and buggy."

"That would be very cool."

Bea sneered. "You were born in the wrong century."

Steely flipped over on her abdomen, pushed up on her hands, repeated the repetition twenty-five times. "The exterminator gave us their first available appointment."

"I'm sure the rats don't mind waiting."

"Wasn't it a little mouse?"

"He has a momma! Country rats are fifty pounders. Yard-long tales, six-inch whiskers. They can chew through steel." Bea picked up a broom and whacked the recliner.

Steely coughed. "I think you can stop beating up the chair, Miss Bea. Anything in it has to be dead from motion sickness." She coughed again and rolled over onto her side for leg lifts. Fifty of those were coming up next.

"Every night I hear them scampering around in the attic." She gave the seat another whack. "We'll wake up one morning, and they'll be at the table eating our breakfast." Bea dropped the broom beside the chair and reclined back, yanking up a lever to elevate her feet.

Steely turned to the other leg. She didn't tell Bea the exterminator would find something, but it wouldn't be a rat. It would be a raccoon. She had gone up in the attic the night before and flashed a light on the scared creature, cowering in a corner. The raccoon had managed to crawl in but couldn't get out.

"How much time have you spent in the country, Miss Priss?"

Steely sat up, stretching out her legs. "One week."

"That's what I thought. You don't know anything about country rats."

"Rats aren't only in the country."

"No, but they're like people, twice as big in the country."

"I don't think that's right—"

"Are you questioning me again?"

"No. But you can't generalize like that. I grew up ten minutes from downtown Houston. One day I lifted up a box in our garage, and a rat the size of a cat flew out. It ran off faster than I could drop the box. They're more scared of you than you are of them."

"I doubt it."

Steely curled up in a crunch, working her abs. "I understand fear," she said, bopping up and down. "Most fears are irrational. I've had fear before."

Bea glared at Steely. "Are you calling me irrational?"

"Not exactly."

"Well, what exactly?"

Steely briefly stopped. "It would be like waking up every night for six months, sweating, in a room full of people, thinking someone was going to attack you in your sleep. Irrational. It never happened. Then you end up being awake when the knife wielder shows up to slit your throat."

"Well, that's loony."

"It's reality." Steely angled her foot to lace up a loose shoestring. "Would you like to take a walk? It'd get your mind off the rats. You haven't left the house since we got here."

"You want me to get a heat stroke?" Bea fanned herself with a newspaper.

Steely bolted for the door.

Bea sniffed. "Did you make a poot?"

"No. I did not."

"I smell something." She sniffed again.

"It's not me."

"Don't be so touchy."

Steely pulled on the door. "Miss Bea, you ask me that every day. I don't make poots."

"Everybody makes poots. Some people are just real sneaky about it."

Steely stepped outside. "Miss Bea, I'll be back in a little while."

"Hope you don't pass out."

Steely shut the door.

"I smell something nasty." Bea hit the remote.

Steely ran a good five miles around the property. Never saw a single rat. That night, she pulled Jack aside. They needed to make an adjustment before there was a situation. Jack agreed to start a rotation with her. She'd go with David three days out of the week while Jack stayed home with his lovely wife, starting the next Monday.

The last day of the week, Jack and David had finished working and were heading home when thunderstorms suddenly barreled in toward them. The wind pushed hard on the truck, swaying the trailer in and out of the two-lane stretch. Hunter held steady to the steering wheel. He had seen worse storms on that highway.

Hunter's phone buzzed. He flipped it open with one hand. "Nick?"

"Sir, he wants it now." Nick spoke with urgency.

"Already?" Hunter asked.

"Yes sir, he wants a P & L and balance sheet for the last thirty days. He wants them every thirty days after that. He trashed the audit. It never left the boardroom. He's moving the assets in fast, like you said. You were right, sir. He's restoring the company."

"So JHI is back on track."

"Looks like it."

Wind blew hard against the truck; rain hit sideways on the windshield. Visibility was not concerning to Hunter. He knew the road blindfolded. Hunter held the phone in one hand and gripped the wheel securely with the other.

"Sir, he's fixing the problem faster than anyone we could have brought in. No one could work that fast. He's telling everyone you took a planned retirement. We'll beat the analysts' projections. Our stock will soar."

Hunter's tone was solemn. "He's falling into his own trap. Don't discuss this with anyone except Pierce. Did you reach him?"

"No, sir. But he should be back in a few days."

"Where is he?"

"No one knows. I'll have him call you when I reach him. And, sir, would you call my dad? He's asking for you."

"I'll call Vince when I get back to the house in about ten minutes."

"Thank you, sir."

"Nick, I'm going to sue Harry for the false and misleading statements he made to the board. Then I'll let the auditors take over. He'll be indicted when they're done."

"Perfect move! Also, Mr. Keaton and Mr. Qualls took the jet to Geneva. We don't have any business interest there, do we?"

"Sure don't. Try to find out what they're doing."

"I'll hack into every computer in this building if I have to."

"I'm sure you will. Got to go now. It's a mess out here."

Hunter tucked the phone into his pocket. The truck's headlights barely lit the road.

"Dad, be careful. Canyon Drop is ahead."

Hunter knew the curve, knew how it got its name too. He stomped the brakes. But the truck raced on. The wind blew harder. They heard a train. A funnel cloud could make its debut at any second. The trailer swayed.

"Dad, please slow it down."

Hunter stomped on the brakes again, pumping them.
David pulled on Hunter's jacket. "Dad? Please slow down!"
"The brakes are out, Son." Hunter hit them again, hard.
"We're too fast. Put it in neutral."
Hunter answered, "I did."
David hollered, "The curve!"
"Hold on, Son!"

CHAPTER TWENTY-FIVE

Nick hated malls, especially crowded ones. He sure didn't want to be in one on a Saturday. It took some manipulation to get him into a dress shop with Cricket. She could try on a dress speckled with diamonds, and she wasn't getting the accolades she wanted from him.

"Nick!" Cricket called, gaining his attention. "What do you think of this one for the fund raiser next month?" She held up a glistening gown.

He was right in front of her, but his mind was not. "Nick!" she snapped. "Why aren't you paying attention? You're thinking about the Hunters again, aren't you?"

His body sealed his lips. No sense in lying.

She flung the dress on a chair. "Nick, that's all you've thought about for the last year—JHI and the Hunters. They're gone! Out of the picture! Mr. Hunter and David had an accident. The rest of them are on a chicken farm somewhere in the backwoods. They'll never come back. You act like you're obsessed with them."

"I'll tell you what I am," said Nick. "I'm ready to get out of here. Now, why'd you call me down here? It better be more important than this."

"Can we talk about us for a moment?"

"Us? What us?"

She put her hands in his. "We've been dating for over two years."

He jerked his hands back, placing them safely in his pockets. "Dating?"

"Yes, dating."

"We're not—"

"It's time to talk commitment."

"Commitment?" he said, raising his voice.

Cricket curled up next to him. "Don't tease me. Haven't I changed?"

"You almost persuaded me. The way you go and help with the children's home."

"Every Saturday."

"And visiting your grandmother daily. Why is she at Star of Light anyway?"

"Oh, just to be comfortable."

"Most of the residents there don't have family or a home. Why can't she stay with your mother?"

Cricket became jittery. "Mother remarried a few years ago. She needed time with her new husband."

"Is this her seventh?"

"It doesn't matter, as long as Mother is happy."

"I see. What's his—"

She interrupted, "Nick, can we look at rings, please?"

"Rings? Look at anything you want—"

"Oh, Nick!" Cricket jumped up and down and wrapped her arms around his neck.

"What are you—" His hands were glued tightly to his sides.

"You're making me the happiest woman on earth." Then she opened her wide mouth and attached it to his.

Nick unsuctioned her and reprimanded her: "Cricket, why'd you do that?"

She laughed. "Why don't you quit with the prude act? Cricket has needs. And don't tell me you're waiting for marriage. Nicky, I will make you feel things you never felt before. Once I take you to my special place, you'll beg me to go back."

He untied her arms and stepped back. "You make this so easy."

"You don't know what you're missing," she teased, walking away.

"I'm about to get exactly what I've missed." *It's been a year now.*

Steely swayed back and forth in the swing for over an hour. The porch in front of the farmhouse was a peaceful place for her. Bea wouldn't go out there. She said it was too painful for her. Steely tried to get her to go out at least to get some fresh air. But she wouldn't do it. Steely was dozing with a book on her chest when Bea hollered, "Steely!" The screen door was the only barrier between them. "Steely!" she yelled.

Steely jumped up, stubbing her toe on a post.

"Steely!" Bea hollered again. "Where's that girl?"

"I'm coming." Steely hopped to the door. "Be right there."

Bea was wearing her sunglasses inside again. When she wore those sunglasses in the house, it meant she'd had another rough day. "You coming or not?" Bea was riled up. Yesterday she tried to run Steely off for the umpteenth time. Bea hadn't considered how she would survive if Steely left her out there all alone. There wasn't another soul she'd let in the house. Food and supplies would have to be air-dropped to her. In spite of Bea's reminding Steely daily that they were only kin by law, Steely treated Bea better than any daughter she could have birthed.

Steely pushed on the screen door. It sprang back in place behind her. "Give me just a minute." She hobbled toward the bathroom.

Bea's open door caught her attention. "Why is there a suitcase on your bed?"

"I'm leaving."

Steely hobbled back to the living room. "Going where, Miss Bea?"

"Just sit—just sit down here." Bea slapped the adjacent sofa in the appointed spot and then propped herself up in her recliner.

Steely took her place, extended her arms down on her legs, and leaned toward Bea. "Do you need me to get you a snack?"

"I'm not hungry." Bea's foot was hard at work, rapidly tapping the floor.

"You need me to cut your toenails again? I found the jumbo clippers for those thick ones on your big toes."

"No."

Steely's eyes widened. "You have another fungus?"

"Will you please be quiet and listen?"

"Sure, Miss Bea."

Bea rubbed her hands together. "I'm broke."

"We're all right—"

"We always had a backup plan. I never saw a time when we didn't have a plan." Bea shook her head. "We're not making it here."

"Miss Bea, don't worry. I've worked three jobs before. I'll find something else."

Bea cut her hand sideways. "What can you do? There's only one drugstore in town. It's not going to work. You need to go back to your family in Dallas. There's nothing else I can do for you here."

Do for her? For over a year, Steely had taken care of Bea as if she were her mother, although there were no similarities between her mother and Beatrice Hunter. "Miss Bea, I'm not leaving you."

"Leave! You make me nervous, reading those crime books all night. You want to know about crime? I'll tell you about crime. The crooks steal, then lie, and get away with it. That's how crime works."

"Good observation."

"We'll starve to death if we stay here."

"I've never starved before. We'll make it."

"What are you going to do—shoot the squirrels?"

"Guess I could learn."

"I'm not eating squirrels!"

"I was just saying…some people do."

"I'm going back to Houston and find somewhere to stay until I die."

Bea argued like she had a home with a bed and hot meals waiting for her, but there was none.

"I'm staying with you," Steely blurted.

"No, you're not, little girl!" Bea stomped the floor. "You go back to Dallas. I'm sure there's someone there who can help you start over again."

"I'm fully capable of starting over if I wanted to. I've made my decision. I'm staying with you."

"Oh no, you're not! There has to be something you can do— you have a degree in something. You're fair looking—"

Steely reached for Bea.

"Keep your hands to yourself!" grumbled Bea. "You're the most touchy-feely person I've ever met."

"Miss Bea, you're in pain. I'm in pain—" Steely caught herself before she made an unthinkable comparison. "But I know I'm not in the same pain as you."

"The more you say, the worse it gets."

"This discussion is over. I'm sticking with you." Steely crossed her arms.

Bea went off on a tirade. "You're telling me when the discussion is over? You've got your nerve."

"You're my mother-in-law. I love you."

"Nobody loves anyone these days—especially a worthless old woman like me!" She exhaled, sat back, and pulled up the leg rest.

"That's not true."

"Please go on off to Dallas." Bea pointed to the door.

"Miss Bea, I'm from Houston. I've been to Dallas a few times, but I'm a Houstonian."

"Well, then go there, but not with me! I lost everything."

"I'll find us a place to live."

"Where?"

"In Houston, if that's where you want to go."

"Where?"

"They have housing in Houston. It's a big city."

"You'll dump me in another rathole!"

Steely ignored the voice in her head screaming, *Run, Steely, run!* "I'm not going to put you in a rathole. And I'm not abandoning you."

Bea wagged a finger. "I'm going to the old folks' home. That's where I'm going."

"You're too young. They won't take you."

"I want to die," Bea said, weeping. "My life is over. Dig a hole and throw me in it. Just let me die in peace." She was having a meltdown.

Steely stayed close, keeping her hands in her lap, until Bea took a tissue out of her pocket, blew her nose, and dried her eyes.

"Miss Bea, it isn't time for you to die."

Bea reared up. "Do you think you're God? How do you know it's not time for me to die?"

Steely spread out her hands. "Because you're not dead."

Bea faintly grinned, pushed her silver roots off her forehead, revealing new creases. "You're the most hardheaded girl I've ever seen."

"My dad used to say I was just like him."

"Now you're going to bring up your daddy? What am I supposed to say?"

"'Steely, I'm so thankful you're here with me.'"

"Oh brother. Let's get out of this rathole—you wore me out."

Steely wasn't sure what a rathole was supposed to look like, since the exterminator confirmed there were no rats in the farmhouse, just the misguided raccoon. Steely had a place to go in Houston. She hoped Bea wouldn't consider it a rathole since there were no rats there. Steely understood there was always the possibility that she might.

CHAPTER TWENTY-SIX

Donna Kaye dutifully guarded Keaton's office from unwanted visitors. Everyone who entered the executive floor passed by Donna Kaye. Most would get a nod since they were employees or had already been screened by security.

Nick usually received her wave plus the status of her current boyfriend when applicable. He'd nailed her last beau. The boyfriend called the $25,000 he took a "loan." When he disappeared the next day, HPD called it theft. Donna got her money back within a week. He got a reservation for an extended stay at the Texas Department of Corrections.

Nick's mind was racing, and so were his feet. "Mornin', Donna," he said, hurrying past her toward his office. Every minute of his day was taken, appointments lined up in his mind.

She charged after him. "Nick, hold up!"

He flat-hand waved and kept moving. "Donna, I'll have to catch up with you later."

"Nick, stop!" she yelled.

He swung back around. "Did that bum show up at your door again?"

"Yes, but that's not it."

"Then what is it?"

"They moved you," she blurted.

The last time someone told Nick he'd gotten moved was fourth grade. He was confused. "Moved me?"

"You're on five now." She squirmed, looking in need of a restroom.

"Five?" He approached her.

"Yes, five."

"Nothing is on five but maintenance and bats. Is this a joke?" He leaned down toward her. "Did Jason find out I searched his cubicle?"

"Mr. Qualls moved you."

"Qualls?"

"He said you're on your way out. Mr. Keaton said he couldn't fire you. You searched Jason's cubicle?"

"He can't fire me."

"I heard them fussing for over an hour late yesterday. They had a man on the speakerphone who sided with Qualls, and you got relocated."

"Somebody is running Keaton." Nick looked down the hall toward his office and then back at her in a panic. "Where's my stuff?"

"Monte packed up everything for you and took it down a few minutes ago."

He sprinted to an open elevator and held the door attempting to close. "Where are the keys?"

Donna cringed. "There are no keys. It has a combo lock. Seventeen-six-seventeen."

The elevator pushed against Nick. He pushed back. "A combo?" Nick let loose of the door. He dropped forty-five floors and stepped into obscurity. No one was in sight since nobody unnecessarily went to the fifth floor. Maintenance didn't even want to be on five. It was off-limits to the public and almost everyone else. It was dubbed "the dungeon." Every mechanical operation was on the floor. Ten years ago, the mechanics were in the basement. Floodwaters from a tropical storm rose two feet in the hull of the building, knocking out the power for weeks. After that, all electrical components were safely banished five stories up. It'd take a flood big enough to float Noah's ark to reach them now.

Nick forged around a maze of electrical panels, finally reaching the only substantial light source, a kitchenette. Two tables, four chairs, a small fridge, and a vending machine with products containing not much more than sugar and white flour were crammed into the small room. Next to the kitchenette was a fire escape. The next door was cracked open, with a padlock dangling on the frame. He flung the door back hard enough to squash a roach on the wall behind it, startling Jason inside. Jason dusted a clump of webs off his suit. "So you ticked off Qualls?"

"Means I'm doing something right." Nick surveyed the oversized closet. Nothing but boxes stacked around a distressed desk with a single chair pushed underneath it.

"That's why I report to Keaton. Qualls is kind of nuts."

"Keaton's in that same food group."

"Kevin questioned some of Qualls's business expenses. The next day his hard drive was toast."

"A virus?" asked Nick, surveying the room.

"A fire. Made it look like spontaneous combustion."

Nick slid out the chair. "This place looks like a spontaneous combustion."

"Does Cricket know?"

"No, she's touring the Caribbean, planning a honeymoon. Hope she finds a groom while she's down there."

"You know she's telling people you're engaged. You better set her straight before she picks out your tux."

"She's lost her marbles."

Nick searched around for an electrical outlet. He found a single one on a light fixture above his desk. He plugged in the power cord, dangling it down from the ceiling to his computer, and tethered his cell to his laptop for an Internet connection.

Nick hesitated and gazed at Jason. "You've been island-hopping."

"Island-hopping? What do you mean?"

"I've seen the flight log. Swigging margaritas? I have the bills too."

"Nobody is supposed to see that but me and Keaton."

"Did you forget I'm still VP of finance? It cost some kind of coffee beans to fly a jet."

"Right." Jason slowly bobbed his head. "It was authorized by Mr. Keaton."

"I've tracked every trip on those planes for the last two years." Nick poked at his keyboard. "I know where they went and who was on them."

Jason spun around. "Man, this place is dark. Can't you get more light in here?"

"Did you see the wiring? Ten more watts would put my life at risk."

"Not any more risk than what you're doing at that computer." Jason kicked at a box and flapped an arm over another. "I can get Mr. Keaton to bring you back upstairs today."

Nick quipped. "I'd rather be here with the bats."

"This is pathetic." Jason leaned over the desk at Nick. "Is there anything I can do to stop you before you ruin your career?"

"I'm in a closet with cockroaches the size of my foot. What career?" Nick ran his hand across his desk, gathered a layer of dust, and dumped it onto the floor. He logged onto the computer. He entered his pass code and scrolled down his e-mails, deleting most of them.

"Everything is fine now. Nobody cares about the past."

"Some do."

"Our dividends will be the highest in the history of the company. This place is amazing. And you're searching a black hole, trying to find something to complain about." Jason slapped Nick's desk, moving a few papers. "Nick, you need to join the party."

Nick lunged out of his seat "Party? This is no stinkin' party." Nick propped his hands on his waist. "You know Keaton is a crook. You may look the other way, but you know it, Jason."

"I'm not the corporate police. I'm doing what I'm supposed to—my job. And that's what you should do too."

"That sounds really nice and sweet, but there are guys in prison today who were just doing their jobs."

"Show me, Nick. You think you know more than the authorities, who can't find anything wrong. You think Mr. Keaton doesn't know you've tried to get anyone you could to investigate him. Oh, he knows."

"Good!" Nick sat back down, focusing his monitor.

"Mr. Keaton wants to bury the past and forget it."

"Why not? He might have picked up a shovel and dug a couple of graves himself."

Jason shook his head. "Think about the money."

"I don't care about the money."

"Sure, you don't. Your parents are loaded. If you didn't make another dime, you'd still pay your bills, buy your cars, and take your European vacations. You don't know what it's like when you can't pay your bills. When you barely have enough food to eat. Knowing your family is one paycheck away from losing its home. Working your way through school and ending up with student loans you'll be paying back with your social security check. Then you see Mr. Hunter showing the rich kid favoritism. You don't have a clue—"

"So, I haven't had a tough time, but that doesn't disqualify me from caring about those who have. Or caring about what injustice was done to Hunter and his family. Yeah, my parents are wealthy. You want to know what my filthy-rich parents taught me? That being poor and having wealth have something in common. They both magnify your character. And I promise you this: I'm going to make this right."

Jason brushed off his jacket. "Make what right? Why won't you play the corporate game? Nobody does everything perfect. There's give and take. No business would be profitable if they followed all the rules. I guarantee you, Hunter didn't."

Nick ran his fingers around the keyboard. "I guess it's better to be stupid than involved."

"Are you calling me stupid?"

"I hope so." Nick hesitated, giving Jason a chance to respond, but he did not. "I'm looking into hundreds of bank accounts Denison didn't even know existed. It wasn't easy, but I found them."

"Hundreds?" he mumbled, looking disturbed.

"Yes."

Jason tightened his lips.

"You know how you catch fraud? You follow the money."

"Corporations are complex. I just do my job. That's it. I'm not into anything sinister."

"Did you find out why Mr. Keaton wants you wiring assets all over the place?"

"I'm telling you nothing."

"What computer is he using to post the wires?"

"His laptop."

"Why would he use a device that's not company issued?"

Jason turned to leave. "I have to get back upstairs."

"I'm sure you do."

Nick hibernated the remainder of day. Lunch was forgotten. His shirt hadn't been white for hours. Papers were scattered on his desk in a way that no one but him could find anything. There were no visitors. No interruptions, until his cell lit up—Donovan. He answered quickly, "Donovan, I'm really tied up now."

"You might want to listen very closely." The sergeant's authoritative tone would scare most people.

Nick drank from a cup. "OK, shoot."

"I had a visit from a young lady named Candy. She was waiting for me when I got to the station this morning. She's a receptionist at JHI. And she's scared to death."

Nick lifted the cup halfway and stopped. "There're a couple of new girls down there. I don't know them. What's she scared of?"

"She's making some wild accusations."

"They're all lies. What does she say I did?"

"Not you, kid, it's your CEO—Harry Keaton. She says he's a murderer."

Nick swallowed, held up a framed picture of himself and Hunter. "Does she have evidence?"

"You think she's credible?"

"Wouldn't surprise me."

"She tapped the phone in Mr. Keaton's office."

"I knew I should have done that."

"It's called illegal wiretapping. I can't use it. She says three guys were arguing. Two in the office and one over the phone. They talked about some people they toasted. Get this—one of our undercovers saw Zev Chevoski coming into your building."

Nick inhaled. "That gives me the creeps."

"We've been trying to get that son of a gun for years. It's difficult when he keeps so many layers between him and his criminal activities. We just haven't been able to nail him. Witnesses mysteriously disappear. Nobody will talk. Had a guy looking at twenty-five years for sex trafficking and still wouldn't deal. We have undercovers around him. The problem is they haven't been able to make a direct contact. Would you check to see if anyone from the company is missing? Or left abruptly? I don't want to come down there and cause a stir until I get some facts."

"You want a favor?" Nick angled his head.

"Just get it done. Working with rumors is great for movies. I must have probable cause."

"Movies?" Nick rolled his eyes. "You think I sit around here dreaming, like this is a movie?"

"Wouldn't surprise me."

"This is real-life stuff."

"Just find out if anyone vanished or left under strange circumstances. Maybe I can figure out what they were talking about. One phone call. I mean it. I'm not keeping you out of jail this time. I'm the investigator. Not you. Don't go chasing criminals!"

"Just remember, that works both ways."

"What's that supposed to mean?"

"For the good guys and the bad guys."

"Just get the info and don't put anyone in the hospital doing it."

"I'm always glad to assist HPD."

"Never mind—"

Nick hung up.

CHAPTER TWENTY-SEVEN

Three quarters of the bungalows on Saint Ambrose had already been torn down. The original homes built in the 1930s needed major renovation or bulldozing. The old Fitzpatrick place across the street had been replaced by a two-story, forty-two-hundred-square-foot stucco. The street was lovely, with mature trees reaching across the cement and gracefully embracing. Trains randomly rattled along the tracks parallel to the west side of the street.

Steely was just as surprised as Beatrice Hunter was about to be that they were going to live there. The home was a place of great memories, as long as she stayed out of the back bedroom. Beatrice hadn't been told about the last time her mom was there. It would be her room.

Steely stopped in front of the house and cut the ignition. There was no reason to give Bea advance notice of where they were going. Bea might try to escape. Jump out of a running car. Who knew what she might do? And the thought of Bea complaining for 110 miles might have caused Steely to jump out of the car.

The look on Steely's face was the same as when she'd swallowed one of Bea's BLTs. Her stomach pains were something she wasn't sharing with Bea. They'd both have stomachaches if she did.

Bea glared at Steely. "You have gas?"

"No."

"You constipated?"

"No."

"You sure have a lot of gastro problems for someone your age."

"I'm fine."

"It's getting dark. Why are we out here like sitting ducks?"

Steely looked over at her and calmly said, "Miss Bea, we're sleeping here tonight—that is, unless you call nine one one."

Bea swung around toward the house. "Is this your old place?"

"Yes."

She swished her head from side to side. "Take me to the funeral parlor!"

"Not just yet…"

Bea peered at the home for a few seconds, took a deep breath, and slowly exhaled. "Are there rats?"

"Not inside. But there are some in Houston. They're in every city." Steely chuckled awkwardly.

"I've never seen bricks fall off a house. A strong wind—a weak breeze—could blow it down."

"The foundation is sinking into the earth. Other than that, it's good," Steely said confidently.

"You think you're funny?"

"It's livable, as long as the plumbing works. I know how particular you are about doing your business."

"Having a working toilet is not exactly a modern convenience."

"It is for some people." Steely cracked open the car door. "I'm going inside, where there's a really cold air conditioner, which I'm sure you know is more important than a foundation in Houston. The tenant is here with the keys."

The conversation had gone better than Steely had envisioned. Bea was still breathing. Thoughts of Bea's dropping dead in the car had crossed her mind. She calmly got out of the car and went inside.

The house had a familiar smell. Not a bad odor, a good one. The entire place could burn down and be rebuilt, and she'd still be able to detect her dad's aftershave and her mom's perfume.

Steely glanced out the front window.

Bea flung open the door and rushed inside.

Guess she's not sleeping in the car.

"I'm not sitting out there and getting knocked over the head," Bea said, catching her breath. "I'll stay the night. That's it."

"Wise decision," Steely answered from the kitchen. "Why don't you take a look around?"

"The tenants were probably a bunch of slobs," Bea grumbled. "Bet they left a big mess. I'm not cleaning up after a bunch of slobs."

Bea went first to the room she utilized least. The kitchen. Appliances had been updated once, in the sixties. They were sparkling clean avocado green. Then she moseyed down the hall, like an inspector, to the biggest bedroom, which was across the way from Steely's. She swung her head toward the bathroom between them. Ended up staring in a framed mirror hanging on the living-room wall. "Guess this will do," Bea said, posing. "Do I look fifty?"

"Aren't you sixty-two?"

She snapped, "That wasn't the question."

Steely didn't answer. Even a carefully arranged compliment could be construed the wrong way. "What do you think of the house, Miss Bea?"

"You think you're smart, don't you?"

"What do you mean?"

"Moving my furniture in here. What if I didn't come?"

"We had to get it out of storage. Did you want me to send it to Grey Canyon?"

"Everybody's a comedian." Bea settled into her recliner, strategically facing the TV. "I can do without a lot of things, but not without my chair and TV." She eased back. "I missed this chair."

"So what do you think?"

"No offense, but this has to be the worst home in West University."

Steely replied, "There's plenty of room for two people. Right? And it will only cost twenty-one dollars and sixty-seven cents per day. Don't you think it's cute?"

"Is that slang? Like 'sick' meaning 'good'?" Bea went over to the back windows and stared. The shades were up and windows open. "Somebody's out there. Eee, that's a wide load," she said loudly.

Steely ran over and slammed the windows.

Rosie, a full-figured woman with a tight perm, marched toward them and joined them inside. "Who are you calling a wide load, missy?"

Bea bent down to Rosie, magnifying the height difference. "Huh, what's wrong with being stout? I was stout once."

"Stout?" Rosie angrily asked.

Steely put her arm around her tenant. "Rosie, this is my mother-in-law."

"Bless your heart," Rosie replied. "You got stuck with her?"

Steely had never seen a wig tossing fight and sure didn't want this to be her first. She maneuvered Rosie around to the front door. "Rosie, it's so good to see you." Steely hugged her, nudging her at the same time.

"You too, honey." Rosie squeezed Steely's hand, almost spraining her pinky, and whispered, "Are you safe here with that woman?"

"Yes, it's fine." Steely mouthed, "She's elderly."

"Well, I sure hate leaving this house." Rosie rubbed her eyes. "Me and my husband felt a lot of love here."

"TMJ," spouted Bea. "I don't want to hear about your sex life."

"TMJ?" Rosie whispered to Steely. "You need to lock her up."

Steely caught Bea's attention and crossed her finger on her lips. "Miss Bea, why don't you check out the bathroom?"

"I don't know what there is to check out," she said, scanning the room. "That can is a can." Bea went in and flipped on the light.

"I'm sorry, Rosie," Steely said, inching her toward the door. "She doesn't realize what she's saying."

"I understand. My aunt Ruby is like that. She used to be so sweet; now she just insults people. Is it old age?"

Steely shook her head. "We don't know."

"Well, we cleaned up real good for you, honey. Everything went great here, except when those vandals broke in last year."

"That was strange. We never had a bit of trouble before."

"They turned the place upside down and pulled everything out of the drawers but didn't take a thing. Figured it must be some troublemakers. Mrs. Yost came over and helped us put everything back together."

"She's a good neighbor."

Bea stepped out of the bathroom and snipped, "I'm going to have to do my business with the door open. I'd get claustrophobia in there. Better pick up some air freshener. The breeze blows out of here straight to the kitchen table." Bea directed her arms like the airflow.

Rosie scrunched her face. "That's gross. Who wants to hear that?"

Steely moved Rosie out the front door. "Rosie, thank you for taking care of the house."

"To clean up this place"—Bea circled the living room—"is going to take a staff of seven. What are those little—"

"Miss Bea!" Steely screamed, as she quickly followed the tenant out onto the steps. "Rosie, I'll have your deposit check ready for you in the morning. Don't worry about leaving Fur Ball. I'll take good care of her."

"There'll be a check in the mail every month to cover the cost," Rosie said.

"I really appreciate you and Joey." Steely went back inside and held the door.

Bea slapped her foot. "I think—"

"Bye, Rosie." Steely slammed the door, turned the dead bolt, and leaned against it.

Bea slapped her foot again. "A flea bit me. Fur Ball is a flea ball!"

Steely went and plopped down on the sofa. "Miss Bea, you can't insult people like that. You have to be kind."

Bea scooted back in her recliner and scratched her foot. "I just speak the truth." She picked up the remote control and flipped on the news. "There's nobody kinder than me, little girl."

"That kind of kindness will get you a spot on the six o'clock news."

"People didn't used to be so whiney. You have to watch every little word, or somebody gets offended. People need tougher skin. They're nothing but a bunch of titty babies."

Steely lifted up. "I wouldn't repeat that in public either." She lay back, covering her head with a pillow.

"A bunch of weenies," Bea grumbled.

"That either," Steely said, muffled.

CHAPTER TWENTY-EIGHT

Pierce stretched the phone around his desk, caught Nick's attention outside his door, and waved him in. Nick wasn't interested in hearing the fireworks going on between Pierce and Muffy, but he came in as directed. Pierce had finished reading the last decade of board minutes. Nick waited for his opinion. Had Keaton overstepped his authority or not?

"Calm down, Muffy," Thibodaux said, with his Cajun twang. "It's our first child. Who would have known an eight-month-old could repeat words that fast?...Oh, I see. So it was your sister who heard him." Pierce's eyes rounded in defense. "I've never heard him say it...Well, tell your sister babies aren't supposed talk that fast. Probably broke the record for a baby's first words. I didn't talk that fast. Did you?" Thibodaux couldn't express himself without his hands. "Certainly...I'll never say it again...Yes, tell your sweet sister she won't ever hear him say it again...Yeah, she was such a sweetie for bringing this to your attention. Sure, wouldn't want him to get kicked out of his play group...No, I'm not being sarcastic. Play groups have boundaries."

Nick was short on time. But even if he weren't, he would rather be punched in the face than to hear another word of this conversation. He tried humming but still caught every awkward word. He eased out of his seat. Thibodaux waved him back. Nick ignored him and bolted for the hall.

Thibodaux covered the receiver with one hand, erroneously thinking it was a muting devise. "Nick, I need to talk to you. Get back in here."

Nick reluctantly returned to the chair across the desk and covered his ears with his hands, using them as mufflers.

"Yes, Muffy, I'm listening...Whenever I think of that word, I'll think of your sister. She's such a sweetie...See you tonight, my love. I'll be home in thirty minutes." Thibodaux puckered up and squeezed a kiss through the receiver. "Muah." He hung up and turned to Nick.

Nick was thoroughly irritated. "Pierce, you warn me the next time you're gonna kiss a phone. It's bad enough just listening to you."

"Children are parrots."

"I know people like that."

"And that sister is a real sweetie. We let her stay with us for a few days. Now she critiques everything I do. Last night she barged into the bedroom and crawled in the bed next to Muffy. Gave me the creeps. Totally ruined the atmosphere."

"Enough!"

"I don't know if I—"

"Another word and I'm running out the door and not coming back."

"I have to vent."

"Not to me. Not today. Did you finish reading the minutes?"

"Yes."

"How many of the subsidiaries did the board approve?"

"Only three in Saint Stephen's."

Nick slapped the desk. "The ones my dad set up?"

"That's right. It's like you said. The other hundred or so Keaton directed. Decisions of that magnitude are way over his authority level. He should've brought it all to the board."

"So we have him for overstepping his authority?"

"Not exactly. He could argue that Jack gave him the authority to expand the subs."

"He'd be lying."

"Can you prove it?"

"Can he?"

"Probably not. But if you accuse the new CEO of fraud, you better have some rocks in your slingshot."

"Well then, how about the audit before Jack left? That's a boulder."

Thibodeaux stretched forward. "It's a no-good piece of sh— a no-good sweetie report."

"Isn't deception a crime?"

"Maybe."

Nick flung himself to the edge of his seat. "Maybe? So Keaton could walk off with a couple hundred million in assets?"

"Sure could."

Nick shot back. "Maybe I should just confront him."

"For being a pathological liar? Nick, it's like you said. This was set up to unravel after Denison got sick and you came in. They slowly cooked the frog and then took advantage of the transition. I believe you were a major piece of the plan. Your position is a liability for you." Thibodaux dropped his head back, rubbed his eyes with his palms, and said, "They used you, Nick. Think about it. You did the audit that got Jack fired."

"I didn't volunteer," Nick said indignantly. "In fact, I objected."

"Jack can't testify. If anything goes down, you're the guy with his hands in the books. You, my friend, are in a grievous situation. This mess could be dumped in your lap and made to look real nasty. Keaton could say you were the mastermind. He'd be convincing. He believes his lies more than the truth."

Nick put his head in his hands. "You're right. I'm not sure I'd even believe me."

"We've chewed on this for a year now. I hate to admit it, but you should consider Jason's advice."

"I have one chance."

Pierce swung his chair toward a window and quickly swung back. "How often does it snow in Houston?"

"Almost never."

"That's about your odds. Almost none."

"Then I don't need to be concerned about risk. Do I?"

"Guess not."

Nick stood. "You going to help?"

"It's only snowed once since I moved here eighteen years ago."

"But when it did, even a few flurries shut everything down."

"Sure did." Pierce powered off his computer. "Now, Mr. Dichiara, I'm going home to my lovely wife and her sweet sister. Would you like to come for dinner?"

"Nope. I have to go get a heavy coat and pray for snow."

Nick went back to his office. He prepared a timeline from the information he had gathered so far. If it was accurate, Keaton's plan worked only if Jack left and never came back. Jack had patiently waited and planned on coming back at just the right time. His testimony would have blown up Keaton's plan. But Jack didn't come back. And Keaton succeeded.

Nick stretched his legs over the printer below his desk. Sleeping in a chair was a Dichiara trait. It served him well. He zoned out for a few hours. Then he opened his eyes and blinked several times, adjusting to light. For breakfast, he sipped stale coffee and ate cake filled with cream from a vending machine. Having checked the time, he reached for his phone and tapped in a number. The line rang twice.

"Tucker here."

"Sheriff, this is Nick Dichiara. Were you able to reach your contact at Energy Oil?"

"Yep. She pulled the last canceled check paid to JHI. The back was stamped Saint Stephen's Bank. Then, she randomly pulled checks from the last four years. Same stamp on the back. Ever heard of INS1, LLC?"

"No."

"Well, that's who they're paying. Added up to over five million dollars."

"That much?"

"Yep. By the way, we had to shut down the excavation of the Hunter vehicle. The cliff isn't stable enough to hold the truck. It landed in the only canyon without road access in all of central Texas."

"Do you have another plan?"

"I'm going to cut it out. I didn't want to do that since there's still some risk to my people. But we're going to be very careful and go for it."

Nick hung up. He did a quick web search and found Saint Stephen's Bank. The institution's assets on deposit were $450 million, the largest independent depository on the island. He punched in another set of numbers on his cell.

"Saint Stephen's Bank, how may I help you?"

"I need to speak to the bank president, please."

"Yes, sir. May I ask what it's regarding? Maybe I can help you."

"I'm calling about a few hundred fraudulent accounts—amounts could be higher than two hundred million."

"One moment, sir, and I'll connect you."

CHAPTER TWENTY-NINE

"Here's your breakfast, Miss Bea," Steely whispered, setting a plate of food on the table next to a cup of coffee.

Bea viewed the spread. "What do I look like—a glutton?"

"Just eat what you want. I'll save the leftovers."

Bea staggered to the table, still not seeing straight. Dry eyes, she complained before. Bea's first night in the Paupher house had been rough. She couldn't get situated. Her hair was in a wild tease from fighting with a blanket half the night. Steely could hear her during the night tossing around. No more than a handful of words were spoken until she finished wolfing down her second helping. Bea tapped the corners of her mouth with a napkin. "Well, I guess I was still hungry from last night. Those weeds you call a salad didn't stick to me."

"I bet this will stick." Steely picked up Bea's plate to set it in the dishwasher, since there was nothing left to rinse off. "You ready for the store?"

Bea carried her cup to the bathroom. She grabbed the newspaper off an end table along the way. "I need a few minutes to digest my food and relax my bowels." She left the door opened and plopped down.

"We sure don't want any more episodes like we had at the drug store." Steely ran a damp rag around the kitchen table.

"I told you. I don't use public bathrooms. People wet all over the seat." Bea turned a page.

"The security guard looked like he might chase after you when you ran out of the store."

"He needs to mind his own business. You shouldn't have left our basket."

"I didn't know what was going on. He might have thought you were a shoplifter running out in a frenzy like that. May still..."

Bea cleared her throat and turned another page. "Just give me a few minutes."

Steely rinsed the rag and laid it across the faucet.

"Eee, this man's been missing for a year. I bet somebody knocked him over the head. His wife and son are missing too. Their wrecked car was found last year in a river near Grey Canyon. They're all out in the Gulf of Mexico by now. A bunch of nuts out there. That's why I keep my gun by the bed."

"Miss Bea, I'm taking it away if you point it at me again."

"You had no business snooping in my bedroom."

"I was checking on you. Please don't point it at me again."

"Quit your fussing. Jack said I have too many nightmares to keep it loaded."

"Probably saved my life."

"Huh. Get the car started. Nothing's moving until we get back."

"You sure?"

"Just go start the car, please."

If she runs out of the store again, leave the basket in a corner and go back.

Sampson's Grocery was the size of a football field. They sold everything from bread to auto tires. Steely pushed the cart down the aisle. Bea tagged along, which was good and bad. Good if they kept moving. Bad if Bea grabbed the cart, jamming the handlebar into Steely. They would have been on their way home thirty minutes ago if Steely hadn't had to battle Beatrice Hunter on almost every item.

They circled to the next aisle. Jars and cans. The only thing they needed was pickles. Steely wasn't expecting a battle over pickled cucumbers. Bea picked a jar from the shelf and dropped it in the cart. "Miss Bea, may we get the Sampson pickles?" Steely held up the jar. "This is the store special, fifty percent off. I have a coupon too. We'll get it for almost nothing."

"The best pickles in the world are Southern Springs." Bea poked at the jar in the basket. "Period. Nobody pickles like Southern Springs. I've been eating those pickles all my life. My mother ate those pickles. My grandmother and my great-grandmother even ate them. It was her cousin's friend's sister's neighbor who started the company. She knew pickles."

Steely thought for a second about the conversation she would need to have with Bea. The one telling her they were out of money. "Miss Bea, I admire your loyalty to the pickle lady. My family, most likely, ate the cheapest pickles. I don't really know. We weren't pickle connoisseurs."

"Are you mocking me?"

"I just hope you can adjust to a different pickle since we need to buy the cheapest. It isn't Southern Springs." Steely made the switch and pushed on.

"It's seventy-five cents."

"If we take care of the small things, it will take care of the big things."

Bea huffed, "You're driving me cuckoo with those coupons."

Steely whispered, "Think of it as free money. If you work for twelve dollars an hour and you save seventy-five cents, it's like getting three and three-quarters minutes of pay for free."

Bea's forehead creased. "A tank of gas must take a month."

"Two hours, fifteen minutes."

"We need a quart of milk."

"Fourteen minutes."

"Out of butter too."

"Eleven minutes."

"You've gone bananas."

"Seven minutes."

"How long did it take you to figure that?"

"It just comes to me."

"You're one odd cookie."

"Five minutes for a big one."

"Enough!"

They swirled around a corner to the next aisle.

Bea rumbled, "Your budget is unrealistic. I bet a homeless person can't eat for three dollars a meal."

"Their meals are free at shelters." Steely headed for the bread. "Nutritious too."

Bea slowly tagged along, barely making forward progress. Steely dropped a loaf of Sampson's bread into the cart. Bea wedged her shoe in a wheel. "Wait just a minute. You can't force me to eat that bread."

"Why not? It's baked fresh in the store." Steely tugged on the cart.

"You buy seafood at a seafood restaurant, steak at a steak house, Mexican food at a Mexican restaurant, and bread at a bakery. This isn't a bakery."

"Have you ever tried it?" Steely whispered.

"No!" Bea dislodged her foot. The cart flung forward. Steely pushed without resistance. A lady passed them, giving Steely a grimacing look. Steely smiled and pushed on. Bea stood behind flatfooted. "Are you trying to run off?"

"Just keeping it going."

Bea caught up, and they moved in unison down the last aisle.

"I'm ready to go home," complained Bea. "It takes you forever to get through a store. When I used to shop, I was fast." Bea snapped her fingers. "I'm not pokey like you."

"I am moving slower than usual." Steely stopped at the toothpaste section.

Bea surveyed the array of boxed tubes. "When my parents ran a general store, we had the best and the cheapest of each item." She held up a box. "We had two different brands. Not ten. The stores these days act like toothpaste is snack food." Bea placed the tube back in its spot and read from the boxes. "Orange, cherry, vanilla, cinnamon, peppermint, spearmint, winter mint, and bubble gum. Gels, creams. Some whiten, kill bacteria, stop gum disease, control tartar. I guess the others let the tartar run wild. Fluoride, no fluoride. All this for a little dab on some plastic bristles."

Steely matched a coupon with a paste that Bea didn't use since her teeth were set in a plastic cup at night.

"You need to get yourself organized," grumbled Bea.

"I've got an idea. Miss Bea, why don't you get in line while I find the last item."

"Did you make a poot?"

Steely looked around. "Shh…no."

"You're the type that gives people no warning."

"Miss Bea, please be civilized." She pushed on to the next aisle, swooping up a small jar. She dropped it in the basket and darted toward the checkout line.

Bea grabbed the basket, causing everything in it to fling forward. "Are you trying to poison me?"

Steely scrunched her face. "Are you allergic to peanuts?"

"How would I know? I haven't had peanut butter since I was five. I hated it then. I hate it now."

"Miss Bea, I'm trying to stretch our funds. Let's be flexible. OK?"

"If you get your peanut butter," Bea said sternly, "then I'm getting my pressed ham."

"Ham squashed up in a can?"

"I've been eating that ham since I was born. My momma said it was my first baby food."

"How much per ounce?"

"Not as much as peanut butter."

"Then get it and meet me in the checkout line."

Bea left grumbling. "All this shopping makes me nervous."

Steely rolled the cart in line with the others. She gazed at a rack of magazines.

Bea came back with two cans and dropped them into the cart. "There. Come on. I have to go."

Steely was disengaged, staring at a cantina pictured on the front of a periodical. The bartender donned an apron standing behind a long bar. Steely had never seen where her dad died.

Bea nudged her. "You going to start drinking?"

Steely shook her head. "I need to run an errand tonight."

The cashier called out, "Next, please."

CHAPTER THIRTY

She made her way through dozens of pickups. Hers was the only sedan in the parking lot. Last time she'd called Sergeant Donovan was two years ago. Her dad's case was ice cold. Whoever killed her father was most still likely out there, living an unrestricted life.

The sign on the door was still there: *NO ADMITTANCE UNDER 21.* She was now old enough to push open the door without being stopped. She was of age.

The inside was identical to the pictures she'd memorized. Beat-up and dingy. Packed with more men than women. She surveyed the room from the mental image that never left her mind. The wall in question was to her right. A lady, with a grease-stained apron, greeted her. "Can I get you something?"

"Have you worked here long?"

"Ten years. Too long, in my opinion."

Steely thought about the best way to bring up the incident. She had played it out in her mind hundreds of times.

The woman folded her notepad and stuck it in a pocket on her apron. "Can I help you with something?"

"Were you here when a man died, nine years ago?"

The lady's face broadened. "Your pop?"

Steely preferred to be anonymous. "How'd you know?"

"You don't look like anyone else in here. And who else your age would be asking about the man who passed nine years ago?"

Steely slowly circled the area to get a general look. Then she squeezed her view back toward the lady. "What happened?"

"Your pop came in by himself." She pointed out a table against a wall. It was the same one Steely would have picked. "He had a large envelope in his lap. Sure didn't want to be here, kept looking at his watch. Sat there a good ten minutes waiting before a bushy-haired man and a rail of a woman came in and sat at the table next to him. He didn't seem to know them. It was real strange. The man tried to give your dad something, but he threw it back at him. I went to the other side of the room to take orders since they didn't want anything. The next thing I heard was screams. Then fists flying, tables turned upside down, and chairs tossed in the air. When things settled, your pop wasn't the only one on the floor. He was just the only one who didn't get up. I called nine one one. The man and woman vanished."

"Is there anything about them that stood out?"

"Yeah, they looked as much out of place as your pop. The man had an accent, like German or maybe Russian. I don't know for sure."

"Anything else? Even if it seems insignificant."

"She called him Steve, or something. I couldn't hear too well. I don't know for sure."

Steely's face reddened.

"You all right?" The waitress passed her a rough napkin.

Steely squeezed it. "I'm fine."

"Oh, and another thing. Some guy came in an hour before, plopped down a grand, and covered all bar tabs. People got drunker than usual. Then, the fight. Some guys are mean drunks. HPD

179

left a number for me to call if the two ever showed back up. They're not showing back up here. Curley would give them what they got coming if they did."

Steely cleared her throat. "Did you see where he hit the wall?"

"Right there." The lady pointed to a nail hole.

Steely stood adjacent to the wall. Her father was six inches taller than she was. The wall proved he was standing and shoved on purpose, just as Donovan said.

"HPD took the nail. Not another one like it on the entire wall. Who would put a double-pointed nail in a bar?"

She tilted her head. "Double...pointed?"

"Yeah, you know—pointed on both ends."

"I've seen enough. Thanks for your time." Steely was leaving with a graphic visual she would rather not have. The envelope Fred brought with him had disappeared before HPD showed up. She knew what was in it. Bank statements can easily be reproduced. They don't disappear forever. Banks keep them for years.

As long as you know they exist, you can get them.

The late-night trip to Curley's confirmed what she knew at fourteen. Her dad wasn't murdered over another woman. The woman was a coconspirator.

It was late when she arrived home. But she couldn't go to bed until she combed the attic one more time. Obsessively, she yanked up the insulation, taking a flashlight to it. There was nothing that surprised her, only the exoskeletal remains of a few roaches. She gave up, shut the garage, and crashed on the sofa. Thirty minutes later, Bea ran from her bedroom screaming.

"The rats! The rats!" Bea flipped on the lights and circled the living room. "The rats are after us!" Bea darted to the front windows and beat on the wooden blinds. "The rats are killing us!"

Steely jumped up, trying to get hold of her. "Miss Bea, there are no rats." Steely couldn't restrain her arms, flailing aimlessly in the air. The blinds were crumbled. She tried escaping through a window that was never going to open. But even if she managed to break the glass, she couldn't hike herself up enough to get out of it. The living-room door, a couple of feet away, was an easy escape, needing only a flip of a lock.

"Miss Bea, wake up!" Steely said, finally pinning Bea against the wall. "You're having a nightmare again."

Bea looked frightened and confused at the mangled blinds. Then she viewed the room around her and calmed. "The rats want us dead."

"Let's have a seat, and we can talk about those bad rats." Steely helped her to the chair and then lay back on the sofa and pulled a blanket up to her neck.

"The rats aren't real rats," Bea began.

"That's reassuring."

"They're people."

Steely lifted her head. "Real people?"

"It's a man, a woman, and a girl who looks pretty and ugly at the same time."

"Maybe this is just a bad dream because you're afraid of rats."

"No, it's more than that. The man's face is shadowed. He's a gorilla. It's not Harry Keaton. I'd like to slap that girl. She took control of everyone, including the wicked woman." Bea stopped and looked around the room. "What did you do with my things?" she asked, irritated.

"They're stacked in the dining area. Some on the floor of the garage, where you can easily reach them."

"I hope you didn't throw anything away."

"Only the trash. Miss Bea, please try not to holler anymore. I was up late—"

"My voice naturally projects. When I sang opera, they could hear me without a microphone."

"I'm sure that's true."

181

Bea sniffed. She squeezed the arms of the recliner and leaned back. "This chair smells strange. You didn't mess with it, did you?"

"I dug enough food out of it to fill a grocery sack. Some looked petrified. I sprayed it with disinfectant."

Bea lifted her arm to check the seat below. "How'd food get in there?"

"It jumped off your plate." Steely shut her eyes, tucked her head under the blanket, blocking out the bright light. "I'm going to sleep a little bit longer."

Bea grunted, "You need to sleep in your bed. That's what beds are for—sleeping."

"Do you see that key on the coffee table? It fell out of one of the boxes."

Bea sprang forward and grabbed it. "It's for a safety deposit box. We had a box. Then they demolished the bank, right before we left town. I don't think there was much in it." Bea rotated the key between two fingers. "I have no idea where Jack got another box. There's a hundred banks in town."

"You might want to start looking. Just in case."

"Huh," Bea grunted. "I'll tell you what's in it. The cob. The big fat cob!"

Steely sat up and folded her blanket, placing it neatly on the end of the sofa. "I guess it's time to get dressed and find a job since nobody's sleeping here."

"Don't be snippy, Miss Priss. I told you to sleep in the bed."

"It was just an observation. I meant no disrespect."

Bea squeezed the key in her hand. "I hate having nightmares about rats. This isn't my first, you know."

"At least you got some exercise."

"Did you really make something positive out of a nightmare that almost gave me a heart attack? I wake up in a frenzy 'cause someone is trying to kill us, and you make something good out of it? I can't take it anymore! You're driving me nuts. My nerves are shot." Bea rubbed her neck. "When I get tension in the morning, it lasts all day."

"Screaming probably gives your nerves a shock. I'm sure Mrs. Yost heard you. She's probably setting out rat bait as we speak."

"That nosy old woman," Bea said in a loud voice. "She lurks outside the windows!"

"It's her duty as the neighborhood watch captain to keep an eye on things."

"Huh. Neighborhood busybody. Sticks a five-dollar flashing light on her car and snoops in everybody's business. What's a hundred-year-old going to do when there's real trouble?"

"Call HPD. Fastest dialer in town. Plays the piano. That lady can hit those keys when she needs to. I think she got a medal in college. Was going pro—"

"Do you like to hear yourself talk?"

"Sometimes I find myself entertaining." Steely hopped over the back of the sofa. "I'm getting excited about looking for a job."

"Excited?" Bea adjusted a pillow behind her and then rested up against it. "Why?"

"I like working. Everybody works at something—the difference is whether you get rewarded monetarily. Sometimes you do something for someone just because they need help. And you're the only one who can help them."

"Caca."

"You mean that in a nice way?"

"Jack always helped the strays. And they bit him. If he hadn't helped Harry, he couldn't have taken advantage of him. Then he and David wouldn't have been out there mowing grass. And they wouldn't have had that accident." Bea folded her arms tightly.

"Miss Bea, I can't explain why bad things happen. But I do know we must still keep doing the right thing."

Bea paused for a few seconds. She grunted, unfolded her arms and hit the remote control to flip on the news. "I don't know if I can do this."

Steely went around the sofa. She knelt by Bea. "Miss Bea, we have to continue living. It's been over a year."

Bea muted the TV. Her eyes teared. "You don't need to remind me how long it's been. Part of me went off that cliff too. I almost lost my mind. Who dreams about gangster rats? I think I've lost my mind."

Steely gently answered, "I can't imagine how you feel. But I know what it's like to be alone and not have anybody...to lose everyone you love most in this world. To have no one to list on your college emergency card. To not know where you're going to sleep at night. I know what that's like. And I know you must move forward."

"I think I'd feel better in the old folks' home with the depressed people."

"The residents at Star of Light aren't depressed."

"They're more depressed than you. You're just too peppy for me. Bubbly all the time. I heard you last week when you stepped in dog poop." Bea pointed outside. "Right there, in the yard. 'Oh, good thing I didn't have on new shoes.' I've never heard anyone in my life say something positive about dog poop!"

"Miss Bea, what do you think Jack and David would want you to do?"

Bea hushed.

"You'll never forget your son or your husband. Ever. You may even think of them every day for the rest of your life. I do. I think of my parents too. Every day."

Bea turned her head toward her. "You do?"

"Yes, every day."

"I would've never known. You seem so insensitive."

"You know, God has something He wants you to do, or you wouldn't be here."

"Now you're bringing God into this?"

"Why wouldn't I?"

Bea reached over the side of the chair, flipped up the footrest, and reclined. "When I die, you'll probably put a jar of peanut butter on my headstone. The cheap one with the coupon." She peacefully closed her eyes. A few seconds later, her phone rang. "I can't move. You better get that. It's on my nightstand."

Steely thought about letting the call go to voice mail, but the caller would get a message saying, "This mailbox has not been set up." Steely hurried to the bedroom and picked up.

"Hello?"

"Mrs. Hunter, this is Sheriff Tucker."

She cringed.

"Hello?" Tucker said.

Steely whispered, "Sheriff, this is Steely Hunter." She took a deep breath and went to the far corner of the bedroom.

"Did you leave town?"

"Yes. We left last week."

"I see. Well, I have some bad news. Someone broke into the farmhouse."

"They did?" Steely slid down in the corner, behind the drapes.

"Yeah, real strange. Somebody tried to get in there last year, on the day of the service. This time they tore open the drawers and closets. You have any idea what they were looking for?"

"No. Everything we left is old and doesn't really have any value."

"Maybe it was some kids acting up. Also, we finally managed to get the vehicle out of the canyon. I'm sorry it took so long, but we tried to minimize the risk to my deputies."

"I understand, Sheriff. We didn't want anyone else getting hurt, either."

"We're going to check out each piece then—"

"Check for what?" she said, interrupting him.

"The base was lodged into the rocks so deeply it couldn't be examined in the initial investigation. It's standard procedure that we check out every part of a vehicle in an accident like this. I'll contact you when we finish."

"I see. Thank you, Sheriff." Steely placed the cell beside the bed and headed back to the living room.

Bea was up staring out the living-room window. "Now we'll finally know what really happened!"

Steely looked back at the bedroom and then the living room. "Miss Bea, could you hear that?"

"What does he think I am? Some kind of fool?" Bea said, irritated.

"Fool?" Steely looked puzzled.

"Well, I'm no fool!"

"He's routinely checking out the vehicle."

"Routine? Is your life routine?"

"No. Not exactly."

"He's suspicious of something," she said, pacing.

"He said the accident was caused by poor weather conditions."

"Why didn't I see it? Something's not right."

"With the truck?"

Breathing rapidly, Bea moved abruptly around the room. "Someone caused Jack to veer off that cliff. I'm telling you, it was no accident, and it wasn't Jack's fault."

"Why don't you have seat?" Steely said gently. "And I'll get you some iced tea."

Bea calmed enough to sit. Her hands nervously shook as Fur Ball curled up in her lap. "As kids, Jack and I rode horses down that road. He knew that curve well. He was always so careful." Bea nodded.

Steely wrapped a napkin around a glass of tea and handed it to Bea.

Bea sipped. "I guess I've been too upset to think straight. Jack didn't miss the curve. Somebody killed my husband and my son. You think I'm nuts?"

"No, Miss Bea. I don't. Please try to sit back." Steely had heard Bea say some wild things. She had been insulted and almost run off. She chalked it up to Bea having a bad day more often than not. Today was not one of those days.

Beatrice Hunter wasn't always wrong.

CHAPTER THIRTY-ONE

Nick Dichiara bypassed parking by hiking the eight blocks from the JHI Tower to Harris County District. Attorney Macini's office. He bypassed the waiting too, since Louie Macini was his first cousin, once removed. Being a cousin was both good and bad for Nick. The good part meant Macini would see Nick with no notice at all. The bad was that Macini was fifteen years older than Nick, and he still viewed Nick as his baby cousin who ate dirt.

The office was tired, like almost everyone there. Macini had his head stuck in his computer monitor, viewing the contents of the flash drive. He clicked and scrolled down the page. The computer was slow. Working with an eight-year-old program was a century old in software life.

Nick pointed at the screen. "Keaton drained the company. Can't you see it?"

"Sure, I see it. I would assume he's funding the affiliates and then wiring the funds back as profits come in. JHI makes some kind of cheese. Nobody would really care about this except the IRS. Are they OK with it?"

"No problem there. We overpay. It's like payoff money, if you ask me. Can you investigate this?"

Macini yanked off his glasses, pointed with them, and eased back. "Nick, you've been asking the same question for a year. You have nothing. You think that's what I do? Go after people when there is no crime? Cuz, we're not short on crime here. My desk is loaded with legit cases. We haven't laid anybody off in the twenty-eight years I've been here. Doubt we ever will."

"But you can see it. Right?"

"Yeah, I see what you're talking about. So what?"

"So I could walk off with a few hundred million by jockeying the assets?"

Macini shook his head. "I wouldn't advise it."

"So Keaton can manipulate Jack Hunter into selling for nothing—and there's no crime?"

Macini folded his hands together. "Jack Hunter was one of the best men I've ever known. I loved that man. Who didn't?"

"Well, there are a couple of guys..."

"He made the decision to sell his shares to Mr. Keaton. He personally would have been better off letting the company go belly up. The argument that the person in charge doesn't know what's going on with his people is irresponsible management. A leader is always responsible for the people below them. Period. Jack Hunter needed to protect his company. And it looks like that's exactly what he did." Macini stood, indicating the meeting was over. "Anything else?"

Nick lightened up. "You know, you're right. He did protect the company. He said he was doing that. It's exactly what he did." Nick got up to leave. "It's just hard to rationalize. No CEO ever does that. They take care of themselves first. Insulate their personal wealth. Then let the company and everyone else lose. But Jack didn't do that. Did he?"

"Nick, hold on." Macini walked out with him. "The last time I saw that look on your face, you put two guys in the hospital."

"Should I have just let them rob Mr. Lin?"

"What happened was Jack's decision. You need to respect that and give it up. That's my advice to you. Leave this alone. Jack Hunter can't testify as to why he did this."

Nick reached the door and stopped. "Just maybe I can make it seem as if he could."

Macini got in Nick's face. "I don't know how you want to make that happen."

"Everything would have worked out for Jack if only he had lived."

"How?"

"Cuz, just stay out of my way."

"Don't cross the line again. In fact, don't even get near the gray area. I know Uncle Vince isn't himself. Nick, don't get yourself in trouble."

"Trouble?"

"I'm calling Donovan if you do anything—"

"Relax." Nick shrugged jovially. "There's no crime here. So you can't create a crime where there is no crime."

"I mean it!" Macini headed back to his office, shaking his head.

Nick pushed out the front door and briskly made his way down the sidewalk. He was suddenly confident he could nail Keaton. He wasn't sure how. But if he had nothing, he'd still be sitting in his corner office on the fiftieth floor, drinking the coffee. He gained momentum. He was done with idle threats, done with contacting every possible authority. He doubted Keaton could get ticketed if he parked in a fire zone.

He was ready to make a threat real. No more useless, idle words. It was time to do the one thing that would get the attention of everyone involved. Drain the blood out of every vein.

The only way to do that was to take the assets. Every last cent he could get his hands on. It might get him killed. You don't mess with that kind of money and not have someone pay a fatal price.

Nick was ready to risk his life to trap the people involved in the cat-and-mouse game.

Most of the customers had cleared out of Cohen's Coffee Shop by midmorning. The late-morning regulars were reading newspapers and drinking their old-school coffee. The red-speckled, laminate tabletops and metal chairs were more sturdy than comfortable.

The counter stools were used mostly by customers who were alone. Steely settled in at an end spot. Her laptop was open as she scoured every job posting in the Houston metro area. Many were listed. It appeared three to five years' experience would open many more doors than a college degree.

An interesting ad popped up: *business development for a major company.* It sounded promising. *Fulfilling work helping people when they need it most.* She liked helping people. Last line: *Burial planning is the job for you!*

Business development for a funeral home? I don't think so.

The next one sounded better: *career advancement—don't miss the career opportunity of a lifetime—mature applicants only—you be in control of your income. Call today for an appointment with our friendly representative.*

The office was fifteen to twenty minutes away. She planned to leave early to avoid traffic. She wasn't familiar with the area. She'd called and set an appointment for eleven o'clock. Then she ran home to get dressed for her first interview.

Steely zipped the blinds shut in her bedroom. She changed into a skirt of perfect length—not floozy short or unaltered long—and a collared blouse, with a light sweater draped across her shoulders. Her Mary Jane shoes announced she was as young as she looked. She stood in the living room, asking for Bea's approval. "Do I look professional?"

Bea took a glance from her recliner. "Brush that hair of yours."

"I did." Steely checked in the framed mirror on the wall. She used a hand to pat down a few strands.

"Get me a brush. Get the spray too."

Steely rushed to retrieve the items from the bathroom. She sat on the floor with her back to Bea. "Miss Bea, please don't mess up what I did. I need to get going."

"Mess it up?" Bea pressed the remote, pausing the TV. "I could stick a brush between my toes and make it look better than this. My arms aren't ten feet long. Scoot back where I can reach you."

Steely moved in between Bea's spider-veined legs.

Bea brushed for a few seconds then sprayed. "Done. Now get going."

"Thank you, Miss Bea. Have you ever been to Mauly Street?" Steely hung her purse over her shoulder and headed toward the garage door.

"No." Bea scratched her chin. "It sounds familiar, but I can't place it."

"I have a job interview there at eleven."

"Great. Have fun. Now shush!" Bea unmuted the TV. The news was back on, loud and clear.

Steely locked the door behind her and took off.

Bea reached for a glass of iced tea on the end table beside her and sipped. "Now I can focus on what's going on in the world. Eee, what's that?" She turned the volume up to a blast.

A reporter standing on a sidewalk announced: "HPD operated a successful sting operation on Mauly Street last night. Prostitution and drug trafficking is rampant in the area. More after this message."

Bea spewed the tea, tossed the remote control, and ran out the front door. She reached the curb and looked both ways. Then she darted back inside with her cell to her ear.

CHAPTER THIRTY-TWO

The neighborhoods surrounding the area were in transition, for the better, but transition hadn't yet reached Mauly Street. Steely stopped in front of a wood-frame house in need of painting and got out of her car. She tiptoed through the overgrown grass to the front door. Neighbors watching across the street shook their heads in disapproval.

Why are they staring? People have businesses in their homes. I hope Mr. Wolcox doesn't have inside plants. They'd die without any sunlight...Must be his van parked in the driveway.

Steely gave the sturdy door attached to the wood frame two swift knocks. The curtains were pulled apart and then quickly shut before the lock was released and the door opened.

"Steely?" the man asked, barely sticking his head out.

"Mr. Wolcox?" she asked.

"Yes, come in and have a seat." He showed her to a stubby chair situated in front of his massive desk taking up half the living room. She had been on dozens of interviews but had never seen anyone in a slinky purple shirt and yellow pants, with bleached, bristled hair.

"I hope I'm not too early," she said.

"Perfect timing." Wolcox leered at her from across the desk.

"Nice shoes you have there."

"Thank you."

Floral wallpaper...carpet matches his shirt.

"You have an excellent résumé," the man said, looking over the single page.

"Thank you, Mr. Wolcox."

"Steely Hunter. Just for the record, is it Miss or Mrs.?"

"Mrs."

"Mm...husband?"

"I'm a widow."

He seemed pleased and made note. "I'm so sorry. Mother, father? Just for the record."

"Both passed. What difference does—"

He edged out a grin. "Too bad," he said.

"Mr. Wolcox, your ad says 'recent college grad a plus.' What exactly would I be doing?"

He kept writing. "We'll get to the details. I pay well."

"How well? That wasn't included either."

"I pay well for loyalty."

Steely perked up. "You won't find anyone more loyal than me."

"I pay well for following directions."

Steely replied, "I follow directions to the tiniest detail."

"I pay well for wearing the clothing we provide."

"I prefer uniforms. Saves money."

"I pay well for taking care of rough customers."

"Nobody too rough for me. I went to Juan Seguin Middle School."

"What would you do if someone touched you?"

"I'd use mace."

"I pay well."

"I'd use mace."

Wolcox slammed down his pen. "Mrs. Hunter, you will comply with all our clients' requests!"

"Mr. Wolcox, it's illegal. You didn't want four to five years' experience."

"Nope. Newbies are more malleable."

"This interview is over." She strapped her purse on her arm, held tightly to the mace in her side pocket, and darted for the door.

Wolcox idly watched her tussle with the knob.

"It's stuck!" She ran to the window, pushed the shade out of the way. They were nailed down. She ran over to the only other door. It might as well have been a wall. No movement at all.

"It's against the city code to nail down your windows and key lock your inside doors." Steely bounced her eyes around the room. "Guess you're more concerned about the vice squad than the fire marshal."

"I wasn't finished talking," Wolcox said. "Since you're not going anywhere, set yourself down."

Steely complied, still gripping the mace.

Wolcox glared at her. "You'll be ready when our clients need you," he said sternly. "I have zero tolerance for customer complaints. It's your job to keep them satisfied."

"I don't exactly know what you mean by 'satisfied,' but I'm certainly not satisfying anyone."

He laughed. "Oh, so you want to be a tough girl? I'll have you so dependent on white powder that you'll do anything I ask."

Wolcox yelled, "Theo! Ralph! Get in here!"

The back door opened. Two guys in tight T-shirts, with tats on their necks, converged on Steely.

There was no way out. Kicking and screaming would get her nothing but cuts and bruises. They could pick her up with one hand and toss her through the roof if they wanted. Theo could chew up the can of mace and spit it back at her.

"She needs an attitude adjustment," Wolcox said. "Cage her for a few days. Shouldn't take more than that. I want her working by next week. Now get her out of here."

Steely closed her eyes and bowed her head.

Wolcox slammed his fist on the desk. "You became my property the moment you walked in that door. You can go easy, or you can make this difficult. But you're going!"

Steely lifted her head, shook it in defiance.

"Really?" Wolcox's neck veins swelled, his eyes enraged. "Drag her out!"

The guys reached for Steely. She pushed them off and stood on her own. "You're not going to get away with this." She was flanked by two bulldozers. They shuffled her to the kitchen. Theo lifted a hidden floorboard.

"This time, make sure the lock is on tight," hollered Wolcox.

Theo jumped down. Ralph lowered her in and followed. The hole was dark, with only the kitchen light brightening it. The space was tight, barely enough room to move through in single file. There were no support walls, just a shoveled-out tunnel leading to a sewer line and a wired cage pushed into a corner.

The cage was sized for a large dog. There was room for Steely to twist and turn, but not straighten out. It wouldn't matter if she could. There wasn't much she could do after they gagged her and bound her wrists and ankles with twine. Ralph was no scout, but he sure tied knots like one.

Theo filled a used syringe with a hallucinogen that would send her soaring to places she would never want to go. What was left of the needle looked like it could be contaminated with hep C or something worse. He aimed it at Steely like he had a dart in his hand.

She made a quick roll away, rattling the cage and causing him to fumble the syringe.

"You shouldn't have done that." Theo picked up the instrument. "The other needle is older."

Ralph's cell buzzed. He checked the ID and answered fast. "Yeah, dude…Get out? Wolcox is out on bail. Theo's about to hike up the new asset…Got it!" Ralph dropped the cell back in his pocket. He turned to Theo. "We need to go now!" He lifted up halfway out of the hatch. "Wolcox! Cops in route!"

"Then we need to toast her," Theo said. "Boss says never leave them talking."

"I'll take care of her. You get a head start. You always slow us down."

"It's your fault for throwing that punk kid on my knee."

"Just go!"

Theo lowered his head to travel through the tunnel. Wolcox sat on the side of the hatch and then jumped down with a briefcase in hand. He tugged on the rope, closing them in. The only light now came from an open manhole at the end of the escape route.

Ralph opened a small toolbox on the floor, took out a syringe, and gave it two quick taps.

"You got her?" asked Wolcox.

"Got it! Go!"

Wolcox went over to Steely. "Guess you're terminated!"

She kicked at the cage.

Wolcox took off, following Theo.

Ralph grabbed hold of the cage, rotating Steely from side to side.

"Settle down, girl." He shook the cage violently for a few seconds. "Now be still!" He pressed his face close to hers. "I'm Officer Nettles."

She closed her eyes and relaxed her head on the bottom of the cage.

"Don't make a sound. I can't let you out yet. I'll be back to get you by tomorrow. You'll be OK in here till then." He emptied the needle onto the floor and left.

Steely stared at the syringe lying in the dirt.

The ropes got tighter as she twisted and turned. It was best just to lie back and breathe lightly. High-pitched chirping sounds meant she wasn't alone. But she was alive. And whatever was out there wasn't as dangerous as Theo or Wolcox.

The doorbell rang. Then someone began beating on the front door. It wasn't a regular knock. It was an urgent banging.

A few seconds passed before someone crashed through the door, splintering it apart with a furor. It sounded as if the house went with it.

Voices, some soft, others deep, were speaking among themselves. Footsteps, light and heavy, shuffled above her.

"Find that girl!" hollered a woman.

"You sure they didn't take her?" a baritone asked.

Steely didn't rattle the cage. What if these people were worse than those who'd just left? Officer Nettles was coming back tomorrow. She needed to be still.

"Tear this place apart!" ordered one of the weakest voices. "Find that girl!"

Furniture was flipped over. Doors opened and slammed. Feet stomped around for several minutes until a chair scraped the kitchen floor.

"What's that?" said a raspy voice. "There's no basement in any of these houses! Open it!"

Light slowly beamed in when the hatch was pulled back. Heads leaned in. Some tatted, some not. Some with stockings rolled above their knees. Old and young.

Steely froze.

A man jumped down beside her. "It's locked. Hand me the crowbar. I think she's breathing."

The man jimmied the door and snapped it open. He lifted Steely out and passed her limp body up to those watching. The ropes were cut. The gag ripped off her mouth. Her eyes were sealed, until she heard a tender voice. "Baby, are you OK?"

The crowd softly cheered when her eyes flapped open, and she began to cry.

"You're OK now." Mrs. Jennings held her closely for a few minutes until she calmed.

"Young lady, what are you doing here?" a man asked in a scolding tone.

"Getting a job," Steely sniffled. "Who are you?"

"I'm Pastor Ladue. That awful man rented this house a few weeks ago. We've been trying to get him out ever since. Mrs. Jennings lives across the street. She watched you come in. She called us when she saw those men crawl like rats from a manhole."

Jennings barely topped ninety pounds, three more than her age. Steely was pinned between Jennings and her sixtyish daughter, Cecilia. "Young lady, you need to be more careful where you go."

"I've been told that before," she whimpered.

"Did you come to this crazy man's house because of a ten-dollar ad on the Internet?" Jennings asked.

Steely squeezed her face together and shivered.

Jennings embraced her. "You're the third one we caught. Got him arrested two days ago. He lies—says he would let them go if they wanted. Most girls on drugs don't want to press charges. You on drugs?"

"No, ma'am."

"Makes me so mad! Destroying our girls while they rake in the money."

Steely thought about Jenny Dix.

"Let's get her out before they come back." Ladue rushed to a window. "It looks clear. Calvin and Dirk will walk you to your car."

"Thank you for breaking in," Steely said, leaving.

"Don't you come back here unless it's to visit me," Jennings said.

Steely shook her head. "Thank you."

Calvin kicked a few splintered boards out of the doorway and led her out. Steely jumped in the car, ground the transmission, and sped off.

CHAPTER THIRTY-THREE

S teely printed off another fifty résumés. The ones she couldn't hand deliver she e-mailed, faxed, or mailed. They either stayed in the decision maker's hands or were tossed in the trash. She thought most likely the latter, since she had no callbacks. The excuses she heard were all the same. Too qualified or not experienced. That was when she managed to get a response. It had been easier to gain employment when she was fourteen. If she wasn't hired by the next Monday, she would take the funeral-home job.

After all other options had faded, she was ready to try her last resort—the Fitzpatrick CPA firm. The family she had been the closest to growing up had been out of her life for several years. Whatever apprehension she had was nothing compared to being locked in a cage about to be stuck with a needle recycled from the seventies.

Mr. Fitzpatrick appeared successful. The family had a dream home. They drove luxury cars the cost of an average house. Steely wasn't looking for special treatment, just a regular job—one that didn't land her at HPD.

The office was contemporary. Chrome legs on a sofa, two chairs, and a coffee table brought the setting together. This was a small business, not one of the five big CPA firms. Steely timidly made her way to a single desk, where a college-aged girl sat reading a mass-produced paperback. Her name tag read Brianna, but it might as well have said "Gatekeeper."

"Hi, I'm Steely Hunter. Is Mr. Fitzpatrick available?"

Brianna flipped the book over, keeping her place intact. "Was he expecting you?"

"No, I just wanted to say hello and give him my résumé."

Brianna smiled. "He's in a meeting right now. You may leave your résumé with me. I'll see that he gets it." She held out a hand.

Steely glanced down at the basket under her desk, holding a résumé that was on its way to the city dump.

"How about Erin? Is she here?"

"Do you have an appointment?"

Steely shook her head.

"She's busy. May I give her a message?"

Steely leaned over the desk, eyes level with the girl's. "Brianna, I realize you're just doing your job. Believe me, I've been in your position for over a year. I know how to run people off in the nicest way."

"I didn't mean—"

"How about you just let her know I'm here? If she's still busy, I'll walk right out the door without any other discussion."

"One moment." The girl bopped down a hallway and disappeared. She could have saved herself a trip and pushed the button on her phone. But she was, most likely, told not to do that. Steely leaned around to see the book titled *Take Control: Get What You Want from People*. She hoped that wasn't the company motto.

Brianna reappeared with Erin trailing along in a tank top, stretch pants, soft-soled shoes, and a thin purse. "Steely! You're a blast from the past!"

"How are you, Erin?"

Erin held out an arm for a side hug. "Terrific! I'm on my way to a yoga class. We'll chat on the way?" Erin popped open the door. "Brianna, I won't be back today."

The girl nodded, as if that were the norm.

Erin briskly led Steely onto the sidewalk.

"Did you hear about Jessica?" Erin asked.

"Jessica from high school?"

"Yeah. She has this great new job. Her boss is out of town most the time, usually takes her with him. Don't tell anybody, but I'm so excited for her. They're dating!"

"I don't know Jessica very—"

"He's telling his wife this week that he's getting a divorce," she whispered, as if the people around them were listening, but they weren't.

Steely double stepped to catch up. "She's dating a married man?"

"It's OK. Emotionally he's already divorced. He's so good to Jessica. Just a super sweet guy."

"I doubt his wife would think so."

They crossed the next block. Erin's cell rang. She answered and confirmed her dinner plans for the next few blocks. She clicked off when they reached the yoga studio.

Steely blurted out, "Erin, I'm trying to find a job."

"Really?"

"Yes, I'll do anything ethical and legal. Last year, I got a BBA like you. I worked on campus, in the business office, the coffee shop, and some of the sporting events. I learn fast. You know that. Erin, are you or your dad looking for help? I'll do anything. Mop the floors. Clean the toilets, if I have to."

Erin swirled her hair around toward Steely, glared over her shoulder, and said, "Our maid has twenty years' experience."

"I'm not trying to get anyone fired. Erin, please, if there's anything you can do to help, I really need to work." Steely stood in place for a few seconds, briefly gaining Erin's full attention.

"Steely, I'd give you a job if I could. But Father isn't hiring until he gets some silly cash-flow problem resolved. He's even pushing me to find another job. Good thing Cricket has connections and can put in a good word for me."

"Where? Do they need anybody else?"

"I can't say just yet. Cricket said to keep quiet about it. I gotta go. My class is starting." Erin swung open the door. "Bye, Steely. You keep in touch. Let's do lunch."

Steely gazed through the window. The class had started. And her last option was on a mat stretching out her gluteus maximus.

The week had ended with a dramatic life-saving rescue, worn-out shoes, and a wheeze when she inhaled. The shoes could wait. A stop by the Ready RX Pharmacy on the way home should take care of the wheeze.

The neighborhood store was empty except for one customer. Didi, a strawberry blonde in her forties, stood at the front register. Didi waved. "Steely, go on back. I'll be right there."

Steely acknowledged her. She went through the store to the pharmacy counter and waited. The cash register light was on. Drugs labeled in alphabetical order sat on six rows of shelving lined up against the back wall. An unlocked half door was the only deterrent keeping someone from walking off with the shelved bottles. Steely stared at the bottles for a couple of minutes until the pharmacist put her white coat back on and gave the door a bump.

Didi picked up a rectangular box, slipped it in a miniature white bag, and set it upright on the counter. "All ready."

"Sorry about the short notice, Didi."

"Didn't matter at all. I had the right milligram in stock." Didi scanned the tag stapled to the bag. "What you been doing, kid?"

"Mostly looking for a job." Steely set her empty purse on the counter. "Looks like you need help."

"I've been double-dutying it for years." Didi tapped the keyboard, totaling the order. "You look tired."

"Just need a good night's rest."

Didi took the pen from above her ear and pointed at a bottle displayed on the counter. "Want some vitamins? These are made from food, supposed to be better absorbed. Might give you more energy."

Steely caught a glimpse of the $29.52 price tag. "No, thanks. That would give me a headache."

"I don't believe that's a side effect." Didi picked up the bottle and then set it back in place. "Yours will be nineteen dollars thirty-nine, ma'am."

"Gone up?"

"Like everything else. We barely turn a profit. The next higher dose would double the price."

"Higher dose? I didn't know there was a higher dose."

"Sure is."

"I'm glad I don't need it. Didi, put it on my account, please." Steely reached for the bag.

"Sorry, kid, we don't have charge accounts anymore."

Steely released the bag, leaving it wavering. "You don't?"

"No, too many people don't pay."

"They don't pay?"

"They run up a bill and then go off to another drug store. It puts us in a real bind."

Steely swiped her eyes on her sleeve. "Didi, I've always paid."

"Steely—"

"Even when my mom was sick. You know I was in here every week. Paid the bill after she passed. I paid every penny...not one time late. You know that." Steely squeezed her purse.

"Steely, you're right. No argument there. But too many people don't pay. That's why I don't have help. The new management said we had to cut it out for everybody. We have to be fair. We can't do it for some and not for the others. Steely, I'm really sorry. If you don't have the money, I'll buy it for you."

"Didi, it's OK. I have it." She dug in her skirt pocket and un-wrapped a worn twenty-dollar bill from a clear plastic bag. She held on to it for a few seconds and then set it down. "Here you go."

"Are you sure?" Didi picked up the bill. "You look like you're about to cry. Really, I'll pay for it."

"It's just a twenty-dollar bill. It doesn't matter if Mrs. Dichiara gave it to me. There are four point three billion more of them. I could have gotten this one from anybody. It's just a regular twenty-dollar bill. Please take it."

Didi opened the register, merged the bill with the other twenties, and handed Steely a few coins.

Steely took the bag and glanced at the shelving behind the counter. "Didi, I have a question."

"What is it, baby?"

"Do most drugs come in different milligrams?"

"Sure do."

"I would imagine you could get very sick if you took a double dose of some of those."

Didi closed the register. "Most certainly. It could make you very sick or even worse. Could be fatal."

Steely glanced over at the half door and nodded. "Thanks, Didi."

CHAPTER THIRTY-FOUR

Steely snuggled up to the counter at Cohen's Coffee Shop, booted up her laptop, and sipped complimentary coffee. She was starting the day earlier than most businesses opened. Being the first applicant to call on a job listing could be an advantage.

Every type of business was getting her consideration except the cemetery job. She called to accept the position and learned she'd be going to hospitals to consult with customers. Anything medical still made her queasy. You could blindfold her, spin her around, and she'd still know the moment she set foot in a medical facility. It wouldn't matter if the place had been sterilized and deodorized—she could sniff out any place medical.

She downed a third cup and checked for new jobs. Nothing but repeats so far. Knowing which job postings were old and which were new saved hours. Her last search was oil and gas. The offshore jobs looked interesting. They paid well. Working in an office, on a rig, would be OK with her. But she figured Bea couldn't handle her being gone on a three-week hitch. How would Bea react if Steely was in the middle of the Gulf of Mexico and she had a nightmare about rats?

She scrolled down the page and located a listing for an accounts-payable clerk downtown. She tapped the number in her cell.

"Jack Hunter Industries," a woman's voice answered. "How may I direct your call?"

She clicked off. Checked the caller ID. The number was stored as "JACK HUNTER—OFFICE." Steely set her phone aside. She stared at it for a few seconds. Then she lifted her cup, indicating a need for a fill-up. The server responded. "Thank you," she said, nodding and taking a quick sip.

How could I work there? They fired Jack.

Staring at her laptop, she spaced out. Suddenly, she envisioned a sixty-two-year-old woman in a kitchen lurking around the pantry reaching for a jar. The woman opened the only jar she found. From the woman's view, she could see the inside of the jar. It was empty. The woman picked up a knife and scraped the jar, mining for remaining residue. She pulled the knife out. It was clean. The jar had been scraped before. The woman reached into the trash for an empty can of pressed ham. She pulled on the open lid, ripping it off. The rangy woman licked her finger and stuck it in the can, retrieving a missed speck hidden in a crevice.

Even if they hired me and then fired me, I'd get some kind of paycheck for a few days. It'd be illegal for them to fire me because of my last name. Maybe I shouldn't use my last name?

Steely hit redial. The call was answered and forwarded to the senior vice president of human resources.

"Benita Ray here," Ray answered curtly but professionally.

"Mrs. Ray, I'm interested in applying for a job," Steely said, trying to sound at ease.

"We have several. Which one in particular?"

"The accounts-payable clerk. Have you filled that one?"

"No, not yet. Today is the last day to apply."

"I would like to apply, please. May I come in now? I can be there in ten minutes. Maybe eight."

"Hold on. Let me ask you a few weed-out questions first."

Weed-out questions?

"Certainly," Steely said, pressing. "But may I come in? I will answer all your questions then."

"Let's talk first."

"OK. Please go ahead."

"Name please?"

She hoped she wouldn't be disqualified on the first question.

Should I use Paupher? No, I'm not manipulating my name.

She confidently said, "Steely Hunter."

Ray paused.

Steely squeezed her cell.

"Your phone is dinging in my ear. Are you pressing the numbers?"

Steely relaxed her grip. "Oh, I'm sorry."

"My ears are ringing. Now, where were we...highest level of education?"

Steely wondered if Ray had heard her name correctly. Maybe she was distracted.

"Answer the question, please. Did you finish high school? Yes or no? These aren't difficult questions."

Steely quickly responded. "Yes, I did. Then I went to college."

"How long did you last?"

"Four years."

"Oh, how far did you get?"

"Graduated."

"Degree?"

"BBA. A bachelor of bus—"

"I know what a BBA is. So why are you applying as an accounts-payable clerk? You should have applied for the executive training program."

"I don't think—"

"This training program would have helped you get into management or assisted you with an MBA if you are fortunate enough to be chosen. The problem is I've already made my choice for this year. But I will let you apply for the next year."

"I think I'll pass on that."

"Pass?" Ray huffed. "Nobody passes on this opportunity."

"It doesn't pay. Does it?"

"Certainly not," Ray clipped. "Do you think you should get paid when the company is giving you six months of priceless training? Some applicants have offered to pay us!"

"Pay you? That won't work for me. I've spent all the money I can on an education."

"Depending on how well you do, the program could advance you ten years up the ladder."

"Working my way up the ladder is not my top priority. May I have the accounts-payable job, please?"

"Hold on just a minute—it's a red flag when someone with your credentials wants a job that doesn't require a higher education. The job is an important one that requires knowledge, dedication, and people skills, but not a college degree."

"This shouldn't be a red flag."

"Why not?"

"I have bills to pay."

"I see. Is there anything about you that would hinder your job performance? Do you get along with people? Can you handle pressure? Are you dependable? These are important traits."

"I could live in a pressure cooker. You could clap down the top and turn on the stove. I'd be fine. I'm one of the most dependable people you'll ever meet."

"I see you don't lack confidence."

"That's what I've been told."

"OK, young lady. Quickly, tell me how you get along with people in less than thirty seconds. Time starts now."

Steely had never used the orphan card. But she needed this job so badly she was putting that card on the table. She was an orphan. And it was time to tell it. She'd use the widow card too, but it could backfire.

"The clock is ticking!"

"Mrs. Ray, I get along with people even when they don't get along with me. My father died when I was in middle school."

Ray hushed.

"My mother died before I finished my senior year in high school." Steely poured out the facts. There was no need to embellish when sharing her history. It was more than ample to prove her case. "Mrs. Ray, one day in high school a girl saw me praying. I like to pray. Do you pray?"

"I do," Ray whispered.

"She told the entire high-school class that I had mental issues. That I spent the summer in a state hospital. You know the one in Rusk?"

"She didn't."

"Sure did. My mom and dad, before they passed, used to tell me to let things like that roll off my back. That's what I did, Mrs. Ray. I let it roll off my back. You can't control what other people say. And you sure can't control what they think. I never one time said anything rude back to the girl. Treated her as if I didn't know what she did. Mrs. Ray, if I can get along with her, I can get along with anyone."

"You didn't say anything to her?"

"I told her privately that what she did was wrong. That was the end of it."

There was a long period of silence. Steely waited for Ray to announce her time was up, but Ray didn't, so she continued. "Most of the time in college, I worked three jobs. I lived in a general shelter my first semester—not a women's shelter, a general shelter. And I learned there's a big difference between the two."

Ray groaned.

"I never missed a day of work. Missing a day might have meant skipping a few meals. And, Mrs. Ray, I don't like skipping meals. If you hire me, I promise I will get along with everyone."

Ray, the seemingly impatient, go-by-the-book senior vice president was speechless.

"Are you still there?" Steely asked.

Ray cleared her throat. "I have allergies. Just be here in two hours."

"Yes, ma'am, I can start working immediately."

"Hold on. You can have the job if you can pass the tests and a background check. Takes about three weeks to complete the process."

"Is there any way to speed up the process?" Steely pressed.

"No, ma'am," Ray said firmly. "It's company policy. No way around it. Just be here on time. Tardiness tells me you don't respect my time."

"Mrs. Ray, there's not a chance of me being late."

Steely closed her laptop. She hitched a ride on the light rail to the JHI Tower.

She had a job at the company founded by Jack and Beatrice Hunter.

Bea might consider her a backstabber. She wasn't sure. But if so, this backstabber was getting a paycheck to put food on the table and pay the electric bill, so Bea could eat bacon and eggs and watch the news nonstop.

CHAPTER THIRTY-FIVE

The JHI Tower was a half-block structure of steel and glass. Steely stood across the street, casting her gaze up to Jack's old window in the executive suite. Then she continued across the street, toward the lobby. A revolving door whirled her inside, where a half dozen guards in blue uniforms with guns attached at their waists watched for trouble. Security was tight. But it hadn't always been. It sure wasn't on Steely's first visit when Jack Hunter was CEO.

The security team checked everyone into the tower. Employees with ID badges had their ticket in. Visitors were sent to the reception desk, where two employees directed them to sit and wait to be escorted inside by whoever authorized them to be there. The thirty-foot ceilings created a noisy entrance extending to the sprawling reception area, where swayback chairs were aligned in rows.

Knowing she lacked the needed credentials for entry, Steely veered toward the reception desk.

"May I help you?" asked a woman identified by her badge as Candy.

"I have an appointment with Mrs. Ray," replied Steely.

Candy was observant enough to spot the interview outfit: black skirt, jacket, white blouse, and dress shoes. "New hire?"

"I hope so."

"What spot?"

"Accounts-payable clerk."

Candy elbowed Kristi, her coworker. "See, I told you accounting is a revolving door."

Kristi nodded. "How long for the last guy—two days?"

"Three hours. My friend in HR said he went to lunch and didn't come back." Candy looked at Steely. "If you last a month, I'll buy you lunch."

Steely agreed.

Candy picked up the phone. "I'll call Mrs. Ray and let her know you've arrived. Name?"

"Please don't call yet. I'm early."

"Then have a seat. Let us know when you're ready."

Steely found a chair situated where she could watch the employees line up and swipe their badges. It was a lively place. She wondered how long it would take Mrs. Ray to figure out who she was. She planned on laying low. Blending in. Maybe no one would pay much attention to her or her last name. Just do her job the best she could and collect a paycheck. The magazines, stacked in the chair next to her, held her interest for the next hour until Nick Dichiara zigzagged through the crowd and stooped down beside her.

"Steely?"

She lit up. "Nick! It's so good to see you."

He wrapped an arm around her shoulder. "Did you move back?"

"Yes, Miss Bea missed the city." She stared at his face. "How'd you do that?"

"It's a battle scar," he said, brushing it off. "What are you doing here?"

"I'm applying for a job."

"Applying for a job here? At JHI?" He squatted on his polished oxfords, pointing one hand to the floor. "Are you serious?"

"I really need a job. Nick, I tried to call you."

"You did? When?"

"A few weeks ago. I left you a couple messages."

"I didn't get them. You know I would have called you back."

"I figured you were busy. I was a little short on personal references. I saw the job listing this morning, and here I am."

Nick lost his balance. Pressed his fingers onto the tile preventing a fall. He asked seriously, "What would you like to do here?"

"Be an accounts-payable clerk."

He tilted to one side and then straightened up.

"I need the job."

"I see. You know what? I have just the right place for you."

"You do?"

"Yes, the executive training program. That's where I'm going to put you."

"Nick, thank you for trying to help, but I can't go six months without pay. I'd rather have the accounts-payable job."

His ears turned dark red. They looked feverish. "There are some things we need to talk about."

"I don't know how long I'll be here. I have to pass some test today and then a background check that could take three weeks."

"Background check? This is a screwball place. Who told you that?"

"Mrs. Ray in HR. And she was adamant."

"Does she know who you are?"

"No."

"Good. I assure you, she'll get you set up today—insurance, benefits, everything. You're starting today."

"Really?"

"Yeah, you have a job. But let's keep it quiet as long as we can—you know, who you are. Would that be all right?"

"Sure, I was thinking it might be awkward."

"The word will get out soon enough. You wait here. Benita will be right down to take care of you." Nick squeezed her hand. "I need to run upstairs now. But I'll catch up with you later. And Steely...I want you to stay close to me."

"You want me to stay close to you?" she said in a high pitch. "I don't have a problem with that."

"Good. See you tomorrow."

She watched him vanish through the executive entrance.

He wants me to stay close to him, and I'm getting paid. And I considered selling graves.

CHAPTER THIRTY-SIX

Nick shot up to the second floor. Convincing Ray to hire Steely as his executive trainee and to start her today was going to be a battle. First thing he had to do was backtrack since he had declined to take on a trainee, as Ray requested.

He approached the last hallway to Ray's office with no strategy. He was almost relieved when he turned the corner and found it empty. Pictures of Ray, with children in crisis, were framed and scattered around her desk. Some had medical issues, some financial, and many family needs. Ray might be a rough talker, but if you could get through the brick wall around her, you'd find a compassionate heart. Her jacket draped on the back of her chair meant she hadn't left the floor. An empty saucer next to the keyboard clued him to her whereabouts.

He sprinted toward the kitchenette in the back corner. Inside were a table, three chairs, a fridge, and Ray watching a cup circling in a microwave. She stood elevated on four-inch heels, a thick black belt squeezing the midsection of her suit.

Nick knocked gently on the wall. He didn't want to startle her. He had done that once before. "Benita? Do you have a moment?"

217

Nick sounded mousey. His game plan changed the moment she glared back at him.

"Mr. Dichiara," she said firmly, "I'm on my way back to my office to finish the payroll for a few thousand employees. Some of them won't make their bills next week if I don't get this done. Do you think that should wait while I take an unscheduled visit from you?"

There was no good way to answer the question. Ray had the skill to purposely word it that way. If he said yes, he was arrogant. If he said no, he was out. This was not a good start. So he cut the finesse and threw out his request.

"I need a favor."

"A favor, Mr. Dichiara?" she snarled, twisting her head to one side. "I don't do favors. You should already know that." The microwave dinged. She yanked the cup out, drowned a tea bag, dumped in sugar from a box, and stirred.

"I really need a favor like right now."

"Hearing tests are covered by your health insurance. You need to get yours checked."

"Benita, there's a young lady waiting to see you—a new accounts-payable clerk."

"I told her she could have the job if she makes it through the application process. She's early." Benita checked her watch. "Over an hour early. Was she complaining?"

"No. If she hasn't complained by now, she'll never complain."

"Mr. Dichiara, cut the chitchat. Tell me what you want or get out of my sight!"

Nick dropped his arms to his side and stood up straight. "Benita, I need you to take care of her right now. Hire her today in the executive training program working with me."

"You declined to take on a trainee. Remember? So I made the decision." Ray threw the spoon in the sink and shot daggers at Nick. "I'm giving that job to someone else. Plus she doesn't want it."

"She'll want it when we pay her as if she has completed the program."

Ray's bifocals slid halfway down her nose. She looked over them at Nick.

"Oh, and full benefits too."

Benita did not immediately react. He would rather that she did. Just go ahead and blow up. Get it all out. But she didn't.

She stewed.

Steam smoked her face as she lifted her cup to sip. "You looking for a fight?"

"Not in particular."

She rattled the cup on the counter. "Well, that's what you're about to get. You should be ashamed of yourself."

"Ashamed for what?"

"She has the accounts-payable job if she passes the tests and the background check. Now, I'm deleting this conversation from my memory and getting back to work." She took a step toward the door. If Nick didn't come up with something fast, the battle would be over. He'd have to go back to the lobby and explain. He couldn't let that happen.

"One question, please," he requested meekly.

"What is it?" she snapped.

"You know corporate policy better than I do."

"That's not a question. That's a fact."

"Yes..."

"Then what? You're dragging like the five-o'clock traffic."

"Tell me. Do I have the authority to hire her to work directly with me? And if I do, you must hire her unless she doesn't meet the corporate hiring policy. Here's the question: is that correct?"

"Technically, yes. It doesn't matter if they put you in a closet with bats, you're still an SVP."

"Then trust me. She's very well qualified. Please do this for me."

"Nope!"

"Benita, please consider this a formal request to hire her today."

Every word steamed out. "Mr. Dichiara, you're pushing me to my limit. We have to follow corporate policy."

"And if we follow corporate policy, your only alternative is to report me to my superior. That'd be good old Harry Keaton." He nailed it.

Her face maddened. The only thing Benita hated more than breaking corporate policy was Harry Keaton. Reporting Nick to Keaton would be like reporting him to the devil himself.

"You're not going to turn me in to Keaton, are you?"

She glared.

"Now, please, don't keep our new employee waiting. And one more thing: please start her today."

"Can't do that." Benita planted her size elevens. "We have to do a background check. We can't hire anyone without it."

"Her background is better than mine."

"At the moment, I'm thinking yours needs further review!"

"Oh, and one other thing: please give her a sign-on bonus."

"Did we have to compete for a trainee?" Benita clenched a fist.

"No. Label it as a relocation bonus. She relocated to Houston."

Benita bumped her cup off the counter, causing it to tumble onto the floor. Nick bent down to help. "Get your hands off my cup!" She grabbed it and sent it spinning in the sink. "Is there anything else you need to tell me?"

"It's a pleasure to work with you."

"Get out before I change my mind!"

CHAPTER THIRTY-SEVEN

The traffic in the reception area had slowed. Steely sat quietly, with a ruffled magazine, ignoring the four eyes planted on her.

"Did you see the way he hugged her?" asked Candy.

"It was only a side hug," said Kristi.

"Yes, but definitely personal."

"Bet he has a twelve pack under that shirt," said Kristi.

They lowered their headsets to their shoulders.

"Look how fast she turned those pages," said Candy.

"It's not a novel, mostly just pictures," said Kristi.

"I knew I should've bugged those chairs."

"Didn't security turn down that request?"

"They don't need to know everything."

Kristi snipped, "You in some kind of gang or something?"

"We're not here just to smile and nod. We're the initial point of entry for every nonemployee who comes through those doors. We don't know who's coming in here. None of these people have background checks. There's more mentals out there like that crazy man the other day."

They nodded.

Kristi asked, "What's Beef Ribs doing with that old ugly fiancée?"

"The Lizard Girl? Monte said he dumped her. Then she tore his face up."

"Beat him?"

"Didn't you see him?"

"No, I had a bad angle."

"Probably will leave a scar. The Lizard Girl is nuts. Always talking about herself in the third person."

"Why is she hanging around here?"

"I don't know. Security lets her come right in. But I'm calling HPD if she ever acts up again. Walking through the lobby with those hips swinging at everybody. Yesterday, she knocked an elderly fella over. Hit him and kept going."

"A hit and run?"

"Never looked back. I reported her to HR. Mrs. Ray wrote it up. Oh, and if an ambulance ever comes again, I'll hold the door while you watch the desk."

"Got it."

"Standard procedure."

They moved their heads in opposite directions, minding their posts. Steely glanced over and smiled.

"Alert!" Candy flashed her eyes away. "She saw me. I'm bringing binoculars tomorrow."

"This ain't bird-watching. You can't sit here ogling people through binoculars."

"I'll take a break, get behind those columns." She pointed to the support beams. "My cousin taught me how to read lips. When the girl comes back tomorrow, I'll know everything she says."

Candy spoke through her teeth, "Alert! Here comes that other big-mouth girl."

"She's friends with the Lizard."

"I'm Erin Fitzpatrick," the girl said, approaching the desk. Her head tilted upward, her chest out. "I have an appointment to see Mrs. Ray. Please inform her that I'm waiting."

"Sit," Candy said sharply. "Oh, and you better lower that nose. You don't want to drown in the rain."

"What's your name?" Erin said in a raised voice.

"Candy. C-a-n-d-y. I'm the chief receptionist. Now go sit yourself down."

"Was that supposed to be a joke?" Erin scathed. "You're not funny. You're rude." She took a few steps away, flipped around at Candy, looked daringly, and then went on.

Kristi covered her mouth. "Drown when it rains? I almost laughed."

"Did you see that shotgun stare that turkey gave me? She doesn't understand authority. Hope she's comfortable. She's going to be there awhile."

"You're not calling Mrs. Ray?" asked Kristi.

"Who's in charge of calling?"

"You."

"Then I'll call when I'm good and ready."

"You don't play."

"No, I don't."

They nodded.

Ten rows of eight chairs were in the lobby. There was an 80 percent chance Erin wouldn't even go to the same row. If Erin went left, the odds tripled.

But she didn't. She cut right and plopped herself down directly across from Steely. "Steely?" she squealed. "Is that you?"

Steely lowered the magazine covering her face. "Hi, Erin."

Erin pitched an air kiss in Steely's direction and then pulled out a mirrored compact and checked her face.

"Erin, is your new job here?"

"Yes. I'm launching my career in the executive training program—best one in town, maybe the entire US. But the billion-dollar question is, what are you doing here?" Sour-faced, she added, "Isn't this kind of creepy for you?"

"Not when I need a job."

"Which one are you going for?" Erin peered over her compact powder.

"I was applying for the accounts-payable clerk, but I—"

"Perfect." She dabbed her nose with a cotton pad.

Steely laid the magazine on the chair beside her folded her arms. "I'm just glad I'm getting a paycheck again. Finances have been tight."

"I know how you feel."

"You do?"

"Yeah, we're kinda going through the same thing."

"The same thing?" Steely shook her head. "I don't think so."

Erin said, "You took that the wrong way." She angled the compact near her nose, checking for stragglers. "My father cut me off without any warning—cut me right off."

"No money?" asked Steely.

"It's just not right for me to struggle."

"You know the executive program doesn't pay, right?"

"Mother is making Father pay me for another six months, until I finish the program. Good thing I have parents."

Steely remained quiet for a few seconds. "Erin, you know…"

Everyone in the lobby suddenly stopped and directed their attention to the heels hammering their way toward the reception desk.

"Here comes Mrs. Ray," Erin said airily. She closed her compact and winked. "I'll be calling her Benita in no time."

"Where's Steely?" Ray blasted at the receptionists.

"She wants you?" Erin slouched.

Maybe this wasn't a good idea.

Ray went up to the desk, commanding Candy's and Kristi's attention. They rolled their chairs in her direction.

"Where is Steely?" Ray barked.

"We don't know," replied Kristi.

"Yes, ma'am," agreed Candy. "We don't know her."

Ray had their number. "I bet you saw Mr. Dichiara. Didn't you?"

"Yes, ma'am," they said in union.

"I hear you call him Barbecue Ribs."

Kristi naively corrected her. "Beef Ribs."

Ray wasn't amused. "Stop stalking him and pay attention to what you're doing. Now, where's the girl he was talking to?"

They pointed to Steely.

Ray drilled halfway toward her and hollered, "Steely, come here please!"

She's as loud as Miss Bea!

Security acknowledged Ray and then went back to their duties.

Steely scurried over. "Yes, ma'am?"

"Follow me!" Ray marched toward the elevators with Steely following. Ray didn't stop to get a guest a badge. Didn't check her in. There was no chance of anyone questioning her. They burst through the gate and waited for a lift to the second floor. Ray's silence made Steely more uncomfortable than her hardy voice.

Ray finally announced matter-of-factly, "I'm Mrs. Ray, the senior vice president over HR."

"Good to meet you, Mrs. Ray. I guess you know who I am, or you wouldn't be taking me through security unscreened like that, not knowing if I had a weapon or—"

Ray swung around to Steely. "Do you have a weapon?"

Steely shook her head. "Oh, no, ma'am."

"Then don't be insinuating that we should run you through a scanner."

A few seconds passed.

"Thank you for your time on the phone this morning," Steely said, rattling on, "never can tell what someone's going to be like on the phone. You meet them in person and could get a whole different—"

"Anybody ever tell you that you talk too much?"

"Yes, ma'am." Steely hushed.

Time lingered until Ray said, "I'm setting you up for your new job."

"Yes, ma'am." Steely tempered her excitement.

Ray vented, "I feel like slapping someone."

"Hope it's not me." Steely stared at the metal doors.

"This place has been bizarre since Mr. Hunter left. I don't know how long I can last. People doing stupid stuff. This is a business! They use the company plane like it's a recreational vehicle! I'd fire that Mr.—just understand, from now on, you'll be treated like everyone else."

Steely glanced back at the revolving door leading outside.

"I worked directly with Mrs. Hunter from the beginning of this company to put solid hiring practices in place that we could use until Jesus comes."

I should have guessed.

"I don't think she would mind." Steely smiled, attempting to lighten the aura. "And I know for sure Jesus hasn't come."

"Nick's being all secretive. He's supposed to tell me everything that goes on around here." She softened. "Well, I hope you're ready to work hard as an executive trainee."

"Mrs. Ray, remember I need to get paid." She braced herself for Ray's response.

Ray spoke through clenched teeth. "You're getting paid."

Steely smiled. "That's perfect."

"Perfect? The college grads who get offered that job give their blood, sweat, and tears, working with no pay for six months. Only the best make it to the next level."

"I see."

The elevator doors spread apart. They marched in: Steely, stoic; Ray, flaming and facing out. Steely had been more comfortable in Donovan's side chair with felons chained outside the door.

Ray grumbled, "I hope you realize you've been given a free ride."

"A free ride?" She looked over at Ray as the doors slammed together.

CHAPTER THIRTY-EIGHT

Ray placed Steely in the vacant office next to hers. Ray stacked a ream of paper in front of Steely on the bare desk and sounded off orders. "Start your paperwork. You're allowed thirty minutes for lunch. Then at two o'clock, a lab tech will be here to draw blood."

"I donated last week. I think you have to wait at least six—"

"This isn't a blood drive. We don't want anyone doing drugs here. Oh, and they take a hair sample too. People tried to switch the samples on us."

"They may take my blood, my hair, or anything else you want. It's fine."

Ray handed her a clipboard. "Here's the schedule. After the paperwork comes the test. Math, spelling, psychological testing. We need your transcripts too."

"No problem. I have a certified copy here with me." Steely lifted a sealed envelope from her purse and passed it to Ray.

Ray ripped into it. "This will do for college. But we need your records all the way back to kindergarten."

"Kindergarten?"

"We want a complete history."

"From kindergarten?"

"Yes, people don't change that much."

"I liked to play grocery store," she snickered. "Will that enhance my job skills?"

"Being a smart aleck to a superior. Do you want to be written up before you start?"

"I thought a little humor might help your tension."

"I don't have tension. And I don't find humor funny."

She's Miss Bea's twin.

"Now get started. You don't want to be the first to take three days." Ray went to her office. She stood over her desk, picked up her phone, and pressed three digits. "Tell Miss Fitzpatrick I must reschedule her for tomorrow morning. Same time." Click.

Filling in answers, checking boxes, Steely ran through every bit of two hundred papers. She carefully read the company regulations. Ray wasn't letting her slide. She worked fast. No breaks for her. She just wanted to finish. At 3:55 p.m., she shuffled the papers together and stood at Ray's door, waiting for attention.

Ray ran her fingers around a keyboard. Steely wasn't sure if that was her normal speed or emotion causing the rapid reaction. Ray didn't look up. "Work five more minutes."

"I've completed everything, Mrs. Ray."

Ray leered up at her. "Did you finish the math test? Those take most applicants half a day by themselves."

"Yes, ma'am. I'm done."

"Did you answer every question?"

"Yes, ma'am. But I don't think you're allowed to ask some of those questions."

Ray growled, "Do you want to tangle with me?"

"No, ma'am," Steely said earnestly. "I most certainly do not."

"I've been doing this for twenty-six years. I have a stellar reputation. And a new trainee wants to instruct me on how I should conduct myself?"

"I really don't want—"

"You're on a slippery slope."

Steely shook her head. "Mrs. Ray, the reason I mentioned the questions is because they could offend some people."

Ray rolled out her bottom lip. "They can build a bridge and get over it!"

"I just didn't want you to get into trouble. There are laws—"

"I haven't been in trouble yet!"

"Yes, ma'am. But many things have changed in twenty-six years."

"You're still sliding. You want to keep going with this?"

"No, I regret bringing it up. They took my blood. My hair. Am I finished?"

"Not just yet. We found a blemish on your records."

"What blemish?"

"What is this assault you committed in second grade?"

"Assault?" Steely was puzzled. "I've never assaulted anyone."

"Says you were in a physical altercation with a girl."

"Physical?" Steely looked down for a second. Then she slowly lifted her head. "They put that on my record?"

"Sure did. We don't want any violence in the workplace. Are you hot tempered?"

"No—"

"What exactly did you do to the little girl?"

"We were at recess playing softball. This girl in my grade was mad because I caught the ball that got her out on second base. The game was over, and everyone was going inside. I forgot my sweater on a bench and went back to get it. Then, out of nowhere, this girl came at me with a baseball bat. I grabbed the bat and pushed her back. She tripped and hit a bench. The loudest scream I ever heard came out of her mouth. The teacher ran back and saw me holding the bat. Then the girl told her I had come after her. There I was, uninjured with the bat in my hand. I wasn't trying to hurt her. But what was I supposed to do? Let her beat me over the head and then tell the teacher? You never know what Cricket's going to—"

"Cricket?"

"Yes, Cricket. Do you know her?"

Ray slammed the folder. "We're done."

"Are you firing me?"

"No." She glanced at her watch. "I'll check your test tonight. As long as you passed, you may start with Mr. Dichiara tomorrow. You're the first to finish this fast. You didn't cheat, did you?"

"No."

"Steely…" Ray waved her up close. "No one else is to know about you. Me, you, and Nick. That's it."

"About me?" Steely eased back.

"That you're getting paid. Do you have any questions?"

"Just one. Does Mr. Keaton have to approve my hiring?"

"No. He doesn't have anything to do with this."

CHAPTER THIRTY-NINE

Keaton perched his feet on the corner of his desk forty-eight floors above them and chewed the end of a cigar. He would have lit the thing if the tower weren't equipped with the most sensitive smoke detectors ever made. He was one proud man.

Qualls bolted in, interrupting the euphoric moment. "Harry, I warned you about that pest."

"What has you worked up?" Keaton retorted, puffing the unlit Cuban.

"Did you know Dichiara ordered the account statements from Saint Stephen's?"

The tobacco dropped in Keaton's lap. His feet fell to the floor. "All of them?"

Qualls erratically darted around the desk. "Yeah. What if he links the accounts? We have over six hundred million floating around the world."

"It can't be all of them."

Qualls was unhinged. "Are you certain Wilkerson didn't get the account numbers?"

"Yes, I'm certain. He sets up the wires on my laptop. The numbers never leave me. They're locked up."

"I still can't find that stupid agreement you signed."

"Don't worry about it. Beatrice doesn't know it exists. And Nick has no idea what's in his hands."

"I still don't like him having the statements. What if he takes the assets?"

"You mean embezzle company funds? He'd go to jail."

Qualls grunted. "He'd be roadkill before he ever saw a jail cell. If this thing goes south, Chevoski would have a dozen cartels after him. Us too, for that matter."

"Don't tell me anything about cartels. Mr. Chevoski said they were legitimate businesses."

"They are now."

"They better be."

"What about the Swiss accounts? Doesn't Jason make those transfers?"

Keaton reclined confidently. "Yes, but I'm telling you he doesn't have the account numbers or the pass codes. I watch him shred the list every time he sends out the wires. I could leave the pass codes sitting on my desk. Nobody would even know what to do with them. What are they going to do? Search every bank in the world?"

"You're telling Chevoski."

"Why? Nick looks foolish trying to prove there's something wrong with the company. Nobody is paying any attention to him."

"Doesn't matter. The boss needs to know. Just in case the blind squirrel gets hit in the head with an acorn. Now call him."

CHAPTER FORTY

Nick powered down his desktop, pulled the string turning off the light, walked out, and shut the door behind him. Clicking the padlock, he gave it a few spins and glanced down at the floor. He scraped at a dark spot with his shoe. Just as he thought. Dried blood. His head was still sore from Cricket's assault. It wouldn't have been so bad if she hadn't worn a five-prong ring.

He went down to the lobby and outside for the short walk to his condo. He was out of the building, but his mind hadn't clocked out. Keaton had won. He picked the only bank in the Western Hemisphere with no online services. It would take a team of forensic accountants six months to get through all the accounts. The timing didn't matter. Keaton would never authorize hiring professionals to uncover a crime he committed. And there was no way Macini was asking a judge for a court order to investigate.

Every law enforcement agency with any kind of jurisdiction had already turned Nick down. He had made more enemies than he could count. He'd told the last guy with a government-issued badge pinned to his jacket that he was incompetent. The guy should have been glad Nick left it at name calling.

Nick darted across four lanes of traffic. Suddenly, his life wasn't worth three extra minutes. Headlights illuminated his body like a spotlight. Drivers, irritated they had to brake, sat on their horns. Cars swerved around him until he reached the sidewalk.

He was drained.

Eighteen minutes to go. One more block and then a straight path home. He waited on the corner to cross the pokiest light in town. His soaring pulse—a good thing—meant he wouldn't pass out right there on the curb.

He watched for any hint of a light change, but nothing happened. His heart sped up a few more ticks. The thought of jumping into the street crossed his mind. Cars would either hit him or stop. But he'd get moving again if he survived. He assessed the risk and stayed put. Cars passed the corner filled with people who wanted to get home as badly as he did.

A jogger complained, "I'm moving to Canada if they don't get this light fixed!" The jogger stayed steady, running in place. Less than a breath away, a man wearing a red cap passed the time by watching the blue dress impatiently jiggling in front of him. Nick hoped he wasn't a creeper. Straightening that guy out would take less than a minute. But he didn't have time for that tonight.

The light suddenly turned. The stick man lit on a pole meant "walk." The corner came to life. The crowd cheered. The jogger retained his US residency. Walking fast, Nick would be home in twelve minutes. The timing was tight but feasible. The capped man kept watch on the blue dress as it shifted with every lean-legged movement.

Sicko.

"Help!" screamed the lady in blue dress. "He took my purse!"

The capped man was also a thief.

The endorphins kicked in. Nick felt no pain from his bum knee. He hadn't sprinted that fast since college. This wouldn't be his first citizen's arrest. Last one occurred when he was seventeen, the night he walked home from a friend's house. Mrs. Yost, at 102 pounds, was no match for a 260-pound muttonhead. But she packed a powerful scream. Nick sneaked up on the guy, wrapped his arms around the unfortunate soul, picked him up off the ground a little too high, and dropped him a little too hard. The guy ended up in Ben Taub County Hospital for a month. Yost had a sprained wrist.

Donovan didn't nominate Nick for a good citizen award for his bravery since it wasn't the first time Nick had put someone in the hospital. It was his sixth.

The thief tossed the cap. But it wasn't hard to spot the only guy running with a sparkly clutch tucked in the back of his pants. He made it one more block before he looked back and saw Nick closing in.

People stared. Police were jammed with calls.

The thief pressed harder, taking a gutsy leap over the front end of a sedan and landing facedown flat on the asphalt. Nick pinned him down, placing a foot on his back. The thief struggled until he realized he wasn't going anywhere.

"You took something that doesn't belong to you."

"Get off me!" the thief complained. "Probably twenty bucks in that bag. Big deal. Let me up."

"I don't care if it's twenty dollars or two hundred million."

The crowd gasped.

Nick applied measurable pressure. "Someone worked for that money, and it doesn't belong to you!" He reached down to yank the guy up but missed the van following a few yards away. The barrel of a .38 eased out of a slit in the driver's window. One round whipped in Nick's direction.

The crowd screamed. Everyone hit the ground but Nick. He dropped the thief and spread eagle toward the van like he was secret service. The van screeched off. Nick ran to the street but could see nothing through windows tinted darker than the law allowed.

The crowd rose cautiously to their feet. Most were already on their cells conveying what just took place. The street quickly became a parking lot. Nothing was moving.

"I've been shot!" cried the thief.

"Stay down and be quiet," said Nick.

The crowd pushed in to observe.

"It was just a purse!" the thief whined. "I don't have a weapon!"

Nick lifted the thief off the ground, yanked the purse out of his hand, and passed it to the lady. "You got a bullet in your arm. It's not life threatening. Now shut up."

"I'm bleeding!" the thief whimpered. "I'm suing the shooter. Did anyone get his license plate?"

Nick held the man tightly by his jacket. "You gonna shut up or what?"

The thief pushed back. "I'm the victim here. Don't tell me what to—"

Nick lifted him a foot off the ground. "Quiet!" He then shoved him to the jogger. "Hold on to this twerp. HPD is coming up behind us." Then he rushed out into the street, squatted, picked up an empty shell case, examined it, and closed it in his hand.

Most people wouldn't be grinning after someone tried to take them out. He had made people nervous enough to do something stupid. "I can capitalize on this." Hyped, he dashed across the street back to the tower. Sleeping fell off his radar.

Minutes later, he stormed onto the fiftieth floor. The only light came from one partially closed door. Keaton sat perched in what Nick would still call "Hunter's chair." The view alone irritated him. A hard pounding on the door, rattling the hinges, startled Keaton.

"Nick, you almost busted down the door." Keaton viewed an array of self-portraits lined up across his desk. He picked up one in each hand.

"Would you like me to call maintenance?"

"Who threw you in a sticker bush?" Keaton held up another picture. "Do you think this one is better?" He placed the picture up next to his face.

"I'm thinking about what you'd be doing right now if they hadn't missed."

Keaton picked up a two-hundred-dollar pen and wrote "Use this one" on the back of the picture, making it his official company portrait. "Now, what's your problem, Nick?"

"They missed, Mr. Keaton."

"The projections?" He smiled. "They were higher than expected."

"The projection of the bullet."

"Bullet?" Keaton appeared anxious, avoiding eye contact.

Nick took the shell out of his pocket. Spun it on Keaton's desk. "Mr. Keaton, you almost had a murder investigation in your lap."

Keaton stuttered. "Murder?"

"Capital murder."

Keaton buttoned up his jacket. "I don't know anything about any murders."

"Then there were more. You're pulling your nails off your fingers. You should be afraid of what I'm about to do. It almost scares me." Nick scooped up the shell, turned, and left.

He speed walked home and slept like a baby.

CHAPTER FORTY-ONE

The far right of the lobby was the executive entrance. Steely had gone that way once before. Nick's corner office, as she remembered, was down the hall from the CEO's. Today, she'd have her picture taken for credentials to get past security.

Steely felt a tap on her shoulder.

"Hey, Steely." Erin was speaking softly.

"Hi, Erin. Are you feeling OK?"

"Peachy." Erin flopped down across from Steely. Her hair was mangled. Clothes disheveled. She dropped her designer bag on the floor, scattering an imported hairbrush under her seat. That bag had never touched the floor before. It either got its own seat, like it was a person, or hung on a portable hook the girl carried with her at all times. Erin stretched her legs into the aisle. Her hair mushroomed over her face, splitting across her nose. "I'm ticked."

"What's wrong?"

"I had the executive training job wrapped up."

"There's only one?"

"Only one left. Some tramp stole it. Mrs. Ray wanted me."

Ray had been overridden. She wanted Erin. Nick gave her Steely Paupher Hunter with no background check. This was a first. Steely never beat Erin out of anything. Never wanted to. Steely scooted to the edge of her seat, hoping Erin wouldn't feel the need to yowl when she gave her the news.

"Maybe a tramp didn't steal it," Steely whispered.

"Mrs. Ray rescheduled my orientation for today. I didn't get it. All I needed was some stupid background check."

"That's too bad, Erin." Steely reached for her purse and casually zipped up her employment contract, listing her as a paid executive trainee. Maybe this wasn't the best time to share.

"Father thinks she found out I got suspended in high school. Wasn't even my fault. You remember, right?"

"Perfectly."

"Cricket cheated on *my* science test," Erin pouted. "Not my fault she grabbed it off my desk."

"But Mrs. Koller pegged you as the cheater."

"Then that witch, Koller, got a promotion. The most unfair person I ever met. Well, at least I wasn't a snitch."

Steely nodded. "That's right, Erin. Cricket got an A, and you got summer school."

Erin pushed her hair back above her catty eyes. "The same thing is happening now."

"What?"

"It's not fair that some piece of trash got preferential treatment by doing vulgar stuff with one of the executives."

"No, she didn't!"

"Benita might as well say it." Erin made air quotes. "An executive decision. Hint, hint."

Steely leaned in. "Hint, hint—what?"

"A bunch of executive bull. I'm going to find out who did this! I'm furious! There are no more training spots until next year." She slouched and closed her eyes.

"I need to tell you something." Steely was going to get it out. Tell Erin sitting right there in the lobby. Let her pitch a fit, holler, roll on the floor, kick her legs up into the air, and get it over with.

"It's not right," Erin barked. "Just not right! Misleading someone like that. They deceive you, build your hopes up, and then dump you at the last minute. It's nothing short of emotional abuse. I'm filing a formal complaint. Maybe I'll sue!"

Steely shook her head. "Erin, I wouldn't do that."

"First, I'm telling that lying Benita Ray what I think about the way she conducts herself. Unprofessional, to say the least."

"Sometimes things just don't turn out the way we expect."

"At least things are going great for Cricket."

"Cricket?"

"Yeah, Nick Dichiara works here. Remember when you wrecked his car?"

"Scratched."

"Yeah, well he's crazy about Cricket. They're getting married."

Steely flung forward and slipped off her seat. She scrambled back up, shivering.

Erin continued babbling. "Nick wanted to help me with this absurd background check, but there wasn't anything he could do. It's company policy. No way around that."

Steely gasped for air.

"Nick asked Cricket to stay home instead of going to UT, so she could be with him. Told her she was the most amazing woman he ever met. Said he couldn't live without her. He wanted to get married immediately, but Cricket's holding him off until she can get a decent wedding. She practically lives in his condo. Decorated his bedroom. Might as well, since that's where they spend most of their time."

Steely muttered, "I don't believe it."

"It's true. I thought Nick was a 'waiter.' Guess not. Cricket just got back from a three-week trip, searching for the perfect spot for a destination wedding. Nick got himself in a mess while she was gone. Mr. Qualls threw him in a black hole."

Steely's mouth dropped. "Kidnapped him?"

"No, silly. He moved him out of his office into a closet. Mr. Qualls took Nick's office."

She scratched her head. "Nick and Cricket?"

"Cricket will get him moved back up. She has some major pull around here."

"She works here?"

"No. Her mother married one of Mr. Keaton's best friends. So she can do whatever she wants around here. Nick wouldn't have a job if Cricket hadn't stepped in to save him."

Steely squeezed her eyes together. "Cricket saved Nick?"

"Yeah, and he better keep her happy. Wait…" Erin sat up. "I just had a thought. Maybe Cricket can talk to Mr. Keaton for me."

"Nick and Cricket?"

"Oh, and I hate to be the one to tell you, but I got the accounts-payable job. Sorry, girl. Benita called me yesterday. She thinks I'll be perfect for it." Erin rested her chin on her folded hands, elbows on the arms of the chair. "I heard there were a few openings in housekeeping. See, Steely, you don't have my ambition. It's in my genes. My lineage always rises to the top. You can set us anywhere." Erin pointed. "We shoot right to the top."

Steely rolled her lips and said, "Erin, then go ahead and shoot right up."

"Oh, look," Erin gleamed. "Here comes my BFF, the Cricket!"

If Steely didn't need the job, she would have run out the revolving doors.

Cricket bulldozed her way through the crowd toward them. "Erin?" Cricket glared down at the girl crumpled up in the vinyl seat. "Are you drunk?"

"No. I had a nip, but no." She swooshed her hair back. "I was upset this morning."

"You look like dookie. You better get it together."

"Sure, Cricket." Erin gathered her purse and stood at attention.

"Now, let's see this cubicle of yours. I had to fight Benita to get you one with three sides."

"Thanks, Cricket." Erin smiled. "I couldn't tolerate an open space."

Cricket gawked at Steely. "Pauper? What are you doing here?"

Erin chimed in, "She's working in housekeeping."

Cricket smirked. "Perfect fit." Her belittlement was benign compared to what she just heard.

"Her 1950s hair looks better than yours, Erin." Cricket aimed her profile at Steely. "Nick needs to come to his senses, or he'll end up in housekeeping like you. But I bet you'd like doing a little housekeeping with Nick. Maybe play house in the broom closet?"

Steely lifted her head. "I've been told harassment isn't tolerated in this office. You need to quit. Or I'm filing a complaint."

"I don't work here, dimwit."

"One day you're going to say that to the wrong person."

"Pauper, one day you're going to learn to keep that sassy mouth shut." Cricket swung around and walked off. Erin wagged along with her through security.

Cricket whispered, "Don't tell anyone who she is. I want to be the one who gets Pauper fired."

Erin shrank back. "Cricket, why don't you leave her alone? Let her have the housekeeping job. She's had enough trouble."

Cricket sternly replied, "I'll leave her alone. Right after I get her fired. She better not try to mess with Nick either. He's off-limits to her."

"Nick's engaged to you. I don't think he would cheat, and neither would she."

Cricket cleared her throat. "She'd be dead if she does!"

Erin abruptly stopped.

Cricket nudged her forward. "It's just a figure of speech."

Erin looked back over her shoulder at Steely. Cricket cupped her arm and pushed her on.

Steely was exposed. Nick was marrying Cricket. Things were not going well.

CHAPTER FORTY-TWO

Steely said to herself, "Focus...focus...I have a job; let it roll off my back. I have to stop Nick from making the biggest mistake of his life. How can I stop him? He's a grown man. It's his decision. I'm staying out of it."

"Steely, did you say something?" Nick approached her.

She flew up. "Nick, you can't do it!"

He looked around. "You know?"

"People make dumb decisions all the time. Sometimes, they realize it before it's too late. I've done it myself. Your personal life is your own business."

"My personal life?" He looked around, confirming no one was near them.

"How can I stand by and let you destroy your life? You're too great of a guy—you're so..." *Kind, thoughtful, muscular—engaged to a cuckoo bird.* "I just can't let you do it."

"Steely, don't worry." He leaned down and whispered. "They wouldn't dare take another shot at me—"

"Somebody shot at you?"

245

"They missed."

"That's a toss-up to marrying Cricket."

He held up a hand. "Is she still telling people that? I'm not marrying her. We're not even friends."

"You're not?"

"No!"

"I thought you had lost your—who's shooting at you?"

"Let's go upstairs and talk."

Maneuvering through the executive entrance, he directed her with one hand, the other barely on the center of her back. Then they caught an elevator that wasn't going anywhere until he ran a plastic card across a reader.

The doors closed and then seconds later opened into a maze.

"This way." He wound her around panels sparkling with miniature lights. At the end of the path was a control box screwed to a wall. He put in a four-digit code, opened the lid, flipped a switch, and continued.

"Are we checking on some sort of electrical problem?" she asked.

"I'll explain when we get to my office."

The path narrowed. The tiny lights crawled to the ceiling. After several more turns, they reached the only standard light source on the floor: a small kitchen. Next to it was the fire escape, and adjacent to it was an insignificant door with an insignificant padlock restraining it.

Nick palmed the lock until it dropped open. He pulled on a skinny pine door that opened into cave-like darkness. If this were anyone but Nick, Steely would have tested the mace in her left pocket and run for her life.

What is he doing here?

The light from Nick's cell was used to locate a string attached to a naked forty-watt bulb. "Steely, this is my new office." He pulled out his chair and booted up his computer. He pointed to the smaller desk and chair butting up to his. "That's for you. Give me just a sec…"

Steely instantly sized up the eight-by-six room. No windows, in the hull of the building, behind the elevators. Two discarded desks, two discarded chairs. Each had a decent computer with a monitor. Abandoned by their makers, the cobwebs that had infested the room were harmless and provided no purpose except producing dust, like most everything else there. Boxes stacked at chest level left almost no floor space.

Mounted on the wall, behind Nick, was the head of a deer. The reproduction would have frightened a small child. He creepily watched her every move.

Stinkin' Erin was right.

"Nick? One question: why are you in a rathole?" This was no metaphor.

Nick jumped up. "Did you see a rat?"

"There are droppings."

Nick slouched back down. "They're only here at night, with the bats." He tapped on his keyboard.

"Do I really have a job?"

He looked up at her. "Yes, you do."

"The bats are chirping."

"They're above us, between the floors." Six numbers from a fob gained him access to JHI's most secure intranet site.

Even a first-year trainee could deduce the only logical reason Nick Dichiara was in a closet. Someone wanted him out. And if someone wanted Nick out, the person certainly would want her out.

Nick quit staring at the monitor and looked at her. "Steely, excuse me. I had to check the account balances. They're up again."

"You sound like you're disappointed. Isn't higher balances a good thing?"

"Please sit down and let me explain."

Steely dusted off the chair, glanced around the room, and sat.

"Thomas Qualls dumped me down here to intimidate me."

"Can he just do whatever he wants?"

"Just about."

"Nick, you're in trouble."

"Yes, but it's good trouble."

Steely scrunched her face. "That's an oxymoron."

"Not in this case."

"Why are you working in a utility closet? I smell pine cleaner."

"Did you sign your employment contract?"

"Yes, I don't think they can fire me unless I'm convicted of a felony."

Nick nodded. "Jack didn't want anyone afraid to speak up."

"What happened to this company?"

"Keaton hired Qualls right after I got here. Then a short time later, he promoted Qualls to executive vice president of acquisitions and mergers, supposedly for global expansion, which was never gonna happen. Then he talked Jack into appointing Qualls to the board. This was the beginning of the end. Hundreds of millions were then drained out of the company into some phony LLCs. Keaton held the board hostage to force Jack out. After that, the funds were funneled back in. Every day the balances go up." Nick pointed at the computer. "We have assets flooding our accounts."

"Jack sold his interest in the company to save it."

Nick tilted his head, surprised at her understanding. "Yes, the company would have cratered if he hadn't stepped back and allowed Keaton to fix the mess he created. How do you know this?"

"I've been putting bits of pieces together for over a year."

"I've been working for over—Mr. Keaton took total advantage of his position. I want him to know I'm on to him."

She perked up. "Are you?"

248

"Yes and no. I haven't convinced anyone to do anything about it."

Steely raised a brow. "You have nothing?"

"I have too much. The answers may be in those boxes behind you. They're filled with bank account statements we didn't even know existed. The problem is they're no help. Thousands of transactions passed through those accounts. It's almost impossible to track them. So I had to get creative. I had to find another way to get their attention." Nick checked his cell and then adjusted the deer.

Steely stared up at the deer. "Why is he looking at me?"

"Old buck will tell us what goes on when we're not here." He held up his cell. "Smile."

"Deer-head security app?"

"Yes, ma'am. How long do you think it would take to go through those?"

She knocked on a box. "Two years."

"What can you do in week?"

"Come up with a random selection." She pulled down the first box, popped it open, and took out a handful of large yellow envelopes. "I did this in college. It's like taking a survey. The margin of error should be less than five percent."

"OK. Do it. Maybe it'll help keep me out of prison."

She turned sharply toward him. "You're not kidding."

"I'm not the one going to jail over this."

Nick returned his focus to his keyboard. An airline boarding pass rolled out of the printer under his desk. He folded it quickly and tucked it in his pocket and looked back at Steely. "I'm going to be out for a little while." He took a deep breath, exhaling slowly. "This project should keep you busy enough."

She raised a brow, figuring he meant he'd be gone for an hour, maybe two. He didn't elaborate. And she didn't ask a follow-up question. She tore open the envelopes, lined them up on the floor, and began.

"This closet isn't so bad. Not nearly as bad as an office in a dark house on lockdown."

"Prostitution?"

She was baffled that he knew that.

"It's all over the news." He opened an e-mail, and his facial expression turned serious. "Keaton wants updated financials in the morning. Mr. Clayton and Mr. Denison are pressuring him."

"Is that bad?" She took her hands out of the box, stopping briefly.

Nick combed his fingers through his hair. "The financials will show the most profitable year ever. What they won't explain is the missing reserves—two hundred thirteen million dollars. Keaton won't get away with this. I'll dangle him off the top of this building and make him talk before that happens."

"That would be coercion. HPD can't use anything he says."

"I'd like to hang him off the top of the building until he starts flapping his tongue."

"You know embezzlement could get him a long sentence." She spread out a few more papers. "In the last twenty-five years, the top fifty largest corporate embezzlers received sentences as long as some murder convictions."

"Really? You've been studying corporate crime?"

"My dad. He's the reason I studied it." Steely unfolded a statement and looked closely at it.

Nick had his head in his monitor.

Steely quickly grabbed another envelope and took a glance at its contents. She ripped opened the next one and scanned down, pulled out another. She ran through ten of them. It was the same bank. No doubt about it. She didn't need to check the account numbers. The names on the accounts were something she hadn't forgotten.

The statements matched the ones her dad had hidden and the ones she'd found in the abandoned warehouse. For several minutes, she thought about the ramifications of what lay in her hands.

There was a tangible link from Fred Paupher's death to the JHI fraud.

She dumped out another box and spread out the envelopes. A new wave of questions sent her scrambling on the floor. She sat on folded legs and stared for a few seconds at what she had found.

This was a game changer. All those late-night hours she'd studied, learning things she didn't know she would ever use, were now the most valuable assets she had to offer on her first full-time job.

Studying account statements had been useless to Nick. They were priceless to her. Helping Nick sort out the fraud at JHI was linked to her dad's death. This connection was real. It was tangible. It was at her fingertips. Nick's previous corner office on the fiftieth floor had nothing on the rathole on five.

For several minutes, Steely struggled internally about sharing what she had found with Nick. Fred's character had already been butchered once. She didn't want that to happen again. But she either had to trust Nick or get out of there.

Steely gathered the statements and set the box back on top of the others.

"You done?" He scrolled down his computer. "I don't blame you. It's a mess."

She stood at the edge of his desk and crossed her arms. "I've seen these accounts before."

He slowly zeroed up at her, as if he'd misheard. "What?"

"My dad had statements from the same bank hidden in our attic."

"How would he have them? Jack Hunter didn't even have them."

"My dad was a good guy. He wouldn't have done anything wrong. Witnesses lie."

"You don't have to defend your dad. But where did he get them?"

"He was contracted by Flash Away to shred them. That's where he got them."

"Mr. Keaton hired them to work for JHI. Paid them way too much. And I don't think they delivered anything."

"Dad gave them back every cent they paid him."

"He knew something wasn't right."

"Sure did." She went back to the box and wadded a few envelopes together. "I don't need to open another box to tell you there are two hundred thirteen accounts at the Saint Stephen's Island Bank. Wires move two hundred thirteen million dollars in and out every ninety days. And I assure you, it's not the same two hundred thirteen million dollars. It's new money coming in and out," she said confidently. "Assets are transferred to Geneva. Whoever is doing this is laundering money."

He looked as if he were hit with hurricane-force winds. His eyes bulged. His mouth hung open. "You figured this out?"

"That much. Do you know what to do with it?"

"You have statements from Geneva? I don't know anything about Geneva."

"I'll e-mail you the account numbers tonight."

"You have the account numbers?"

"I had to dig through trash bags in a warehouse and watch a man give a kid a concussion to get them. But I have them. I'll e-mail them to you tonight."

"You did this in just two minutes."

She shrugged.

He focused back on the monitor, opened an e-mail, and scrolled for an airline confirmation. Another destination was added to his itinerary. The printer spit out a new boarding pass. He would be making two stops before circling back to US soil.

She wondered what his quick reaction on the keyboard meant.

"I know you're not going to hang Mr. Keaton off the top of the building. So what do we do?"

"Take a vacation. You earned some time off." He tucked the boarding pass in his pocket and looked over at her.

"I just got here."

A question she knew he wouldn't answer satisfactorily went through her mind: *What is he doing?*

"You'll know when you see it," Nick answered, before being asked. "I'm going to run out for a bit and then come back and take you to lunch."

She found his answer was satisfactory, for now.

CHAPTER FORTY-THREE

The faint sound of mariachi music played from speakers mounted along the colorful walls. The server one-handed the empty
plates and carted them off. Steely set her napkin on the table. Nick
pulled out a plastic card, which the server swiftly scooped up.

They stared at each other for a few seconds.

"Now let's talk about you," he said. "How are you?"

"Good," she said.

"I know you're good. Steely, you're always good. But really, how
are you?"

Steely was caught off guard. The "I'm good" answer always
put an end to the "How are you" question. Not with this man. He
meant it.

Her right hand quivered on the cleared table. She wished it
were in her lap, out of sight, and wondered why she'd put it on
the table. Her mom had always told her to keep her elbows off the
table. Then her hands would be invisible. If only she had followed
that etiquette. She inched her arm slowly away, but her progress
was halted when Nick put his hand on hers, holding it in place.

Suddenly, it was OK with her if they sat there till Jesus came. She was no longer moving.

"I know you're not a complainer," he said.

Her heart pounded.

"I'm so glad you came back," he said.

Her vocal chords froze. She wasn't trying to sing an opera, just utter a few simple words. But even a slight squeak wasn't manageable. The most observant man in the world would certainly be aware of her struggle.

"Are you all right?" he asked.

She nodded.

"You're the kind of woman…" He slowly lifted his hand, releasing hers.

She screamed inside.

Then she gasped for breath as if she'd swum so far out into the ocean she couldn't get back. Nick watched her agonize. Surely he couldn't guess what caused her distress. They were a man and a woman sitting together. And now he'd confirmed it.

For a few seconds, neither had words to express their respective thoughts. They stared at each other, saying nothing.

"What kind of woman do you think I am?" She poked at him with a spray of flirtation.

The elderly man and woman at an adjacent table adjusted their hearing aids well above normal. They chewed on pralines, listening to the intense conversation going on a few feet away.

Nick never made an accidental slip of the tongue. His words were pointed. "I know all about you, kid."

Her emotions ping-ponged from high to low. "Woman" then "kid"? It was torturous. "You don't know about my wild college days."

Why did I say that?

"Yeah, working three jobs is pretty wild behavior." He smiled.

The server brought him a receipt that needed his signature and a tip if he was giving one. He added the total and scribbled his signature. Steely purposely glanced down at the $21.53 tab with a $10 tip.

No wonder the servers fought for our table.

"People change," she said.

"Some grow better, some worse. You were your mother's caretaker after your father passed."

"Have you been stalking me?" she teased softly, with a grin.

"It doesn't take a stalker to know what you've been doing." He used a napkin to dab his eye. "You're transparent, not invisible."

Is he crying?

"I am?" She didn't try to be transparent. It was just what she was. Crystal clear.

This young lady related very well to this golden boy with blue blood running through his veins. But if there were genetic markers for loving, caring parents, DNA tests would have proved they were kin.

"Anybody else would have dumped Mrs. Hunter and run."

"That wasn't an option. She's my mother-in-law."

"How is it? Living with her in your home?" He held up a hand. "You don't have to answer that. One thing I know about her is she's never phony. You always know how Mrs. Hunter feels—'cause she's constantly telling you. One day though, I hope she realizes you're better to her than any daughter she could have birthed."

His assessment stunned her to silence.

He continued. "If I searched the world, I wouldn't find anyone like you."

"You wouldn't?" she squealed.

"No, I wouldn't."

The elderly lady had heard enough. She got up and poked Nick's shoulder, her husband beside her. "You better not let her get away."

Her husband agreed.

Nick respectfully stood. "Ma'am, we're coworkers."

"Hogwash," the woman said as they walked off. Even strangers had recognized the difference between a date and a business lunch. Friendship and romance. Even if no one else was ready to admit it.

Nick flashed a boyish grin. "We better start walking back."

Externally, Steely was reserved. But that was not the case internally.

They quietly made the five-minute walk back to the tower. Nick stayed close. She hoped it would always be that way.

CHAPTER FORTY-FOUR

Candy poked Kristi. They watched the couple make their way through the lobby as if they were a security threat. Candy slid off her chair, held on to a side desk, trying to get one last look at the couple. She scrambled back up and stretched her neck over the desk.

Kristi, on the other end of the counter, had less visibility. "See anything else?"

"Looked flirtatious to me." Candy tucked her blouse back into her skirt. "Something funny is up with those two."

Kristi glanced over at the executive entrance, where the couple had disappeared. "I don't see anything funny. They're just walking and talking. Girl, you gettin' crazy."

"I have information," Candy said pretentiously, "that I can't disclose."

"Oh no, you don't!" Kristi screeched. "Out with it, now."

A man in a blazer with gold buttons waited impatiently for someone at the desk to acknowledge him. "This is nonsense," he scolded. "Make a call and announce me to—"

"Sir, we have a problem here," Candy remarked. "Please take a few steps back." She pointed to a yellow line taped on the floor. "We'll be with you in a minute."

The man checked his watch. He took a step backward, almost to the line. But he wasn't crossing that line. He wasn't completely complying. Several people gathered behind the man. He checked the time again and used his cell.

"I promised not to tell," said Candy.

Kristi whispered, "You know those extra fifteen minutes you take at lunch with Rick?"

Candy said, "My friend Tiffany works in HR. She talked to a girl who knew that girl in high school." She glanced at the executive entrance and then back at Kristi. "She wouldn't reveal her source, but it's reliable information. Beef Ribs was driving his new one-of-a-kind sports car a few years ago. That girl was driving intoxicated and smashed into him—almost totaled it."

"She's a drunk?"

"Yep. Almost caused him to run over a little girl on the sidewalk."

"She looked so innocent." Kristi shook her head. "Why would he have anything to do with someone like that?"

"Looks can be deceiving."

The phone buzzed and lit up another line. They were all blinking now.

Kristi picked up. "JHI Tower. May I help you?"

The man stomped back to the counter. "Young lady, why am I waiting here like a dummkopf?"

Candy righted herself. "Sir, we don't use that kind of language here."

The phone beeped. Candy reached for the receiver. The man knocked the phone off the counter, disconnecting all the calls. "I'm going through security right now." He glared at them, sounding as if he was chewing on gravel. "Which one of you wants to risk her life to stop me?"

The waiting line had doubled. The crowd watched Candy's bold stand against a force three times her size. "Sir, don't be coming in here acting like some bully threatening us." Candy pointed in his face. "We'll have you tossed out of here. Now, get back in line like everyone else."

The man's bushy brows shook below a slash mark on his head. His thick fingers pressed down on the desk with enough force to take him over it. "I can have you eliminated with one phone call."

The crowd gasped.

Kristi caught the attention of a security officer. He could read the distress signal in her expression and rushed over. "Is there a problem here?" He was even more concerned when he recognized the problem. "Mr. Chevoski, sir."

Chevoski read from a plastic badge and said mockingly, "*Candy* was having difficulty announcing my arrival."

"Please come with me, sir. I'll take you right up to see Mr. Keaton."

Chevoski taunted, "Candy dear, don't forget where we left off. I'm a man of my word."

Security escorted Mr. Chevoski through the executive entrance like he was royalty.

"I'd feel safer in prison with felons," Kristi whispered.

"Probably where some of these people need to be."

"Why does the CEO want to see that thug?"

"I've got one foot out the door. If he comes back out here talking all crazy, I'm gone." Candy went for her cell and tapped in a number.

"Who you calling?"

"My source in the executive suite. I'll know all about that crazo in about two minutes. Then I'm reporting him."

"To HR?"

"HPD. He threatened us."

"Sure did." Kristi glanced back, making sure he was still gone.

CHAPTER FORTY-FIVE

S teely pulled up close to the garage. She climbed out of the car, retrieved a recycling bin from the curb, and set it on the front steps. Then she headed back to the car for a grocery sack. She still hadn't told Bea about her new job. There was no easy way to announce she was working for the enemy. Bea was doing well. She seemed content, almost happy. And Steely did not want a relapse. It was a scary thing when Bea quit drinking iced tea and watching TV nonstop. The thought of Bea relapsing halted Steely from telling her yesterday. It'd be worse if Bea found out on her own and accused Steely of keeping another military secret.

Halfway to the front door, a pop rang out loud enough to send two squirrels scrambling up a tree. The neighborhood kids set off firecrackers a couple times a year. They seemed to forget the city ordinance allowing fireworks applied to the Fourth of July and New Year's Eve. Today was neither.

Steely checked Mrs. Yost's yard for her granddaughter or her friends and then glanced down the street. No one was causing any mischief. She dropped the sack, ran to the front door, pushed it open, and hollered, "Miss Bea?"

"I got him!" Bea, with her pistol in tow, shifted her muumuu from the bedroom to the living room.

Steely went for control of the firearm. Bea didn't resist her, as Steely carefully removed Bea's finger from the firing mechanism. "Miss Bea, is someone in here?"

"Not anymore," she said satisfactory. "He won't bother me again. I decimated him."

"Did you call nine one one?"

"They won't come out for cockroaches. I checked."

Steely opened the chamber, dumped out the bullets, and closed it. "Miss Bea, you can't shoot cockroaches with a three-fifty-seven. This gun is only for life-and-death situations. You can't exterminate bugs with it."

"Come see, Miss Priss." Bea marched Steely to the bedroom that she didn't like to go in. Bea's assessment was correct. The cockroach was dust. "I blew him away," Bea said, proudly.

Steely looked intently at the half-dollar hole in the wall. She shook her head. "Miss Bea, two squirts of roach spray—that's all you need: two squirts."

"That guy could guzzle that spray, burp, and keep on going. It wouldn't even make him drowsy. He wasn't going to get the best of me. This was personal between me and him."

"Personal? With a cockroach?"

"He's been tormenting me ever since I got here. I smashed him with a broom three times. He flipped me a leg, crawled a wall, spread his wings, and glided down after me. One night I woke up, and he was sleeping on my pillow!" Bea angled a foot toward the bug and proudly stated, "I won the war! He won't be tormenting me again."

Steely opened the drawer beside the bed, set the gun inside, and closed it. "Miss Bea, you can't shoot at anything again unless it's a life-threatening situation. A cockroach is nasty, but not life threatening. You have to follow the rules, or I'll have to take the gun away."

"Huh."

"The only time you can shoot is if someone breaks into the house. Don't shoot if someone is in the yard. Or if they knock on the door. You don't shoot. Only if they break inside the house. Then you can shoot. OK?"

Bea followed Steely to the den, grumbling.

"If Mrs. Yost was home, HPD would be knocking on the door. They're arresting you next time."

"That nosy old woman needs to mind her own business. What is she, a hundred?"

"She's your age."

"Huh." Bea shuffled to the kitchen.

Shaking her head, Steely went back outside and picked up the bag and the bin.

"That girl thinks she's the boss of me," she spouted.

"I can hear you," Steely yelled back, coming inside.

"Good! I hope you didn't buy any more of that stale bread."

"It's not stale. It's only a day old."

"It tastes like it's a month old."

"We can toast it."

Steely placed two loaves of bread and two blocks of expired cheese on the table. She placed the recycle bin beside the wastebasket.

"Listen here, I don't care if you recycle. But don't be buying me any of that recycled stuff," Bea said. "I want new."

"Why? It's good for the environment."

"People let their dogs poop on newspapers. I'm not wiping my tush with anything recycled with dog poop."

"Miss Bea, I would imagine they want only clean paper." Steely coughed. "What's that smell?"

"I fixed blackened chicken."

"You cooked food?" she asked.

"I used the chicken tenders you bought on the highway. Sit and eat." Bea set a plate on the table.

"You made me a plate?"

"I do plenty of things for people, Miss Priss. I'm a nice person."

Steely unwrapped the foil from the dish and jabbed a fork into the meat. She examined the dark specimen, lifted the fork, and sniffed.

"Don't forget to say your prayers."

Definitely not telling her today. I might end up like that roach.

The meat was dark even before it was fried to a crisp. Almost 90 percent of the protein that entered Steely's digestive system was chicken. This wasn't chicken. She was certain of that. And Bea's smeller was broken. They had ten packages of the meat in the freezer. The rancher they bought it from, along the highway, did not sell them chicken. But whatever varmint it was, they were eating it. She chomped down on a slice. "It's nice and chewy."

Bea leaned back against the sink. "Maybe it's the stuff they're feeding chickens these days."

"What stuff?" Steely held her breath and attempted to consume another chunk.

"You know, all that organic stuff and then letting them run around."

"You mean free ranging?"

"I bet they're feeding them tofu. Roaming around with tofu in their belly. That'll make a chicken taste funny."

"How much was this meal?" Steely poked at the gamy texture.

"I figured from the stickers you put on everything. Tofu chicken, ninety-nine cents; peas, fifty cents; carrots, thirty-five cents; salt, five cents; flour, twenty-five cents; cayenne pepper and other spices, twenty-five cents; sugar, ten cents. I didn't put it in a calculator."

"Two forty-nine. We're under budget. I like tofu chicken."

"I bet you do, cheapskate. This brings back memories for me. It's what the poor people in my family used to eat."

"I doubt they ate this." Steely snickered.

"Well, you better get used to it—since we're poor." Bea turned on the faucet, rinsed out a rag, and wiped the stove. Then she plugged up the sink with the rag. She turned on the water and squirted in liquid. Bubbles formed.

"What'd you do today?"

Steely didn't answer.

Bea shut off the water, turned around, and stared. "I asked you a question."

"What did you do today?" asked Steely.

They stared at each other for a few seconds.

"What'd you do?" Bea said sternly.

Steely stretched over the table toward Bea. "What's that around your neck?" It wasn't Bea's standard pearls.

Bea lowered her chin.

Steely leaned in. "What is that?"

"This place is a fleabag." Bea tossed another rag into the water. "I have to use protection."

"You're wearing a flea collar?" said Steely in a high pitch. "They're for animals, not people."

"Huh."

Steely watched her affluent mother-in-law, in a muumuu, wearing a flea collar matching the one Fur Ball wore daily. Beatrice Hunter didn't know it, but she didn't have flea bites. There were no fleas in the house. Unless Bea rolled around in the front yard for hours at a time, she wasn't getting fleas. What Bea had was a nervous itch.

"Are you going to tell me what you did today? Why is it sometimes you won't shut up, and sometimes I have to drag stuff out of you?"

"I found a job. I started working today."

Bea glared. "You pouring coffee again?"

"No."

Stern-faced Bea said. "Is this job legal? I'm not bailing you out of jail."

"Miss Bea?"

"Don't act like that's a silly question." Bea leaned back on her arms. "You have a shady résumé, little girl."

"It's legal."

"Then they're desperate."

"They're not desperate." Steely bit into another piece of meat.

"You can't adequately process a prospective candidate that fast. You need time to check personal references, job history, testing... Then comes a background check, drug test. Takes a couple of weeks at least."

That screening was her idea. "That's what they said at first."

"I don't care what they told you." Bea pitched a wadded paper towel into the trash. "I wouldn't trust them."

"I'm working as an executive trainee."

"Huh, you won't make a plugged nickel for six months." Bea turned back to the sink, dunked a dish into the water, and scrubbed.

Steely set her fork on the plate and then took it to the sink. "I'm working at JHI," blurted Steely. "I'm getting paid."

Bea twisted around.

Steely braced for her reaction. "Are you OK with that?"

Bea paused and then said, "JHI?"

They were silent for a few seconds.

"What do you think?" Steely pressed. "They're paying me a great sign-on bonus."

"Is it two hundred seventy-five million dollars? 'Cause that's what Harry Keaton owes me."

"It's a little short of that. Nick Dichiara forced them to pay me. We had lunch today."

"I sure like that boy. I need to call Nancy. She must have called a dozen times."

Bea snickered. "I wonder what Benita said about Nick's breaking the rules."

"I don't know, but she sure thinks you could run the place."

"She's the most intuitive woman I've ever met." Bea pulled the rag out of the sink, draining the water. "Come on. We need to get you fixed up." She tossed her apron on the table and pushed a chair toward the bathroom.

"Wait. What? You're excited about me working with Nick? You weren't this excited when I married your son."

"You're not marrying my son. Now get moving! First thing, I'm giving you a hot-oil treatment for that ratty-looking hair."

"My hair's not ratty." Steely weaved her fingers through her locks.

"Then you're getting a facial and a mani-pedi.

"A pedi? *You're touching my toes?*"

"No daughter-in-law of mine is going around looking raggedly. I'll fix you up, and then you're off to bed for some beauty rest." Bea jammed the chair into the bathroom. "Get in here!"

"It's still daylight." Steely squeezed in the chair, wedging her legs between it and the vanity.

"Sleep is as important as makeup. We have to get rid of those puffy bags under your eyes." Bea trotted off to her bedroom, grabbed a flowered zipped bag, and laid the contents out on the counter.

"I don't have bags." She felt her face.

"I'm patting those down with guacamole." Bea took off for the kitchen. "Stay put."

"Can I have some tortilla chips, please?"

"Nope!" Bea brought back a small bowl of guacamole and pushed in behind Steely. Nobody was getting out of there in a hurry.

Steely dipped a finger in the bowl.

"Quit eating that!" snipped Bea.

"Ah! It's got a kick to it!" Steely fanned her mouth with her hand. "Miss Bea, I didn't know what you would think about me having lunch with Nick. Sure didn't think it'd get a makeover."

"You didn't cheat on my son, did you?"

Steely twisted her head up at Bea.

Bea turned her back around. "Do you think my son is in heaven eating PB and Js?"

"I don't think they eat—"

Bea whispered, "Did he kiss you?"

"Of course not. He's not like that."

Bea flung her head back. "We might have to have one of those talks."

"Oh no, we don't!"

"Well, I don't know…"

"I'd have sense enough to know if it was a date."

"Did he hold your hand?"

Steely wrinkled her nose.

Bea straightened up. "Let me explain. Hand holding is a crossover."

"A crossover?"

"From a no-touch business meeting to a date. We had our first date."

"We?"

"From now on, the way you look should be your top priority. You're a woman, aren't you?"

"I'm a serious, well-educated woman. I don't need to manipulate someone with the way I look."

"Don't you understand marketing?" Bea wiped Steely's face with a moist cotton ball.

"Yes, actually I minored in marketing."

"Huh! A kid with a lemonade stand has enough sense to know it's all about the presentation. When was the last time someone came up to you and said, 'Awww, look at that beautiful brain? Steely, you're so smart. I just want to help you'?"

"Where'd you learn this stuff?"

"Common sense."

"I don't think—" Steely felt her face.

"Stop!" Bea screamed. "Don't touch your face. There's bacteria on your hands!"

"It's my bacteria."

"You want to look like you're going through puberty?"

"It's my skin."

"And you're going to be the only one looking at it if you don't stop."

Steely moved her hands safely to her lap, where bacteria didn't matter. Bea scrubbed up to her elbows. Steely knew better than to smile. You didn't smile when Bea was serious.

"Would you like my medical history and insurance card?"

"Be quiet or I'll hurt you." Bea dabbed a cotton ball, soaked in pink liquid, around Steely's face and repeated the process with three different solutions, clearly killing every speck of unwanted bacteria.

"Where'd you learn how to do this?"

"The Grey Canyon Beauty Shop. I was running it when I was twelve."

"You got a job at twelve?"

"Started at ten. The beauty shop was attached to my parents' general store. I'd go every day after school. It was fun."

"This makes you happy, doesn't it?"

"Will you quit moving your mouth?"

Beatrice Hunter cleansed for the next forty-two minutes. Steely just listened, since moving her mouth was forbidden, while her face was slathered in mayonnaise. Bea rattled on.

"Everyone worked. Nobody gave a flip about your age. Rich, poor, and everyone in between. If you planned on eating, you worked. You played too. But you worked first, so you could play and eat."

Steely finally had to chime in. "You get fired here if they find out you're a day short of sixteen."

"Quiet." Bea patted her face back down. "It's a shame. The only people hiring kids now are criminals."

Steely stared blankly at Bea in the mirror. *How'd she know that?* Bea flew around from making ludicrous assumptions to wise statements and everything in between.

"Harry Keaton has been a thief since he was five. We had to watch him every time he came in the store. He'd stuff his pockets with sodas, candy, anything else he could get away with. Older kids would get him to steal for them, so they wouldn't get caught. You can't compare that to what he's done now. One day he's going to get back all the trouble he's caused. You watch and see."

Steely hoped that was the case. This was not the time to add accelerant to the disdain Bea had for Keaton. Informing her about a connection to the accident might cause her to drop dead right there on the bathroom floor. Or load up the gun and do something that would put him in the grave and her in lockup.

She did as ordered and kept quiet.

CHAPTER FORTY-SIX

The whites of Nick's eyes were now red. He'd never had eye-strain before, not even when pulling all-nighters in college, studying for exams. He printed out the transactions for the day, stopping at twelve dozen pages and carefully spreading them across his desk. The daily wires were multiplying. Every transaction was automated. Preset, in motion. That was the only way someone could float that many wires in twenty-four hours. And it happened every working day. Monday through Friday. The assets went from JHI to Saint Stephen's to Geneva. Some leaving out JHI and going straight to Saint Stephen's and then off to the Swiss slopes.

The company did not *need* to send that many wires. JHI was a wholesale operation. Only large sums in fewer transactions should be transferred, not all the nickels and dimes shifting around, like they were a retail establishment. And nothing should be going to Geneva.

But there were bigger questions: Whose assets were coming into JHI? And whose assets were going straight to Saint Stephen's? The company was the pinnacle of success. It'd take some funny math to say they earned revenue of $213 million per quarter. This was money laundering on steroids. A small-time hoodlum couldn't do this. Certainly not anything Keaton could navigate. He was a pawn.

Keaton had been questioned before. He couldn't explain anything in a language anyone could understand—because it didn't make any sense.

Nick no longer cared. He was backed into a corner. And he sure wasn't going to stay there. The only thing he could do was take a risk that was much more life threatening than interrupting a robbery in an alley in the middle of the night. This time he had more than grit. He had account numbers and pass codes.

He grabbed the phone, checked the time, and then set it back in place. The banks had closed hours ago.

Pressed and dry-cleaned, Jason came in and positioned himself into Steely's chair. He propped his loafers on Nick's desk. He'd apparently torn himself away from his cappuccino maker long enough for a visit with his battered pal.

I'm going to knock that "all leather" stamp off the bottom of his shoes.

"Nick, let's grab some dinner before everything closes."

"Not yet," Nick said, refusing to look up.

Do I start with facts or speculation? They're probably the same.

He gripped the papers between his fingers. "Not one subsidiary formed in the last ten years has ever been profitable. Not one. Then suddenly they all have a positive cash flow. How do you explain that?"

Jason dropped his feet. "Profits are good. Don't have to explain it. Stockholders don't fire CEOs because they're too profitable. Nick, don't let your career go down the toilet over this."

"The wires are spreading like a plague."

Jason scanned the room. "Maybe this dust is getting to you. More revenue is not a plague."

"I found two hundred thirteen million dollars in two hundred thirteen accounts unknown to Mr. Denison."

"You did what?" He stirred, swishing his arms back and forth. "Bet we're getting bigger bonuses this year." He calmed.

"Jack didn't know about these accounts. How does your CFO not know about them? There's never been a transaction, except for the initial deposits opening the accounts about a year ago. These were our reserves. Moving assets without a detailed explanation is a big fat no."

"This is a huge company. Assets are moved around from one sub to another all day long. It's standard business practice. You're overreacting, as usual."

Nick walked around his desk, rubbing his head. "My limbic system is about to blow a fuse. Sending two hundred thirteen million to accounts your CFO didn't know existed is not an acceptable business practice. It's misappropriation of funds. What are we doing sending thousands of wires? Then he lumps them together and diverts a million here and a million there."

"I don't know anything more than what I'm told. Transfer the assets. I tap a few keys and keep it moving." Jason motioned toward the door. "Come on, let's get a burger. What's that burger place you like?"

Little buddy, you're about to lose your appetite. "Here's a perfect example: INS83, LLC." Nick picked up an account statement and tossed it back on his desk. "This partnership is only a few days old. We have no information on it. There's over eight million sitting in this account. What is this?"

"Pocket change," touted Jason.

Nick shook his head. "That's two and a half percent of the company assets. Margin of error is one percent, not two and a half. Any CFO would be incompetent losing two and a half percent of the company's liquidity. Good thing I'm not incompetent. This is criminal."

"Criminal? There's probably just a miscalculation. Now, print that thing up for Mr. Keaton, and let's get out of here. I'm hungry."

"Calm down. It's printing." Five pages slid out of the printer. Nick shook the pages together, placed a clip on the top left corner, opened a large envelope, and shoved them inside. "The company's been scrubbed—cleaned up, like the crisis never happened."

Jason stuck his hands in his pockets. "Looks like Mr. Keaton turned things around."

"Camouflaged assets." Nick powered off his computer. "Who's helping him?"

Jason squirmed. "I don't know what you mean; lots of people help him every day. He runs this place."

"Who's calling the shots? Keaton's so inept he can't even send a wire. Qualls looks like a hit man."

"He's OK."

"Qualls couldn't make change for a dollar. Have you ever tried to have a conversation with him? Why'd Hunter let him in?"

"I hear he had a rough childhood. His father abused him."

"His father died before Qualls was born. I know who rose from the dead, and it wasn't his dad."

"How do you know that?"

"At thirteen, he was the prime suspect in his mother's brutal death."

"Didn't he pass a background check?"

"He was never arrested or charged. You're cozying up to a hit man."

Jason fidgeted, tapped on the desk, and headed for the door. "I do what I'm told, and I mind my own business. That will keep me out of trouble."

Nick climbed up on his chair and pulled the string, turning off the light.

"The company's on solid ground."

"Uh-huh, and they give to widows and orphans."

274

"I think they did give to—"

Nick slammed the door. "Jack's accident wasn't an accident."

Jason became sullen. "You've lost your mind. Are you just going to make stuff up?"

"There's physical evidence. Jack and David were murdered." Nick locked the room and faced Jason. "I'm sure you've overheard things you shouldn't have heard, seen things you shouldn't have seen. You know things you shouldn't know."

Jason couldn't stand still. He was visibly shaken up. "Nick, if there were any proof Mr. Keaton had anything to do with Mr. Hunter's accident, he'd be in jail. This time, Nick, you're dead wrong about Mr. Keaton!"

Nick replied, "I'm not wrong about Mr. Keaton. And I'm not dead—yet."

CHAPTER FORTY-SEVEN

Keaton held up the report, kissed it, and set it carefully down on his desk. He opened a drawer, extracted a bottle, and poured champagne into a glass. He toasted himself and drank. He was one proud man. Yesterday, analysts touted JHI stock as a "strong buy," sending the price soaring to an all-time high. But wealth and success weren't enough for Harry Keaton. He wanted a legacy. That meant a name change. Every piece of letterhead, every envelope, pen, picture, and sign—especially the one flashing on the top of the building—had to go. Jack Hunter had been replaced. Now he was being erased.

Outside his office, Donna tiptoed into the suite late again. Just yesterday, Keaton chewed on her for being three and a half minutes tardy. Five minutes would surely get her a tongue-lashing. She put her bag away and powered up her computer. She would have been in the clear if the machine hadn't made that awful chime.

"Donna!" hollered Keaton.

"Yes, sir?" she replied from her desk. "I'll stay late."

"Just get Pierce in here. I need to see him!"

"Yes, sir. Calling him now."

She reached him on the first try. But it took Pierce Thibodaux forty-five minutes to comply with Keaton's urgent request and ride up four floors.

"Good morning, beautiful," Thibodaux said, approaching her. "Is Harry still here, or have they hogtied him and hauled him off?"

Donna half cupped her mouth. "He's been calling for you since I got here. He's in a rare mood. Maybe he won't scream at you today."

"No chance of that happening." Thibodaux winked and then blasted into Keaton's office. "What's the big emergency, Harry?"

"I'm the CEO of this company," he said, toasting.

Thibodaux shook his head. "That's a constant nightmare."

Keaton ignored him and motioned for Pierce to sit.

"Nope. I won't be here long." Thibodaux checked his watch. "You have five minutes."

"Did you see Nick's report?"

"Yep."

Keaton's chest swelled. "I'll be up for CEO of the year. I've done the impossible. No one could pull this company out of the disaster it was in but me."

"No one else could put it in one either."

Keaton continued ignoring Pierce. "We've crossed over to a new horizon. It's time to put away the past."

"I'd like to put away the present," Pierce said, irritated.

"Under my leadership, we'll have a great future."

"You have three minutes fifteen seconds."

"Long after I retire, I want to be remembered." He angled the chair toward the window and gazed out. "I want to be remembered every time someone drives past this building."

"Like the throw-up virus? You got it."

"For me to be effective, to the maximum of my ability, there must be a name change."

"Change it. I was sick of hearing your name anyway."

Keaton arched his head toward the clouds. "I'm changing the name of the company to Harry Keaton Industries—HKI!"

"*Hicky?* You might as well name it sh—" Pierce bit on his bottom lip. "You're an arrogant, self-absorbed old man who thinks he's entitled to what someone else worked over twenty-eight years to create. And with one report you think the company should be named after you?"

"I'm in control here. The board will do whatever I want."

"You're full of bullsh—" Pierce stopped and then burst out, "Bull sweetie!"

"Is that Cajun?"

"You put this company in some kind of bull sweetie."

Vessels swelled in Keaton's neck. "I don't know what you're saying, but I don't like the sound of it."

Thibodaux snapped his fingers. "You're going to prison, not paradise. See, Nick has all this bullsh—sweetie figured out. Didn't he tell you? Oh, maybe it was a surprise? Oops. Well, since it's out— Nick knows everything."

"He should."

"This was one big swindle, and we know it. He should?"

Keaton replenished his glass. "Maybe you need to listen to yourself."

Pierce made a fist. "What are you talking about?"

Keaton smiled. "Nick knows everything. He prepared the report that trapped Jack. I'm helping him stay out of jail by locating the assets and sending them back to company accounts. He shouldn't have messed with the assets. That's criminal."

"I was right about you. You're dirty enough to set up Nick. It won't work. I'll defend Nick until the day I die."

"Mr. Thibodaux, are you forgetting who you represent? Defending Nick, who embezzled company assets, would be a conflict of interest. You must defend the company."

Pierce said, "This was your plan all along. Denison gets sick. Jack holds the CFO post for Nick. You send me on vacation. Jack has an accident. Just a remarkable concurrence of events. A lunar tetrad."

"Be careful. You could go down with Nick. If anything goes amiss, Nick had his hand in everything. You took off when all this went down." He held two fingers together. "You guys are tight. Right?"

"You're going to fall into your own trap. You'll spend the rest of your life in prison."

Pierce stomped past Donna. He took his cell out of his pocket, poked at the numbers, and held it to his ear. "I'm on board." He hopped into an open elevator.

Keaton barked on the phone.

Donna looked curiously at Keaton's door still swinging and then back at the elevator's closing. She kept her head down. She whispered, "Did he call Mr. Keaton 'sweetie'?"

CHAPTER FORTY-EIGHT

His original plan to head straight from his condo to Bush Intercontinental Airport was nixed. Nick was wide-eyed by 4:00 a.m. Exhaustion is what he should have felt, but he was hyper, not the least bit tired. Playing out his every move for the next two days over in his mind like a big-screen drama had energized Nick. And he especially liked the ending when the good guys won. He hoped that would be the case in real life.

The airport was less than an hour from his condo and about the same from the JHI Tower. His flight wasn't lifting off until ten. He could stop by his office, run a report of any overnight transactions, and confirm the routine wires hadn't mysteriously halted and the assets hadn't disappeared. It was possible to get in and leave before Steely arrived. She'd have too many questions that he did not want to answer, especially if she saw his suitcase and carry-on. If anyone deserved to know what was going on, it was Steely. But for now, not knowing was her—and his—life insurance.

He took a shower and went to his closet. The rack of suits hanging on the left was bypassed for a pair of jeans and the cotton pullover. He laced up a pair of running shoes, picked up a light-weight jacket, and went to the front door to fetch a small suitcase he'd packed the night before. There were only two sets of clothes in his bag. If he were not back in three days, wearing dirty clothes would be the least of his worries.

The intruder alarm was set. He rolled out the bag and hit the stairs. Getting a taxi in front of his condo at five in the morning wasn't a problem. The hotel facing his condo had cabs lined up, waiting their turn, 24-7. He whistled, and the next one raced over. Nick got in and explained his plans to the driver. The cabbie didn't mind taking Nick a few blocks to the JHI Tower when promised the long haul to the airport and a cushy tip.

The cabbie bore down on the accelerator. He never braked until he reached the tower. The driver offered to hold Nick's bag, but he declined. That bag wasn't leaving Nick's sight. The cabbie swung across the street and waited as ordered.

The night-shift officer waved Nick past the barriers to the executive entrance. Nick was relieved to see he was not yet on the security watch list. He swiped his key card and shot up to the fifth floor. The path to his office was routine until he took the last turn. The door was open. The light was on. This wasn't the time to have a brawl and get security involved, but someone was in there. He propped his suitcase against the wall, veered around a corner, and dove in.

Steely jumped back. Papers shot out of her hands. "Nick, I didn't hear you."

"I didn't mean to scare you." He stooped to help her pick up the mess. "I just didn't expect you to be here."

"What are you doing here?" She crouched on the floor and continued to gather the papers.

"I was about to ask you the same thing." He helped her up and went back for his suitcase.

"I came in a little early."

"A little early?" Nick set his bag by his desk. He hung the jacket over the luggage, hoping she didn't notice. But she did. "Didn't Benita tell you not to be here at odd hours?" He booted up his desktop.

She glanced up on the wall. "That deer's a gossip," she said, casually putting the papers back in a box.

"Don't do as I do," he said seriously. "You have to protect yourself."

She circled around him. "No suit today?"

He jotted quickly on a notepad and held it up. "Be careful what you say. I think we're bugged." He mouthed, "Information is getting around way too fast." He scrolled his computer. The assets were still there.

She panned the room and mouthed, "Where are you going?"

He wrote, "Don't ask."

She mouthed, "Are you stealing the assets?"

He went around his desk and put his head next to hers. His five o'clock shadow brushed her face. "The assets were already stolen. I have this under control. Just be safe and keep your eyes open."

She cleared her throat and breathed in his ear. "Don't go."

"I have to do this."

He began to move away. She pulled him back. "We'll figure out another way. Please, you don't have to go."

Nick was flushed, his breathing rushed. "I found the reserves in Saint Stephen's. They are the exact amounts in the accounts you gave me in Geneva."

"You accessed them?"

"Yes, I had the pass codes." He spoke with more expression. "There's over four hundred million floating around. This is much larger than JHI."

She rubbed her chilled arms.

Nick placed his hands on hers and whispered each minty word. "Taking away their assets will be worse than jail time. Prison is nothing more than a reunion to these creeps." He waited for her to respond.

She didn't.

He cleared his throat. Then he went back to the keyboard and logged off his desktop. It was staying put. His handheld device was making the trip.

Steely stood by. She crossed her arms, hands wrapped tightly around elbows, and whispered, "Did you warn Jason?"

"Every day for the last six years," he said loudly. "I'll send him a text." He tapped the screen on his cell.

Steely whispered, "Every move you make will get riskier. We can figure out another way. Give me one week. Who knows what we can do with an entire week."

"The risks are layered. I'll get through them one step at a time."

"Do your parents know?"

He raised his voice. "My parents don't know anything I'm doing and neither do you."

They both knew his response was not just for her hearing.

Nick whispered, "Steely, just stay quiet. Whatever you do, don't confront anyone. Don't do anything to bring attention to yourself." He put on his jacket and rolled the bag to the door.

She was in a prolonged stare. He came back and held her arms. "There will never be a crime without Jack's testimony. So I'm going to speak for him." He embraced her tightly for a few seconds before letting go.

"Bye, Nick," she whispered as he left.

Candy and Kristi had a visual of Nick dashing out the front door. If he had looked over his shoulder a second time, he would have seen Qualls tailing him.

Kristi said, "Where's he going so fast?"

Candy looked over and observed, "He's calling for a cab."

"First time I ever saw him in jeans," giggled Kristi. "Come to Momma, cowboy! It's rodeo time!"

"Next thing you know, you'll be listening to country music!"

Kristi nodded. "Already kicking it!"

"You bought boots?"

"Yep."

Qualls crept through the revolving doors, close enough to see Nick jump into the open cab and yell, "Go!" The tires spun around twice before gripping the asphalt.

Qualls couldn't hitch a ride on a bus. Every vehicle bypassed him. He took a few more steps into the street in an attempt to gain attention. Everything sped by. He raised a fist and then stomped directly in a water-filled gutter. He cursed it. Beating the ground back into the building, he hit the revolving door with enough force to spin it faster than he could move. The door hit his backside, sending him facedown to the floor.

"That man fell right on his face," said Candy, rising. "Oh, never mind. He's getting up." Candy straightened her collar. "Hey, we better quit goofing off. Mrs. Ray could come down and start barking at us."

"Ruff, ruff!" Kristi said, cackling.

They made enough ruckus for security to gaze in their direction. Qualls was roughed up. Blood dripped out of one nostril.

"This place is too serious," said Kristi. "People are so uptight. Their faces crack if they smile."

"Some of the managers act like they have a burr in their—" Candy locked eyes with Qualls. He limped a few steps away. He wasn't laughing. He was lethal.

"You think that's funny? I'm really good at shutting people up."

Candy froze with her mouth half open.

Kristi stuttered, "Sir, we were only—"

"Shut up!" Qualls ordered. "I don't want to hear another sound out of you!"

The girls quickly rolled their chairs back. Candy considered screaming at the top of her lungs, before watching him leave, unchallenged, through the executive corridor. She grabbed her cell and then looked at his disappearing shadow with the phone to her ear.

Kristi was shaking. "Where I grew up, 'shut you up' meant dead. You think he meant dead? I don't make enough money to be threatened on the job. Nuh-uh, they can't pay me regular to take physical threats. No, ma'am."

Candy firmly gripped her cell. "Rick, get down here. I found another one of the murderers."

"Murderers?" Kristi rose halfway to make sure he was gone.

Candy hung up and made her next call. "Sergeant Donovan, please...Yes, I'll hold."

Kristi rattled. "Who'd he murder?"

"I don't know."

"Why don't we tell security?"

"What can they do?" Candy visually traced his steps. "I want him locked up!"

"These people are crazy." Kristi opened her e-mail and started typing.

"What are you doing?"

"Asking for a raise."

CHAPTER FORTY-NINE

The bank statements were packed away. They were no longer needed for Steely's purpose. Nick had given her access to the JHI accounting system. Accounts-receivable and accounts-payable information in the *known* company accounts could provide what she needed. Her focus was on amounts paid to vendors all the way back to her dad's death. Flash Away was central. She knew that. Keaton had connected Flash Away to JHI. There were certainly tentacles reaching out to others. It was time to tie them together.

JHI's other 107 vendors proved legit. She quickly dismissed them and took a magnifying glass to Flash Away.

There were no receivables from Flash, and rightly so. There should not have been. Only payables. Her head stayed in the monitor. Her fingers tapped on the keyboard for most the day. She hadn't taken a break until there was a noise at the door.

She casually put her monitor to sleep and turned to welcome her incoming guest.

"Mrs. Ray! You startled me," she said, standing.

"Well, I'm surprised you heard me."

"Mrs. Ray, I usually hear more than I should."

Benita gazed at the phone on Nick's desk. "Does that thing work?"

"Yes, ma'am. Did you call?"

"A hundred times."

Steely picked up the phone, turned it over, and flipped a lever. "Oh, Nick—I mean, Mr. Dichiara must have accidently cut off the sound."

Ray placed one foot perpendicular to the other. "Do I look stupid?"

"No, ma'am."

"Don't 'Mr. Dichiara' me. I know you two have fuzzy lines between employee and employer." Ray viewed Nick's desk butting up to hers. "I don't even want to know what's going on in here."

"Mrs. Ray, no—"

"Keep it to yourself."

"Mrs. Ray, really, we—"

"Didn't I just say keep it to yourself?"

Steely zipped her lips.

"You're in here hibernating together." Ray looked up at the deer. "How do you concentrate with that thing staring at you?"

"We're on friendly terms."

Benita scanned the room. "This is the last time I'm going to tell you. Don't come in before eight a.m. or stay past five."

"Yes, ma'am. I was just trying to work ahead."

"Well, quit it. And if you see anyone on this floor, besides Monte, call security. I told him to watch out for you. Not one minute early. Not one minute late. I'm not your babysitter. Do what I asked you to do."

"Yes, ma'am. I sure don't want—"

Ray gave Nick's desk two quick taps with her solar nails. "Where is he?"

"He's out."

"Where? Or are you not supposed to tell? Because I'm the human-resource vice president. You'd better answer me. Now, where is he?"

"He's out on business."

"Where?"

"I really don't know."

"Uh-huh. Can you take a message? Do you know how to write the antiquated way?"

"Yes, ma'am." Steely searched the desk for a pen and paper. "Just one second." She ran around to Nick's desk. She pulled out the middle drawer, picked up a pen and a pad, and pushed the drawer in. Steely grabbed a cup and headed for the kitchen.

Ray rubbed her head and followed. "Where are you going? I'm talking to you."

"My coffee is cold. May I get you a cup?"

"I don't drink coffee."

Steely stuck a filter into the machine, positioned her cup under it, and turned around. "Now we can talk."

Ray caught up with Steely. "Bugged?"

"I don't know."

"I'll get it swept." She looked back at the closet.

"I think Nick wanted to leave it for now." Coffee dripped, filled the cup.

"I don't like it, but fine. When you hear from Nick, tell him Jacqueline Dupree, who was an accounts-payable clerk, quit showing up. She and her entire family went missing about a year ago."

"Got it."

"Tell him I finally found Juan Rios. He's in the Harris County detention center, awaiting trial for dealing drugs. Never would have thought it…"

Steely shook her head. "No. Mr. Hunter's assistant?"

"More like a friend. He wouldn't see me. Maybe Nick can talk to him."

"He's not a drug dealer."

Ray got in Steely's face.

"Mrs. Ray, he's not. I know he's not a drug dealer."

Ray whispered, "You should have told me who you were, Mrs. Hunter."

"I couldn't risk you not hiring me."

"That would have been a reason to hire you."

"I see."

"Now, you be careful down here. Dial zero-one on that phone if you need help. It'll go directly to security. I've instructed them to run up here if you call. It appears as if some of our executives are nothing more than hoodlums. I've got two very disturbed receptionists downstairs. One of them almost walked out a few minutes ago. The other wants a raise."

"Mrs. Ray, do you know anything about Flash Away?"

"Mr. Keaton hired them over my objections. Alexis Canker is as crazy as her daughter."

"Who's her daughter?"

"Cricket Maunder."

Steely quickly inhaled. "Cricket?"

"I had a nightmare the other night. She was in handcuffs, getting hauled off. It'd be a dream come true."

"That's why she has been coming in and out of here. I've never seen her mother. Her name has changed several times."

"When I found out the person who owned Flash Away was married to Zev Chevoski, I was ready to pitch a fit, but it was too late. Mr. Hunter resigned before I could tell him."

"Who is Zev Chevoski?"

"A sociopath who claims Mr. Hunter was his father. He tried to buy the company once."

"Does Miss Bea know about this?"

"Of course. She used his DNA, taken from a wad of gum, to prove it wasn't true. What does Bea think about what you're doing here with Nick?"

"I didn't tell her. She's too fragile." Steely sipped from her cup.

"Fragile? I've known Beatrice Hunter over thirty-five years; I've never heard anyone call her fragile. A heart of gold, maybe."

Steely shot her eyes at Benita. "Heart of gold?"

"You know she and Mrs. Dichiara pitched in to send you a check every month after your father passed."

"*They* did it?"

"I mailed the checks myself. They split it right down the middle. Arranged for your housing in college when they found out you were sleeping in the library."

"How'd they know?"

"Nick found out."

"He's so...Mrs. Dichiara is really nice. I can't believe Miss Bea."

"You mean 'cause she pitched a fit about you marrying David?"

"Well, that and—"

"She didn't want anyone emptying her nest. She did your make-up and hair, didn't she?"

"You can tell?"

"She wouldn't fix you up if she didn't like you. Oh, before I forget. Let Nick know Jacqueline Dupree's husband, Warren, was an employee of Energy Oil—one of JHI's biggest accounts. I don't—"

"The Energy Oil in Grey Canyon?"

"Yes. Mr. Dupree commuted back and forth from Houston on the weekends."

Steely composed herself. "Mrs. Ray, do you know when Mrs. Dupree quit showing up for work?"

"It was about a year ago," Benita said.

"I see."

"I better get back downstairs. Don't forget what I told you."

She indicated she wouldn't.

Benita left.

Steely rummaged for her cell. "Nick, please pick up." The phone rang three times. No answer. She put it away. She woke up her computer and started a new search in payroll. Only Keaton,

Ray, and Nick had access to payroll. And now Steely—thanks to Nick's leaving the pass code and a fob.

Her first search: former employee, Jacqueline Dupree. Her hire date was five and a half years prior to Jack's accident.

All amounts paid to Dupree should have been the same, since she was a salaried clerk. Steely scoured every pay statement. It proved to be a swift search.

Every pay slip was the same, except one categorized as a bonus.

Dupree had never received a ten-thousand-dollar bonus or even a ten-cent bonus before the week she went missing.

Was that normal for the company?

Steely quickly searched to find out. Every other bonus was disbursed in December. Not another one was disbursed in May. She scrolled back to view the line-item description: *major issue eliminated*. The check was issued the day after Jack's accident. Dupree hadn't been seen since. Steely's heart raced. Keaton signed the check. This was significant. Coincidence was not in her vocabulary. Nailing Keaton was not about money to her. It was about murder. And maybe he was vulnerable in both.

Juan Rios had to be cleared of any of this. He received regular pay except a bonus paid in December, just like every other employee except Dupree.

Flash Away received monthly invoices for $30,000, which seemed exorbitant but consistent, until she hit on a $150,000 check. She breathlessly checked the description: *major issue eliminated*. The check was issued the day after her dad died.

It took several minutes to regain her composure. Maybe this was all circumstantial. Maybe something that would be meaningless to a judge or jury. But not to Steely. See had waited patiently, for years, for this kind of information to be in her hands.

This was confirmation that Cricket's mother was connected to her father's death. Fred had cut all business ties with Alexis and her bogus Flash Away the week before he passed. He returned the income he earned. And he was ready to report what he knew to Mr. Hunter.

Emotionally, she was relieved, proud of what her dad had done. This confirmed, at least in her mind, that he was murdered. If it were even possible, she was even more resolved to get those responsible.

Nick's voice mail was full. He had suspended communication with the world. Most likely, he wouldn't be answering until he took the final blow to Keaton.

No longer caring if Keaton or anyone else was listening, she parked herself in front of the deer. She might as well chuck her deductions, like mud at the wall, and see if they stuck.

She ran to the stairwell and called Sheriff Tucker. He picked up quickly. "Tucker, here."

"Sheriff, this is Steely Hunter. Did you retrieve the truck?"

"We tried two other cranes. They couldn't hold the weight. They're setting up a new one as we speak. It should be stable enough to hold the weight. You'll be the first call I make when I get it checked out."

"Thank you." She ran back to the office. Her pain had eased. It didn't matter if she had no hard, incriminating proof. Bonus checks could be explained away. And even if they couldn't be, she knew no grand jury would recommend Keaton and Canker to stand trial.

CHAPTER FIFTY

"Bold lettering," Keaton said airily to the caller. "Harry Keaton Industries!" He wrote it out on a pad. "I don't care how much it costs…yes, every letter capitalized. Get the permits. I want to see it in one week. Do you know who I am? I'm one of the most successful CEOs in the country! I'll call the mayor if I have to…You have one week." Finally, he was getting the recognition he craved. He shaded the block letters and held it up by the window.

Donna knocked and then cracked the door. "Mr. Keaton—"

Keaton hollered, "Just a minute! I'm on an important call."

Donna rolled her eyes toward the lobby and tilted her head in that direction. "Mr.…uh, Mr. Keaton, I think you'd better let these officers in."

"Unless it's the president of the United States, tell them to wait." He continued the call. "That's right. All letters lit…How bright? Bright enough to see from the moon!" he said.

Donovan shoved the door open. Two bulletproof officers were at his side. He was dressed like everyone else in the building until he flipped over his lapel and brandished a shield. The two staring uniformed officers waited by the door as Donovan marched in. "Mr. Keaton, I'm Sergeant Donovan with HPD. I'm not the president, but it'd be a good idea to answer my questions unless you prefer me to take you by your suit tail and haul you in."

Keaton dropped the phone and stood at attention. His important call dangled off the edge of his desk. He buttoned his tailored coat. "Is there a problem, Officer?"

"I have some questions for you, sir."

"There's nothing you need to talk to me about." Keaton gnawed on a fingernail.

Stone-faced, Donovan was abrupt. "Last time. We can talk here, or you can take a ride in my backseat. You won't be the first CEO who has and probably won't be the last. Now sit yourself down. I don't want you leaping out that window."

Keaton complied, dropping into his seat as ordered. He scraped his fingers, frantically, on the arm of the chair. "I have nothing to hide. Ask whatever you want."

Donovan towered over the desk. "What do you know about Jacqueline Dupree and her family?"

"Jacqueline who? I don't know any Jacqueline anybody!"

"She was an employee here."

Keaton swiped at the sweat dripping down the side of his face. "I don't know all the employees in this company."

"According to the Grey Canyon sheriff, Warren Dupree and his wife, Jacqueline, and their eight-year-old son had an accident on the day of the Hunter funeral. Someone ran them off the road and into a creek. They're all missing. So I'm going to ask you again. What do you know about them?"

"I...don't...know...them. I've never even heard their names. Officer, I'm a successful man." Keaton drew blood ripping off a fingernail. "I'm telling you, I don't know a thing about this woman." Keaton loosened his tie, took off his jacket, and laid it on the credenza behind his desk.

"That's all for now." Sergeant Donovan motioned to the officers. "Let's go."

"Good." Keaton dabbed his face with a tissue. "I'm glad we cleared this up."

Donovan twisted his head back at Keaton. "This is not cleared up, Mr. Keaton." He turned and left.

Keaton pounded three numbers on his phone and chewed his bleeding finger. "Get down here!" he shouted and hung up.

Seconds later, Qualls stomped in, rattling the wall when he slammed the door. "What'd you do? Take a shower with your clothes on?"

"Who is Jacqueline Dupree?"

"You don't need to know."

"The police came in here asking about her accident. I've never been questioned before, and I don't ever want it to happen again."

"Don't worry about it. Mr. and Mrs. Dupree's only friend was a plastic bag of escape from reality."

Keaton dropped forward, cradled his head in his hands, and groaned. "What happened to them?"

"They got greedy."

"Where are they?"

"Mr. Dupree had a terrible driving record."

"Had?"

"Drove his family right into a creek," Qualls sneered. "Doors popped opened. They're in the gulf by now."

Keaton stood up. "I can't take this! Being questioned by the cops?"

Qualls gruffly replied, "Why? You don't know anything."

"That's right. I don't. I didn't agree to anybody getting hurt." Keaton pounded a fist on the desk. "We had a plan. Everybody wins. Even Jack, if he hadn't paid off the company debt. You and Chevoski should have stuck to it."

"You screwed it up by signing that idiotic agreement. I've been cleaning up your mess ever since."

"You agreed. No more murders!"

"You can't bind me. I'll take care of anyone who becomes a threat."

Keaton stood. "I won't be a part of this!"

Qualls darted around the desk and knocked Keaton back into his leather chair. "Don't you know the law?" He leveled himself, eye to eye. "You're an accessory to everything that goes on around here." He grasped a fistful of Keaton's shirt, pinning him, and then shoved him toward the windows. Qualls jammed his left forearm between Keaton's chin and chest. Keaton felt faint. The glass was the only thing between him and sudden death. He could die three different ways in a matter of seconds. Slightly more pressure could sever the miniscule amount of air seeping into his lungs. His heart could lose the ferocious battle it was waging to push blood through his cholesterol-laden veins, or he could fly, like a bird with clipped wings, out the fiftieth-floor window.

"You're no better than me." Qualls was out of control. His mind seemed to have snapped. "You're bought and paid for. Mr. Chevoski owns you." Qualls released his hold. Keaton wilted, sliding to the floor, gasping for air. "You're pathetic," Qualls spit at him.

Keaton was plagued with regret. He was involved in everything they did, whether he agreed or not. He had blood on his hands.

And for a handful of people, it was too late to reverse anything. His solution was to play dumb. He was really good at that.

CHAPTER FIFTY-ONE

Bea fiddled with a newspaper in her usual spot. A few feet away, the local news blared from the TV. Steely came in the front door and locked it behind her. "Hi, Miss Bea. Please remember to lock the door. Anyone could walk in."

"If they do, they won't walk out," Bea said, flipping a page.

"You don't want to invite trouble."

"It doesn't seem to need an invitation." Two more pages were uninteresting to her. "You missed dinner."

"Did you cook again?" she said in a high pitch.

"Chicken enchiladas."

Steely crossed over the crack in the living-room floor that grew every time a train vibrated the tracks behind the house.

Steely set her purse and keys on an entry table and went to the kitchen. On the stove was a foil-covered casserole. She lifted the silver wrap and peeked inside at the green sauce she was not fond of.

"How come you're always late when I fix chicken enchiladas?"

She quickly sealed the foil. "I am?"

"You come in here sniffing like a bloodhound. You don't like the smell, do you?"

"I'll get some in a minute. Thanks for cooking."

"I'm getting to bed in a few minutes. You know I start doing hair at the old folks' home tomorrow. They're desperate for me."

I should have thought of that a year ago.

"That's right, Miss Bea." Steely lay back on the sofa, across from Bea. "You seem kind of excited."

"It's no wonder the old folks are depressed. Their hair looks like doo-doo. There'll be a smile on those old crinkly faces when I get done with them."

Steely laid her head on the armrest and briefly shut her eyes. "They could call you a pooper scooper."

Bea chuckled.

Steely shot up. "You laughed at my joke?"

"First time one was funny."

"One out of a thousand."

Steely relaxed. Bea put a crease in the paper, folding it in half.

Steely cracked open an eye. "Why do you read the obituaries every day?"

"To see who departed." Bea looked distressed. "Eee...too bad about that Fitzpatrick man."

"What Fitzpatrick man?" she said casually.

"You know. My old neighbor. He passed over the weekend."

Steely sat up. "Not Erin's father? I just saw her on Friday."

Bea pointed at the paper. "Survivors: one daughter, Erin. Weren't you friends with that girl?"

Steely bent forward and folded her hands. "We sort of grew up together. We were very close at one time. May I see that?"

"Huh. He was so young—still in his fifties." Bea passed the paper. Steely stared in disbelief.

"His visitation is tonight. Miss Bea, do you want to go?"

"Nuh-uh! I don't want to see any more dead people. No, ma'am. I've seen enough dead people to last until the day I die."

"I'm going to run over there." Steely grabbed her keys and opened the door. "I'll be back in an hour. Maybe sooner."

The Santa Maria Funeral Home had two viewing rooms. Steely had seen both. Her dad had been in the large one, her mom in the smaller. The small room was locked. Fitzpatrick had to be in the large room, farther in. She turned a corner and saw a few people bunched together, all appearing thirty years or more her senior. Rose and carnation sprays displayed on stilts stood by a closed casket flush against a front wall. Floral couches lined the perimeter of the room, along with a few scattered chairs. This could be a formal living room in any nice home, minus the casket and flowers.

Erin was propped up in a corner between two couches. She fidgeted when she caught a glimpse of Steely coming up on her left.

Steely moved in precision toward her, watching for any indication that she was welcome or not. She hoped not to be the first person ever thrown out of the Santa Maria Funeral Home. She bravely put one foot ahead of the other and moved forward.

Erin hadn't budged. Steely had reached the point of no return. Erin couldn't deny she saw her. If Erin didn't respond right away, she was going to give her condolences to Mrs. Fitzpatrick and leave. Either way, she would have no regrets for coming. She'd been in Erin's shoes. Two more steps, and Steely was within an arm's reach of Erin. If she didn't react in about two seconds, Steely would go to plan B. She softly said, "Erin, I'm so sorry about your father."

Erin grabbed Steely, leaned on her shoulder, and wept. Steely cried too. The same way she had when it was her dad lying there.

"Steely, I didn't think you'd want to come."

"Of course I was coming."

Erin held on to her as they moved to a couch and sat. Suddenly, they were in a time warp. It was as if they'd never parted.

Erin opened up. "Father was filing for bankruptcy and restarting his business. He lost his biggest client. He barely had any other business since they took so much of his time. It really freaked him out when the secret service started investigating him."

"For what?"

"Organized crime."

"Your father wouldn't be involved with organized crime."

"I know!"

They nodded.

"It's very scary to be questioned by law enforcement," added Steely.

"He was a stinking number cruncher. That's it. He was scared even to talk about it. But he didn't do anything wrong. It just doesn't seem right that he committed suicide."

"I'm so sorry, Erin." Steely guessed he'd had a sudden heart attack. He had avoided one with a stent a few years back. The last thing she wanted to do was ask the wrong question. Listening was the safest route.

"He just told me he was going to get a clean start and build his business back up. He already had two new clients. He only needed a few more to replace the big one he lost. I just don't know what to think. It was just awful, finding him like that."

"You found him? That's a tough thing to deal with…"

"He was at his office, working late. He wasn't answering the phone. Me and my mother got worried, so we went to check on him about midnight. Mother waited in the car while I went in. There he was, in his office, sprawled out on the floor. An empty pill bottle and a bottle of whisky beside him." Erin whimpered. "I've never seen my father drink whisky. Maybe a beer or two…"

"I'm so sorry, Erin." Steely held tightly to her hand.

"Why would he delete his hard drive? I'm so confused."

She had to ask. "Erin, who was the client he lost?"

"Flash Away."

For a few seconds, Steely saw Erin's mouth move but didn't hear a word she was saying. It wasn't the time to tell Erin that her father's largest client was involved in racketeering, murder, and money laundering. Just not the right time to send her emotions on another wild ride.

"Are you OK, Steely?"

Steely opened her eyes widely and took a deep breath. "Yes, I'm listening."

"We don't have the autopsy report yet. I don't even know if I want to see it. I tell you, I'd gladly give up everything I have if I could have my father back."

"Erin, I loved your father. He was always so kind to me."

"He loved you too. I was too busy thinking about myself to pick up on Father's desperation."

"Your father was crazy about you. He was so proud of you. Try to focus on that."

Erin agreed, looked at Steely, and sincerely confessed, "I wish I was more like you."

Steely scrunched her face. A few minutes earlier, she'd worried about being a visitation crasher. "Me?" she breathed.

"You took such good care of your mother...and now Mrs. Hunter."

"Oh, Erin..."

"Remember how mean I was to you?"

"No, I don't remember."

"I hate the way I acted. Will you forgive me?"

Steely glanced at the casket and then back to Erin. "Maybe we should talk about this later."

"I need to know." She grabbed Steely's arm. "Please, will you forgive me for all the mean things I did to you?"

"Erin, I forgave you long ago. I don't think about it. You could say I have offense amnesia."

Erin used her sleeve to dab a few straggling tears. "What's that?"

"I don't remember being offended. It's a condition I like having."

"Then you might not remember most of high school," Erin whimpered. "I treated you just terribly."

"Here's what I remember. We rode our bikes to school together, played kickball in the park, and then went to get ice cream. I remember when we went roller-skating for the first time. I fell down and spit my knee open. I remember you ran home and found some medical tape—practically wrapped up my whole leg because you didn't want it to hurt anymore. That's what I remember."

Erin laughed through the tears. "I used that whole roll of medical tape on your leg."

"Yeah, I had to walk stiff-legged all the way home."

"Remember when we made those mud pies in your backyard?"

"Yeah, they tasted terrible!"

Erin giggled. "Why did we eat mud?"

"'Cause, Allen, the teenager who knew everything, told us they tasted like chocolate."

"Well, he found out they didn't when we threw them at him!"

"Hey, I still have our rock collection in my attic."

"I want to see them. We had some beautiful rocks."

For the next thirty minutes, they remembered the past. The good times overshadowed the not-so-good times. Steely made sure of it. She gave Erin just what she needed most on the night of her father's visitation.

Forgiveness.

CHAPTER FIFTY-TWO

Bea ran out of her bedroom in a frenzy. "Steely? Where are you?" she yelled.

"I'm out here," Steely hollered from the garage. "You having a nightmare again?" She climbed down from the attic and came inside. "I got up early to look at some old—"

"How do I look?" Bea twirled.

Beatrice's twenty-four-hour muumuu had been replaced with a dress. Nicest dress Steely had ever seen her wear that wasn't black. It was pleasantly pink. Her flea collar had been replaced with a string of pearls and matching dangly earrings.

"You look great. Aren't you going to work?"

"Yes. When Alice called last night, she said it'd cheer up the old folks. They need hope. I'm giving them a vision. I forgot to ask her how she got my number."

Steely cleared her throat. "What does it matter?" She circled around Bea. "You look stunning. I don't know how else I can put it. I've never seen you look so good. The people at Star of Light will be thrilled you're doing their hair."

"And doing their makeup."

"You giving them a pedicure too?"

"I have boundaries."

"Just seeing if you had lost it."

Bea was almost jolly. "They'll look ten years younger after I sand them down and polish them up." Bea rushed to the bathroom. She checked herself out in the mirror, touched up her makeup, and came back giggly. "You sure I'm OK?"

"Really, I've never seen you look better."

Bea was radiant. "Do I look forty?"

Steely stepped back. "How old?"

"Fifty. Do I look fifty?"

Steely rubbed her chin. "Do you feel fifty?"

Bea eyed herself in the living-room mirror. "I do. Do I have a youthful glow?"

"You're glowing, for sure."

"I took your advice and called Nancy Dichiara. I should've called her months ago."

"Really?"

"Nancy's trying to reach Nick. Tell him to call her when you see him. She doesn't want him to do something that will get him arrested. Most everybody has been arrested, at least once."

Steely leaned a shoulder down. "You've been arrested?"

Bea winked. "Just one of those misdemeanor things—total misunderstanding."

The doorbell rang.

Steely flashed her head suspiciously toward it and then back at Bea. "You expecting someone?"

"Pepe's picking me up."

"Pepe Martinez from Grey Canyon?" Steely said with an escalating pitch.

"Yes, he moved here a few days ago," Bea said with a twinkle.

Steely lit up. "He's here for you?"

"Get your mind out of the gutter, and go let him in. I have to check my face." Bea trotted around the corner to the bedroom. Steely never saw Bea trot before. If the house was on fire, Steely doubted Bea would trot.

"Check your face?"

Bea hollered from the bedroom, "Get the door!"

"I'm going."

Steely unlocked the door for the only person Bea had ever invited in. Bea and Steely were more than antisocial. They were nonsocial.

Martinez held flowers wrapped in green paper. He was Latin charm. Perfectly peppered silky hair, in a comb back, with a splash of aftershave.

"Mr. Martinez, I'm so glad you're here." She pulled him in.

"*Gracias*, Steely." He kissed her on both sides of her face.

"Please, have a seat. Miss Bea will be right out." They sat adjacent to one another. Steely quizzed him. "What brought you to Houston?"

"Bee-Bee."

"Bee-Bee?" She looked over at the bedroom, leaned down, and whispered, "You're living dangerously, calling her Bee-Bee. She hates nicknames."

"She likes my pet name."

"She does?"

"I waited a year to call on her. I wouldn't disrespect Jack. Now I'm going to vigorously pursue her until I catch her."

"Catch her? May I help?"

"I missed out on that foxy lady forty years ago." He grinned.

"Foxy?" Steely straightened up. "I don't know what to say to that."

"She isn't slipping away from me again. There's no one like Bee-Bee."

"Agreed," Steely said, with one brow raised higher than the other. "So you're not going back home without her?"

"No way. I'll stay in Houston and sell my house in Grey Canyon, if needed. I have money. I can take care of her."

Steely moved in closer, putting her hand on his arm. "Mr. Martinez, stay here. Take my room. I'll sleep on the sofa, in the garage—I don't care. Just stay."

Martinez patted her hand. "Thank you, dear, but I'm staying with my cousin, a few blocks away. Bee-Bee doesn't want us to co-habitate." He inched up a little higher. "Bet I'll have a ring on her finger in thirty days."

"Ring?" Steely said hurriedly. "Thirty days? Really, let me help."

"Thank you, *señorita*." He winked. "But I got this."

Steely stuck out a hand. He shook it. "Let me know if there is anything I can do."

CHAPTER FIFTY-THREE

The closet light seemed to have lost a few watts. The desk had accumulated another layer overnight. Steely had shut herself up studying spreadsheets until her cell jiggled. "Hello?" she answered.

"Mrs. Hunter, this is Sheriff Tucker."

Her face became serious. "Yes, Sheriff?"

"We retrieved the truck. The axle was wedged so deeply in the rocks that the fire didn't get to most of it. This was no accident. We're certain of it."

Steely visualized the fireball. The frantic calls she and Bea made to Jack and David. The panic that grew every second they didn't answer. Then the knock on the door the first time she heard Tucker's voice.

"Mrs. Hunter, are you there?"

"Murder? Sheriff?"

"Yes. There was an electrical device attached to the brake line. Someone remotely signaled it to explode and bust the line. Hunter couldn't stop because he had no brakes. This must be a shock to you. It sure is to me. I'm working with HPD to scour the remaining pieces. We're going to find out who did this. I'm sorry to tell you over the phone, but I can't get to Houston tonight. I didn't want this to wait."

"Sheriff, we needed the truth."

"I would have never guessed this. Mrs. Hunter, will you tell Bea? You'll do a better job than me."

"This may not be the best time. She just got on her feet. I'll tell her as soon as Nick gets back."

"I couldn't reach him," said Tucker.

"He's kind of busy right now."

"He wanted us to review the surveillance tape from the Energy Oil parking lot. It shows Warren Dupree appearing to change a tire on Jack's truck. He and David were out all day on the tractor, so he had easy access to the vehicle. On the day of the service, I got two strange calls. One about someone prowling around the Hunter farm and the other about the Dupree vehicle, almost completely submerged in a creek off Highway 90, less than fifty miles away."

"Dupree?"

"Yes. Dupree, his wife, Jacqueline, and their young son have been missing ever since."

"Sheriff, I need to go now."

Steely closed the phone and pushed a trash basket between her legs. The smell of rancid dumpling soup was strong. She pushed it back, wiped her face with a tissue, used her arms as pillow, and laid her head on her desk. Two minutes later, someone opened the door.

"Pauper?"

"Please stay out of here." Steely didn't look up.

Cricket came closer. "Nick's phone goes straight to voice mail. Where is he?"

"Get out." Steely pulled the receiver from Nick's desk.

"Everyone's looking for him." Cricket inched in. "Pauper, what is he doing?"

Steely poked numbers in the phone. "I need a security officer on five, please." She closed the receiver and laid her head back down.

Cricket taunted, "So you don't feel like talking? I bet you'd talk about what happened the night your dad died. You tell me where Nick is, and I'll give you every last detail."

Steely turned her head toward Cricket.

"Nick and Vince Dichiara met up with him. Your dad accused them both of defrauding the company. See, Mr. Dichiara set up the LLCs. Nick's the one who siphoned millions from JHI. Can't believe the self-righteous Nick Dichiara could do such a thing? Why do you think his dad brought him to a business meeting? Mr. Dichiara roughed up your dad. Nick tossed him against the wall. Looks like Nick's the green-eyed monster. Where do you think he is right now? He took off with over two hundred million. Do you really think he's coming back? He's a criminal, just like his parents. And you'll be charged as an accessory."

"You know so much. Yes, my dad hit the wall. Everyone knows that. But what actually killed him?"

Cricket blurted, "A headless nail. Now, what do you know about Nick?"

"You want to know what I know? You're a sociopath."

"Maybe so, but I'm a really good one." Cricket's mouth opened, teeth and gums showing, like a vicious dog, ready to bite. "You're going to lose Nick, the assets, everything. You're nothing but a Pauper, and you always will be!"

Steely popped up and, in a lightning quick gesture, swung the trash can and sprayed its contents on Cricket.

Cricket shimmied. Some of the liquid dripped off. "Oh! You're disgusting!"

The elevator dinged. Security had arrived.

"You're going to regret this!" Cricket took off for the stairs.

Steely lay back in her chair. "That almost shut her up."

The situation was unraveling fast. She picked up a damp cloth from the kitchen, cleaned herself up, poured a fresh cup of coffee, and went back to her desk to figure out her next move.

CHAPTER FIFTY-FOUR

Steely didn't usually talk aloud to herself. She could no longer sit there and keep smelling floor cleaner in the utility closet. It was her turn to do something no right-thinking person would advise her to do. The moment had come to blow the lid off this place and ensure that Keaton or no one else could go after Nick Dichiara.

Cricket had blabbed to her cohorts by now. If $200 million was missing, it was probably in Nick's hands. Who else would have guts enough to take that kind of money? She rubbed her neck, thinking of Bea's assessment of Keaton. He was a liar and a petty thief. But he didn't have the stupids to try a fraud of this magnitude. This thing had accelerated beyond his control. She was sure of that.

Steely thought about getting to the speaker system and rattling off what she knew. The emergency system was in a locked box a few steps away. Everyone in the building would hear. But maybe throwing out a wide net wasn't the wisest move. Chaos and confusion could work for or against Nick. Public opinion was too risky. She settled for an inalienable weapon. The truth. And getting it to those who had denied it for years was about to be the easiest thing she had done in a long time.

The deer and Steely were about to have a serious talk. She positioned herself to get a perfect visual and good voice projection. Nick and whoever else was listening were about to get an earful.

"Nick, my dad was murdered when he found out about the fraud. The bar fight was a total setup." She spoke perfectly, highlighting every word. "There was no other woman. David and Jack were murdered too. The accident was no accident. Sergeant Donovan will have arrest warrants issued. Who knows when—maybe today. Jacqueline Dupree worked in accounting here. The authorities found her and her husband, Warren. They rigged the truck. Nick, hold on to the two hundred million until we meet up. Then we'll run hard and far. The money trail leads to Mr. Keaton and then traces back to Mr. Chevoski and various individuals. They were using the company to launder revenue from drug and human trafficking. It's getting a good washing, so who will care if they never see it again?"

Steely pushed a flash drive into the computer and clicked. She ejected it and stuck it in her pocket. "It's all right here on this flash drive. The drama will start when the so-called clients call for their assets. We'll get some popcorn and enjoy the movie from our special spot. See you soon!"

CHAPTER FIFTY-FIVE

Switzerland is warm in May. Nick vacationed there once. Skied too. But this trip was no vacation. He was here to conduct business. The kind of business that could land him with a roommate in a Swiss lockup half the size of the utility closet if things didn't go as planned. But Nick didn't focus on risks. If he did, he'd rightly have fear written on his face. There's nothing more suspicious than a frightened guy trying to transfer $426 million into new accounts.

The bank wasn't much bigger than a branch in some US grocery stores. The structure had probably been new when George Washington was in office. You didn't see marble floors like these in twenty-first-century buildings.

Most of the bank's account holders were faceless. The very reason the accounts were there to start with. An account holder's ID number and pass code were like a debit card, allowing them to move assets in and out with ease. No questions asked. But the bank wasn't as secretive as it once was. The war on terror ended total anonymity a few years back.

An elderly lady in a black wool dress and hair in a tight bun greeted Nick at the door. "This way, Mr. Dichiara," she said. "Mr. Rohr will see you now."

Rohr, the bank president, occupied the only private office on the floor. He was a stick figure with suit sleeves slightly longer than his arms. "Please have a seat, Mr. Dichiara."

Nick relaxed in a single chair angled across the desk from Rohr. "Mr. Rohr, I need to move half the accounts to the US and transfer the remaining to new accounts here, since all of these accounts have been breached. This knucklehead thought he could outsmart us by wiring the assets here."

"His miscalculation."

Nick caught a glimpse of a photo of Rohr, a woman his age, and a large dog posed pleasantly. "Yeah. He poisoned his neighbor's dog last week."

Rohr shook his head. "A real sicko."

"The neighbor's kids are still crying."

"Can't they lock him up?"

"That's my number-one goal when I get back to the States. Can you accommodate my request?"

"Most certainly, sir. We don't want our accounts funded with illegal transfers."

"I appreciate your cooperation. I have my paperwork in order. It shows that these funds were moved from a US corporation without authorization from Mr. Jack Hunter. He was the only one who could have authorized the transfer at the time. The wires came from our accounts in the U.S., then to Saint Stephen's Island Bank, then here, during his tenure."

"Very clear, sir. We've already reviewed this. Our auditor agrees with your findings. We moved the funds to a holding account yesterday."

"Perfect." Nick reached into his jacket. He opened four sheets of folded paper and passed them to Rohr. "Each account marked is to be wired to a US account or to a new account here. All corresponding pass codes are adjacent to the account numbers."

"We have the new accounts set up for you and will take care of it immediately."

"Here is the original affidavit, signed at the time, saying I was authorized to receive any and all funds on behalf of the company. No one else is to have access to the pass codes for these accounts except for me. Is that clear, Mr. Rohr?"

"Yes, Mr. Dichiara. Quite clear. You will be the only one with access. But please secure your pass codes. Anyone could access these accounts with them."

"Very clear, sir."

Rohr began to leave and then stopped beside Nick. "This won't take long."

"Mr. Rohr, one more question. Is there a waiting period to access a sum of that size?"

"No, sir. When the funds are wired, they are as good as cash."

It's like I'm robbing the bank. "Oh, and, Mr. Rohr, we're not certain we have plugged the leak on our end. If any additional funds are deposited in any of the old accounts, please have them automatically transferred into one of the new accounts."

"Certainly, sir."

"Thank you for your cooperation."

"There is one very important thing you need to know, Mr. Dichiara."

Nick moved around, facing Rohr. He envisioned the cantonal police swarming in with guns drawn, yelling, "Hit the floor!" He glanced at the back of the office. No door. Front was clear too. "Yes?"

"We have superb chocolate lattes. May we get you one?"

Nick eased back. "Absolutely. They're my favorite."

"My assistant will prepare it, sir," Rohr said, leaving. "You won't be disappointed."

Nick nodded and relaxed a little. *Lord, I'm going to make it out of here.*

CHAPTER FIFTY-SIX

Chevoski rammed his car over the sidewalk to the driveway. There was no need to jump the curb. The driveways into the JHI garage were wide and easy to access. He braked long enough for Monte to open the door and let Keaton in. Then he peeled off into the street, cutting off all the traffic. Several drivers slammed on their brakes to avoid a collision. Chevoski thanked them with an obscene gesture. If they had been road ragers, somebody would be dead.

"Do you have to drive like a maniac?" complained Keaton.

"Why not?" Chevoski ran through a solid red light.

"Gee. Watch it. Would you?"

Chevoski turned sharply into an alley, stopped short, and killed the engine.

"Why are you jerking me around?" Keaton demanded, shaken.

Chevoski bent a leg up on the console between them. "I'm going to ask you this one time. Where's my money?"

"In the bank," Keaton snapped. "Are you still freaking out about the eight million missing from the Saint Stephen's account? I told you I'd get to the bottom of it."

Chevoski glared at Keaton. "The Swiss accounts are gone."

"Gone? They can't be gone. Jason took care of the transfer right before he left for vacation. I watched him do it myself. Just like I always do."

"The Swiss accounts are empty, you imbecile. I'm missing four hundred twenty-six million. You'd better have it back in twenty-four hours."

"Maybe the funds crossed each other in transit. When you're dealing with over six hundred million dollars, you can't expect everything to be perfect. I'm sure the assets are secure. It would be impossible for anyone to get to them. Nobody even knows they are there. Jason couldn't even do it without me. The funds are there."

"They better be. 'Cause I'll take care of you and everyone you know if I don't have them back by tomorrow."

Keaton was breathing heavy, huffing like he was short of breath, holding his chest.

Chevoski wanted him scared but not dead. "I know you have sense enough not to lie to me."

"You do?" Keaton muttered.

"Yes. Now tell me. Who had access to the account numbers and pass codes?"

"Nobody. I'm telling you. Nobody."

Chevoski eased the tension, saying, "Think real hard. Did anyone have access?"

"Nobody." Keaton's pulse soared. "Jason put in the account numbers. I put in the pass codes."

"I should have worked with a smarter idiot who could wire funds," Chevoski grumbled. "Where is he?"

"I don't know. He's taking a few days off."

"We'll find him. Now tell me why David Hunter's widow is working with Nick."

"A Hunter?"

"Steely Paupher Hunter. Does Paupher sound familiar?"

"Did you tell Thomas?"

Chevoski slapped the console between them. "Are they still breathing?"

Keaton was afraid to ask.

"I should have let Qualls take care of them all when he had the chance. The Hunters traveled in that truck together. They could have all gone over that cliff. The Pauphers drove an old, beat-up car. Easy pickin's. I won't make that mistake again."

Keaton listened, afraid even to move.

"If the funds are clearing overnight, they'll be there by tomorrow." Chevoski smirked. "The people who own these funds would kill you for taking five dollars. Do you get the picture?"

Keaton used a facial expression to indicate he did.

"Why are you ordering signs with your name on them?" Chevoski laughed cynically. "You're nothing but a talking head. I put you in this position, and I'll take you out when I'm ready." Chevoski lowered his leg and turned the key. "And I still haven't found that stupid agreement you signed. I didn't authorize you to sign that. Dumbest thing I've ever seen anyone do. You better hope it doesn't appear. Two pieces of paper that you so stupidly signed could destroy us all. You'd better find Jason."

"I'll reach out to him."

"And call Nick Dichiara."

"Why?"

"If the funds don't show up, he has them."

"I don't think so. He's been wandering around in the dark."

"That's exactly what he is doing." Chevoski shifted to drive and made a left turn, banging Keaton's head on the window. "Call Nick Dichiara."

Keaton struggled holding the phone.

"Call him!" Chevoski yelled.

"It's going to voice mail."

Chevoski snatched the phone. He spoke loudly into it. "Mr. Dichiara, you have something of mine. Now I'm taking something of yours. You better have my money back by tomorrow, or we both lose what we value the most." Then he threw the phone at Keaton.

Keaton whined, "What if he doesn't have it?"

"Covering my bases."

"His dad is already half dead. His mother is his caretaker."

"Oh no, I don't want the half-dead parents. I'm going to rip his heart out and take that little girl."

Chevoski turned into the garage. Keaton rolled out of the car.

"Stay close to your phone!" Chevoski yelled. "Or you'll be the next thing that disappears." Chevoski smoked his tires and took off.

Keaton's knees buckled. He went down hard. The parking attendant ran over and helped him up.

CHAPTER FIFTY-SEVEN

Steely teetered two boxes on one shoulder with one hand and used the other to carefully take the five steps down from the attic to the garage floor. Each foot safely touched a step, skipping none. She opened the door to the kitchen, placed the boxes beside the sofa, and began sorting through them. These were her things. She'd saved them since she had left for college. A fourteen-year-old doesn't exactly know what's relevant and what is not. That's how long it had been since she had opened the boxes, containing every written report about her dad's death.

The six-o'clock news had Bea's attention. She was reclining in her normal spot, her feet propped up since she had been on them all day. During the next commercial break, Bea would surely be asking why Steely was digging through the old boxes. But Steely ended up being the one with the first question. "How was your date? Did he hold your hand? Did he kiss you?"

"Smarty-pants." Bea poked the device that never left her possession and paused the TV.

Steely had one box emptied. "Did you like fixing hair today?"

Bea curled her mouth up enough to smile. "Gray hair is too coarse to work with. So I dyed them all blond."

"All of them?" Steely laughed.

"Not a gray hair left in the place. They liked the chicken pot pie too."

Steely flashed her eyes at Bea. "What chicken pot—"

"Same chicken as in the freezer."

"You took them the tofu chicken?"

"Pepe drove out to the rancher and picked up fifty pounds of meat for the old folks' home."

"Miss Bea, that wasn't chicken."

"There's one thing good about being raised in the country. You know the difference between chicken and possum."

"Possum?" Steely flexed her head back. "I wish I didn't know that." She continued going through the box.

"Their stomachs are cast iron. A little possum won't hurt them. They've been eating bacon and eggs every morning for the last eighty years. They didn't get all put out about the smell, like you. You could make a poot, and they wouldn't know. The possum even put them in a good mood."

"You didn't put any alcohol in it, did you?"

"I didn't spike the possum. Sometimes you act like I don't have any sense."

"I'm just asking." Steely went back to sorting.

"Most of them hadn't worn a lick of makeup for years. Their skin was like burlap. I took a flap at a time, sanded and moisturized it. See, when you have a good disposition, like me, it rubs off on other people. Alice said the old folks did activities today that she hadn't been able to get them to do. They exercised and enjoyed it. I showed them how to do those balates."

"You mean Pilates?"

"Then I did their hair while Pepe cooked."

"Good team."

"Now I need some peace and quiet to catch up on the news. Why are you digging in those boxes anyway?"

"I have some unanswered questions."

Bea clicked the remote. "What questions?"

Steely held a cutout of a wrinkled newspaper.

Bea glanced over it. "What you got here?"

"There is a company called Flash Away that did business with my dad and JHI. It's a common denominator between the two."

"Flash what?"

"Away. They store documents on a USB."

"Isn't that a Swiss bank?"

"A flash drive. Most companies use them. It's an efficient way to store important documents." Steely unraveled a newspaper clipping and pointed. "Do you know him?"

"Vince Dichiara?"

"Yes. Now whose shadow is next to him?"

"I think we both know. It's Nick Dichiara," said Bea. "Vince and Nick were there the night your dad died. Steely, I didn't know. You want me to ask Nancy?"

"I'd rather ask them myself. I need some answers." Steely picked up the car keys and went out the back door.

CHAPTER FIFTY-EIGHT

Nick rolled over on his stomach and draped his arms off the sides of the lounger. The masseuse hovered over him, rubbing an oily mixture into his back. A man in a white uniform set a drink with a slim straw in a narrow glass on the table beside him. He was being treated like royalty on Saint Stephen's Island.

"May I get you something else, sir?" asked the uniformed man.

"I'd like a few more lobster bites, please. I worked up an appetite out here in the sun."

The waiter bowed. "Yes, sir."

The masseuse picked up the frosted beverage and held the straw, allowing Nick to sip without moving anything but his lips. Then the masseuse set the glass down and went back to work. "Sir, your muscles are knotted up. Try to relax."

Nick closed his eyes. "I'm doing all the relaxing I can until the hurricane hits."

"Sir, there's no need for concern. There are no tropical disturbances anywhere near us."

"Maybe not for you." He turned over. "But a cat five is about to hit near me."

The masseuse looked puzzled.

"That's all for now." He slid down his aviators. The masseuse picked up a towel and left.

Pierce Thibodaux threw a towel at him and settled in the adjacent chair. "Working hard?"

"It's about time you got here. Where's Muffy?"

"I can't bring my wife when I'm on the lam."

"You're not on the lam." Nick chuckled.

"Remember, I'm an officer of the court."

"We're not in the court."

"Hey, did you hear Steely's message?"

"Yeah. I heard Keaton wet his pants. I didn't expect them to deposit another two hundred thirteen million into the Swiss accounts."

"Four hundred twenty-six million."

"Too bad. He's about to hit a recession."

"The feds say the money is clean. They're not touching it."

"Fine. We got what we came for. If the feds don't want the assets, it will be a bountiful year for various charities in Houston."

"Keaton wanted to be more charitable."

Nick rose up on an elbow. "Now who's the bigger thief? Me or Keaton?"

Thibodaux laughed. "You."

"Who's going to jail? Me or Keaton?"

"Keaton, if Chevoski doesn't grind his coffee beans first."

Nick sat up and planted his feet in the sand. His disposable cell beeped. "Yes?" he answered.

"Mr. Dichiara, this is Melvin at the bank."

"Yes, Melvin."

"He's coming tomorrow morning, sir. Eight thirty."

"Well done, Melvin."

"Mrs. Farnsworth sends her apologies and wants me to relay again that we will fully cooperate with you and the Saint Stephen's authorities. Our bank will not be involved in fraud."

"I understand. Please remind Mrs. Farnsworth about the importance of a flawless meeting."

"You can count on it, Mr. Dichiara. We'll see you tomorrow, sir."

"We set?"

"Yep, our first guest is arriving tomorrow morning. Whoever doesn't make it out in time will become a permanent resident in a US prison. I've got them this time...Or else they've got me."

Thibodaux nodded. "And me too."

"But it's worth the risk."

CHAPTER FIFTY-NINE

Steely stared at the stained-glass door, wondering what Nick would think about her being there. This wasn't a social call. It was personal. Anything Mr. Dichiara could tell her about the night her dad died would make the trip worthwhile. She knew what she wanted to ask but struggled with how to say it without sounding accusatory. Or insinuating something she didn't mean to insinuate.

The pondering time was over. She gave the doorbell a quick press. A shadow formed in the glass and grew increasingly prominent until the door opened.

"Hello, Steely."

"May I come in, Mrs. Dichiara?"

"Of course. I was wondering if you were ever going to ring that bell."

The wool carpet had the wear and tear of one thirty years newer. The decor from the seventies looked as if it had been preserved in a time capsule, the unworn, upholstered furniture as though no one had lain on it. Custom swag drapes covered every living-room window.

"What can I do for you, honey?"

"Mrs. Dichiara, may I please speak to your husband?"

"Come in and sit down." Nancy looked placid. She motioned to the sofa.

Steely stayed put. "Mrs. Dichiara, I need to ask him some questions about the night my dad died. I only need a few minutes. May I please speak with him?"

"Honey, his memory isn't good. Talks in riddles most the time."

"Let him answer in riddles. I'll figure them out. This is very important. If he could remember even the slightest detail, it might help." She rubbed an eye with a closed fist.

Nancy reluctantly called, "Vince, can you come in here?"

Wheels began rolling toward them. Nancy rubbed her hands together at the sight of her husband in a motorized chair. He was sickly thin, with just enough muscle to direct the control stick. His hair was white straw. His undershirt hung well below his neckline, meant to fit a much larger man.

"What is it, Steely?" His speech was shaky at best.

It was understood that Steely's time for questioning would be short. She gently quizzed him. "Mr. Dichiara, what happened the night my dad died?"

Even after being impaired from a stroke, Vince remembered that night. "I don't know. I never made it inside. HPD pulled up before I could get out of my car."

"What did you see?"

"People passed out in the parking lot. Some throwing punches." Vince suddenly appeared disturbed. "Nancy, has the newspaper come?"

"Vince, you read the paper this morning."

His right leg shook erratically. "I did?"

"Vince, I'm sure you forgot because you were in a hurry to get outside. I would've forgotten too." In the gentlest way, Nancy U-turned her husband, rolling him toward the bedroom. "I'm

327

going to set up the laptop Nick brought you. You can read the news in Sicily if you want. How about that?" She winked at Steely. "Could you excuse us for a minute?"

"Yes, ma'am." Steely now understood Mrs. Dichiara's apprehension. Any information coming from him would be unreliable at best. "Mrs. Dichiara?"

"Just a moment, dear." Nancy closed the bedroom door but soon came back in the living room. "He comes and goes."

"Mrs. Dichiara, do you remember anything he told you that night?"

"I was a sitting state judge at the time. He didn't even tell me he was going there. Sure didn't tell me what happened."

Steely squeezed her lips together. She briefly closed her eyes.

"There's one thing I can tell you. Your father wasn't a cheater, honey. He was set up. I can't tell you anything else about that night, but I can tell you this. Bea said—"

"Miss Bea?"

"I told her not to tell me. She didn't listen. Once something goes in your ear, the damage is done."

Steely nodded.

"Your father called Jack and asked to meet, but he was out of town. Harry Keaton got involved and set up the meeting with your father at the cantina. He definitely planned on going. But Jack wanted Vince to go instead. Vince had been Jack's personal attorney since he graduated law school. If it was business or personal, Vince would be the best choice; Jack trusted him. The meeting venue seemed strange. Why would they meet at a cantina? So Vince had Nick meet him there fifteen minutes early. The ruckus inside had ended before he and Nick arrived. This talk about your father fighting over a woman is nonsense. He was there to talk to Vince and nobody else. Someone stopped him from doing it. That's all I know."

Steely agreed. "So Nick and Mr. Dichiara weren't inside when the fighting started?"

"HPD had the place sealed off. Vince told the officers that he was there to meet with your dad. But since he didn't go inside and wasn't a witness, he wasn't much help. Almost everyone in the bar that night was as drunk as a tick. What kind of witnesses do a bunch of drunks make? The news said they were carried off in paddy wagons. Steely, I'm so sorry about what happened to your dad. It was a terrible tragedy."

Steely felt relieved by Mrs. Dichiara's candor. "Nick and Mr. Dichiara weren't inside."

Nancy folded her hands. "Oh, I see. You weren't sure if they were involved."

Steely shrugged. "I've been told otherwise, but I didn't believe it."

"I understand." Nancy nodded, reassuring her. "I don't blame you. It looks bad. Everybody's all hush-hush."

"Mrs. Dichiara, where's Nick?"

"Since I can't reach him, I'm sure he's doing something that he knows I wouldn't want him doing. He's helping somebody who can't help himself. He's been like this all his life. I can't get him to stop. It's just in him. Maybe the cautionary part of his brain doesn't work right. But the compassion part goes full speed. He's always the one who stands up to the bullies. He just can't sit back and watch an injustice. At one point, he was making a citizen's arrest every week! Please pray for him."

"I do. Mrs. Dichiara, do you have a gun?"

"Yes. And I know how to use it."

"Have you ever shot a roach?"

"Is Bea doing that again?"

CHAPTER SIXTY

B ea rolled over in bed. Yawned. Clinically, she was still asleep since she didn't hear the banging on the front door. The alarm clock hadn't gone off yet.

The back door creaked.

Bea rolled on her back.

The door was pushed open.

Her eyes popped open. Bea had excellent hearing. She could tell the difference between outside noise and inside noise. Pressure applied to the floor made squeaking sounds. Every movement brought forth a reciprocal sound. There was no way to control it. An intruder could tiptoe and still make a sound on the rickety floor.

Steely left hours ago. Pepe would have knocked. There was no way he would walk into the house unannounced. Whoever was there shouldn't be there. Bea was certain. She was no longer alone. She tugged on the bedside drawer. Her pistol was there, if Steely hadn't moved it as threatened.

The intruder was moving slowly. The squeaks were several seconds apart. It shouldn't take that long for him to get from the back door to the bedroom in the small house.

The hinge on the drawer was older than Bea. Another tug inched it out. Opening it too fast could alert the intruder and send him running. Too slow and he could crawl to the bedroom before she had the weapon out.

The barrel was in sight. Bea sighed in relief. Her big hands were useful when she was a teenager playing volleyball, but not when she was trying to fit her giant paw into a stubborn drawer. Someone was approaching her with bad intentions.

Pepe would be there in half an hour. He had located Jack's safety deposit box in a bank in Grey Canyon. They had agreed to check it out. He wanted to leave early. But the extra hour of sleep Bea insisted on had come with a high price.

She twisted her hand inside the drawer. She clasped the grip and slowly moved the gun out. She opened the chamber and sighed.

Empty.

Steely had removed the bullets. The most likely spot for them was a dresser drawer a few feet away. Bea eased out of bed. The bedroom door was half open, enabling her to hear even the slightest movement. The bad part was the intruder would hear her if she made more noise than the rustling of the trees on the rooftop.

She slid over to the dresser, never lifting her sock-covered feet. She opened the drawer and hoisted the narrow box out. She quietly filled the chamber, closed it. The safety latch was flipped off.

"Nobody's getting my TV," she mouthed. With her back against the wall, she eased toward the hall, granting her a full view of most of the den. Whoever was out there would be facing her in a matter of seconds. Bea slid closer to the bedroom door. She took a deep breath and made the turn.

"Mr. Qualls? You came for breakfast?"

He had a knife in his hand. A gun stuffed in his waist.

"You should answer the door when you're home. Where is the agreement? Give it to me, and I'll let you live."

Bea correctly assessed that he had no intention of letting her live, even if he got what he came for.

"Mr. Qualls, you don't take a knife to a gun fight. I'm trying to figure out how to shoot you so you don't splash blood on my recliner."

He went for the gun.

Bea squeezed the firing mechanism. Hit him in the shoulder. The gun fell out of his hand. He ran out the same way he came in. Bea fired again, striking his left side. He was hit but not down. He stumbled outside and down the driveway toward the street.

Bea trailed behind him all the way to the sidewalk. Panned the street.

He had vanished.

CHAPTER SIXTY-ONE

Steely heard nothing from Nick. He had been silent for the last twenty-four hours. If he were an enlisted man, he would be labeled AWOL. He was on an unapproved leave of absence. He had to come back successful or not bother to come back at all. The number of people wanting a piece of him was escalating. But his life wasn't at risk yet—unless some loco did the dumbest thing ever and assassinated him before regaining control of the money.

The assets, floating into oblivion, were leverage for Steely. Sergeant Donovan didn't know it, but he was her backup. One call from her would draw him to the tower in minutes. Her plan, like Nick's, could be a huge win—or a disaster. But one thing was for certain. It would be a turning point.

The tower was virtually empty when Steely arrived an hour earlier than Ray allowed her to be there. She wasn't concerned that the only person she saw in the building was a security guard. Getting to the tower before normal working hours was the least dangerous situation she'd be facing that day.

Steely's cell lit up. She almost didn't answer, but it was unusually early for a neighborly call from Mrs. Yost.

"Mrs. Yost, I really can't talk right now. Is everything OK?"

"No, it isn't!" Yost said shakily. "Your mother-in-law is shooting up the neighborhood again! This isn't the Wild West, you know!"

"Shooting?"

"She ran out the back door. Bang! Bang!"

"Is she OK?"

"OK? Zipped down the driveway like she was running track. Didn't you call the exterminator? You know I've tried to be patient because of her mental condition. But I had to call HPD this time."

"I warned her. I'll call her right now and take care of it."

"She'll have to explain to Officer Montgomery when she gets there."

"Mrs. Yost, I'm so sorry she troubled you."

"Troubled? Me and my granddaughter are held up in the bathtub like we're under a tornado warning!"

"Stay put. I'm calling her now."

Steely ended the call. She pressed in Bea's number as fast as she could move her fingers.

It rang only once before Bea said, "You wouldn't believe what just—"

"Miss Bea, are you OK?"

"Yes."

"Are you trying to get arrested?"

"Just defending myself. It was a five-foot-ten rat!"

"A man?"

"Yes, although calling Thomas Qualls a 'rat' is an insult to the rodent."

"He broke into the house?"

"I had to shoot before he climbed in my bed."

"What's he doing there?"

"He rambled on about some agreement."

"An agreement?"

"I told him he couldn't have it. Then I shot his old, ugly self—twice. Oh no! I hear Pepe outside. We're going to the bank in Grey Canyon. I'm not even dressed."

"Miss Bea, listen to me. Get out of the house now and go to Grey Canyon. Don't come back until you hear from me."

"I don't even have my makeup—"

"I don't care if your face is bone-dry. Get out now!"

"Not until I'm fixed up."

"Officer Montgomery is on her way. Get out now before anyone else comes back!"

"All right, I'm going! I'm going!"

"And don't come back until I call you."

"I'm going!"

Click.

Bea was now safe with Pepe.

CHAPTER SIXTY-TWO

Steely focused back on Keaton. For two hours, she strode around the closet debating how to approach him. All scenarios were covered.

Total denial.

Blaming Jack.

Nick.

Mr. Dichiara.

Her dad.

And even herself.

She memorized counterresponses, and then she dialoged in her mind. She played Keaton. Then herself. She'd be ready for whatever he tossed her way.

Steely checked her cell. Five missed calls from Erin. She redialed. Erin promptly answered. "Steely? I've been trying to reach you since yesterday. Where are you?"

"In Nick's office. Service here is spotty. Sometimes it rings and sometimes it doesn't. My mind has been on lockdown all morning. What do you need?"

"Cricket has gone nuts. I heard her on her phone."

"More than normal?"

"She ordered a hit on you, Nick, and Mrs. Ray. I've never heard anyone order a hit."

"A hit?"

"You have to get out of there. She wants you all dead—I'm mean really dead! Not just a figure of speech. She wasn't joking. You've got to get out of there!"

"I'll go. But there's something I have to do first." She hovered in a corner and whispered, "I can't explain now."

"I'm coming down to you. I'll be there in a few minutes. We'll leave together."

"No, don't wait for me. Go on."

"I'm not leaving without you. What do you have to do? I'll do it with you."

"No. Please go."

"Are you trying to test my loyalty? I'm not leaving."

"OK, Erin. You can wait in Nick's office. Use the combo on the door and let yourself in."

"Got it."

Steely ended the call. She redialed Nick. Got his voice mail again, but it was no longer full. His messages had been retrieved. "Nick, I'm ready to meet up with you." Her perfectly worded prose should get both his attention and anyone else who was listening. It didn't make sense that she hadn't gotten a response from yesterday's talk with the deer.

She circled the closet, stopping to set her view on her cell. Then the deer. The time of sitting and waiting was over. Donna hadn't given her the nod that Keaton was free, but she could no longer wait.

It was also time to give Donovan his invitation to this party. Calculating every second for his arrival was critical. If he got there too soon, she wouldn't have time to confront Keaton. Too late and well...Who knows?

Donovan's cell number, which she had memorized, was by-passed for the main line at HPD headquarters. He would answer his cell and make an emergency run to the tower or send a barrage of officers in his place. Messages left at his office, marked urgent, were immediately forwarded to him. This, hopefully, would be just the right timing.

"Sergeant Donovan, it's Steely. Mr. Keaton is about ready to turn himself in. He'll confess and name names. Please meet me in his office. See you in a few."

Steely pressed an indention on the side of her phone to stop all sounds. Vibrating was the only alert it would be making until after she had talked with Keaton. She slipped it into her pocket, locked the closet, and took off for the stairs. The elevators weren't the best mode of transportation. They could stop on any floor and could possibly pick up the wrong person. The stairs were isolated, rarely used; even when going up or down one floor, occupants used a lift.

No one was around to see her enter the stairwell, close the door behind her, and bend her knees. "Father, I've prepared all I know how to prepare. Please help me get the truth from this man. That's all I want is the truth, Jesus." She lifted herself up and took off for the forty-five-flight climb.

Every costly step echoed up and down the steel structure. Her job as an executive trainee was over. She hoped that would be the worst of the consequences. Accusing the CEO of murder was not specifically mentioned in her employment contract, but Keaton had Jack fired using the company as leverage. It was the time to use that same leverage on Keaton. He had to go. The tables had turned. Hopefully they wouldn't turn back.

She rubbed her eyes and pressed on. Her emotions were fully caffeinated. She picked up stride, running up another dozen floors before taking a break.

On the thirty-eighth floor, her cell rattled. She ignored the number. It was not one she recognized. It vibrated again. She thought about the handful of people who had her number. What if Miss Bea was in trouble? She cautiously answered.

"Hello?"

"Miss Paupher...Hunter...Whatever you call yourself, my name is Chevoski."

Steely stopped short. She leaned over the rail and scanned below. Then she looked up as far as she could see. No one was there. He wouldn't be calling if he knew she was alone in an enclosed stairwell.

"I need proof my money is on its way back in my accounts by six o'clock tonight. I'm giving Nick and Keaton the same demand. One of you has it. Today I'm taking care of Keaton."

She began moving faster up the next flight.

"He'll cooperate. I hope you have sense enough to respond in the correct manner. I'll take care of the big mouth, Beatrice Hunter. If the money still hasn't shown up, I'll make a jigsaw puzzle out of you. I've never had anyone not cooperate after the first cut. Six o'clock tonight is the deadline."

She ended the call and took off.

Her thoughts gained speed, along with her pace. Bea had left for Grey Canyon with Pepe. No one would find her there. Chevoski must not know where Nick was, or he wouldn't be calling her. Donovan should arrive in a few minutes. Her focus was back to cracking Keaton.

It was time for Steely to be combative. Her nature was anti-combative. It was a desirable quality. One of her best traits had to take a backseat for the next few minutes. She was confronting Keaton.

She stopped for a few seconds and caught her breath. For the most part, her argument would be factual. Some of it would be deduction, substantial at best. She hoped her assertions were correct. Keaton would have to deny the truth to argue.

Her emotions, high with anticipation, carried her all the way up to the forty-ninth floor. Her cell rattled again. This number she knew.

"Donna, I'm almost there."

"Mr. Qualls just left. He was bleeding badly. Somebody shot him!"

"Is that right?"

"He said the cartels are after them because some money disappeared! Don't come up here."

"I'm on forty-nine."

"Did you take cartel money?"

"Be there in two minutes."

"Don't come here. Mr. Chevoski is after you. Mr. Keaton is packing his bags. Don't come! I'm leaving too."

"I'm here."

The door to the fiftieth floor sprung open outside Nick's old office. She gazed at it before moving down the hall. There was no time for reflection. No time for good or bad memories. She had to focus on the man who had ripped the pictures of Jack and Bea off of the walls. He was about to bolt. The door to Keaton's suite was in sight.

CHAPTER SIXTY-THREE

Donna was standing outside Keaton's door, shaking. Steely checked her phone. Time wasn't on her side.

Donna flashed her eyes at Steely. "Cartels?"

Steely's brow rose. "Speculation, at first."

"They're going to come in here and kill us all!"

Steely put an arm around her. "Go on home. Sergeant Donovan should be here any second."

Donna grabbed her purse. "Let him fire me! I'm never coming back. This place is too dangerous. Cartels after them." She took her nameplate off the desk and threw it in the trash. "You come with me." She ran and pushed a button and an elevator popped open. She held it. "Come on! Let's go!"

"I have to talk to Keaton first."

"Come on," she whispered.

"Go on."

"Are you sure?"

"Yes, please go on."

Donna hesitantly let go of the door.

Steely stuck her head in Keaton's office. He gripped a duffel bag and raced around the room, picking up useless plaques and framed photos.

She took a deep breath and boldly entered. "Mr. Keaton, I'm Steely Hunter. We need to talk."

He glanced over at her and kept moving. "Ms. Hunter, if you or Nick took their money, you better put it back before there is a massacre."

Steely swished her head from side to side. "It won't be the first."

Appearing at a loss for words, Keaton stared at her for a few seconds. Then he swung back into motion, picking up magazines, books, and artifacts.

Her carefully planned spiel needed to be even more condensed.

"Mr. Keaton, you're partly responsible for the murder of my dad."

Keaton paused, dropped his chin to his chest. "I…I don't know anything about that."

"You knew about Mr. Chevoski."

He shook his head and moved faster. "He is a businessman. That's all I knew."

"Everyone in town knows what he does. You knew people weren't just scammed but murdered. It will go better for you if you're the first one to confess."

Keaton yanked a pen set off his desk and crammed it into his bag. "I don't have anything to confess except my poor judgment in trusting Alexis. She introduced me to Chevoski. I only agreed to make the company temporarily look bad. What's the big deal? I moved some assets around and then put them back." Keaton stuffed a paperweight into his bag, along with two framed photos from his desk. "Things just got out of control."

"Out of control? The game went lethal the day my dad was murdered. This is no petty crime, Mr. Keaton. Look out the window." Steely leaned in that direction. "Take a look."

342

He stared at her and then at the window.

"Go on and see! You better help yourself while you can and tell the truth, or you'll die in prison." This was a risky move. If Donovan wasn't down there, with at least one car flashing its lights in the street below, Keaton's glance would be benign.

Keaton's face reddened. His eyes protruded as he dashed to the window. The show of force from three cruisers, their lights wildly flashing, briefly paralyzed him.

Steely exhaled and confidently moved closer to him. "Mr. Keaton, they're here for you."

Keaton turned away. "They have nothing on me." He recklessly bounced around the office, gathering framed documents with meaningless scribbles.

Steely stayed on him. "You set up hundreds of bank accounts for phony subsidiaries of JHI. Then you allowed drug and prostitution money to pollute the company assets. Technical name is money laundering. And that makes you part of the conspiracy that resulted in the murder of my dad."

"I didn't know about your dad until after it happened. Same thing with Jack and David. No one was supposed to harm them. I can't control other people."

"There are only a handful of people who know the truth about what happened to Jack and David. You, Mr. Keaton, were not one of them."

Keaton inhaled and tightly closed his eyes. "I didn't know until after the fact. I'm telling the truth."

"A polygraph hooked up to you would be exploding."

He went back to his desk and did what he does best. He deflected. "Vince Dichiara set up the subsidiaries with Nick's help. Maybe you need to talk to them."

"Everything Nick and his dad did was legit. You made two hundred thirteen million in reserves disappear. That's called embezzling."

He pulled out drawers for a second look. "I was investing operating capital in our subs."

"Your venture capitalist group consists of murderers, human traffickers, drug dealers, and money launderers. They're not upstanding members of the chamber of commerce! Do you know how many of these crimes are solved?" Whether this was a rhetorical question or not, he wasn't answering. "You follow the money. The money trail, Mr. Keaton, leads to you."

Keaton circled over to the window. He took another disturbing glance down. He flipped back around, zipped up his loot, and continued his exodus.

"Did you know the DA released Mr. Rios? All charges were dropped."

Keaton shot his view downward and made a dash for the door.

"He's going to sue you and Mr. Qualls for framing him."

"I had nothing to do with that." He gripped the bag tightly.

"Mr. Keaton, you can't prop yourself up in Jack's chair and take no responsibility for what happened. You pointed the finger at Jack. Remember, you even agreed that the CEO is responsible for what goes on around here."

Keaton paused at the door. His recollection of the past had been recreated in his mind to forget what he couldn't erase. But his narcissistic bent hadn't left him totally unscathed. His eyes glassed over. His body trembled. Facing the truth was something he hadn't done for most of his life. He was a thief. A sleaze. A lazy leech. But worst of all, he was jealous of Jack Hunter. And now he was being destroyed for it.

CHAPTER SIXTY-FOUR

Saint Stephen's Bank had a Polynesian flare. Pink stucco, clay roof, and palm trees blowing in the wind surrounded the property that was stumbling distance from the beach. The interior decor was made of twine-tied bamboo. Anyone unfamiliar with the island might perceive the bank as the perfect place for a heist. Their assessment would be dead wrong. The islanders were an independent people whose rule of law made international standards look feeble. Law enforcement was swift, and punishment, harsh. A perpetrator would risk being shot on the spot if the bank president, Sheila Farnsworth, was in her office.

Nick Dichiara stood angled in a back corner. Farnsworth gave him the signal.

The first customer had arrived.

The possibility of spending the rest of his life in a federal prison hadn't deterred Nick. He had accomplished something no one else could: he'd ripped off the crooks. And now he was ready to bag his first one.

His risks were far from over. He could still be the one convicted of grand larceny, plus a half dozen other crimes. The new Saint Stephen's and Swiss accounts were explainable. But what judge and jury would believe a rogue CFO with $213 million sitting in the business account of Nick's Lawn Service? The highest balance in the account had been $2,093.04 until yesterday. The account had been used for the lawn business Nick ran from the age of ten until his freshman year in high school.

If Nick didn't trap Keaton by this time next month, he could be the one indicted. No one walks away with that kind of money without heads rolling. He had no indictable proof of anything Keaton had done. Absolutely none. In his possession was $639 million—more than the gross national product of many civilized countries.

He cringed when he saw a man in a hooded jacket heading to the teller window. Nick knew the jacket. He had given it to Jason for his birthday just last year.

Jason yanked a printout from the teller's hand. He examined it. Then he turned aggressively, like he was about to slug him, before demanding to see his boss.

Sheila Farnsworth was prepared to respond. "May I help you, sir?"

Wilkerson crumpled the printout. "My name is Nick Dichiara. There's been some mistake on my account," he shouted. "I had over eight million in here. I transferred it a few days ago."

Farnsworth didn't need to examine the account statement. She'd studied it for the last two days. "Sir, we no longer have an account for INS83, LLC. You closed this account."

Wilkerson was livid. "What do you mean—closed it? That's my money! And you'd better find it!" He leaned into Farnsworth.

She retreated a step and opened her jacket to reveal a filled holster. "Do not make another erratic move."

He indicated that he understood. He took a deep breath and calmed his rage.

"Sir, there's someone here who can explain."

Nick moved out of the shadows and into the light.

Wilkerson twisted his head around and rolled his eyes. "Nick, what are you doing here?" Jason asked nervously.

"I'll be the one asking the questions," Nick said, moving closer.

Jason did his usual two-step. "There's been a mistake."

"Really?" Nick made a fist and sent Jason to the floor. "I kept hoping you were just stupid. I wanted you to be stupid. You bugged my office. Cloned my phone. Cloned Steely's too. Then you opened an account in my name. You were my best friend, Jason."

Jason scrambled up. His chin split and oozing blood.

Farnsworth tossed him a tissue. "Don't mess up my bank."

"What are you all steamed about?" Jason blotted his injury. "It wasn't your money. I put it here for safety. I had to use your name because nobody would think anything about you having that kind of money. That's all I did. Really, I earned this money."

"What'd you do for eight million?" Nick stood flat-footed, restraining himself.

"It'd interest me too," added Farnsworth.

Jason groaned. "Nick, I didn't know they were doing anything wrong. I told you everything I did. I wired funds. That's it. Mr. Keaton wanted me to set up thousands of automatic wires. That's all I did. It's not illegal."

"You were their pigeon, flying back and forth, drinking their coffee. When did you figure out what they were doing? Before or after they murdered Jack and David?"

Jason wiped his hands on his thighs.

"Before? You knew they killed them, and you still let them use you. We're done."

"I didn't know for sure they killed people. We're innocent until proven guilty."

Farnsworth buttoned her coat. "Not here, blockhead."

"Nick, remember I saved your life when you almost drowned? You wouldn't be here if it wasn't for me. Help an old pal out. Let me go."

"I almost drowned because you knocked me in the head with a paddle."

Jason was ready to sing. "It was Cricket's mother, Alexis Cankor."

"Alexis Cankor?" Nick bobbed his head and acted like he wasn't shocked.

"She wanted Cricket to marry David Hunter. But he wouldn't have anything to do with her. Alexis picked up on Mr. Chevoski's hatred for Mr. Hunter and used him. The original plan was to funnel out the liquid assets and run. But they didn't do it because of Cricket. She didn't want to be on the run for the rest of her life."

"Cricket made these decisions?"

"She wanted to be free to go and do whatever she wanted. She convinced her mother and Mr. Chevoski to launder money through the company. It worked well. Chevoski gave up his businesses to do this full-time. His clients are the top drug dealers and human traffickers in the Southwest. He takes twenty percent off the top. Then he nets the rest back to his clients."

Nick tightened his face. "And you didn't know a thing?"

"I hacked into Keaton's phone and personal e-mail. I had to for my own protection. No one would ever find that account. Chevoski killed Mr. Paupher. Warren Dupree followed his orders and rigged the brakes on Mr. Hunter's truck. Mr. Qualls activated the device that severed the brake line. Cricket's grandfather had Mr. Chevoski investigated and found out the truth about him. He was going to report Chevoski. That's what the grandfather told Cricket, right before she killed him in the garage. She's the one you need to go after. Not me. I'm a bystander."

Nick stared at Jason. He was shocked at how fast Jason spilled his guts. He should have dangled him off the top of the building. This information would have come out before his hands got tired.

"Everything I found out was after the fact. That makes me innocent."

"Not here," assured Farnsworth.

Nick snapped back, "Who else is coming here?"

"I think they all are. I came to get my money and get out before they get here. Keaton doesn't even know I took it."

Nick crossed his arms. "You ripped off the crooks. Who would do something that dumb?" He shook his head. "It's time to say good-bye, Jason."

"What?"

Nick stepped aside.

"Nick, please! It was the only way I could reach my goals."

"I hope your goal was prison," Nick snapped.

Thibodeaux charged in, accompanied by two police officers. "You're in deep, sweetie," he hollered.

The officers surrounded Jason and directed him to spread out. They frisked him. Secured metal cuffs around his hands and ankles and started moving him out.

"You're quiet for a guy who may get hung," quipped Pierce.

Jason went limp. "Hung? They don't hang people in the U.S."

"Saint Stephen's doesn't have an extradition agreement with the U.S.," Pierce said. "You're being arrested for breaking their law. They'll give you a speedy trial. You may make court tonight." Pierce smirked. "Saves them money to give you a speedy trial."

The officers shoved Jason outside to a waiting car. The islanders watched from a distance. He struggled, irritating the officers, until they clubbed him. His resistance ceased. The officers held open the car door and shoved Jason inside.

Nick glanced at him and then looked away. Thibodeaux leaned over and waved. Jason departed, crouched inside. The onlookers dispersed.

Pierce and Nick hustled toward a waiting cab. Pierce elbowed him. "I was starting to think we'd be waiting here a while."

"I took out a little insurance yesterday—you know, to lower the risk of the situation dragging out," said Nick.

Thibodeaux clapped his hands. "I think four hundred twenty-six million definitely put this thing on steroids."

"Make that six hundred thirty-nine."

"Six hundred thirty-nine million?"

"If I had to be a fugitive for the rest of my life, they weren't going to get away with this."

"It's not over yet. I hope you have the assets where they can't find them." Pierce continued alongside him.

Nick nodded.

"What do you want to do with Jason?"

Nick shrugged. "He's better off here. Max ten years. It's more than fair. He'll live."

Pierce agreed. "Now how are you going to live on US soil?"

"It's me or Chevoski. One of us won't see tomorrow." Nick opened the cab door. He unfastened a wire from his shirt and wound it up. "I'll take the recording back with me. Jason can be questioned via video. HPD may not even need him. The roaches are scattering fast."

"They'll all be dead if their business associates get hold of them."

"Even if I could, I wouldn't save them from their business partners. You can finish this up, right?"

"I'm an attorney. Of course I can do this."

Nick tilted his head and got into the cab. "Just call the cops if anyone else shows up." He held the door and leaned out. "Don't forget to send a boat for me. I don't want to be in the gulf after dark. The jet's going down when we get over water."

"Due south from Galveston. Right?"

"The trackers are in my parachute."

"Do you have to crash a jet?"

"If it gets off the ground, I'm going to give them a spectacular ride." Nick tightly grinned, closed the door, and tapped the driver. "Hit it!"

CHAPTER SIXTY-FIVE

The Grey Canyon Bank still passed out toasters to their new customers. For the last thirty-two years, Mrs. Billings had been in charge of the safety deposit boxes. She knew exactly where Jack's box was located. It was the same one his parents had rented. Billings inserted the bank's key into the slot and turned it, releasing the box. It was left on a table for Bea to open at her pleasure.

"Mrs. Hunter, let me know when you're finished." She exited the vault and went back to work, allowing the customer her privacy.

Beatrice plugged in the second key, lifted the lid, and then slammed it back.

"What's wrong?" asked Pepe.

"I almost wish we hadn't found this box. I have a bad feeling."

"What could it be?"

"I don't know." She leaned down on the lid, as if it could pop open by itself. "Why didn't Jack tell me it was here? Maybe he had secrets."

"What secrets?"

"My nerves are shot! I can't take any more surprises. What if he committed fornication?"

"Bee-Bee, Jack wasn't like that."

"I always trusted him. He could have—"

"Why don't you quit speculating and open it?" Pepe prodded. "There must be something important in it."

"I guess you're right." She slowly flipped the lid over. Inside were two legal-sized envelopes.

"Papers?"

The first one had no exterior markings and wasn't sealed. She slid the document out and read for a few seconds. She jumped up and down, waving the two-stapled pages. "This is our safety net." She leaned over for Pepe to kiss her cheek.

"What is it?"

"A buy-back agreement." Bea held it close to her chest before passing it over. "Jack knew what he was doing. That Jack. He was faithful and smart."

He scanned the first page. "Jack could buy the stock back at the same price he sold it?"

She cheered. "We're back in business!"

Pepe kept reading. "This is the original. It's notarized on the last page. It says the option passes on to his heirs. You can buy your stock back from Harry."

Bea sang, twirling in a circle. "I'm getting the company back!"

Pepe smiled. "Jack was one smart guy."

Bea calmed down enough to pick up the second envelope. The return address read: "Vince Dichiara, Attorney at Law." She ripped into it. "Wait until that Harry..." Her arms sprung out. Clasping the envelope in her hand, she stumbled back against the wall.

Billings came running in. "Is she all right?"

Pepe said, "Bee-Bee?" He waved a hand in front of her stoic face.

Billings said, "I'd think she was passed out if she wasn't standing and her eyes weren't open. She's still breathing, right? I don't want anybody dying in here."

Pepe held her in place. "Just give us a minute." He pried the document from her fingers, held it up to the light, and read. "Yours and Jack's will?"

Bea used her hand to signal for him to continue and then dropped back.

He speed-read the first page. Then he covered his mouth with it. "Oh my goodness. He left everything to David. Including JHI stock. Did David leave everything to…"

She took a deep breath.

He folded the will back into the envelope. "Netting out the company debt, your stock wasn't worth that much. Was it?"

"Seventy-nine million."

"That much?"

Bea opened her purse. Took out a pack of matches and began striking one.

Pepe grabbed her hands.

She struck again, got nothing but a puff of smoke.

"Bea, stop! You can't burn it."

She tossed the matches in the air and dropped her head on the table and moaned. "Steely can claim my stock!"

Pepe smiled. "I hope you've been nice to your daughter-in-law."

Bea stood up. "Just as nice as I am to everybody else."

Pepe put his arm around her. "Bea, don't worry. I have plenty for both of us." Pepe closed the box. "Marry me?"

Bea flexed her arms at her waist. "Are you proposing to me in a bank vault, after I just lost the company for the second time?"

He shook his head. "I guess not."

"My emotions are scrambled eggs, and you're proposing?"

"Definitely not."

Bea snatched up the documents. "I guess we better go find the little rich girl."

"Didn't she tell you to wait for her call?"

"She might be rich, but she's not the boss of me."

"I'm sure not," he said, following her.

Pepe motioned to Billings that they were done. And then they fled.

CHAPTER SIXTY-SIX

Steely was the only barrier between Keaton and his exodus. He was short of breath, gasping. "Jack would have had plenty of money if he hadn't paid off the company debt." He looked away and shook his head. "I was giving him what he always wanted— early retirement. I didn't want anyone to get hurt." He ducked his head, attempting to maneuver around her.

Steely held out a stiff arm, impeding him. "Mr. Keaton, you could get a death sentence."

For a moment, Keaton didn't resist. "I may already have one." He pushed past her, opened the glass door to the lobby, and pressed an arrow for a ride down.

"Mr. Keaton, where are you going?"

"Out of the country. You'd better get going too. Mr. Qualls could walk in here and kill us both. Mr. Chevoski thinks I double-crossed him. He's gone crazy." Keaton jabbed at the button several times.

Steely dogged him. "You can't run for ever. Stop and make things better for yourself. You can start by telling me who killed my dad." She paused. "Who killed my dad?"

"Where's that elevator?" He panted. He beat his fist rapidly on the door. There was no movement from the cables. He ran for the stairs.

Steely thought about tripping him, tackling him. He was a big guy. But if she could trip him up, he'd fall hard.

"Mr. Keaton, please tell me who killed my dad." She stood dauntlessly between him and the exit. He wasn't getting past her without someone getting hurt.

Keaton spit out, "Chevoski. I swear I didn't know."

"Who killed Jack and David?"

"Chevoski ordered Dupree to rig it up. Qualls set off the electrical charge that punctured the brake line. I didn't know. I'm telling the truth. I had no idea."

She moved out of the way. He swung open the stairway door and ran like a madman.

Where is Donovan?

The elevator dinged. Steely squatted in a dark corner with a visual on the lobby. Nobody was coming in or out without her seeing them first. Keaton wasn't coming back. She was sure of it. Even if he didn't get caught leaving, he'd have to hide for the rest of his life. Miss Bea was safe with Pepe in Grey Canyon. Nick was hiding out, somewhere around the world, with laundered money. He'd be drawn out when today's drama hit the news. She sunk lower when she heard the door slide open.

Sergeant Donovan and his entourage of two had arrived. Steely lifted her head up. "Thank you," she whispered, rising.

Donovan ran to her. "Are you OK?"

"Yes, Sergeant."

Donovan ran into Keaton's office. Panned the room. "Where is he?"

"Down the south stairwell." Steely pointed.

Donovan ordered the officers, "Bowman, down the stairs. Wylie, take an elevator to the lobby." Then he glanced back at Steely. "Where's Qualls?"

"He left."

The sergeant squeezed the mouthpiece attached to his shoulder. "Seal off the building." Then he spoke firmly to Steely. "We're going to have a talk later. First, I'm searching the floor. Go lock yourself in Keaton's office until I get back."

"Yes, sir."

Donovan drew his weapon, turned right, and began his search. Steely did as directed. She almost had the door shut when Chevoski gripped her wrist with his brutal hand. His fingers were as wide as they were long. He stuck his boot in the door and shoved it open. "Quiet," he whispered.

Her fingers were becoming numb. She pulled back. He let loose. The impressions his hands left were identical to those on her dad's neck. This was the hand that killed her dad. This man had ordered the murder of Jack and David, commanded the lethal drug and alcohol mixture that stopped the heart of Mr. Fitzpatrick, and blew the gaping hole in Jenny's chest. He was the boss.

Screaming was an option. Donovan would be there in seconds. She quickly dismissed that scenario. He didn't have his assets. She was safe for now. And there was no way she was going to miss this opportunity. He was about to commit a crime that the victim could live to tell. Assuming she lived through it.

Taking her against her will was a felony. The gun in his other hand meant aggravated kidnapping. They were in a high-security building. By the time they got out, there'd be enough film for a documentary. He couldn't get the death penalty, but he could get life. For the moment, that was good enough for her.

Chevoski stuck the semi in her gut. "Not a peep," he whispered, twisting her wrist, causing a burning sensation.

"Mr. Chevoski, I got your message."

"You recognize me?"

"I've seen pictures," she spouted bravely.

"Let's go." He yanked her, almost pulling her arm out of its socket. "You're always helping people. Now you're going to help me get my money back." He directed her to the executive lobby. Glanced left, then right. Both were clear. He decisively headed left. Unless he planned on bungee-jumping out a window, the only thing in that direction was the north stairs. He prodded her along, bruising her ribs.

She said, "These stairs end in the main lobby." His answer would tell her if taking her was a spontaneous opportunity or planned. Spontaneous would be to her benefit.

He smiled with clenched teeth. "We're walking out the front door."

Spontaneous.

He pulled a lever on the stairwell wall, setting off an alarm. A voice over the speaker system began repeating an emergency message: "This is not a drill. Please exit the building. This is not a drill. Please exit the building."

"Now get moving," he said. "The building's on fire."

The tower occupants were well trained in emergency drills. Fire captains assigned to every floor ensured that everyone got out quickly. Drop what you're doing and leave by the closest exit were the instructions. Workers split off between the north and south stairs. The building was suddenly in chaos. Chevoski shoved Steely hard, sending her diving to the second step, totally missing the first. The handrail saved her from an uncontrollable fall down an entire flight. She complied with his request. They blended in with the other evacuators until she stopped on the fifth floor.

"Keep going," said Chevoski.

She wasn't budging. "I smell smoke."

He pulled on her. "Did you know they don't put smoke detectors in closets? Now don't act up."

"I'm not leaving until I know Erin's OK." She pushed off from him and beat on the locked door.

Monte cracked it open. Chevoski moved down a few steps, out of view.

"Where's Erin?" she asked.

"The medics are coming to get her. She's awake and breathing now. Smoke was coming from inside the closet. I thought you were in there. Someone locked the door from the outside. I came by and busted in. You better go."

Chevoski nudged her back.

Steely hesitated and then proceeded to the lobby.

People were pouring out of the building. Word had spread. The alarm was not a drill. Security personnel guarded the propped-open doors, making sure all who entered were emergency workers. Chevoski and Steely were almost out when Candy caught a glimpse of them.

"Act normal," he advised.

They passed by the rescuers without incident. Calling for help would have been less risky for her than leaving with him, but she stayed quiet. He tightened his grip on her and pushed toward the street, which was more hectic than the lobby. Dozens of emergency vehicles were lined up around the building. Any hint of a fire at the tower triggered an automatic five alarm, sending over forty firefighters.

Candy kept her eyes on Steely and Chevoski. She called for Mrs. Ray a third time, but she was out of her office, like everyone else. She still had a glimpse of them when she spotted Ray, several feet away, talking with a security officer. She left her post and ran over to Ray.

"Mrs. Ray, Steely just left, out that door, with Mr. Chevoski." Candy pointed.

Ray raced outside.

Candy followed. "I lost them in the crowd." They both stared at the people shuffling around them.

Ray stepped up on a pillar, getting a better view of the street.

"I'm sorry, Mrs. Ray."

Ray climbed down. "You did exactly what I told you to do. I can figure out what direction they're going. Come upstairs and help me. We need to find Sergeant Donovan."

CHAPTER SIXTY-SEVEN

Chevoski hustled Steely down an isolated side street toward a parked car. Sirens blared loudly behind them. Lights beat against their backs.

"Now let's see if you're worth six hundred thirty-nine million."

She jerked her shoulder back. "Six hundred thirty-nine?"

"I don't think you're worth ten cents. You better hope Nick feels differently."

Steely angled her head to pose for the last security camera before they reached the car. The first seven had gotten a shot of them, but the last one had a perfect view. Chevoski opened the driver's-side door and shoved Steely over the console. Her legs rammed into the windshield until she settled down in the passenger seat. He got in, hit the gas, and skidded off. Steely was in her most vulnerable spot yet. Alone in a car with a man who would kill her for dinner. She was his captive. He appeared in control.

He set the pistol in his lap. This move made her more comfortable than his waving it at her while he ranted on about how he had been a victim. He had been treated poorly his entire life, misjudged and abused by most. He was a textbook sociopath. She sat quietly, taking mental notes.

Chevoski headed south on I-45, staying within five miles of the speed limit. He wasn't giving law enforcement any reason to stop him. But anyone interfering with him and his destination would find themselves in more danger than Steely.

The JHI jet was housed at the Southeast Regional Airport, immediately off the highway about halfway between Houston and Galveston. After a half hour of listening to his insane raving, Steely had a visual of the jet. It was not their destination. Chevoski whizzed by without so much as a glance.

"Where are we going?" she asked.

"I'm not stupid enough to take the company jet," he snapped. "I have a charter."

"At the airport in Galveston?"

He scoffed. "No one will look for us there."

The next half of the trip was just like the first. Chevoski poured out his life history nonstop. He gave deep details, like someone telling a close friend. He had no conscience of wrongdoing. Everything he did was a reaction to the horrifying things that were done to him, and worse.

Fred Pauper wasn't his maiden kill. He was twelve when a kid made fun of his no-name sneakers. That kid was never seen again. He started selling drugs at thirteen. Bought himself some new clothes. By the time he was fifteen, he took over the territory, and no one dared to challenge him until one night when he was leaving a restaurant with his girlfriend and three friends.

Gunfire sprayed rapidly in their direction, mortally wounding everyone but him. Chevoski wasn't hit, but he was covered in his girlfriend's blood. He rushed to his car, followed the perpetrators to a rural area, and ran them off the highway. His evening was spent cutting them into little pieces. In the most painful way.

After that evening, he always kept layers of associates between him and his vocation.

The killing of those Steely loved hadn't caused Chevoski to blink. He was talking to the daughter of a man he'd brutally killed. The widow and daughter-in-law of men burned beyond recognition. He had no remorse. No normal compassion. If it took basic human emotions to keep a heart pumping, he would already have been dead.

If this man wasn't stopped now, he would rack up even more on his kill list.

Steely thought about grabbing the gun from his lap. She'd get a kill shot or die trying. He'd be incapacitated, wreck the car, and maybe hurt someone else.

Her hand quivered and then calmed. That's what he would do. She leaned back in the seat. She wasn't him.

He slowed when they crossed the causeway to Galveston Island. He used the blinker to signal a lane change. He was exiting.

Maybe I should have thought this out. How could I think this out? I was kidnapped!

She briefly closed her eyes and prayed.

Jesus, help me.

Steely wasn't afraid. This was nothing compared to finding her mom that day in bed. Or listening to Sheriff Tucker tell her and Bea about the truck wreck. Still she kept quiet. The airport was in sight.

The car shimmied in the sand when Chevoski made a quick right toward the airstrip. "We'll be out of here in ten minutes," he boasted.

The airport was isolated. Nothing but private carriers used the facility. All the hangars were tightly locked up. A single aircraft was out of its housing, engines warming, and stairs extending up to an open cabin. Chevoski passed through a narrow driveway, several yards from the aircraft.

"You and your father should have minded your own business. You'd be rich, and he wouldn't have died in a bar. You don't mess with me. I don't mess with you. That's how it works."

Steely didn't engage him. He was talking, and that's exactly what she wanted. Information. Any details he blabbed, she'd remember.

"Your father caused his own demise when he called Jack Hunter. Good thing Harry found out about the meeting with Vince Dichiara. Me and Alexis offered him a great deal. Who wouldn't take three million over ten years to mind his own business? I was paying him to live. Then we could do business again."

"It was blackmail."

"I've mellowed in my old age. I was just going to scare his moral convictions out of him—send him to the hospital. One good concussion should've convinced him. Surprised me when I saw blood. He could have been a rich man. Nick Dichiara was a pain from the beginning. We knew there wasn't a chance he'd figure this out. I'm an entrepreneur." Chevoski was starry-eyed. "We put together a worldwide operation. We'd all be set for life. No need to run. We could've been upstanding citizens. No one could've touched us. Whoever took my money will be dead by tomorrow. I will find him. And when I do…"

Chevoski advanced past where cars were allowed on the runway, stopped at the stairs, and cut the engine. He rushed to the passenger side and yanked Steely out.

"It's time for the ride of your life."

Steely was getting on a jet with a man who wanted to make her the next slash in his belt. She pushed his arm away, the one holding the gun. If it went off, it wasn't hitting her. "Mr. Chevoski, tell me one thing. Why did you pick my dad for the job?"

Chevoski flashed a menacing grin. Everything about him was disturbing, but especially the look on his face when asked a serious question.

"Cricket recommended him. She was a conniver, even when she was in seventh grade. I can understand why she hated you."

"Where is she?"

"Catching up with Old Lady Hunter. We'll send a plane to pick her up in Beaumont tomorrow."

The pilot was sitting in the cockpit. His back was toward them. He was suited with a captain's hat. A petite shadow stirred in the cabin. Steely grabbed the railing when Chevoski jolted her up the stairs. "Hurry up," he commanded. "You're going to enjoy your last ride."

"Your plan lacks sense."

"Do you think stealing six hundred thirty-nine million makes sense?" Chevoski gripped her right arm tight enough to rupture vessels. "There'll be a sixty-million-dollar contract on my head if I don't get that money back by tomorrow."

"Good," Steely snapped. "Your business destroys people."

"I help them escape their miserable lives. They'll risk every-thing for a pouch of powder. It's not just the poor slob on the street anymore. Doctors, lawyers, CPAs, chefs, bankers, politicians. Fine, upstanding citizens are my customers. It's the way they survive."

"Survive? They fry their brains. Then they steal, kill, and de-stroy for their addiction. They end up in a prison or dead."

He shoved her up another step. "Stop lecturing me and move!"

Steely resisted, forcing him to drag her up every step. There had to be an air traffic controller, mechanic, or someone around. The pilot fiddled in the cockpit, appearing disinterested in his passengers. She stalled. "You know you're not Jack Hunter's son. I've seen the DNA results."

Chevoski paused. "There was no DNA test."

"Mrs. Hunter had one done from a glass you drank from."

"That's a lie. Jack Hunter hid me. Every time I heard a news report talking about how great Jack Hunter was, it made me sick." He shoved her up the next step.

"Your mind has caught that bug too."

"On her dying bed, my momma told me Jack Hunter was my father. I believe her over him. Now go!" He knocked her up the next step and then another.

Steely pushed back, dropping down a step. "Leo Chevoski—your mother was in a relationship with him—he was your father. He killed a family of four right after you were born. He was executed a few years later. Your mother probably didn't want you to know."

"Jack Hunter sent my mother child support. Guilt money is what it was. Now go!" They went up another step to reach the platform at the cabin door.

"Where's Alexis Canker's stepsister, Jacqueline, and her husband, Warren Dupree?"

Chevoski was smug. "Mr. Qualls sent them on a river-rafting trip."

"In a car?"

"You know how treacherous a river can be." He yanked her inside.

The cabin had four rows, two seats on each with an aisle between them. The cockpit door was open, unlike commercial flights. The captain's hands were moving around the controls.

The shadowy figure was Alexis Canker. She had nothing to say to their guest and took her seat. Chevoski pointed Steely to the place across from Alexis. The woman had her hand in her lap on top of a snout-nosed gun. The six shells would be more than she needed to control Steely. "She'll go for your extremities," bellowed Chevoski. "I don't want you dead just yet."

The captain, with an Australian accent, sounded off. "Everything's ready, mate. We are ready to secure the cabin."

"Then do it!" Chevoski secured himself in the first seat, facing opposite the others, and closed his eyes. "Lock us up," he ordered the captain.

Steely leaned over, catching a glimpse of the pilot's arm. He was not a pilot. She had been in a flight simulator at NASA. Holding on to the lever controlling the landing gear was not on the takeoff list. She braced herself to drop to the floor or run out the door and jump, if she could.

The pilot sounded alarmed. "Sir, you need to see this." Chevoski glared at Steely and then strutted to the cockpit. Leaning over the pilot's shoulder at the panoramic view, he slid his pistol in the pilot's back.

"They were waiting for us. Did you do this? Get this thing moving, or you're dying with me." He shouted, "Alexis, lock the cabin!"

The captain whacked Chevoski's arm against the dash. The man squeezed off one round, barely missing his target. The man charged at Chevoski, grabbing his arm and twisting until it snapped. The firearm was chucked into a corner, out of reach. The fight was now physical. The captain slammed the cockpit door, locking them in.

Steely ran forward, blocking the control panel. Alexis pointed her weapon at Steely, her finger wobbling on the trigger. "You have two seconds to get out of my way."

The boots shuffling outside were getting closer. They were either law enforcement or cartel. Steely wasn't going out to check. Her back was against the wall. Alexis exposed herself in the gaping door, following Chevoski's instructions.

The riot in the cockpit briefly distracted them. Glass was breaking, bodies were flinging around—until they heard a single shot.

Steely dropped to the floor and rolled up in a tornado crunch. Whoever was outside was coming in. Three shots whizzed by. Alexis dropped to her knees. She bent forward, bleeding out. She was no longer a threat to anyone. Steely fell sideways, away from her.

The plane was being invaded. Dozens of boots marched toward them, up the stairs, armed with automatic rifles. The boots stopped at Steely's feet.

"Steely, are you all right?" Donovan squatted beside her.

She popped open her watery eyes. "Yes."

"You need to get out of here, right now." Donovan pulled her up and passed her to an officer, who helped her out.

Donovan beat on the cockpit door. His crew jammed in behind him. "Open the door before we rip it off. This plane isn't going anywhere." Donovan hit the door again. "Last chance."

The cockpit door slowly opened. Donovan pushed it the rest of the way, with a shotgun aimed inside.

Nick held up his hands. "It's me!" A gash above his eye had torn open. He was bloodied but standing.

"Of course it's you." Donovan viewed Chevoski slumped in a corner. "Well, did you leave him with a pulse?"

Nick kicked the limp body. "Guess not."

Donovan squeezed his mouthpiece. "I need the coroner and a bus." He turned back to Nick. "You need to thank Mrs. Ray for calling me."

"Mrs. Ray?"

"She said they leased this jet on a company card, or we would have never found you."

"I was going to call."

"Sure you were." He ordered, "Move back and let us out."

Donovan and Nick maneuvered out of the cabin and then down the stairs. The remaining officers stayed to process the plane. "Mr. Qualls died on the highway a few miles down. Mr. Keaton had a massive heart attack. He's in intensive care. We got…"

Nick panned the area from the hangar to the runway.

"Don't be taking off. I've got a bus coming to transport you to the hospital."

"Where's Steely?"

Donovan caught up with him. "There's nobody out here but my people and some Galveston County deputies. Where could she go?"

Nick blotted his head with his arm, removing enough blood to gain better sight.

Donovan rotated around the area again. "Chevoski's car is missing!" He ran for his cruiser and jumped in. He turned on his radio and called in a BOLO. Nick hopped in beside him. Donovan flipped on the siren and fishtailed out to the interstate. "Where'd she go?"

"Have you picked up Cricket?"

"Nope. We really don't have anything on her. She might be the one who slips away. I hope Steely didn't…"

"Where are we going?" Nick said, worried.

Donovan floored it. "I'm heading toward town. We've got a few minutes to figure out where she is. I hope Steely has enough sense not to go near Cricket."

"She knows Cricket was involved in the death of her dad, most likely Jack and David too."

"Oh dear God."

CHAPTER SIXTY-EIGHT

Steely didn't bother hiding Chevoski's rental. She left it in the driveway in front of her house. The only person she would hide it from was already inside. She had passed Cricket's coupe parked halfway down the street. The house shook when Steely burst in the front door.

Propped up on the sofa where Steely's mom used to lie, Cricket pointed a pistol.

"Sit."

Steely passed the two easy chairs, facing Cricket, and moved slowly into Bea's adjacent recliner. She had no inclination that Cricked would settle for her extremities. "How's this going to end, Cricket?"

"You're going to die," Cricket said matter-of-factly.

"That's not your decision to make. Now, why don't you put that away? Nobody else needs to get hurt. HPD is on the way."

"No, they aren't. You came alone, so we could have this little chat. Mrs. Hunter and Mr. Martinez are on their way."

"Then let's have that chat. Why'd you bring my dad into this?"

Cricket tightened her grip, her teeth exposed like a rabid dog. "Simple. I hate you! This time, if I go down, you go down."

Steely placed a hand over heart, as if she could shield it. "Why? I never did anything to you."

Cricket fired at the family pictures, scattering a glass frame.

Steely hardly flinched.

Cricket words were fiery. "You had this perfect little family. Did you know my father beat my mother and me? At six, I still wet the bed. He beat me every time until I bled. My mother kept me out of school until the scars healed."

Steely pivoted her head from side to side. "No. They haven't. You need help. I know who can help you."

"Help? This house will be our deathbed. We'll die together. When I go, you go."

The front door came ajar and then pushed open. Martinez held it for Bea and then closed it behind them. Cricket tucked the gun on her far side.

Bea spouted, "Steely, why didn't you invite us to the party? You know I don't like finding things out from other people. Especially, this little—"

"Miss Bea—" Steely briefly put her hands over her face. "You weren't supposed to come home until I called. Why don't you and Mr. Martinez go have dinner, get a tenderloin? My treat."

"I'm not hungry!" Bea fired back, scowling at Cricket.

"Why don't you go to Mr. Martinez's cousin's house?" Steely looked over at Cricket. "That'd be OK, huh, Cricket? This is between you and me."

Bea folded her arms and wagged her head. "We're not leaving you here with this cuckoo bird!"

Martinez crossed his arms, locked his knees, agreeing.

Cricket barked, "Have a seat, you old bag."

"Listen here, little girl," Bea said, wielding a finger, "you call me an 'old bag' again, and I'll slap you silly."

Martinez struggled to restrain her.

Cricket brandished the gun. "Sit."

Steely waved Bea down, encouraging her to comply.

"They're right," snipped Bea. "She's nuts."

"I said sit!"

"The only place I'm sitting is that chair!" Bea said. "Steely, get up!"

Steely shook her head.

"Sit yourself down," Cricket said. "Boyfriend, you beside her." They complied, a short table catty-corner between them and Cricket. Steely rounded out the semicircle.

"Cricket, now you have three hostages. Think about what you're doing."

Cricket leaned back. "There's nothing to think about. I'm insane."

Bea popped off, "You're right about that, girlie."

Cricket cast her gaze on Steely, Bea, Martinez, and then back to Steely. "So, the last thing I'm going to do is kill all three of you. Boyfriend first, then Mrs. Hunter. Steely you're last. That's the order. I want Steely to watch."

Bea jumped up.

"Sit down!" Cricket screamed. "You're not first."

"Shut up," Bea said. "If I'm dying, it'll be in my recliner. Get up, Steely. Go on, get up!"

Cricket aggressively stood, with her gun arm stretched. "You have two seconds to sit yourself back down, or I'll change the order."

Steely maneuvered around Bea and the table. Bea fell into her recliner, dug her hands down in the seat. Then she made eyes at Steely, who was standing in front of the chair. Steely exchanged looks with Bea. Martinez stayed put between them.

Cricket yelled, "Now sit, or you're first!"

"Listen to me," Steely pleaded. "Nobody else has to die."

"Steely, sit down," said Bea. "You better do what she says."

"Yes," Martinez said, "you need to sit."

Steely argued. "Cricket, please put the gun down and end this peacefully. I know who can help you."

"I'm about to fire!"

Steely raised her hands to her chest. "OK, Cricket, but answer one more question for me. Did you switch my mom's meds?"

Cricked grinned.

"Cricket, I know you did. You don't need to answer."

The revelation seemed to stun Martinez and Bea. They stared at each other and then cut eyes back at Cricket.

Steely calmly pleaded, "Please put the gun away. You don't need to do this."

"My last bit of satisfaction," Cricket mocked. "Steely—begging for her life."

"No, stupid," said Bea, "she's begging for yours."

Steely dropped into her seat. A bullet whooshed through the front window into Cricket's shoulder, leveling her. Donovan kicked in the front door. Nick followed and clung to Steely.

Donovan kept the laser fixed on Cricket. He nabbed her pistol and lowered his guard. She was incapacitated, wounded but not mortally.

"Don't move," Donovan said. "The medics are on the way." He squinted at Steely. She turned toward him, Nick still wrapped around her.

"You saw the laser in the window, didn't you?" Donovan asked.

She nodded.

"Don't ever block a cop from a perp! And taking off like that?" Donovan sounded more scared than irritated. "If you weren't here…We didn't have a second guess."

"I'm sorry, Sergeant, but you got my message."

"What message?"

Steely lowered her tone. "To come to the tower. Then you were following me, right?"

"No! I came with an arrest warrant for Keaton and Qualls. We found Warren and Jacqueline Dupree and their little boy. They were willing to testify. Chevoski died in the fight with Nick. Qualls was found on the side of the highway dead. Keaton is on life support from a heart attack. We had everyone but Cricket."

Steely held tight to Nick. "Guess everything worked out."

Bea stepped in, her tone raised. "Worked out? I almost got shot twice today." Pepe nudged Bea. "Well, at least we didn't all die." Bea nodded.

Steely straightened up. "Wait, what?"

SWAT officers swarmed in, weapons drawn. They lowered their guard when Donovan signaled that the threat was over. He pushed them along. "I need all of you to go out the back, so we can process the scene." They formed a circle outside by the back door.

Bea pinched Steely's arm. "You pushed my gun down in the seat."

"Sergeant Donovan was there," Steely said.

"He wasn't there when we drove up," Bea said.

Steely's face broadened. "He wasn't?"

Bea shook her head. "Nope!"

Nick nodded.

"That's right," Pepe said. "We drove up and saw the girl in the window. Bea ran right in."

Steely looked over at Bea for confirmation.

"She couldn't take us all." Bea poked Nick. "Set up a board meeting in two hours. Let Clayton, Charlie, Pierce, and Benita know that they better be there if they want to protect their ass—"

Martinez elbowed Bea.

"Assets," Bea said. "Tell them this is an emergency meeting, and the majority stockholder will be there. If they have anything smart to say, tell them to read the corporate bylaws and show up. You need to be there, Steely."

Steely cleared her throat. "Miss Bea, I'd rather not. Mr. Cohen is going to retire and sell me his coffee shop. He's never been robbed in the forty-three years he's been in business." She smiled.

"Listen, you can buy that run-down coffee shop if you want. Start a chain of run-down coffee shops, drink stale coffee all day long—but only after you attend the board meeting tonight."

"Fine." She shrugged. "One meeting, then I'm out."

"Huh! We'll see about that." Bea tightened her lips and added, "We'll have to build up our cash again."

Nick rubbed his chin and muttered, "I'm sure that won't be too hard."

"It'll take a few years. Can't make that kind of money overnight."

"It's amazing how fast money can move these days," added Nick.

Bea shook her head. "Pepe, let's get some dinner." Pepe and Bea headed down the driveway.

He whispered, "Bea, are you going to fight Jack's will?"

"Nope."

"Bee-Bee, you're such a sweetie!" Pepe wrapped his arm around Bea's shoulder and kissed the side of her face.

"We're sorta kinfolks. She's like a daughter to me. Who else would share their PB and J?"

Pepe scrunched his face. "What's a PB and J?"

Bea kept moving. "Don't worry. You're never eating one."

Mrs. Yost waved at Steely from an open kitchen window. "Y'all all right?"

Steely and Nick waved back. "Yes, ma'am," said Steely.

They walked concurrently down the driveway, past the HPD cruisers now blocking the street. The entire property was taped off. If they wanted to go anywhere fast, it would have to be on foot.

"You want to see the coffee shop?" asked Steely. "It's only two blocks away."

"Why not?" Nick held her hand tightly as they strode along. "Steely, you know I don't care about you because of your position or money. Right?"

"Is the coffee shop venture that impressive?"

"You're about to expand yourself." He wrapped an arm around her shoulder. She intertwined her hand in his.

"I've already got the budget down. I'm good with budgets."

"I hope so." He stopped. She looked over at him. "Steely, if I had to create what I'd want the love of my life to be like…" Her eyes teared. "I know people aren't perfect. But you're perfect for me."

She let go of his hand and grabbed him in a tight embrace. He wrapped his arms around her. For several minutes, she couldn't speak. She squeezed her eyes together. Her tears had nowhere to go but out. She suddenly remembered what good tears felt like.

Nick wasn't moving until she was ready. She could lift her feet off the ground. She wasn't falling. He had her.

She finally lifted her head. There was no need for words. As always, he could see right through her.

He leaned down far enough for their lips to touch. He was a little choked up. He kissed her again. But this time their eyes brightened. And the tears dried.

The board meeting was short. There were no objections to naming Steely the new chairwoman, which was a place customarily reserved for the majority stockholder. Benita Ray and Pierce Thibodeaux were appointed board members. Nick Dichiara was elected president.

Beatrice Hunter was voted in as an *honorary* board member. Her duties were limited. She preferred spending her time cruising the world with her soon-to-be husband, Pepe Martinez.

Cricket's grandmother was pardoned. Nick saw to it. Cricket was not. She was sentenced to serve forty-five years for her part in kidnapping and conspiracy to commit murder. Alexis was given a life sentence. They were placed in different facilities. It wasn't a mother-daughter camp.

Keaton disappeared from the hospital, a move that proved to be dangerous. He was never seen again. The sharks were very aggressive that summer in the Gulf of Mexico. Rumor has it that it was Keaton that drew them in.

Since the US authorities couldn't prove the funds Nick had gathered were illegally gained, Nick decided to spread the love. He transferred $213 million from his lawn business account to Beatrice Hunter. Another $213 million was placed in a US account for the company's reserves. The Saint Stephen's account was divided among dozens of viable charities. The original owners had a blood bath, blaming each other for trusting Chevoski. Some even thought others had absconded with the assets.

Nick and Steely married. Their family grew to three the next year, when little Freddy was born. They tore down the Paupher house on Saint Ambrose and built a new one with a solid foundation.

They continued eating PBJs. The sandwich with smooth peanut butter and grape jelly remained one of their favorite meals.

ACKNOWLEDGMENTS

I 'm grateful to my Lord and Savior Jesus Christ for inspiration to write this book.

Special thanks to editors Donna Sims, Cindy Davis, and Melanie Stiles for their guidance.

42355376R00214

Made in the USA
San Bernardino, CA
01 December 2016